OUT
OF THE
BLUE

LILA ROSE

USA TODAY BESTSELLING AUTHOR

ISBN: 978-0-6480340-9-4
Print - Paperback

CHAPTER ONE

EASTON

PAST

I sucked back the shot and placed the glass on the bar. University was already kicking my arse, and it was only the start of my first year. Although, what didn't help was my decision to change my degree. My dad hated the fact I switched from pre-law to a bachelor's degree in paramedic science. In fact, he hated it enough to kick me out of the house. Didn't bother me. I had enough cash saved from all my jobs during high school to find my own place. Even if it was a shithole, it was mine. No wonder Mum had left the dickhead and the town a few months ago. She'd asked for my forgiveness, but I didn't need to give it when I understood. The man looked down on everyone around him and any chance he got, he put them down too.

What I wanted in life didn't matter to him, so I stepped out from under his thumb. I wanted to help people and not in a way where I could keep them out of jail, but instead where I could save lives. Becoming a doctor hadn't appealed to me. It was about a month ago and in my science course when I'd changed my mind on where I wanted my life to lead. People who worked in the police, fire, and health systems came in for a recruitment drive, and as the paramedic explained how his job worked, something clicked inside of me. I wanted to feel that pride the paramedic showed when he talked about his career.

While my mind had initially been on the police academy, I soon realised I was more interested in the cop who came in to give a career talk than the actual job.

He'd been so damn fine with his deep voice, tall, buff body, and eyes that I could have gazed into all day.

I shook my head. That was another thing I knew my father wouldn't be proud of—me being gay. He didn't know, and if I could help it, he'd never find out.

"Hey, kid, you want another?" Harry, the barman, asked. I'd been coming to his establishment for a while because I liked to relax with a drink or two while I studied. Some would say a pub was too loud or crowded, but Harry's was different. He had his regulars and pop-ins, but he never got run off his feet, nor did he have the music pounding.

"Sure, Harry," I replied, and then flipped my textbook closed. "Can I also grab some wings and fries?"

"On it." He nodded, taking my empty shot glass and turning towards the kitchen to yell out my order, which brought a smile to my face.

I pushed the textbook away and grabbed another, flicking it open. But then I heard the door to the bar open, so I glanced that way. My eyes widened and I gulped.

It was the cop.

The one I'd admired at university.

Shit.

I quickly glanced down to my book and pretended to read. It didn't stop my ears perking up at the sound of his approaching footsteps. My pulse kicked up. I wanted to look, stare, and eye fuck. But I didn't, knowing I wouldn't be able to hide my desire, and since he was a cop, he could probably smell a lie from across a room.

My gut clenched in disappointment at the thought of him being straight. Something that happened a lot when I was attracted to a particular guy.

"Hey, what can I get you?" Harry greeted after he set my shot down in front of me.

"Two Coors."

I flushed bright red when I hummed in the back of my throat. His voice was one I could listen to all night long. Even in the morning as well.

I kept my head down and tossed page after page aside while listening to the barman filling the order, and then the cop paying for it with thanks. I sensed him move away from the bar, so I let out a deep breath and chanced a glance up into the mirror across from me. The view was of the cop striding towards the back of the pub and sliding into a booth. He placed one of the Coors to the other side of the table, and I wondered who he was waiting for.

As soon as he started to take in his surroundings, I quickly moved my gaze back down to my book. I tried to pay attention to the words in front of me, but they all blended into each other and my mind stayed on the cop.

I remembered his name. Lan Davis.

Lan.

It wasn't one I'd ever heard before, which made it easier to remember. I liked it. It was tough, sexy, and suited him.

The door banged open. I glanced there to see a woman walk in with a soft smile aimed behind me. My heart deflated and sank to my feet. She was there for Lan. In the mirror, I saw his returning grin.

Yeah, they were together.

Another one bites the dust.

I snorted at myself and shook my head. Picking up the shot glass, I tipped it back and went back to my textbooks. My night had just dimmed a little since she walked in and was snuggled up close to Lan in the booth as they talked.

After I'd finished my dinner and a beer a couple of hours later, I slammed my textbook closed and stretched. I needed to get some sleep if I was going to be coherent in class the next day.

"You done for the night?" Harry asked.

I opened my mouth to answer when I heard close by, "See you later, babe."

It was Lan saying goodbye to his *friend*? Woman? Hook-up? He didn't leave with her, though, so I wasn't sure what she was to him. That caught my attention, and I zoned for a moment.

"Kid?" Harry pressed.

Clearing my throat, I looked from Lan in the mirror; he was heading towards the bar to Harry, and I just knew my cheeks blossomed red. "Yeah, heading home. See you next time."

Harry shot me a wave when someone yelled his name from the other end of the bar. That was when I felt a presence at my side.

"So…" was drawn out and it caused me to freeze. "You're just going to leave and not say anything after watching me most of the night? Do I know you or something?"

I sucked in a breath, thinned my lips, and I may have even whimpered a little. Sweat formed on the back of my neck, and I thought if I stayed still long enough, then he wouldn't disappear, and my dream would be true.

His chuckle had me blinking slowly, and I focused on him in the mirror. He'd leaned into the bar on one elbow while looking at me with a smirk on his lips. Throughout that time, I sat stunned out of my mind that he was even talking to me, and I was also embarrassed he'd caught me looking at him most of the night.

"And you still don't say anything." His voice rumbled.

I had to do something so he didn't think I was weird.

"Ah…" Great, I wished to God I wasn't so socially awkward. Maybe I'd grow out of it one day, but it wouldn't be that day obviously. Especially not when a sex god talked to me. I tried again. "Sorry. Um, yeah. Sorry. I didn't mean to stare." *Think, Easton. Think.* I slid off my stool opposite where Lan was taking up the space and grabbed my jacket. I shrugged it on and happened to glance at his crotch, and my damn eyes didn't want to look away. So instead, I explained, "I remembered you calling into one of my classes at uni. You talked about being a cop."

"So you're at university?"

"Yes." I nodded.

"What are you studying?"

"Everything there is to become a paramedic."

"Good career choice, but it can be hard sometimes."

A small smile formed on my lips. "So can being a cop I'm sure."

He chuckled. "Very true. You in your first year?"

"Yeah." I picked up my books and hugged them to my chest. "It was, uh, nice to see you again, and sorry if I annoyed you at all." Sweet mother of Jesus, where had my balls gone? So what if he was good-looking and intimidating with his bigger form. He was just a human being who was trying to have a normal conversation. Thinking that, I met his amused gaze and caught his lips twitching while my face burned. "Well, I better get going."

"I'm headin' off too." He turned and started for the door. I'd look even more of an idiot if I sat back down and waited until he was gone to make it less awkward. Sighing, I waved to Harry and slowly followed behind Lan.

When he stopped just outside and turned to me, I thinned my lips to keep from squawking like a fool. He put my nerves to the highest level they would go for some reason.

"What's your name?" he asked.

"Easton. And you're Lan."

He chuckled again. A sound that licked at my skin and made my stomach tense. "I am." He took a step closer and I nearly fainted. "You shy, Easton?"

I managed a nod.

"Tell me if I'm wrong, but I'm guessin' you like the way I look. That right?"

Christ on toast.

I did.

I *really* did, and he'd noticed.

I hadn't determined yet if that was a good or bad thing.

How did I answer? With the truth or a lie?

Glancing to the ground, I sucked in a quivering breath and bit my bottom lip. I nodded again. Lan hummed under his breath, causing goosebumps to pop up all over my skin.

I felt him step closer again and my body trembled. He was either going to tell me to go fuck myself or say something that would shock me.

His hand reaching up was what I saw next. I kept myself locked tight, trying not to flinch. Two fingers touched my chin, he tilted my face up so our eyes clashed. He was smiling, so I was guessing he was going to say something that would shock me. His teeth grazed his bottom lip. "I like the way you look too, Easton."

Yep, surprise had my heart racing even faster than it already had been. It also caused my dick to thicken behind my jeans.

"Y-you do?"

"Yeah."

I flicked my gaze to the side and then back to his. "Are you gay?" I whispered.

"No," he stated. My stomach dropped and I wanted to look away, but then his thumb ran over my lips. "I like both sexes. Mostly women, but right about now, you." He smiled, leaned in close and ordered, "Breathe."

My mouth opened as I drew in a deep breath. For a second there, I'd forgotten I needed oxygen to live.

"Would you...." Well, polish my nuts and serve me a milkshake, I had just about blurted if he wanted to come back to my place, but that'd be too forward. On the other hand, he pretty much told me he was interested in me, right? I wasn't sure. I'd only ever been with one other guy, and that was for a weekend of testing the waters. The result: I was definitely gay.

"What?" Lan asked roughly.

"Nothing." I shook my head. His hand dislodged from my chin and then—*gasp*—he placed it on the side of my neck while his other one went to my waist.

In a way, I was glad I still held my books to my chest; it saved me from jumping him.

He bent, and I arched back to keep his stare. *His heated stare.* "Yes," he clipped.

"Y-yes?"

"I'll come back to your place."

Tits on a whale.

I hadn't heard that.

"Okay," I muttered. "It's just around the corner."

He smiled and stepped back. "Good."

"Right." I nodded. With my whole body feeling like it had been shot up with caffeine, I practically spun on my heels and skipped off. Lan chuckled, so I slowed and then explained, "It's not the best of places, but it's enough for me."

"It'll be fine."

"Do you, um, live close by?" I asked as we walked side by side.

"Nope. I'm from Ballarat, not far though."

"And…" I cleared my throat. "That woman at the pub?"

He grinned down at me. "A friend. We were catching up."

I nodded and thought it best to watch my steps so I didn't trip. Excitement tingled in my chest and gut. Lan Davis was coming home with me.

With me.

To have sex.

At least that was what I hoped we were going to do.

CHAPTER TWO

EASTON

I stopped just outside my unit and faced him. His gaze ran from my groin, slowly up.

Yes. Heck yes, we were going to have sex.

My dick jerked.

"Keys?" Lan asked.

Only I didn't respond because I was looking at Lan's erection behind his jeans. My eyes flared. He was big and long if the bulge was any indication. When he stepped closer, I lifted my stare to his. It was then I sort of embarrassed myself and started panting because his hand was in my jeans pocket searching for my keys. The tips of his fingers brushed against the end of my dick. It jerked in response.

"Need to get you inside so I can take care of that for you."

Bloody shit.

"Yes please," I blurted.

He chuckled and pulled my keys free. Since I didn't move, he gently shifted me to the side and unlocked the front door. Lan pushed the door wide and stepped back. His brows rose at me, and since I was eager to get things rolling, despite my jumble of nerves causing my hands to shake, I quickly walked inside. I wasn't a very good host either because I didn't wait for him inside the door. No, I made my way down the hall, passing the bedroom, bathroom, and moving into the living room, then the kitchen. There I dropped my books to the table and cursed myself when I glanced behind me to see Lan slowly coming into the room. I'd left him to shut and hopefully lock the front door. I didn't even show him around or tell him where I was going. However, the unit wasn't big enough he would get lost, and he probably heard my frantic long strides down the hall.

Turning, I tucked my trembling hands behind my back. "Hi."

Lan's soft smile widened as he paused in front of me. "Hey."

"Uh, you can probably tell I'm kind of nervous, but it's because you're you and I'm me, and never in my life would I have thought you could be in my house and wanting to—" I coughed. I couldn't say have sex; I'd probably choke over the word in embarrassment. My face was already heated.

He got closer, his hands landing on my hips. "You've done this before, yeah?"

What did he mean?

Have sex?

One-night stands?

"Yes?" God, even I could tell I sounded unsure.

He chuckled. "I know you're young. Probably way too young for me, but tell me you've been with a guy before."

I nodded. "Once."

He groaned, laying his forehead against mine. "I'll try to take it slow, but...." I lost one hand from my hip because he'd grabbed mine from around my back and led it to the front where he pressed it against his erection.

Dear God, thank you, thank you, thank you.

"I'm so fuckin' hard for you right now."

"I'm easy." I blanched. "I mean, I'm not easy, but I'm good with any way you want to go. Fast, slow, medium." *Shut up, Easton.*

Lan grinned and rubbed my hand up and down his length.

"Good to know." With his other hand, he brought it up to cup the back of my neck. "You gonna kiss me then?"

My hand squeezed over him with his question. "Yes," I whispered, and finally relaxed enough to bring my other arm around to slide it against his waist. I lifted up to my toes and softly touched my mouth to his.

Shit, it felt so nice it warmed me all over.

Another touch of his mouth with mine was all I got before he took over and used my hand on his dick to drag me closer so our bodies aligned. Then he kissed me.

Lan Davis kissed me.

He slanted his mouth over mine with a grunt and teased my lips apart with his tongue. I wrapped my arms around his back and gripped his tee. Only they didn't stay there long because Lan was tugging my jacket from my shoulders, and while our mouths tasted each other, I straightened my arms to let the jacket fall to the floor.

What was happening was nothing like my first time. It was slow, sensual, and... more. The first time had been hot, clumsy, and straight to the point. I ran my hands up under Lan's tee, over his smooth, warm flesh while Lan traced fingers up and down my arms, causing me to shiver.

Lan pulled back and blinked down at me. "Fuck, you can kiss."

I bit my bottom lip to stop myself from smiling big. His comment gave me courage, and I felt unsteady from it in my stomach. In a nice way.

"So can you."

"Wanna taste more of you. Where's your room?" he asked, stepping back and taking my hand in his.

Without saying anything because I would probably bugger the moment up, I led him back down the hall and opened my bedroom door. Dropping his hand, I walked in and quickly looked around to see if I needed to tidy or hide anything. "So, this is it. Small, but enough for me, and the, uh, bathroom is opposite here."

"Easton," Lan called.

Stopping near my bed, I turned. "Yeah?"

"You okay with me being here?"

"Yes!" I shouted. "Um, yes," I said more calmly.

His smile was sweet, but it was his eyes that grew darker. "Good. Now I need to know if you're okay I want inside of you?"

My knees wobbled as my body tingled and I nodded.

He smirked and leaned against the doorframe. "Get undressed for me."

Heaven.

I was in damn heaven, enjoying the way he was ordering me around and how he'd spoken roughly with lust riding his voice.

Of course my nerves got the better of me, so even though my hands started to shake again, I lifted my tee up and off, throwing it to the floor. Next, I kicked off my shoes and got rid of my socks. Then I undid my jeans, which took me a couple of tries, and slipped them down my legs along with my boxers. When I straightened, I blushed. I felt exposed, especially with how hard I already was, but the way Lan's gaze ran over me relaxed me.

"Goddamn, you're gorgeous," he growled. Lan straightened and came at me. His lips landed on my shoulder first, where he licked and sucked. Then his hands moved to my waist before running around to my back and then arse where he squeezed. I let out a breath, dropping my head back, eyes to the ceiling, enjoying the feel of his rough hands on me.

I grabbed the edges of his tee and tugged it up. His arms went into the air for me to pull it over his head. Sweet Jesus, he was built and beautiful.

His hands came between us where he undid his own belt and jeans, then pushed them down his legs. When he'd kicked off his shoes, I didn't know, but I was glad he had because his jeans were easier to slip all the way off. He stood before me naked.

My dick leaked pre-cum. I licked my lips, my ears ringing in excitement from the thought of tasting *his* wet tip.

I sat back on the bed, took hold of the backs of his thighs and tugged him closer to me. At first lick, he groaned. When I sucked him all the way in, swirling my tongue along the way, his groan was louder and longer.

"Fuck. You look good suckin' me." His voice was harsh, desire filled. Slowly I glided my mouth back up to the tip and licked over and around it. He chuckled. "Not shy now."

No, I wasn't. Not when I wanted him so badly. Glancing up, I smiled around him but stopped when he pushed his cock back into my mouth, near to the point I was gagging. He quickly pulled back. Slipping all the way out, he bent so his face was in front of mine. Then he kissed me once more.

With his strong body, he forced me backwards. I moved into the middle of the bed still with Lan over me, kissing me. He spread my legs with his hands, and his form moved between them before he settled his weight down. I curled my arms around him, one over his shoulders, the other to his butt where I pressed down and was rewarded with Lan rubbing his hardness over my own.

"Christ, I haven't done this for a goddamn long time," Lan confessed.

"Had sex?"

He shook his head, still grinding against me, his jaw clenched. "Been with a guy."

My chest puffed out, glad he'd picked me.

He leaned in, licked my earlobe and bit it. "Need to fuck you."

"Yes."

"Gonna get you ready for me."

"Please." I nodded. "Lube, drawer."

I lost his heat for a moment and heard the drawer being pulled open. Only he did it so fast there was a crash next when it hit the floor.

"Shit," he cursed and went after the lube on the floor. I couldn't help but laugh. He was just as eager as I was, and I liked that a lot.

Lan grumbled about something as he climbed back onto the bed and between my legs. There he paused and ran his gaze over me. "Love your darker skin."

"I like yours better."

He shook his head, then kissed my stomach, which quivered from his touch. "Like that also."

"What?"

"Your body's reaction to me. Noticed you've been hard most of the night."

"You're hot."

He looked up at me as he nudged the top of my dick with his chin. "Glad you think so or I wouldn't be here." He winked. His warm, hot, and wet mouth then slid over and down my dick. I fisted the sheets in both hands and moaned.

Too long.

It had been way too long since I'd felt this. The pleasure, the thrill and touch of another man.

Lan used his hand to spread me wider for him, and I was more than happy to comply. He ran his lips up and down the top of my dick, then licked the tip before repeating it again and again. His cold fingers touching my ring caused my body to jolt. He kissed my pelvis and gently rubbed two slick-with-lube fingers over my hole.

Finally, as he sucked me into his mouth again, he pressed in with one and gently eased in further, stopping when I resisted the movement. As soon as I relaxed at the invasion, he moved his finger deeper and deeper still, until.... "God, yes," I cried when he touched my prostate.

I rocked down on his finger, loving the feeling, even when another joined the first. I tightened my hold on the sheets, losing my mind in pleasure. "N-need more. Need you," I panted. It had been so long since my first time, my climax was already close, but I didn't want to finish without him inside of me.

His fingers slipped free and his weight lifted from the bed. Then I heard the rustling of a packet. At least he'd remembered a condom. He was back on the bed kissing up my body.

"Last chance to back out," he offered.

I rolled my eyes. "No way."

He smiled. "Good. Wasn't sure I could have let you. Wrap your legs around me, East." I did. "You ready for me?"

"Very much so."

He bent and kissed me. His arm moved between us, and I knew his hand would be wrapped around his cock when the tip touched my ring. He pushed, and I sucked in a jagged breath. He was big. "Fuck, East." He groaned when he slipped in more. "So damn tight."

With a deep breath, I relaxed and pushed down on him more, gripping his shoulders. "More," I panted.

He thrust hard. I cried out from the moment of pain before it turned quickly to pleasure as his cock rubbed against my prostate.

"You okay?" he asked, stilling his body all the way in.

I nodded.

He leaned in and touched his lips to mine. Against them, he ordered, "Want words, East. You okay?"

"Yes." I nodded again. He slowly pulled out and then slipped back in, hitting the right spot. "You feel good."

Lan dropped to his elbow over me and kissed me hot and hard. I ran my hands up and down his sides while one of his drifted under my arse and gripped. His thrusts quickened, and each time he entered, a shot of rapture burst within me.

"Lan," I whimpered against his lips, my balls drawing up. "Lan," I whispered, opening my eyes to see him watching me. "I-I'm going to come."

He grunted. "Close, wait for me."

"Lan."

"Wait," he clipped.

"Babe—Oh God," I cried as cum shot out of my tip landing on my stomach.

"Fuck, you get tighter. Fuck. Yes, shit." He pushed to his hands over me, drilling into me harder. His eyes lowered, focusing between us as he watched himself fuck me. "Coming," he yelled, before his length thickened, and warmth spread within me. He kept thrusting, only to slow after four more hard ones. He smiled lazily down at me. "I could get used to this."

With my hand at the back of his neck, I pulled his body down to cover mine. I kissed him, then thumbed his lips. "So could I," I answered, ignoring the worry threatening to fill me. It would be easy to fall for a man like Lan Davis.

CHAPTER THREE

EASTON

PRESENT

$\mathcal{O}$f all the situations I could have been called to last month, it had to be the one Lan was overseeing where a man got shot in a backyard incident. Honestly, I didn't know what I felt after seeing Lan Davis. What I did know was even though it had been a few weeks since I'd seen him, he remained on my mind. I struggled to forget the way my heart had beat wildly upon seeing him, as if it were thrilled. But then my brain had taken over, and I'd become angry he was there.

Shit, I still had those reactions each time he crossed my mind, which was too many times for my liking. What was worse was how he still managed to look like a sex god, even with the salt and pepper colour he had going in his hair, goatee, and moustache. He was still tall, still buff, and still damn delicious.

The bastard.

However, being infuriated won out over anything because I doubted I could ever shrug off how things ended between us. He'd given me two months of pure happiness. I'd been in love with him by the end of our time together. Only he'd killed it in one night. The night I went to visit him in Ballarat. How was I supposed to know he'd have his mates over when I popped in? I didn't, and the way he handled the surprise visit was gut-wrenching.

One of his cop buddies had answered the door and called for Lan. He came our way with a laughing smile on his face, but it quickly dropped when he saw me.

Dropped.

Like I was nothing, and as far as I knew, we had been something. At least to me.

Unless I imagined all the tender times we'd spent together.

He'd sidled up behind his friend. "Yeah?"

"Um... hi, sorry if this is a bad time—"

"It is. I don't have time to help you out."

My jaw clenched so tightly I was surprised my teeth didn't shatter, much like my heart was. I searched his face for the Lan I knew. The Lan he was when it was just him and me, but he wasn't there. I was staring at cop Lan, straight Lan. One with hardened eyes.

He didn't know it, but he'd just made the decision more manageable for me.

"Right. Of course." I nodded. "Just wanted to let you know..." I flicked my gaze to his friend who was still standing there listening to everything with rapt attention. I shook my head and sighed. "I'm moving away. My mum needs help with some things and..." Fuck you, you arsehole, *was what I wanted to say. Instead, I sniffed and knew I needed to get away from there before I started crying. "Nothing," I muttered. "Goodbye."* You rat bastard.

Turning, I heard the front door close and then his friend asked, "Who was that?"

"Just a guy, I helped out his family in a rough spot. Can't get rid of him now."

Jesus.

I pressed my palm into my chest to try and stop my heart from tearing in two.

Shaking my head, I jumped down from the removal truck and dragged my mind out of the past. It didn't need to linger there. I was over Lan, and if luck shined down on me, I would never see him again. I didn't even know why he was working in Melbourne when he was from Ballarat, and I didn't care for the answer. He may have acted as if he wanted to know why I was back in Victoria, but I'd never tell him because I was determined never to see him again.

Stretching, I stood before my own house and grinned. It was perfect.

I'd always wanted a ranch-style home with some land, only a small amount, and I'd finally got it. There were houses on each side, but far enough away we wouldn't annoy each other and didn't have to get to know one another. It also meant I could be as loud as I wanted and they shouldn't be able to hear me, I hoped. Not that I was a lively person in general, but I had to be when my beasts didn't listen.

I had six dogs, all rescue animals. Some of them were angels and the others liked to try my patience. Another reason I was glad to have extra space was for them to roam and run amuck however they pleased in the fenced-off area out the back. It was better than the small backyard I had in town. I also planned to save more when the time called for it. With a passion, I hated how some people treated their animals. It made me sick to the stomach when I thought about what my guys and girls had been through before I got to them.

Currently, while I moved in, my old neighbour was taking care of them for me.

"Yoo-hoo," was called from my left. A woman in her sixties maybe called from the nearby fence with a wave. So much for not getting to know the neighbours. I liked my privacy, but I would never be rude. I waved and then made my way over to her.

"Hi." I smiled.

"Hello, dear. I'm Mrs Bridge. I thought I would introduce myself."

"I'm Easton Ravel."

She eyed my tattoos running down both arms. "Are you trouble?"

I chuckled at that. "No, ma'am. I'm a paramedic looking to settle down with my rescue dogs."

"Oh, how sweet. It's a pleasure to meet you, Easton Ravel, and if you ever need anything, my husband and I will help. My John is a handyman. He fixes everything around this place."

"Thanks, that's great to know." We both glanced at the car pulling into my drive. "And there's my help. I better get to unpacking."

"Is that your wife arriving?"

Grinning, I shook my head. "No. I'm not married, and he's a friend. We're paramedics together."

"Lovely. I'll let you get to it then."

"Wait, Mrs Bridge. Do you know who lives on the other side of my home?"

She shook her head. "No, dear. He keeps to himself. Actually, he's hardly home. I'm not sure what type of job he has, but it keeps him busy."

Perfect.

"No worries, thanks for the information. Have a great day."

"You also."

Turning, I made my way over to Oliver who stood leaning against his car. He grinned. "Making nice with the neighbours already? I thought you said you didn't want to know them."

I rolled my eyes. "She happened to be outside when I pulled up. I couldn't be rude."

"Of course you couldn't." He straightened and met me at the back to the removal truck, bumping my shoulder. "I have to say, it's a sweet place you got here."

"Told you it was." I pulled the doors open and jumped up into the back.

"But it's too far out for my liking. Though anytime you want to rekindle anything I'd be here in a heartbeat."

I tensed. "Oli—"

He laughed. "Don't. I'm teasing. I know you're right. We're better work partners than bed ones."

That had been my argument. Though we had been compatible in bed together, I just saw him more as a friend than having a long-lasting relationship with him.

"Sorry," I muttered.

He snorted. "Don't worry about it, honestly. Besides, Chris would have my balls if he heard me offering myself to you again."

I laughed. "He really would."

"So you won't tell him?"

"Hell no, he'd punch me in the face while telling me I'm too damn good-looking for my own good."

"God, I love that man."

I faced him. "You do?"

"Yeah." He nodded, smiling softly. "He gets me and knows I enjoy teasing you too much to stop. I get off on getting a reaction out of you. You get this guilty look each time I say something. It's funny as hell." He shook his head. "East, it's been nearly a year. I'm over it and have moved on. You need to stop feeling bad for breaking up with me."

I couldn't help it. I felt like a prick at the time for hurting him. I still did even though I knew he'd moved on. I was wired in a way that I cared too much.

"Come on, throw me some stuff and let's get this moving," he said. I did, thinking how lucky I was that Oliver and I stayed friends. He was one of my closest and had helped make the move back to Victoria easier after losing my mum.

Hours later, I was driving back into my driveway with my dogs in the back of my Ute. Before I'd picked them up, I'd dropped off the removal van and paid for pizza at Oliver and Chris's place to say thanks for helping me out. I left a pouting Oliver with Chris for him to deal with. Oliver wasn't happy because it was the start of my three weeks' holidays and he hated working with someone he hardly knew. He'd have to suck it up though because I was looking forward to the time off.

I got out of my vehicle and went straight to the back of it and opened the tray. Tin, Bell, and Buddy whimpered at me, eager to get out and run. While Astro, Captain, and Nero sat quietly waiting for my order. I quickly grabbed their leashes so I could lead them out the back since the front gate was still open. If the three eager ones got loose, they'd take off wherever they liked and wouldn't come when called. I was currently training them since they were the newest arrivals in our family.

"Come," I called. They jumped down and nearly took my arm off trying to take off sniffing. I walked them to the side of the house where the gate was to the fenced-off area out back and opened it. Around the back of the house, I took them all off their leads, and they bolted in different directions, checking out their new home.

After placing their leashes over the railing on the back deck, I stood a while and watched them.

This was home.

This was mine.

Land, a ranch-style log home, and fresh air.

It was where I'd always pictured myself, and I was finally doing it.

Mum would be proud.

I glanced up at the darkened sky, to the stars shining and sighed. I hoped she could see me. See how I'd finally found my place and was happy. It'd been hell after she'd lost the fight with cancer.

Hell times ten.

When I'd first moved to New South Wales to help her out with bills and such, I'd hated it, but of course, with Mum being there, I soon learned to love it. She helped me through the pain of what I'd been feeling from Lan. I'd been so angry and had played up a bit with drinking, partying, and fucking anyone who'd have me. That was until Mum kicked some sense into me and got me on the straight and narrow. Told me to finish my schooling to become a paramedic. She'd been my rock.

And then I'd lost her.

Dad hadn't given a shit how sick Mum was or what we were going through. So after Mum lost her battle, my "fuck you" to him, and out of wanting remembrance to Mum, I started getting tattoos. Mum had always loved ink, even had some herself after she'd left Dad. I had a couple that matched my mum's, a sun on my back shoulder and an owl on my arm to make sure she was always with me.

A smile lifted my lips when Dad had seen me for the first time covered in them. His nose turned up before he told me, "You're no son of mine." Hearing it didn't faze me; it suited me fine because I had always been my mum's son.

She was all I needed in my life, and now I would live on, taking each day as it came, for her.

CHAPTER FOUR

LAN

"You've been saying this for a while," Parker said, glaring down at me. He hated when I talked about it, but I wanted to. His lips thinned as he spotted me while I did my last set of weights. I had been telling him I felt I'd lost interest in being a detective. I was sick of the hours, sick of the bullshit we got sometimes with certain cases. I wanted a change. Wanted to settle down a bit. Hell, I'd saved enough to even take a pay reduction *if* I found a job that talked to me more than what I was already doing.

Maybe I was just after *something* to change in my life instead of it being the same old.

"You're already on an extended break. This time away could be just what you need. A break."

"Could be." But it wasn't and he knew it. Still, I'd take the time away to figure out what was going on in my head. If I'd be looking for a job elsewhere or going back. What I did know was that it'd suck not working with Parker if I did leave. He also hated change, so I wasn't sure he'd like it if I left in the first place.

"You gonna tell me who that ambo guy was to you yet?" Parker asked for, fuck, the billionth time. One day he'd get it through his head I wouldn't answer, but it was a good ploy to change the subject.

I hooked the weight back into its hold and sat up. "I'll tell you when you tell me where you go every Sunday," I said, then chuckled at Parker's scowl. Yeah, he didn't like sharing as much as I did. I stood, picked up my towel, and told him, "Your turn." We traded places so I could spot him. He set his towel down and lay back on the bench.

It was damn torture.

Parker didn't wear a tee when working out. He thought they got in the way, and for too long now I'd been checking him out more and more. Something I had to goddamn stop because he was as straight as they came. We'd been partners ever since I moved to Caroline Springs. Parker's clipped attitude had been frowned on in the department, and no one wanted to work alongside him. Then I got put with him and soon discovered we worked well together. What helped was the connection we had with the Hawks MC. We were detectives, but also honorary brothers to the club. The only difference was we didn't wear their patch, so we could help them when the situation called for it.

A lot would see it as a bad move, but to us, it wasn't. We believed in their values. They protected their families and did it however they wanted. Family was important. I was taught that by the club back when I used to live in Ballarat. My cousin Stoke was a member of the Hawks MC. At the time, we were both trying to help the same woman, Malinda. She was a good woman, a woman I wouldn't have minded claiming as my own, but she only had eyes for Stoke. When shit happened to her, Hawks went all out to bring her peace. It wasn't exactly legal, but after what she went through, the bastard who'd messed with her didn't deserve to travel along the legal path. Since I had their backs in the situation, I became a part of Hawks. I had proven myself, and as far as I was concerned, they did the same in my eyes.

Most law enforcement officers would balk at the idea of being a part of an MC. But I didn't; I respected their ways.

Parker was a different story. He hadn't known them as long as I had, but he'd got involved when, unbeknownst to him, he was living with the prez's sister-in-law. Crap went down, and he was always in the background willing to help, but the Hawks didn't take him into the fold until he shot himself to protect a brother from going to jail when Low, Dodge's woman, had been held hostage.

"You gonna spot me or stare at me?" Parker clipped.

"Shit." I stepped closer, hands ready to grab the bar.

Shit again. I hadn't realised I zoned out while watching his stomach muscles work. "Sorry, thinking of other stuff. I wasn't staring at you."

"Thinkin' of that ambo guy?" he taunted.

No. But Easton had always been in the back of my mind and now the front a lot since seeing him. Hell, he'd changed. He was a little taller, broader, and with the short-sleeve uniform he'd had on, I'd seen the ink on both arms and damn, it had looked fucking amazing on his darker skin.

Parker sighed, set the weight into its hold and sat up. "Lan, what the fuck is up with you? Is that guy a problem? Do I need to do a background check on him or something? He an ex"—my heart stalled—"crim you put away?"—then it started beating again.

Easton Ravel was an ex, just not the kind Parker was thinking.

I'd screwed up big time with Easton, and I'd done it in a way it took me years to get over. If I were honest with myself, I still wasn't over it because I'd never been with another guy since him. I wanted him to be my final memory with a guy. However, none of it stopped me from fucking women. I did. But Easton deserved to be my last relationship with a guy. That way no one else could tarnish my memory of him; he'd been important to me and losing him had been all my damned fault. I fucked him over because I'd been a pussy.

I shook my head. "No. He's just someone I knew. Don't worry

about it." I tipped my chin up at the weights station. "You done here?"

He eyed me, fully aware I was talking out of my arse. But there was no way I was telling Parker Wilding that Easton used to be my... boyfriend.

No one knew that side of me, and as far as I was concerned, I'd left that side behind when Easton left town.

"Suppose." Parker stood, grabbed his towel and ran it down his chest and stomach. Of course I watched it, then spun and cursed myself for watching. I started for the locker rooms when Parker called my name. Turning back, he asked, "You coming to the compound? There's that thing for Fang and Poppy."

"Nah, I think I might catch up on some sleep." I hadn't been getting much and maybe with extra z's I'd stop thinking of Easton and staring at Parker like I wanted to take a bite out of him. God, I hoped he never noticed. "I'll catch up later there."

He gave me a chin lift, and I quickly made my way to the locker room again.

I groaned as I lay flat on my bed. I'd already had a shower at the gym, so all I had to do was kick off my shoes and socks, then slip off my tee. I felt drained mentally. My mind wouldn't let up for me to actually get enough hours of sleep. Then there was my job. We had shit hours, some days not sleeping at all. Which was why, since it was the start of my break, even though it was the middle of the day, I wanted to rest whenever the hell I liked, then maybe, I wouldn't be fucked in the head.

Yeah, right.

It was easy to blame lack of sleep for why I kept admiring Parker. But it'd been happening too often. Even more after I saw Easton. Now both men kept popping up randomly in my mind.

Parker would cut off my balls if he knew I was attracted to him.

Easton would punch me in the face if I tried to see him or contact him and try to apologise.

Even the thought of…. No, I couldn't go there. Easton would never want anything to do with me ever again, and I couldn't say I blamed him.

Closing my eyes, I cringed as regret stabbed at my gut.

Easton had made me happy.

He'd made me smile, laugh, and damn… love, even in the short time we were together. His shyness had charmed me. When he'd opened up, each time I saw him was something special to witness.

What he didn't know was that the first night I saw him, I'd been there to hook-up with an old lay. That was until I kept catching him looking in that mirror behind the bar. At first, I thought it was at the woman I sat with. Then I realised his eyes stayed on me each time. He tried to hide it, only glancing up for a second or two or he'd bring his book higher in front of him so it looked as if he was reading and not staring at me in the mirror.

Jesus, just thinking of it brought a smile to my lips. I knew if I didn't get rid of the bird I'd been with, I'd lose the chance of having Easton. I would have regretted my choice, which was why I'd got her out of there so I could approach him. He may have been young, but my attention had been zoned on him as soon as I'd entered that pub. He'd looked familiar, and it took me a little time to remember I'd perved on him at university when I had to go and give a talk. He'd appealed to me more than any other guy had. So I faked a text from the station calling me in for work, and as soon as the woman I'd been with left, I'd made my move over to him.

He'd stuttered, floundered, and near panicked at my attention. I'd enjoyed every moment of it, and even more when I'd gotten him back to his place.

Two months.

We'd had two months together, and I had to admit, they were the moments in my life I felt carefree and loved the most from any other memory from my past.

Then I fucked it up.

"Christ," I muttered into my room and ran a hand over my face. The pain I saw on his face still gutted me each time it slid into my mind. I was a motherfucking prick.

Maybe I needed to find him so he could punch me.

Then at least we could look for closure.

But I was kidding myself. I'd want closure, but I'd also want Easton back in my life. If he accepted me as a friend, I'd take it and then long for more on my own time.

Like I'd longed for more from Parker, but that'd never happen, and I'd finally started to get my mind and heart to realise it.

I was one confused dickhead.

Two guys?

Two males?

Where was my dream of a family? Yeah, even men liked the thought of kids, a dog, and a damned white picket fence.

I was forty, and I had none of it.

Shit, maybe it was time I did find my future and put those two men behind me.

Only, I didn't have a clue what in the fuck I was going to do.

Rolling to my side, I closed my eyes and prayed sleep would take me away from my thoughts.

Sleep must have taken me, but something had woken me.

Shifting slightly, I glanced at the alarm clock on my bedside table. Two hours, that was it.

My body locked tight when I heard a floorboard creak. With my lids dipped low, I peeked out to my bedroom doorway.

Fuck.

Shit.

A figure stood in it.

Someone was in my goddamn house.

Two more appeared behind the first.

My heart raced. Thankfully I was already on my back with my arm up over my shoulder. All I had to do was reach under my pillow for the gun I always kept there. In my line of work, I knew I had to be careful.

They moved into the room, spreading out. Fuck. I'd maybe have time to shoot one or two, but the other would have time to get to me, and if the intruders had weapons, I'd be screwed.

"Know you're awake."

No use faking now. May as well play.

Opening my eyes, I glanced at the person on the right. A filthy and what looked like high teenager. My left, the same thing, only a girl, and standing at the end of the bed.... Jesus Christ.

"Miller?"

Miller smirked and waved his gun around. "Nice place you got here."

"When did you get out?"

He chuckled. "Recently for good behaviour. So I thought I'd visit the man who put me behind bars. The traitor." I went to sit up, but he screeched, "You move I start shooting."

With the sun still shining through the windows, I could see he was high on something. All their pupils were dilated.

"Why'd you snitch?"

"Why wouldn't I? You may have been my partner, but we were cops."

Miller and I had been put together fresh out of the academy. To start with, we'd been friends. That all ended the night I saw him dealing while on the job. After I reported it, it wasn't me who broke his door down to arrest him, but it was me who'd caught him fucking an underage girl who was so doped up she didn't know where she was or even who.

"You could have kept your mouth shut or even come to me about it first," he yelled.

Bang.

CHAPTER FIVE

EASTON

I was sitting at the kitchen table eating some lunch when Nero, my boxer dog, got to his feet quickly and started growling. I froze, the fork halfway to my mouth. Nero was my more placid dog, so it was unexpected to see such a reaction from him. It also told me something was wrong.

My fork clattered to the table when dropped. I quickly stood and followed Nero to the front door. Astro picked his head up off his bed, stretched and then went back to sleep. He didn't care what was going on, and thankfully the others were out in the backyard or I was sure Nero's reaction to whatever was happening would have got them worked up.

At the door, I peered out the glass panels on each side of the door. There was no one out there, not even a vehicle coming in the drive.

Nero sniffed under the door and growled low again. He then scratched at it.

My pulse kicked into panic mode and my hands started to sweat.

I grabbed his collar in a tight grip and opened the door. "Shit, Nero, settle," I demanded as he fought to run. Maybe it was an animal he sensed and he wanted to hunt. There was no way I'd let him go to find out though.

My body tensed when a scream ripped through the air. My head spun towards my neighbour's house, and so did Nero's. Then his body followed.

A gun fired.

Fuck, fuck, fuck.

Without a thought to protect myself or Nero, I dropped my grip on his collar, and he bounded forward. I quickly ran after him. I headed for the fence between the properties. Nero jumped it first, and I followed. Before I could make it to the front door, Nero was there scratching, snarling, and nipping at the wood.

My heart sat in my throat, but still, a need to help urged me on. I opened the already unlocked door and stepped in. Nero made a beeline for the hallway to the right, his nails slipping and sliding over the polished floorboards. I bolted after him when I heard his bark, people yelled, something fell to the floor. Another gunshot. Glass shattered.

All of it happened before I made it into the room.

A growling, snarling Nero had someone cornered in the room. Another pushed past me slamming me into a wall. "Nero, guard," I ordered and made after the one running down the hall, ignoring the cry of "No" from someone.

I neared him, reaching out to take him to the ground, but then I heard roared, "Easton, don't."

I stumbled, shock reverberating throughout my body over someone knowing my name. I glanced at the front door to see the man, who had dripped blood along his way, already disappearing.

I spun back to the room and stalked down the hall, where I had the perfect sight of Lan Davis bloody and beaten, struggling to get off the bed.

Bugger the fuck out of me.

As I raced back towards the room, I heard a female scream, but Nero's snarled growl overpitched her. Rounding the doorway, I saw a girl trying to climb out of the broken window, but Nero had his jaw wrapped around her leg.

"L-let her go," Lan panted.

"What?" I cried.

"Do it," he barked.

"Nero, heel."

Nero released and sat his butt down on the floor, and we both watched the girl scramble the rest of the way out the window and limp away.

I swung my gaze back to Lan.

Blood.

All I could see was blood.

My chest ached. I went to Lan's side, and my training kicked in. I picked up his phone I found on the floor next to the bed. "We need to call the police, an ambulance."

"No," he yelled, and lurched forward, only to groan and fall back against the mattress. "No," he gasped. "No police."

"Lan—"

"No. Call Parker."

"Who?"

"Parker. In contacts. Code 451784."

My jaw clenched. He'd rather me call his boyfriend than the damn law enforcement. "Lan, at least let me call an ambulance—"

"No," he growled out. "Parker."

Sighing, I bit out, "Fine. Let me check you over first." He didn't say anything as I threw back the sheet. I winced when it stuck to his leg, causing him to grunt. My hands glided over him, checking his injuries. I ripped the sheet apart and tied it around his leg and his lower arm where there were a small stab wounds'. His shoulder held a gunshot wound, only there was no exit, so the bullet was still inside. His hip was bleeding obviously grazed by another bullet. His left eye was swollen and would probably keep going. There was a cut to his chin, one to his arm, and another to his chest.

I felt sick to the stomach at seeing it all.

Especially on someone I knew.

He didn't say anything as I examined him, but his good eye stayed on me as I worked. I could feel it. Thinning my lips, I stood back and looked at my piss poor job of a patch-up. Better supplies were needed. With the bullet still in his shoulder, his blood started to soak through the sheet. I leaned forward and pressed my palm against it. "You really should go to the hospital," I said again.

"No," he grunted.

Shaking my head, I used my free hand to pick his phone back up, unlock it, and find Parker's number. I pressed his name and placed it against my ear.

It was answered with a gruff, "Yeah?" A charming way to answer the phone to someone he knew. It could even be Lan's boyfriend.

"This is... Lan Davis's neighbour. I just caught a group of people in Lan's house. He was beaten badly before I could come to his aid—"

"What?"

I continued, "He's asked me to call you. He's refusing to go to the hospital which I advise against strongly."

"I'm on my way," he stated coldly and hung up the phone.

I glanced down at Lan. "He's on his way."

"W-what are you doing here?" he whispered, his eye still on me.

Then it clicked.

Screw me with a sledgehammer. Lan and I were neighbours.

"East?" Lan pressed in a gruffer tone.

Sighing, I shook my head and left my gaze on the wound and held the sheet there. "We're neighbours."

His eye widened. Then he winced and settled again. "Neighbours?"

"Yes."

"You're the one who moved in recently."

"Yes." I glanced to Nero sitting at the side of the bed on the floor and then back again to the wound. "Nero heard something. I followed him over here."

"You could have got hurt."

I shrugged. I didn't care if I had. I was happy I stopped what was happening before it was too late for Lan.

Too late for Lan.

I couldn't think about that.

"I'm surprised they ran when I came."

Lan coughed, his eyes closing fully and staying that way.

"Lan," I snapped. He couldn't sleep until he'd been checked over. "Lan," I barked. Nothing. "Lan, dammit you prick, open your damn eyes."

His lips twitched. "Just restin'."

"Jesus," I muttered.

"Not so shy now," Lan uttered.

My body stilled.

"You were—"

If he was rehashing things from the past, I wouldn't let him.

"Why did they run?" I asked instead.

His mouth closed, his lips dipped down into a frown. "Heard you coming. Already shot Miller in... hand. His gun on... floor... tired."

"Lan Davis, you stay awake or I'll kick your arse."

He chuckled, then groaned. "Could be fun."

Darn this man.

"You knew one of the people in here?" I asked.

"Yep."

"Lan, you really should go to the—"

"No. We'll deal with it."

I sighed and clenched my jaw, not only from annoyance but for fear they could come back and finish the job.

"Fine." I wished the Parker guy would hurry the fuck up. "Are you still a cop?" He'd been in plain clothes the day I saw him when we attended a gunshot wound to Jarrod Blackcomb a while ago.

"No. Detective."

"How long you lived in Melbourne?"

"While now."

34

"Why'd you move?" I asked, not wanting to, but if questions kept him awake, then I was willing to ask meaningless ones.

"Wanted a change."

"Nice area to move to."

"Yeah." He shivered.

"You cold?"

"Hmm."

"Lan!"

"Can't a guy get some rest?"

"Not yet." I needed someone to hold his wound so I could get some supplies, though I wasn't sure I had the right stuff at home for it either.

He licked his lips. "You like your place?"

I did. I wasn't sure if I still did since knowing I lived next door to the man I never wanted to see again.

"It's okay." I settled for instead.

He scoffed, then coughed and groaned. After a couple of breaths, he commented, "Sure you liked it more than okay before you knew I lived here."

Observant bastard.

"I don't know what you mean."

"You got more dogs?" he asked. I appreciated the change in topic.

"Yes. Six in fact."

"Six?"

A smile slipped onto my lips. "Six. All rescue dogs, all different in their own way."

"How bad?" he whispered.

I knew what he was asking. "Not too bad. A few cuts and scrapes."

His lips twitched. "You could never lie well."

And damn him for knowing that.

Nero stood and turned towards the door; a low growl dropped from his lips. People were coming. Finally.

CHAPTER SIX

PARKER

I glanced behind me once again as I drove into Lan's driveway to keep my mind off how goddamn sick I felt in the gut with fear. Someone had harmed Lan. They'd harmed a person who was in my life. They wouldn't get away with it. I clenched my hands tighter around the steering wheel.

Pick and Billy followed me to Lan's property on their rides, while Fang sat beside me in my car, and Muff sat in the back.

All of us were alert to our surroundings. Someone had been there, to his house... and I wanted to make them bleed. The need to inflict pain shouldn't come from someone in law enforcement, but they'd fucked with the wrong person. I wasn't only a detective. I was also a person who believed in people paying in whichever way I saw fit. No one screwed around with someone I knew.

Yet, whoever had attacked Lan must have got away or else his neighbour wouldn't have called from Lan's mobile. I was sure the neighbour's voice sounded familiar, but I couldn't place it.

Pulling the car up, I was quick to turn it off and climb out. I was the first to the opened front door on Lan's house.

"Lan," I yelled.

A low growl sounded from down the hall, and then, "Down here. Nero, heel."

With the others at my back, I moved towards the hall and down it. That was when I saw fucking Easton Ravel. The guy from Lan's past. My feet nearly stalled from eating up the floor when I spotted him. Okay, I may have faltered a little but kept going when I noticed he was leaning over a body lying on the bed. Fists clenched, my heart hardened, and I kept walking even when a part of me wanted to turn and not see what pain Lan would be in.

It was when I entered the room and saw the blood coating the bed and some on the floor that I stumbled. Then I locked my body tight.

Recognition crossed Easton's face as he glanced up at me. His body tensed as the others enter the room.

"What the fuck?" Billy growled.

Easton ignored the comment and opened his mouth to rattle off, "I'll need someone to hold his wound. I have to get supplies, get this stitched up. We'll need—"

"Leave," I ordered roughly.

"Parker," Lan cut in, only his tone softer, pain-filled.

Christ.

I dropped my hands to my hips closer to the bed, glaring down at my partner. "You need to go to the hospital—"

Easton snorted. "I've tried—"

"Shut it," I ordered. "You've done your job, now leave."

The big arse dog at his side stood, a snarl vibrating from his lips. "Nero," Easton called. The dog settled.

"Parker," Lan bit out harsher.

I wasn't having it. No matter their past, Easton was an outsider. He had no right to be involved.

"Pick, ring it through—" I started.

"No!" Lan bellowed.

"You," Easton growled low and pointed to Muff. "Get over here and hold this." Muff did, and Easton moved away from the bed.

Only he made the wrong move to get in my face. His expression darkened. "I don't give a fuck who you are to him, but I'll tell you right now, you don't come in here and make shit worse by ordering others around." He flung his hand back towards Lan. "He didn't want anyone called but you. So how about you shut the hell up and listen to what he has to say, then I can get him fixed up." He shoved past me, called for his dog and they both made their way to the door. Then he stopped. "I don't know if any of you can get stuff, but he'll need some hard medication for the pain. A drip, antibiotics."

"You get the things to stitch him up. We'll worry about gettin' the rest," Fang told him.

Easton nodded and strode from the room.

It was silent for a moment.

"I'll ring Nurse," Billy said and left the room.

"Lan, what happened?" Pick asked.

Fire burned in my chest and head. All I could think was I wanted to make someone hurt like Lan was. My hands clenched and unclenched at my sides.

"Miller," he said.

"Fuck," I clipped.

"Who's Miller?" Muff asked.

When Lan didn't say any more, I did. "His old partner when he was a cop. Lan caught him selling drugs. He got put in jail for that *and* for taking advantage of underage girls. Guess he got out and wanted revenge." Lan grunted. "Doesn't explain why you don't report it."

"Mine to handle."

Everyone in the room understood then. Lan wanted the fucker to bleed like he was.

"Then we wait. You get better, and after, we'll hunt together," Pick said, his voice hard like steel.

"We can hunt now, then hold him for when Lan is better," I suggested.

"Lan?" Fang said.

Lan sucked in a breath and cringed. "Don't care who finds him. He's mine when the time comes."

Good. I was too edgy to not look for the motherfucker.

Footsteps sounded down the hall. Easton was back without the mutt with him. His hard gaze stayed on me all the way, and I returned it.

"Fix him up to what you can, then leave. We have someone comin' to help," I told him.

"Parker," Lan groaned.

"He's not a part of this, Lan. He's an outsider."

"Don't," Lan demanded.

"Who is he to you?"

The room thickened with tension.

"Parker," Pick warned.

I wanted to shout, *"What?"* but didn't. I thinned my lips and kept them shut.

I needed to goddamn know how they knew each other. Did this Easton kid cause shit for Lan in his past? There was something uncomfortable between them I didn't understand, and that pissed me the hell off.

"What happens if he says somethin' to the wrong person?" I asked.

"I won't say anything to anyone. I know when to keep my mouth shut." Easton laid some shit on the bed, opposite to Muff. "Now everyone needs to get out while I do this."

"It's all right," Lan told him.

I straightened, arms crossing my chest. No way was I moving when I didn't trust the guy in the first place. For all we knew, he could have been a part of what went down.

Easton sighed. "Fine." He started squirting some type of liquid onto pieces of gauze and then lowered the rest of the torn-up sheet.

I sucked in a breath. His face and shoulder weren't the only injured parts of him. Cuts covered Lan in a lot of spots. What looked like stab wounds were on his lower arm and leg, and a graze on his hip.

Murder was high on my mind.

Easton said, "This is going to sting. I won't touch your shoulder until we have the drugs to numb it." He glanced over at us. "The bullet is still in there. He'll need to be near knocked out to get it out."

Pick or Fang must have nodded or something, but I was locked up too tight to do anything. If I let myself free and let what I felt go, I'd lose it and start breaking shit.

Easton, to my surprise, was gentle as he started cleaning the cuts on his face and chest. Lan grunted a few times, but other than that, he didn't say anything.

"Nurse is here," Billy called from the front of the house.

"Thank fuck," Lan muttered. Meant he was in more pain than what he let show.

"I'll go see if they need help," Fang said. I felt him leave but didn't see it.

"So," Muff drew out, "looks like you'll be as high as a kite soon enough, detective."

Lan grunted.

"I'll text Sarge. Lan's already on break. I'll see if he can pull any strings to get me outta work. Some family emergency or some shit. If I can't, I'll work around it all."

"You don't have to have time off," Lan whispered.

Pulling out my phone, I told him, "I ain't fuckin' doin' anythin' else until this cunt is at the Hawks compound."

I caught Easton's eyes flash for a moment before he blanked his expression.

"You reckon that'll be a problem with the sarge?" Pick asked. "Two detectives out for a while?"

I shrugged. "We're between cases. Before he can shoulder me with another, I drop the idea of me having time off as well. Can only ask." I scrolled through the contacts for Sarge's number when a low hiss snapped my attention over to the bed. "Careful," I barked.

Easton grumbled something under his breath.

I stepped forward. "What did you say?"

His head slowly lifted, his glare sharp. "I said—"

"Looks like the fun started without me." Nurse walked into the room with Billy and Fang following, all carrying something. Easton shifted his attention from me to the other men. His eyes widened a little.

Nurse dumped his stuff on the end of the bed and stopped beside Easton. "Hey. I'm Nurse. I'm here to help. What do we have?"

"Gunshot to shoulder, the bullet's still embedded. A graze from another bullet on his hip. Stab wounds on his left thigh and left lower arm. There are lacerations on his face, chin, arms, and chest."

"All right." Nurse nodded. "Hey, buddy. Looks like..."

"Easton," I clipped.

Nurse glanced over at me, nodded, and looked back down to Lan. "Looks like Easton has already started the clean-ups, but I'm here to give you the good stuff to take the pain away. Then, with Easton's help, we'll get you all stitched up. Sound good?"

Lan tipped his chin up.

"Parker, a word," Pick called. He'd already made his way to the door before I answered. I didn't want to leave.

"Come on, brother. They've got this under control," Billy said.

I glanced back to the bed. Nurse and Easton worked alongside each other cutting at Lan's jeans and getting things set up. Muff still held pressure to the wound and Fang stood in the corner watching it all. I knew none of them would let anything happen if I left Lan with the person I didn't know.

Running a hand over the back of my neck, I sighed and made my way out of the bedroom. I found Pick in the kitchen leaning against the counter. Billy came in after me and leaned his arse on the bench near him.

"Wanna tell us the issue you have with that Easton guy?"

"He's an outsider," I stated, as if that was enough on the matter.

"And?" Billy said.

Apparently, it wasn't enough.

"I don't trust him to keep his mouth shut. Who's to say he wasn't a part of all this? Convenient he's Lan's neighbour and then this shit goes down."

"I caught up to Easton outside when he left before." Billy straightened and crossed his arms over his chest. "He seems legit. You remember him from the day Blackie got shot, yeah?" I nodded. "He's a paramedic, and what I got off him earlier, he was the one who came to help Lan out when his dog heard something. Can't say he'd been in on it when he's stuck around to help Lan."

"He shouldn't know our business. We don't know him."

"Lan seems to, and he also seems to trust him," Pick replied.

My jaw clenched. They were too quick to give their trust to someone who could say shit and get us all in trouble. "Until I know everythin' about the guy, I'm not trustin' him."

Pick grinned. "Not sayin' you have to. But go easier on him."

That wasn't gonna happen. Still, I answered, "Yeah, sure."

They looked at each other, both smiling and then shook their heads. Pick turned his gaze back to me first. "We gotta talk about what's gonna happen next."

"He'll need protection 24/7 and have men out there hunting for the fuckhead Miller."

"Pick and I are headin' out of town tomorrow with Josie. Still, the brothers will pull together to have Lan's back. You and Lan are a part of Hawks; we got you covered. We'll set up a rotatin' shift. Don't stress. We'll get it figured."

I nodded. "I'll stay here tonight, but I want out tomorrow to search for this fucker."

"I'll get Knife and Beast here tomorrow. We'll have church tonight to organise the rest and keep you updated on the outcome."

"Good. Thanks."

"Anything for you and Lan," Billy stated.

Hearing it felt goddamn good.

"We're gonna head out, take Fang and Muff with us. You good to assist in there?" Pick asked.

"Yeah." I was. Even though I liked the extra layer I had with them being there between Easton and me, I'd suck it up without them. Besides, they'd start the hunt for Lan, and that was more important.

CHAPTER SEVEN

EASTON

*P*arker entered the room as we finished setting Lan up with a fluid drip and pain relief. He walked up to the man who I learned was Muff, yet another member of the Hawks MC. I wasn't sure how Lan got involved with an MC or if I liked it, but they'd been nothing but helpful since they arrived.

"I've got it. Billy and Pick are waiting for you and Fang out front," Parker said to Muff. Muff nodded and stepped back. Lan's blood soaked his hands, but it didn't seem to bother him. As he moved away, Parker stepped forward and took his spot leaning over Lan and applying pressure to his wound. He wouldn't have to do it for long. As soon as the drugs hit, we'd take care of the wound.

The room was awkwardly silent.

Lan's eye opened at the shift of movements. He stared up at Parker. "You good?"

Parker snorted. "Yeah, and you will be soon."

"'Kay."

He closed his eye again.

"Lan," I called. "Are you doing all right?"

He smiled, but his eye stayed shut. "Oh, yeah." Then he chuckled.

Nurse laughed. "He's well on his way. Just a bit longer and then we can get to work."

"East," Lan whispered.

Oh hell, I didn't know what Lan was like on any type of medication. I just hoped he wasn't a talkative patient.

"Can we give him more sedation?" I asked, wanting it to work faster. From the suspicious rise to Parker's brows, my tone was on the side of panic. Nurse only laughed. He wasn't leaving me with much of a choice. I seriously contemplated smothering Lan if he opened his mouth and said something he'd regret in front of his hardarse partner and Nurse, who from the club's vest he wore, was also a part of the Hawks MC.

"East," Lan muttered.

"Yeah?" I replied reluctantly.

"Thanks for comin' to help."

My body sagged in relief. "Not a problem."

"Good to see you again. I've—"

"How about you just rest and let those drugs make you sleepy," I suggested.

"How about you shut up and let him talk," Parker snapped.

My glare shot up to him. "And how about you go f—"

"All right, ladies." Nurse clapped. "Let's get this show on the road." I moved out of the way so Nurse could apply a little more sedative into Lan's drip.

Parker thinned his lips and glanced down at Lan. He was already looking up at him with a tired smile. Lan started to reach up to him but winced and dropped his arm again. "Long hair," he muttered.

Was there something going on between those two? Though, from the way Parker's brows dipped, I was sure he was confused by Lan's words. To me, it kind of sounded like he liked Parker's long hair.

Parker shook his head. He opened his mouth to say something, but Lan closed his eyes, and Nurse announced, "He's out." Then added, "Parker, wanna give us a few to do what we gotta. We'll need help after he wakes to get him cleaned up, the bed also."

"Got to call the sarge anyway," he said in his sharp tone, then walked from the room.

"He's a good guy," Nurse said after Parker disappeared.

I turned my attention to Nurse and raised a brow. Nurse laughed. "Yeah, he doesn't seem it right now, but he is. Just got some anger issues." Parker was still on the phone. While I waited, I stood beside the bed and stared down at my gloves with Lan's blood on them.

I could never have thought I'd be in this situation, working on someone I'd known. Someone I *had* cared for, but there I was.

Darn it all, I suddenly felt like crying. Everything caught up to me, and the weight of it dropped down on my shoulders. Pressure built in my chest and my eyes held moisture, but I wouldn't cry then. I wasn't sure if I would at all. In that moment, I just felt too much since things had settled a little and the room lay silent.

I slipped off the gloves and threw them to the floor; they lay alongside what felt like millions of gauze pads covered in yet more blood. Nurse had said he'd get one of the brothers to deliver some blood to replenish Lan's since he'd lost a lot. I didn't question where all his supplies came from; it wasn't my business.

Guess it *was* good Lan knew the Hawks MC.

Although, I wasn't happy with Lan's thirst for vengeance. He never used to be like that. He always played by the book. Then again, I hadn't seen him in ten years. I didn't know what else he'd been through or what he was like nowadays.

I lifted my eyes from the floor to Lan on the bed. It was hard to see him like that. Heck, even when he wasn't injured, it was hard to see him.

I never thought I'd get over Lan.

Deep down, I hadn't.

Maybe that was why I couldn't keep a long relationship. They weren't the first man I loved.

Damn him.

Damn him for living next to me.

Damn him for getting hurt.

Damn him for making me love him. Making me feel again. Making me want him.

And damn him for.... Shaking my head, I pushed my fingers through my hair.

I couldn't be around him. He would end up breaking me even more than he already had, but really, it seemed I hadn't healed in ten years. So as soon as Lan recovered, I would stick to my side of the fence and he'd stay on his.

It had to be.

Someone cleared their throat; I jumped. My eyes shot to the doorway where I found Parker there leaning against the frame with his arms crossed. How long had he been there? "Nurse gone?"

I nodded. "To organise blood for Lan."

"He sent me a text, said we need to clean up." He shook the plastic bag in his hand. "We'll need to burn everything after we're done." He studied me, waiting for my reaction. I didn't have one. I'd already heard enough to know they were covering it all up to hunt the person who did that to Lan. I wouldn't object to it, not after everything. They were men who knew what they wanted, and I wouldn't step in their way.

Even if I tried, I wasn't sure I'd live to see the next day.

That thought alone scared me enough to keep my mouth closed.

I grabbed some more gloves, covered my hands and started picking up the rubbish scattered on the floor. Cleaning the blood out of the carpet was going to be a pain.

"Also, someone will be here to fix the window soon," Parker added as he grabbed some gloves.

I nodded again.

"What, you too good to talk?"

Dropping my head back, I stared at the ceiling and took a deep breath. Rolling my head to the side, I eyed Parker's scowl. "No matter what I do or say you don't like me. How about we just work silently alongside each other?"

"Or you could just go."

Facing him, I asked, "What is your problem with me being here?"

He threw the bag down. "I don't know you, so I don't trust you."

"Lan knows me. *He* trusts me. Can't you trust him enough to accept me being here?"

"How do you know him?" he demanded.

"Lan's story to tell. It's not mine, and I won't be saying anything so don't bother pestering me about it. Now, will you pull your head out of your arse enough to work alongside me?"

"We'll see."

I threw my hands up in the air. "Are you always this angry?"

My question surprised him. His scowl deepened, which I didn't think was possible, but there it was. He growled under his breath, and for some reason, I wanted to laugh.

Shrugging, I went back to work and ignored him. His feet stomped around the room a little louder after that. Like he was a pouty, spoilt little boy who didn't get his way. Again, I wanted to laugh at him, but I wasn't ready to have my nose broken.

Sheesh, how does Lan work with the guy every day?

If it were me, I would have asked to be transferred to get away from him. Unless there was something more going on between the two of them... but a part of me told me I was wrong about that idea. Parker wasn't sending my gaydar off. Then again, neither had Lan that first night I.... Yeah, thinking about that wouldn't do me any good.

Maybe Parker was just protective.

He seemed it.

There could be a reason behind why he was so protective. Did someone important to him die? Guessing what had happened wouldn't get me any closer to figuring a man like Parker out. I was sure he had many, many layers and no one had yet got to the bottom of it. Did Lan know everything about him?

Why was I even thinking about prickly Parker? I didn't care who he was or why he had problems with anger. I glanced to him out the corner of my eyes. He was scrubbing the walls with a frown to his lips. I wondered what he would look like if he did smile.

Hold up. I didn't need to know what he looked like.

He was an arse.

Nothing but a growly Neanderthal.

So okay, he was a good-looking one. Tall, slim build with long dark hair and darker eyes, but that didn't make up for his attitude.

"What are you looking at?" he barked. My body jolted.

Shit.

"You missed a spot," I said and pointed to the wall. Thank heavens there *was* a spot he'd missed.

"Just—"

Lan groaned. We both moved at the same time. I went to the left side, Parker the right.

"Lan?" I called.

"The pain meds would be working, yeah?"

I nodded. "Of course. He's just coming out of the sedation."

"Lan, can you hear me?"

"Uh-huh," he mumbled.

"Good. Nurse and I got you all stitched up. If you can still feel pain, let me know, and I'll up the dosage."

"Good." He smiled.

"Great," I replied. "When you're up for it, Parker and I'll help you get cleaned up."

"'Kay."

Parker's shoulders dropped, tension unhinging them. He flicked off his gloves, and I did the same. I needed a shower myself, but that'd wait until Lan was cleaned and situated in a room where his blood didn't coat any of it.

"Does he have a spare room?" I asked.

"Yeah, next one over."

"With a bed and all?"

"Think so."

I started for the door. "I'll go see if the bed's made up. If not, I'll do it for Lan to get in after his shower." I wasn't sure why I was explaining myself, but I did, and Parker said nothing to it. I was just about out the door when Lan called my name. Turning back, I said, "Yes?"

Lan chuckled. "Remember the last time we showered together?"

Oh, screw me deep and hard.

My gaze flashed up to Parker. Already he stared at me with eyes so wide I was surprised they didn't pop out of his head.

I couldn't answer Lan, not with Parker there, and I also didn't think I wanted to talk about it with Lan either. So instead of saying anything, I bolted from the room.

CHAPTER EIGHT

PARKER

*S*ay what the fuck now?

I was stunned to the spot staring after a blushing Easton. *That* was how they knew each other, but how— Fuck, I didn't mean how, I knew how, but why... wait, I didn't know Lan was gay.... Except, he couldn't be. I'd heard about his dates with *women*. He'd spoken of them.

"East?" Lan called.

My gaze swung down to him. I snapped my mouth closed and cleared my throat. "Ah, he'll be back, and so will I. Just, uh, rest." I stalked from the room and straight into the next one where I found Easton laying a sheet on the bed. "You and Lan?"

He glared across at me. "Talk to him about it."

"When?"

"*Talk* to *him*—"

"I didn't know he was gay."

He rolled his eyes. "He's not."

I snorted. "Yeah, and he just likes to shower with random guys." I was not thinking of those times at the gym showers or the precinct.

Fuck no. I would not let my mind go there.

Easton's brows raised. "Does he?"

He was a frustrating little dick. I growled under my breath. "So he's not gay, but you two had a *thing?*"

His gaze narrowed even more. "*Yes.* Ten years ago."

I jerked my head back in shock. "What, were you fifteen or something? You look like you're twenty now."

"No," he bit out. "I was nineteen. Not that it's any of your business. In fact, you need to get back in that room while I do this. Then when he's more with it, we'll get him clean and back to resting." He turned his back on me, and I knew I wasn't going to get any more out of him.

I supposed I'd got enough anyway.

Lan wasn't gay, but apparently, he was for Easton. And that was ten years ago. Lan would have been thirty at the time, and Easton said he was nineteen. Who seduced who?

My steps faltered. I didn't give a flying fuck who seduced who.

Jesus. Where had that thought come from?

Shaking my head, I walked back into Lan's room and over to the bed. He seemed to be sleeping again. I sighed in relief because I wasn't sure I wanted to hear anything that came out of his mouth right then.

Still, it wasn't like I cared if Lan liked guys. Each to their own and all that. But it was a shock to find out, that was for sure.

Lan shifted on the bed, his good eye opened, and he blinked a few times. Then noticed me and a smile came over his lips. "Parker." He sighed.

"Hey, man. You doin' okay?"

"Yeah."

"We got Hawks searchin' for Miller. We're gonna get you back on your feet real soon."

"Hawks. Good guys."

My lips twitched. "Yeah, they are."

"So's you."

I stiffened. "All right."

"He's awake?" Easton asked from the doorway.

I nodded. I wasn't sure if I could look at the guy without wondering why Lan had picked him or had there been others? *Nope, not going there either.*

Easton came forward, moving around me to Lan's side. "Lan, we need to get you up and clean. I've made up the spare bed for you to hop into after you've showered."

"Sure," Lan replied happily. "Long as you get in with me."

I tensed.

Easton grumbled something under his breath. "Ah, no, but I'll help you… and Parker's here to help as well."

"East and Parker," Lan mumbled and then started chuckling.

I snorted. "Come on, man. Let's get you up."

He laughed harder, then winced. "I already am."

"Uh, no you're not. You're lying in bed," I told him and then glanced to Easton to find he was blushing about something.

Ignoring whatever it was, I pulled the sheet down and clenched my jaw. I couldn't wrap my head around someone being in Lan's house and hurting him. No, it wasn't that I couldn't wrap my head around it; it was more like I wanted to wrap my hands around the fucker who did it and not let go.

I sucked in a deep breath through my nose and shook my head. Leaning down, I gripped Lan's arm where it wouldn't hurt and slid the other under his back. "Let's get you washed." He grunted, and with Easton's help on the other side, we got him up and standing. He rested all his weight my way. His jeans were already undone and hanging low so Nurse could patch up his hip. The wound on the leg already showed through the cut material around it, I glanced over to Easton as we slowly, so damn slowly, made our way to Lan's en suite. "His bandages okay in water?"

"Yeah, they're waterproof. Still, I'll change them again later."

I nodded and kicked the door open all the way.

"You guys are the best," Lan said.

I chuckled. Yep, he was still high.

"Lan, we're going to turn you around, and you need to lean against the counter," Easton told him.

"Sure, anything." He smiled. Once we had him half propped up on the counter, so his injured leg wasn't taking his weight standing on the floor, we stepped back.

"I'll get the shower, you get his pants down," I said, and started to shift around Easton.

He grabbed my arm. "No. *You* get his pants down and *I'll* start the shower."

I narrowed my gaze and clipped, "I don't think so. You've seen his junk before."

He straightened to his full height, and still, he was shorter than me and crossed his arms over his chest. "You can't tell me that during the gym or at work you and Lan have never seen each other naked?"

Fuck.

"Not the point," I bit out.

He cocked a brow. "What, because I've had his dick in my mouth it should be me to undress him?"

I could feel my face heating. My idiot eyes flicked down to his lips, and I wanted to tear them out of my head. Instead, I sneered, "Glad we got that sorted then."

"Hey, hey, hey," Lan said. "No arguing, both of you go. I got it handled." He grinned, then cringed and softly cursed. His hands went into the top of his jeans and started to slip them down, but I saw he was struggling, and Easton also noticed.

"Dammit," Easton muttered. "Stop, you'll rip your stitches," he ordered and stepped towards him. I took the chance to move to the shower and get it turned on. I waited for it to heat and kept checking the temperature. I glanced over my shoulder to see Easton on his knees helping Lan out of his jeans. Lan was smiling softly down at him, then he lifted his head up and glanced over at me and winked.

I jerked my head back around to the shower and pushed what was happening behind me out of my head.

"Fuck," Easton clipped.

"What?" I asked, spinning back around. Easton stood with his hands on his hips in front of a grinning Lan. "What's wrong?" I took a couple of steps over and stopped at his side.

Easton ran a hand over his blushing face before dropping his head back, eyes closed to the ceiling. He cursed again, and I saw his hand lift, gesturing in front of him. I looked at Lan, then down his body.

A laugh abruptly left me. I then snorted. "Seriously, man. You're injured, and you can still get it up."

Lan's grin upped a notch. He was so going to kill himself when he remembered this shit. But right then he didn't seem to have a care in the world with his erection tenting his boxers.

"There's—"

My hand shot up. "Nope, I don't want to hear it. You're going in the shower with your boxers on."

"'Kay," he said lazily.

"Come on," Easton said, exacerbated, and went to Lan's right side. I took his left, and together we got him into the shower. Easton gave me most of his weight so he could help clean him down.

Lan hummed under his breath, then giggled like a little girl. "A fantasy come true."

I froze.

He meant Easton in the shower with him. It had to be it.

It had to be.

Push that fucker way, *way* back in my mind also. I wasn't even gonna open my mouth to clarify it because it was what he meant. Lan wasn't attracted to me.

No.

Hell no.

Jesus, that was just laughable.

He'd never once looked at me in a way that said otherwise.

It seemed Easton wasn't touching on what Lan said either. "You can turn off the shower," he told me over Lan's shoulder.

In the process of it all, our clothes got drenched. Luckily, I carried a spare change in the car. As we got out, I grabbed the towel off the rack and handed it to Easton, he glared but dropped Lan's weight onto me while he quickly dried him off.

Damn, who was going to change his boxers?

It sure as shit wouldn't be me.

"You two are great," Lan mumbled. His good eye opened and closed slowly. Exhaustion had him leaning into me more than he had been.

I grunted my reply, and Easton mumbled, "Uh-huh." Then with a sigh, he wrapped the towel around his waist and put his hands underneath it. A scowl replaced the perturbed look. He seemed to take his damn time getting Lan's boxers off him.

"This ain't the time to jack him off—"

"Fuck you, dickhead. His boxers are wet and stuck on his skin. You want to give it a go?"

"No." I glared down at him. Easton shook his head and went back to work. I wasn't pissed at him; I was annoyed at myself for being a dick when he was there helping but didn't have to.

Still, I didn't trust the guy because I didn't know enough about him.

"East wouldn't do that. Not when I fucked things up with us," Lan muttered.

"Lan, not now," Easton clipped.

Curiosity and all that shit.

"How'd you fuck things up?" I asked.

Easton's gaze snapped up to me. It was harsh, and any other man would have been wary of it, but I wasn't.

"I got sca—"

"Lan!" Easton snapped as he straightened. He cleared his throat. "Step out of the boxers," he ordered. Lan nodded, and with our help, we had him out of his boxers and in the spare room next. Gently, we lowered him to sit on the side of the bed. "I'll grab some other boxers," Easton said, and disappeared from the room.

I stood back, ran a hand over my face and eyed Lan hunched in on himself. "You all right?" I asked.

He nodded and winced once more. "Like your hair long," he whispered. My head jerked back. What was I supposed to say to that?

"Uh, thanks." I glanced around the room. It was bare other than the bedside tables and the bed Lan was on.

Lan snorted, his arm went across his stomach.

Easton came back into the room and knelt in front of Lan. "Lift your feet, and then Parker will help you stand."

Lan smiled softly down at Easton and did as he asked. Stepping up, I helped Lan to his feet, and Easton hiked up his boxers under the towel, then whipped the towel away.

"Right, now I'll change the bandages, up your meds, and then you can rest."

"I'll go fix some food. He should eat before resting," I suggested.

Easton nodded. With one last look at them, I made my way out of the room.

CHAPTER NINE

EASTON

*S*leep didn't come for a damn long time and then when I eventually drifted, it wasn't peaceful. The cause of it was from dreaming of masked men attacking Lan, and I wasn't able to help him.

In the end, I climbed out of bed in the early hours of the morning feeling like I hadn't slept at all. I made my way into the kitchen and switched on the kettle. While that boiled, I went to the back door and unlocked the dog door. Not that the lazy buggers would be up; it was too early for them. I glanced out the floor-to-ceiling glass back sliding door to down under the kitchen window where their beds lay and caught a couple of them lifting their heads to sniff. They checked out it was me unlocking the door and then curled back into themselves to go back to sleep.

Hell, maybe if I had someone to sleep next to, I wouldn't be up so damn early on my holidays either. Snorting, I walked into the living room to peek out the front window towards Lan's house.

I'd left there after settling Lan into his spare bed again. Even though Parker had made me a sandwich, I ignored it because I didn't want to be around either of them. My limits had been pushed. Not only from Lan and his loose lips, but from the aggravating

Parker. I didn't understand the guy, and I didn't want to since all he seemed to do was piss me off.

Well, it wasn't like I had to know him anyway. Even if he was Lan's work partner, I didn't care because Lan wasn't going to be in my life again.

There was no way I would want to put myself through the hurt I'd felt that first time again.

Especially since it was noticeable that not even Lan's partner, who he worked closely with, knew Lan liked women *and* men. God, I hoped Parker would keep it to himself since I was certain Lan didn't want anyone to know about his past with me. Not only that, but about him liking guys.

Had he been with anyone lately?

Shaking my head, I scrubbed a hand over my tired face.

I didn't care either way.

Like I'd told Parker, I'd go back and check on Lan and his wounds. I'd keep it professional. Act like Lan Davis was a patient.

I had to.

My phone rang. I went back into the kitchen, grabbed it off the bench and answered it after glancing at the caller ID. "Miss me already?"

Oliver snorted. "No, okay yes, but that's because Henrietta is bossier than you on the job."

"Only another few weeks and I'll be back."

"Thank God, but I was also calling about tonight. Chris and I were going to bring out takeaway."

"No," I stated, already knowing the real reason Chris and Oliver would want to soften me up with a takeaway since it was usually me who cooked on nights we got together.

"He's a friend of Chris's and really nice. Cute even."

I groaned. "Cute? Oliver the last guy you called cute was Brad, and he had a problem with phlegm."

He chuckled. "I forgot about him."

"How? Chris nearly threw up each time he sucked his snot into the back of his throat and then made that swishing sound as he played with it in his mouth."

More laughter. "Good times. But I promise Simon is different."

Sighing, I pinched the bridge of my nose and thought about it. I didn't really have anything planned for that night, and I only had to check on Lan that day. I supposed I could tidy the house in between.

"Easton?"

"Fine. But he'd better be nothing like Brad."

He cheered. "He won't be, you'll love him. See you at seven." He blew a kiss down the line before ending the call.

Had I just made a big mistake or could Simon be the distraction I needed from a certain someone else?

I'd waited until just before lunch to head over to Lan's. It also happened to be the time after I saw Parker leave when two bikers arrived to keep watch on things. How I knew Parker was gone wasn't because I'd been at the window staring out again. It wasn't. I just happened to be walking by the window to clean the TV when I heard some Harleys coming up the road.

What didn't make sense was how my heart sped as I saw Parker step out the front door wearing a thermal top and jeans. Then I scoffed at the stupid organ and put its reaction down to the fact Parker aggravated me too much.

Once Parker's vehicle was out of sight, I stepped out of my house and made my way over. I knocked on the door because I wasn't sure if it would be unlocked, and if it was, I wasn't keen on walking in and having bikers wanting to kill me for just entering the place without drawing attention to myself first.

Tits on a whale, my stupid mind was running away from me. Then again, I didn't know any bikers, so I wasn't sure how to act around them. The ones from yesterday seemed okay, and they all acted like I was doing them a favour helping Lan.

The door swung open and in it stood Goliath.

The man was huge.

He stood in it scowling, crossed his arms over his chest and loomed over me. If I had to admit, for a moment, I felt like I wanted to run or whimper in fear or squeak out a sorry and hide. Instead, when his brow arched at me, I blurted, "I'm here to check on Lan. I was the one who found him yesterday with, um, my, ah, dog...." I glanced down, expecting to find Nero, but he wasn't with me that time. I looked back up and added, "I fixed Lan. With that Nurse guy. I'm a fixer... uh, I mean, a paramedic. Here to check on Lan." The guy blinked, and I blurted, "I won't say anything to anyone." I wanted to live and was sure the guy could snap me in two with just a look.

It had been years since I'd mumbled and acted like a shy little boy, but with a guy like the one in front of me, I was back to being my teenage self in seconds.

"Who is it, brother?" was called from behind.

The big guy stepped back, his hands moving as another biker came to his side. At least the new one smiled after he chuckled at whatever scary guy signed. "Hey, Easton. I'm Knife and that's Beast. The other brothers told us about you, as did Parker this mornin'. Lan's in bed asleep. You wanna check him?"

I eyed them both. "Yes?"

Knife laughed. "Relax, dude. You're cool, so Hawks'll be cool with you."

"Okay." I nodded. When they both moved out of the doorway, I stepped in. I licked my suddenly dry lips. The two men before me were good-looking, and any other time I would have taken my fill in and admired, but I wasn't stupid. Doing that would be a sure way to sign my death warrant. I looked everywhere else but at them and quickly pointed towards the hall, mumbling, "I'll, um, check out— on.... I'll check *on* Lan."

I heard a snort, and when I was halfway down the hallway, more laughter started, different from Knife's, so I guessed he just told

Beast how awkward I was being. At least they were finding my actions funny. Why in the high heaven had I acted like a timid little boy around them? Yes, they were intimidating, but if shit went down, I'd trained in boxing and martial arts enough to be able to protect myself. I could take them on. All right, maybe one.

What was I thinking?

The whole situation was messed up. First, Lan being my neighbour and what had happened to him, and then how he wanted to take care of the situation on his own. Well, not his own but with the help of Parker and the Hawks MC. Who was Lan Davis?

Was he anything like the person I used to know?

I shook all the thoughts off and entered the spare room. Knife was right; Lan still slept soundly. I checked over his wounds. All of them seemed to be okay. So I made sure to refill his water on the bedside table. On it was also an iPad, Lan's phone, some magazines, cut-up fruit, and bottles of medication. I read a couple of the labels. One was for inflammation, another was for pain, and then there were some antibiotics. I glanced at the IV. He still had fluids dripping into him. I'd have to mention to the bikers if Lan was drinking on his own, which he was more than capable of, we could take the drip out. Yesterday it had been to infuse the harder pain meds into him to knock him out and to make sure he didn't dehydrate too much overnight.

Lan twitched in his sleep. I expected his good eye to open, but it didn't. As I stared down at him, so many emotions flooded me. Anger would always be present, but I couldn't push the small part of me that cared for Lan away. I was happy he would heal, sad it had happened in the first place, and worried about what it meant if I stayed being his neighbour.

Of course I would stay. I loved my house too much to move and start over again.

But I wasn't sure how I'd handle knowing Lan lived just next door. I ran my gaze over him. He hadn't changed much. Back when... he'd always been muscular, and with how the sheet rested down around his waist, he was still built like a stone statue. All contours I used to love tracing with my hands and mouth.

A soft smile touched my lips at a particular memory.

Lan sat topless on my couch; he'd just finished drinking his beer and bent forward to place it on the coffee table. Of course my eyes weren't on the movie we were supposed to be watching together. Instead, they lingered on his chest, his abs, his warm, smooth skin. He'd been visiting me for over a month, and I was well on my way to loving him. Each text, call, or pop in I got giddy over. We talked about everything, even what we wanted in the future. But being able to stare and admire him as I was, I never thought I would get used to. I never thought I would ever have been so lucky to have a man like Lan Davis in my house and bed. Someone who teased me when I blushed, laughed when I stumbled over my words when he'd said something dirty, and looked at me like he was right then.

"You're supposed to be watchin' the movie," he said.

I smiled. "Can't help it when you're sitting there half-naked."

He chuckled and winked. Then his eyes darkened, his tone serious with the next words, "Happiest night walkin' into that pub and seein' you."

"Really?"

"Yep." He grabbed my hand and tugged me closer, and I straddled his waist. "Been thinkin' of movin' to Melbourne."

My body tingled. "Really?" I breathed.

He smiled. "Yeah."

A clatter in the kitchen brought me from my thoughts, and I was grateful for it. My smile dropped, and I bit my bottom lip instead. Thinking about those sweet moments wouldn't get me anywhere. Clenching my jaw, I sighed and then made my way out of the bedroom, down the hall and stopped dead.

The kitchen was an open area that joined into the living room like mine did. I could see clearly into it from where I stood at the mouth of the hallway.

I could see what was happening in the kitchen.

The shock had my jaw dropping, my eyes widening, and me stumbling my steps towards the front door. I didn't want them to know I'd caught them; they could want to beat me senseless to keep my mouth shut.

But they'd heard and parted, both glancing my way. I froze like a deer caught in the gaze of a predator.

Knife slapped the counter in front of him. I jumped from the sound, and my body jolted again when he started laughing. He threw his head back and laughed heartily, then folded forward to slap the counter again. I chanced a glance at the scary Beast to even find him with a smirk on his lips. He rolled his eyes, and then when he gripped the back of Knife's hair, my stomach churned before it tingled and shot that feeling right to my cock. Beast pulled Knife back into his chest and whispered something into his ear before nipping at his neck.

Knife snorted out a small laugh and then said, "Okay, all right. I've had my fun." He grinned. "But you should'a seen your face. Fuck, that was funny."

"W-what?" I stuttered.

Knife started around the counter. "Man, you nearly had a heart attack when you'd said you'd check *out* Lan, instead of on. Probably thought we'd hate gay guys or some shit, had to play with you a bit."

"What?" I whispered.

Both Beast and Knife laughed. "Easton, we're bikers. We have our own set of rules that some would frown on, but what we're not is haters of gay, black, and any type of different people."

Sweat formed on my top lip. I wiped it away. "Um, I think, ah... I could tell."

They'd been lip locked together when I'd walked in.

Knife grinned wickedly. "Beast's mine. We have a kid together. The sooner you learn Hawks is different to most clubs and the members are awesome people, like me, the sooner you'll calm the fuck down around us."

Beast was his.

They had a kid together.

Hawks was definitely different.

Still, what was I supposed to say to that?

"Okay?" I offered.

Knife snorted. "Get your arse in here and have a drink. You helped Lan out. Lan and some of the brothers said you're cool, so let's chat."

Did I want to chat with Knife and Beast?

Bikers?

Men who would do anything for Lan since they were already out hunting for the man who harmed him.

Shit. Yes. I was intrigued by them and even the club.

CHAPTER TEN

PARKER

*B*y the time I made it back to Lan's, it was after dinner, and I had no leads to find Miller. Some would think it'd be easy to find a motherfucker who had a gunshot wound to his hand, but the people I knew—who would do a backyard fix-up—hadn't seen the dick. I would have stayed out later, but Knife and Beast had to get back home to their girl, Nevaeh. At least I knew there were still a couple of brothers out looking for Miller. The sarge had also gotten back to me and told me without a decent amount of notice, I wouldn't be able to have time off. Still, he was a good guy because instead of being out in the field, he'd given me some desk duties I could do anywhere with a laptop for a week. Meant while I stayed with Lan at night, I had something to do when sleep wouldn't come.

I opened Lan's front door, dropped my bag to the floor, and found Knife and Beast relaxing on the couch. "Nothin' to worry about?" I asked, after closing the front door behind me. I took the chair off to the right of the couch.

"All good, brother," Knife said. "Easton checked him out this morning, then Nurse came by this afternoon and took him off the drip. Lan's still on pain meds, but he's drinking and eating on his own and can swallow tablets when prompted."

"He been all right?"

Beast chuckled.

Knife glanced at him, grinning. "Yeah, he's been as high as a kite."

Shit. I wasn't sure if that was good or not. Guessed it depended on what Lan said and if he'd want the brothers to know.

"What'd he say?"

Beast's lips twitched. Knife said, "Just stuff about his neighbour. I nearly dropped his plate when he mentioned about tasting Easton for the first time."

Lan was going to kill himself.

I groaned, sat back further and ran a hand over the back of my neck. "You know whatever you hear outta him you gotta keep it to yourself."

Beast grunted. "Know that," he said and signed at the same time. Beast became deaf after a motorcycle accident. He learned sign language and how to read lips. Even before the crash, he never used to talk either because of his speech, but since being with Knife, he wasn't afraid if he fucked up his talking anymore. It was amazing what the right person could do for someone.

Something I'd never wanted. Bitches were too high maintenance.

"Yeah." Knife nodded. "'Course we do. He ain't fully with it. It just surprised us. You ever knew he liked dick?"

"Jay," Beast warned.

"What?" Knife rolled his eyes at Beast's glare.

"No," I said.

His brows raised. "Do you care?"

I narrowed my gaze. "You askin' me if I care Lan had somethin' with Easton?"

"Yeah, or that he's into dudes."

Leaning forward, I rested my elbows on my knees. "Seriously, Knife? Who was it that told you to man up with Beast after you asked me to run a background check on the guy you were jealous over?"

"I... you.... Shit, yeah okay. Stupid question." He chuckled.

I watched Beast's hands move over his words and nodded. "Yeah, your guy wanted me to check on that Ben dude." We both laughed. Knife grumbled under his breath.

"Anyway," Knife drew out, and I knew he was about to change the subject to get it off him. "Easton seems cool."

Jesus, he could have picked something else to talk about.

"Thought you two had to get home to your girl?"

Knife chuckled. "Yeah, we do." We stood. "Pick mentioned you didn't like Easton much."

I shrugged. "It's not that I don't like him. I don't trust him, and I don't know him."

"Just want to point out how he took the time out today to get to know us. Even after Beast freaked him out and he seemed about to shit himself being around us. He sucked it up and sat down with us."

"That's nice for you."

"Parker—"

"Hey," was called. We all faced the hallway to see Lan stumbling his way over to us.

"What're you doin' up?" I asked, making my way over to Lan and then hooking my arm under his and around his waist.

"Dunno," he mumbled. "Wanted a walk."

Yep, he was still high on pain meds.

Beast and Knife chuckled.

"Come on, let's say goodbye to the brothers, then we'll see about some food."

"'Kay." His smile was a little sloppy. We made it to the door after Knife and Beast had already stepped out and stopped on the front porch.

"Catch you soon," Knife said. "Think Dallas is out here tomorrow." Beast sent me a chin lift before climbing on his ride.

"Thanks, brothers," I called.

"Anytime," Knife replied.

I waited out there until they were on their way out of the drive. The night had grown colder; it made me want to get Lan back inside since he was only in his boxers. But then a vehicle came down the road, I paused, and Lan looked to where I was. We saw it pull into Easton's driveway and stop just out the front. Three guys climbed out and made their way towards the house. When the front door opened, Easton stepped out.

I felt Lan tense.

Of fucking course being out in the middle of nowhere with not much traffic or noise for that matter, the voices were easy to hear on a quiet night. I wished Knife and Beast were still there with their rides idling or some shit to drown out what we'd heard.

"East, we brought dinner and your dessert," someone yelled and then laughed.

"Oliver," was warned.

"I'm kidding. Or am I?" He paused and then, "Easton Ravel, I'd like you to meet Simon Flagon, your date for the night."

Shit.

Lan straightened to what he could and clipped loudly, "The fuck?"

All eyes turned our way.

"Lan, let's go in," I suggested in a low, rough tone and went to turn him towards the front door, but he didn't want to move, and since he was damned injured, I couldn't exactly pick him up and carry him outta there.

"Excuse me?" someone called.

"Oliver, leave it," Easton ordered.

"I will not. Who do they think they're talking to? And looking at us like we're scum." He snorted. "Especially when they're huddled close like—"

"Oliver," Easton snapped.

"It's fine. Everything's fine," I called.

69

"Like fuck it's fine," Lan called. He stumbled out of my hold and down to the end of the porch, closer to Easton's house.

"Lan," I grumbled low at his back. "Get the hell inside."

He gripped the railing and shook his head slightly. "Not until that dickhead leaves. He'll not—"

"What dickhead?" Oliver yelled harshly, taking a few steps our way.

"Oliver," a new voice said calmly.

"Jesus," I rattled off.

"What happened to you?" Oliver asked as he got closer to the fence.

"You," Lan went to point at the Simon guy, but I grabbed his arm and shoved it down. He winced, and I regretted it.

"Parker, get him inside," Easton called.

"I'm trying," I bit out. "How about you move your party inside?"

"Who are they?" Oliver asked.

Lan cursed. "Easton, don't fuckin' think you can—"

"Lan Davis, not another word," Easton growled.

Oliver made a noise in the back of his throat. "Lan Davis? *The* Lan Davis?"

"Oliver. Inside now."

"But, honey, that's—"

"Oliver," Easton warned.

Oliver glanced back to Lan and took him in slowly from head to toe. "I can see why—"

"Ollie, I swear to God, if you don't shut your mouth, I'll kick your arse," Easton hissed, and ran a hand over his head in frustration.

"Fine. Okay." With a final look, he spun and walked back towards the entrance. "We'd better eat anyway before it goes cold." He moved out of sight. I heard the front door open, and then the other two men followed him into the house while Easton dropped his head, sighed, and then mumbled something under his breath before coming our way.

"It's getting cold. He should be inside," he mentioned, as if I didn't know it already.

"We were just sayin' goodbye to people when your friends rocked up. Then Lan didn't want to go in."

"*He* is just standing *here*." Lan grinned at us both. Lan was a dick for that scene, but an amusing one. Never seen him jealous. It was a different side to him, and it made me wonder what made Easton so special to gain that reaction from Lan.

Actually, scratch that, I didn't care either way.

"Then let's get the fuck inside," I grumbled.

He shook his head and faced Easton. "You datin' that guy?"

Easton's jaw clenched. "It's none of your business, Lan."

"Bullshit," Lan clipped. "I'm not leavin' this porch until you tell me."

Silence.

"East," Lan growled low.

He shook his head. "I've just met him."

"Good," Lan clipped, then added, "so you'll not touch him."

This certainly felt awkward. Still, I kept my mouth shut and pretended I didn't hear shit.

Easton's face screwed up. "You don't have a right to tell me what to do."

"Then I guess I'll be stayin' right here." Lan managed to straighten and cross his arms loosely over his chest.

"Just go in," Easton bit out.

"Nope."

Lan was just that stubborn he would wait outside until Easton agreed. Though somehow, I knew Lan would win. Easton was... fuck, I couldn't believe I even thought it, but he was a kinda okay guy, and I knew he wouldn't let Lan suffer in the cold for much longer. The way he dropped his head back and looked to the sky, I figured he was about to give.

He brought his gaze back to Lan. "Fine," he snapped. "I won't touch him."

"And he can't touch you."

Easton threw his hands up in the air. "It's not like you'd know—"

Lan dropped his hands back onto the railing. "Don't make me come over there. The pain meds are wearing off, but I'd still come over to make sure *nothin'* happens."

"You're an annoying arsehole."

I couldn't contain the snort. They both looked to me while I leaned my butt against the railing with my ankles crossed, like my arms were over my chest watching the show. They'd forgotten I was there, but I had to be in case Lan ended up on his face from exhaustion. His body tensed even more, and then he cringed. Yeah, he was telling the truth, the pain meds were wearing off for him.

Easton turned and started for his front door.

"East," Lan called. When he didn't get a reply, Lan added, "I'm coming over—"

"No!" Easton spun back, his hands fisted at his sides. "Nothing will happen. We'll all eat dinner and then they'll leave."

Lan smiled. "Okay."

Easton threw up his hands again and stomped the rest of the way inside. Even slammed his door in the process.

"You ready to go inside now?" I asked, my lips twitching, amused by the scene.

Lan slowly turned to me. "You're going to have to help me. My body's fuckin' killing me."

I chuckled, shook my head and went to his side. I wrapped an arm around his back while he placed one around my shoulders. "Would you have gone over there?" I knew the answer, but I wanted to be sure I was right in my thinking.

He grunted when we started walking. "Yes," he said through clenched teeth.

"Fuck, Lan, did you even take the meds on your bedside table before comin' out?" I asked, making our way into the house.

"I was sick of feelin' fuzzy, and when I got up, I was still high a bit, so I thought I'd be fine."

"Well, you're fuckin' not."

"Know that, dick."

I got him back to the room and lowered him to sit on the side of the bed. I grabbed the water and pills, then handed them to him. "Take 'em."

He did and then placed the glass back on the bedside table. He gently moved back and pulled his feet up on the bed. I flung the blanket over him. He smirked. "You make a good house nurse."

"Shut up."

He laughed and winced, laying his arm across his gut.

"I'll get some food before you crash," I told him, and when he said nothing but nodded, I went back out into the kitchen. As I heated some food I found in the fridge, my thoughts drifted to the scene outside. Lan had obviously had it bad for Easton to demand shit from him like that. Even after, from what I gathered, Lan hurt him, I was surprised Easton listened. But then it came back to my previous thought about Easton being an okay guy.

Still, I didn't trust him fully.

CHAPTER ELEVEN

LAN

I watched Parker walk out of the room. When I'd spoken to Easton outside, I'd forgotten he was there. What was strange was how he hadn't seemed surprised by it. That got me thinking that I must have said or done something to give away my past with Easton in front of him. But what? I should've warned them I was never good on pain meds. How I tended to blurt shit out…. Fuck, I wish I remembered, but I didn't.

Which meant I'd have to ask him and talk it out before the meds kicked in.

I'd also have to get him out of the house in case I said or did something to Parker. Something I'd regret, and he'd freak out over.

Burning pain touched me in my shoulder, side, arm, and leg. Hell, might as well be all over since it sure felt like it. Honestly, I hadn't even seen the pain meds on the bedside table when I woke. I'd heard Parker's voice, and like a ship to water, I wanted to head towards it and see what he was doing. I knew I would've acted the same way if it'd been Easton.

Goddamn. *Two guys.*

Two guys who wouldn't have, and didn't, want anything to do with me.

Though from what I could guess, Easton had stuck around after finding and fixing me up with Nurse, and that was nice. I could recall Nurse arriving but not much after that. How long had Easton stayed? What had he said to Parker? Or what had Parker overheard me saying to Easton?

Fuck me. I felt like an injured, pathetic animal, and all I could think about was Parker and Easton. My mind should have been on Miller and my vengeance for what he'd done to me. I clenched my jaw and fists. It was his fucking fault I was laid up in bed and probably making a fool out of myself.

Shit. Had I said anything in front of the Hawks brothers?

Christ. To hell with it. Right then, I didn't care because my head throbbed with new pain. That motherfucking piece-of-shit Miller. Why in the hell did *I* have to suffer from his bad choices?

He would pay.

He had to.

The Lan who'd been his partner was long gone.

In his place was a man who'd seen too much shit. Too many crims got away with crimes I knew they'd committed. At first, I thought the Hawks values were wrong, but the way they handled Malinda's situation, I knew deep down they weren't. They, as well as Malinda, made me realise I would put the badge aside if I had to so the culprit could be taught a lesson before they were handed over to me, and now Parker. Or if there was a case where a lesson wasn't enough, I turned a blind eye. Hawks dealt with their own problems, and it wasn't over petty shit. Bad things had happened, and they'd sorted it to protect their family.

It was the path I chose to follow.

It was the belief system I chose to live by.

Family was first.

I didn't have much of it, but I saw many close friends and their families as a part of my life, in one way or another.

And one day I would have my own to protect.

But then Easton came barrelling back into my life. After seeing him again, all I could see for my future was Easton at my side. Waking and falling asleep beside him. Smiling, laughing, and spending all the time I could with him. He'd been my only piece of happiness so long ago. Could he be again? Maybe he could if I showed him I wasn't the person I'd been back then—a coward.

My sight shot to the doorway as Parker walked in and my heart skipped a damn beat spotting him. How could Easton be the future I hoped for and still be attracted to a man I shouldn't be?

He carried with him a tray and came to my side to lay it beside me. "Someone cooked today. I found risotto in the fridge. Thought it'd slide down better than anythin' else."

"Thanks."

"You doin' okay?"

"Yeah. Look, I was thinking about how I doubt Miller will make another appearance here. No use for you to stay. I'll be fine on my own."

He straightened and crossed his arms over his chest. "You want me gone?"

I glanced down at the food and then back up to his scowl. "Sure."

"Why the sudden change?"

I clenched my hands and sucked in a breath through my nose, then brought up the damn awkward subject. "How much do you know about Easton?"

He snorted. "This why you want me to go? You're embarrassed? I don't give a shit about what happened between you and the kid."

"He's not a kid," I bit out.

Parker relaxed his stance and sat on the edge of the bed. "Not the point I was gettin' at. You don't need to worry about being embarrassed over it."

"I'm not. But how did you find out? It looked like you knew a lot while we were outside before."

He leaned back on a palm and eyed me. His lips twitched, and I fucking knew whatever happened it was going to embarrass me.

"You wanted him in the shower with you, said something about remembering the last time it happened."

Fuck.

What a way to find out about it.

"Bet you got the shock of your life?"

He chuckled and shook his head smiling. "Yep. So did Beast and Knife."

With my gut churning, I blinked slowly over at Parker. "Shit, I said it in front of them too?"

"Nah, you'd said something else to them when I wasn't here."

I ran a hand over my face with a wince. Weariness pulled at me. "Don't matter who knows."

Parker leaned forward and picked up the bowl. "Eat before you crash."

I smiled. "You're good."

He snorted. "No, I'm not."

"You are." I grabbed the bowl and stuffed a mouthful in, only to cringe when my shoulder twinged. He sighed, grabbed the bowl back and with an eye-roll, he scooped up some on the spoon, and held it out in front of my mouth.

"Shut it," he warned, maybe because my smile had grown.

After I chewed and swallowed, I asked, "You don't care?"

He gave me more before he answered, "Nope."

"Why?"

"Each to their own, Lan. I ain't gonna judge shit like that. You still care for him?" By the quick flare of his eyes, he hadn't expected that question to come out of him.

"Yeah, I do." Did I? I did. He was on my mind constantly, even before I saw him about a month ago. I'd also wondered where and how he was, and who he was with. Though, with that last thought, I always seemed to get pissed.

My gut twisted at the guilt of how I'd ended it with him. I hadn't wanted to, but I'd been scared by how my colleagues would take it. Too concerned about *my* feelings and nothing about his. I'd gone to his place the next day, but he was already gone.

I wished to Christ I'd chased him.

Regret.

It'd always be a part of me, and I could only pray things would change.

Unless he thought I was still a dick. The way I acted out the front wasn't promising or helping me any.

"More?" Parker asked. I hadn't realised I'd still been eating while lost in my own thoughts.

I shook my head. My brain had grown foggy.

"Gonna sleep," I said after a sip of water.

"All good, I'll be on the couch."

"You don't—"

"Shut it, Lan."

I chuckled and slowly slid down in the bed. "See, you're good," I mumbled, my eyes already drifting closed.

Parker

Standing, I took one more glance at Lan and left the room. I pulled the door half closed; if Lan called out, I wanted to be able to hear him. I headed down the hall to the living room and sat on the edge of the couch, resting my head in my hands and sighed. If I was such a good guy…. I shook my head, knowing I wasn't. There was no doubt about it. I wasn't a good guy. Lan saw my fucked-up attitude at the world. I was angry all the damn time.

Angry at so many things.

Lan couldn't seriously believe I was a good guy. It had to be the drugs talking. Then again, he didn't know everything about me. No one did, not even the sarge since I had a different surname to the person I should have called Mum.

Admittedly, before Lan came along, I'd been worse. Since him, and the connection he had to the Hawks MC and the way they were in the world, I'd found something within all of them that resonated in me. Their morals. The way they treated each other and their families.

That was how families should have been.

Not what Erin was.

She'd been nothing to us.

Not that anyone knew where my anger stemmed from, but it wasn't something I could get rid of. At least I didn't think I could. It'd been with me for a long time and for a damned good reason.

Sergeant got me to see a shrink a few times. Not that it worked out. Talking to strangers didn't sit well for me as I didn't trust easy. At least not until I'd had time to read them, and time meant more than a couple of visits.

Yeah, I had issues.

The funny thing was, since Lan, a man who showed me I could trust, and the Hawks brothers as well, they helped cool my anger. It was still there. It would always be there, not only for what happened, but for the stupid choices I'd made and how it had cost not me but a person I loved.

Christ.

I rubbed my palms into my eyes.

Exhaustion pulled at my mind and body. But when I slept after being so goddamn tired, I sometimes dreamed, and I fucking hated those more than the lack of sleep. I snorted. That was another reason I was a cunt most days. I survived more on catnaps than actual sleep.

Jesus. I was so damn screwed up.

Standing, I grabbed my laptop and walked into the kitchen. I poured myself a mug of coffee that was already brewed and tilted my gaze to the front window when music from next door started up. Seemed Easton had decided to have a party. Only a second later, the tunes quickly shut off. Thank fuck, I was in no mood for anything else that night.

CHAPTER TWELVE

EASTON

$\mathcal{I}$'d walked into the kitchen hoping for a moment of silence to think after what happened outside, but I heard the footsteps following so I knew what would be coming.

"Lan Davis," Oliver hissed.

Groaning, I faced him with a frown. "Ollie—"

He shook his finger at me. "No, don't you Ollie me. When did you find out? How do you feel about it? Lan Davis, the love of your life, lives next door."

I rolled my eyes. "He's not the love of my life."

Oliver crossed his arms over his chest and rose his brows.

I glared. "He's not."

He sighed and waved his hands up, then dropped them. "Fine. Okay, he used to be… but he could be again. I didn't miss the way he eyed Simon like he wanted to rip his head off."

"He also listened from the door," Chris called from the living area.

Groaning again, I went into the next room. I should have guessed they would be able to hear us with the open-planned living area *and* that Oliver would listen at the front door.

Stopping at the end of the couch where a smirking Chris and a calm-looking Simon sat, I said, "I'm so sorry about what happened. Can we please just drop what occurred out there"—I pointed towards the front door—"and go on to enjoy our meal together?"

Oliver snorted from behind me. "Sure, but I still want answers."

I spun his way. "Did you not invite Simon here as a blind date? Don't you think it a little rude to talk about this in front of him?"

When Simon cleared his throat, I gave him my attention. "Don't mind me. Oliver already said there was a fat chance you'd want to go out again."

Suddenly, I was picturing the best way to murder someone named Oliver.

"He did, did he?" I bit out. Oliver rolled his eyes.

"Easton," Simon called. "Seriously, don't worry. They just wanted me out of my house so I would stop pining over my ex. It wasn't until on the way here they told me to check you out and see if I liked you."

Closing my eyes, I shook my head slowly. Opening them, I caught Simon's soft smile. I told him, "I don't know if I should kick them out without food or make them stay and eat it all in front of them."

Chris huffed. "Now, come on. It's never *me* doing this."

I pondered it for a second. "True."

Oliver snorted. "Like you'd let me starve." He walked around the couch and snatched up the takeaway bags. "Besides, I'm too cute to make suffer. Let's dish up while you dish out the goods."

"Oliver," Chris sighed.

"What?" he called over his shoulder on the way back into the kitchen.

"Leave him alone."

He laughed. "Why would I do that?"

I shook my head at him again and then told Chris, "Don't worry, I'll have a quick chat and then get him to back off or I'll threaten the Pink tickets I organised."

"You wouldn't," he screamed.

"I would," I shouted back, and then left Simon and Chris chuckling to help Oliver. It wasn't like I didn't and wouldn't talk about Lan to Oliver. He was my best friend, but I didn't understand myself what the hell Lan's actions were about outside. It felt as if he were staking his claim over me, which seemed stupid because it had been *years,* and... I didn't know. I knew nothing when it came to the man next door.

It had to be the medication.

It really had to be.

I wouldn't let my heart get all melty again, like it had moments ago outside when he was demanding I didn't touch anyone and no one was allowed to touch me.

Seriously, what was that about and why did I like it?

I shouldn't, couldn't, *wouldn't* like it because it would all lead to me being hurt.

"You don't look happy," Oliver commented quietly while taking out some plates. "Did I push too far?"

"No. You know I can handle you playing around, and if you did go too far, I'd let you know."

He rested his butt against the counter. "So what is it?" A smile tugged at his lips. He knew what it was. Not what, but who.

With a sigh, I ran a hand across the back of my neck. "He lives next door."

"Yep."

"How am I going to cope?"

"Two options. Steer clear of him, though I have a feeling he won't allow it. Or you can get it over with."

My eyes shot to slits. "What?"

"Do him and see if there's anything between you two still. Although, anyone with eyes can see he's eating you up as a delicious meal every time he looks at you. At first, I thought they were being pricks, but as soon as I saw him look at you, I knew I was wrong. What I don't get is who that other guy is, and did I imagine the bandages on Lan Davis or not?"

"I think I'll pick the first option. It'll be the safest."

Oliver scoffed. "Safe is boring."

"Safe is calming."

"Safe is turning into an old man who lives with his stray dogs and no one else." He looked around the room. "Wait, you're already there."

I chuckled. "Fuck you."

"Been there, done that, no thanks."

"Let's get the food out there before it's completely cold. Also, to answer your other queries, the other guy—"

"Is to die for."

I snorted out a laugh. "He's not bad. But he's also straight and Lan's detective partner."

"Boo."

"Not at all. He's also an arsehole."

"Forget him then and tell me what happened to your hunk."

"He's not *my* hunk."

He waved a fork around. "Semantics."

"He was attacked in his own home, I helped out and—"

"You helped out?" he screeched.

"Everything okay?" Chris called.

"Fine," Oliver yelled, then cleared his throat. "We're good. Tops in fact. One more moment is all we need, and then we can eat." He moved closer and hissed, "What do you mean you helped him out?"

"Nero heard something. We went to investigate and I ended up saving his life."

"Oh God. Oh my God. You could have died yourself, you fucking idiot."

"Ollie."

"Nope. Do not talk to me for the rest of the night." He huffed. "Well, until I'm over the fact I could have lost my best friend. I don't care how hot he is. *You* do not risk your own life."

"We risk it every time we go out on a call."

He glared. He wasn't ready to hear any truth, which was fine by me. I was over talking about it all and I didn't need to defend my actions. A lot of people would have done the same as me in that situation. What mattered most was being in the right place at the right time, or else Lan wouldn't be breathing. To me, excluding my fears of feelings, I knew that losing Lan from the world wasn't an option I could cope with.

Of course, a quiet night of takeout never turned out that way when Oliver was concerned. When he begged to have just one shot, it turned into twenty. It was about the tenth when somehow Simon and I had started dribbling on about our problems. Maybe that had been Oliver's evil plan after all. Therapy of some sort. I just wished it didn't involve a headache when I woke and the dogs were barking up a storm.

What also didn't help was the pounding on the front door. I rolled, peeked, and saw it was seven in the morning.

Shit.

Whoever banged on my front door would get an earful from me. I slowly stood, my head throbbing and my stomach threatening to bring up last night's dinner. I gently rubbed at it as I stumbled down the hall to the front door. "Quiet," I clipped. The dogs heard me through the back door and stopped, going back to whatever they'd been doing. I wouldn't open the dog door until I got rid of the visitor or some of my mutts would go bananas over the new person.

Just as another bang sounded on the front door, I swung it open ready to curse the person standing there, only to snap my mouth shut and straighten.

Lan's eyes slowly slid over my body. "Did they stay the night?" Lan scowled. "The car's still here, so they must have. I swear to fuckin' God, East, no one had better be in your room."

He went to push past me, but I stopped him with a hand to his chest. He glanced down at me. "What are you doing over here?" I asked.

"Car. Still here. What did I tell you?"

I shook my head, trying to clear the fog. "Wait, what?"

He shifted to the side and pointed to Chris's car still in my drive. My head jerked back in shock. They were still there? Had I...? No, I would have known if someone was next to me in bed.

I licked my dry lips, and told him, "We had a few too many last night, that's all." At least I was pretty sure that was all.

Lan frowned down at me. Bugger him for being tall. He leaned in and bit out roughly, "Do you forget I can read you?"

I gulped, not because I was afraid of him. Instead, it was his low voice doing things to me; it always had. "I-I'm not lying."

He straightened. "No, you're not, but you're also not sure. Let me help find out for you." His hand came to my stomach. I gasped and looked down, then realised I was only wearing boxers. Lan's cool hand flattened against my stomach, which clenched under his touch. I couldn't take my eyes off his pale hand against my darker skin. Then, as he slid it to my side, I bit my lip to refrain from sighing, but I couldn't stop my body trembling from his touch.

"East," Lan whispered.

I slammed my eyes closed and shook my head. "You shouldn't be out of bed."

His fingers rubbed gently up and down my waist. "Should I be in yours?"

My head snapped up, my harsh gaze colliding with his amused one. "Don't."

"East, you don't know how—"

"Morning." Oliver appeared at my side like some knight in shining armour. Lan dropped his hand to cross his arms over his chest and he glowered at Ollie. I didn't miss his flinch though. He was standing there dressed in track pants, a loose tee, and flip-flops, but he was doing it in pain.

That just pissed me off.

"Go home, Lan, and take better care of yourself. Have you even had your morning meds?" I ignored how I wished his hand was still on me.

His jaw clenched, his eyes narrowing. "I'm fine."

"You're not."

"You don't look it," Oliver put in.

Lan ignored me and shifted his eyes to Oliver. The injured one seemed a little better and was slightly open. "So you all stayed the night?"

"Sure did."

"The three of you?"

"Yes," Oliver drew out.

"Where did you sleep?"

Oliver grinned wide. "If you're wondering if any of us touched Easton, we didn't. He went to bed on his own. Chris and I stayed in the spare room and then Simon came in early to say he was catching a taxi home. He slept on the couch."

"Not that it's any of your business," I added.

"It is," he clipped back at me.

"It's. Not."

Again, he leaned in. "You know it is."

"Oh, this is fun," Oliver commented.

We all straightened and turned when we heard a car coming down our dirt road. It drove into Lan's driveway and stopped. A buff man in a biker vest stepped out first, and then a gorgeous woman. The back door flew open, and another man stepped out, only he was taller and leaner.

"Shit," Lan muttered.

CHAPTER THIRTEEN

LAN

*J*ust what I needed. Mally would fret over me, while Stoke no doubt would lecture me about making his woman worry and that I needed better security. I didn't have a damn clue why Julian was there.

"Who are they?" Easton whispered. I glanced back to see his arm stretched out towards me, as if he wanted to grab me and pull me inside if I needed saving.

Christ, I wanted to smile, but I held it back. I couldn't get excited at the possibility of a chance between us. For all I knew, he hated me and only put up with me because he'd helped me. But hell, I really *did* want to get my hopes up.

If I were really honest with myself, I could also see Parker there, but that was only because we worked together, and that was it, dammit. It was all I allowed myself to think.

My front door flew open with a bang. I winced knowing there'd be a hole in the wall. Then flinched as pain shot through my shoulder, arm, and leg. Hell, even my hip seemed on fire. Parker stood in my doorway next door, his wild gaze travelling over everything.

"Where in the fuck is he?" he snarled.

"Oh shit," Oliver muttered.

I caught Stoke grin and point our way. Of course he would have noticed where I was. Mally and Julian glanced over as Parker stepped out onto the porch and stood with his legs spread, arms crossed, glaring at us.

"He didn't know you were out of the house," Easton whispered.

"Nope. He was asleep on the couch."

Easton grumbled under his breath, and then I heard his gasp. I looked to where he was. Parker had taken a running leap down to the end of my deck, over the railing, managing to take the fence as well. He landed hard in a crouch and stood slowly, all while scowling at me.

"What in the fuck were you thinking?" he growled out.

"Pinch me," Oliver whispered. "Ouch! Okay, I'll be storing that away for my spank bank."

"I was just next door," I stated. Jesus, they all treated me like I couldn't take care of myself. I had a damn revolver hooked in the back of my pants.

"He hasn't had any medication," Easton supplied.

I glared down at him, and he smirked.

Fuck me. If he wasn't trying to get me in the shit, I would have enjoyed that smile.

"I'm fine," I clipped.

"Help me too," we all heard Julian call, and turned that way. Stoke had just dropped Mally to her feet on Easton's side of the fence and Julian was standing on my side with his arms up as if he thought Stoke would pick him up like a baby and lift him over.

"No," Stoke said.

"Declan," Mally started, but Stoke already started our way. "Come on," Mally said to Julian and took his hand. We continued to watch as he fumbled his way over landing on his arse. Finally, he stood with a pop and brushed his butt off, doing it all smiling. With one arm swung around Mally's shoulders, they started for us.

"What's goin' on?" Stoke asked, stopping at the bottom of the steps next to Parker. "See from the photo Pick sent, you're looking better, brother," he added, eyeing my face.

"Nothin's going on, and thanks, *brother*," I clipped.

"Well, well, well... looks like I've certainly arrived at the right time. Are we having an orgy?" Julian asked.

Mally giggled.

"Can we get him the fuck home? He's sweating, shaky, and needs to goddamn rest," Parker ordered.

"Who're you?" Stoke asked. He lifted his chin towards Easton behind me since I blocked his doorway.

"Neighbours, duh, even I knew that one." Julian cackled. "Hey." He waved. "I'm Julian, the Hawks MC gay mascot—"

"Like hell you are," Stoke barked.

"Did you used to date him?" was asked from behind me.

Everyone froze, and then slowly shifted their eyes to Easton. However, I still stood in front of him. Stoke raised a brow and asked, "Who's he talkin' to?"

"I so have to get Chris for this," Oliver said, and then he bellowed, "Chris. Chris, come quick."

I moved to the side and shot daggers at the man, but he seemed immune. We all heard heavy footsteps pounding and then Chris saying, "What? What's wrong?"

"There's more of them." Julian gushed.

"Nothing, just watch," Oliver told Chris.

"You called me like the damn house was on fire for nothing."

Oliver snorted. "No," he drew out.

I looked to Parker. His scowl had been replaced by an amused smirk. I glared. "Need to get back home and take meds."

Parker shook his head. "It can wait a bit longer since you wanted to take a walk over here in the first fuckin' place without cover or any drugs to take away the pain I'm sure you're feelin' right about now."

Fuck you. I sent him the message with my gaze. I clearly wasn't going to get any help from him.

"Stoke, Mally, Julian," I snapped. "This is Easton, Oliver, and from what I heard, Chris."

"Your neighbours?" Mally queried.

"Just him." Chris thumbed at Easton, who looked a little pale. He probably didn't mean to ask that question earlier, but it was too late now.

"Hey there, Easton." Julian waved again. "Cute name by the way. But who were you asking that question to? I mean, I know I'm totally smoking, but I'm unsure—"

"No one," he blurted loudly. His hands rose and covered his burning cheeks. "Nothing. Don't know," he added, and then, "Dressed. Shower. Headache. Drinking."

Oliver curled his arm around Easton's waist. I glared down at it. He quickly removed it and cleared his throat. "I think what Easton's trying to say is that we had a few too many last night. He woke with a headache, and he needs a shower before getting dressed."

"Yes." Easton nodded.

Pink spread across his cheeks despite being scared and that was my fault. He was probably worried about my reaction after he'd blurted his question, and in front of Stoke, a biker. I didn't want him to worry. I hated the look of fear in his eyes. It reminded me of the time I lost him because I'd been a fucking fool.

"Me," I said.

While I was sure everyone's stare shot to me, all I wanted was Easton's, and when I caught his gaze, I gave him a soft smile, and to hell with it, a wink also.

"Lan," he mumbled.

"I *wanted* to get the truth out there," I stated.

Oliver sniffed beside Easton.

I glanced at my cousin Stoke and told him, "Easton asked *me* because he and I used to date ten years ago."

Somewhere close by, a slow rising rooster let off his morning greeting.

Stoke stared at me with no expression showing. Mally smiled, and Julian gaped like a fish out of water.

There was another sniff. I saw it was Oliver once again. Only he had tears in his eyes, and when I spotted Easton's bottom lip wobble, my heart stuttered over a beat. My confession had meant something to him.

"You could have told me," Stoke said.

I glanced back and shrugged, only to damn wince. "Had too many issues back then."

"So," he drew out, then his lips twitched. "Used to date. Like when he was fifteen? He looks about eighteen now. Lan Davis, my cousin, the cradle robber."

Parker snorted, then chuckled. He wasn't the only one. Chris and Oliver joined him, while Julian swiped away tears and Mally's smile grew bigger.

Meanwhile, I sent Stoke the finger, and said, "Fuck you."

"I'm twenty-nine actually," Easton said, and more chuckles were added to the first.

"And now?" Julian asked.

"Friends," Easton shouted.

Parker scoffed, shook his head and came forward. "How about we worry about all that shit later and get this dickhead back to his house and drugged up."

"Can I just say, I love your tattoos," Julian piped up. His eyes were running over Easton appreciatively. Not liking it, I stepped back in front of him.

"East, you wanted a shower, and you'd better get back to your friends," I said.

Julian and Mally giggled with each other. I ignored them.

"Nice to meet you all. Bye," Easton called quickly, then shoved his friends back and shut the door.

"Just friends?" Stoke asked.

"Shut it," I said, as Parker stopped at my side to help me down the steps. I'd already started to feel like a damned weak kitten. My legs shook with each step I took.

"Fuckin' idiot," Parker mumbled.

"You can shut it too," I told him.

"Just to say, I've never stood in front of a woman, as friends, if another man was eye fuckin' her," Stoke mentioned as we all made our way back to the fence.

"Stoke," I warned.

"It was only a thought." He helped Mally over and then came to my side. With both his and Parker's help, I was over the fence and Mally came to my side, sliding her arm around my waist.

"Hey, babe," I said.

"Good to see you." She rubbed her hand up and down my waist, and I waited for it. "But if we ever get a call hours *after* an incident that involved you—someone in our family—I'll never talk to you again."

With my hand on her shoulder, I squeezed it. "Got it."

"You'd better. We were worried sick."

"I'd hit you if you weren't healing for making my woman panic," Stoke added.

Mally gasped. "He wouldn't." Glaring over her shoulder, she snapped at her man, "You wouldn't."

Stoke chuckled.

I started up a step, only to stumble. I would have fallen on my arse if it wasn't for Parker rushing forward to grab me.

"Can I call you a dickhead again?" He shook his head and helped me the rest of the way inside. I sat on my couch after Mally moved the blankets down and then she sat next to me. Parker ordered, "Julian, the room with the door open down the hall. Grab the pills on the bedside table."

"Got it, Loki. By the way, loving the longer hair on you." Julian was another man who was immune to glares. He walked off with a smile on his face.

Parker hovered in front of me, scowling with his arms crossed. It was the usual look for him, only most of the time I wasn't on the receiving end.

Leaning forward, I pulled the gun out and sat it on my free side. "I'm not stupid."

Stoke laughed and took a seat in the chair. Parker raised his brows at me. "No? Hmm, let me fuckin' think about that." He dropped his head back, eyes to the ceiling. After a second, he straightened, even dropped his arms down at his sides, his hands fisted. "Not stupid would be for an injured person to stay the fuck in their bed and take their medication. Not stupid would be stayin' in a house where he'd be the safest. When someone's *not* stupid, they wouldn't walk goddamn next door to demand to see if his ex has a guy in his bed. Not stu—"

"Enough," I snarled. "I get it." Shit, if I had enough energy, I'd get up and in his face, maybe even punch him… or grab him and kiss him. *Crap, erase that bloody last thought.*

"Do you?" he bit out. He faced Stoke. "You lot hangin' about for a bit?"

"Yeah, brother."

Parker stalked to the kitchen where we heard him grab some keys. "I'll be back," he announced, and then stormed out the door, slamming it closed.

"Ah… someone has their knickers in a knot," Julian said from the hallway entrance. He came over and handed me the pills and a glass.

"You worried him, Lan," Mally said.

I wasn't ready to think about Parker being worried for me. We were work colleagues, brothers in a way, but that was it. That'd be all there ever would be.

Fuck. I was too tired for anything more.

"I have an idea. Let's talk more about your neighbour," Julian said. Closing my eyes, I rested my head back on the couch and gave him the finger.

Once again, Stoke chuckled.

CHAPTER FOURTEEN

PARKER

*F*uck Lan goddamn Davis. Fuck him. Stupid goddamn motherfucking idiot. Did he not think I'd have thought he'd been taken from the house if he wasn't in it when I woke the hell up?

Seriously, what in the Christ was he thinking?

I wanted to punch him.

I would have if he wasn't damn injured.

Dread and I had been friends before and feeling it always made me angry. I was fuming. When I'd still been half asleep and stumbling down the hall to Lan's room to check on him, only to find the cockhead gone, it was like I'd been stabbed in the gut or shot with fear so high I got dizzy.

Slamming on my handbrake, I rubbed at my chest. The screwy idiot could only worry about Easton. Fuck, even when Lan had shown he'd been armed, it didn't matter since he was already harmed enough to slow his reaction time.

I banged my hands against the steering wheel and cursed up a storm. Getting out of the car, I slammed the door shut and stomped off into the distance.

When I come to a stop, I said, "Sorry I wasn't here on Sunday, brother." Shaking my head, I closed my eyes. "Always sorry for so much." With a sigh, I scrub a hand over my face. "You see, Lan had some trouble. He was shot up and beat." I clenched my jaw. In a crouch, I asked, "Why does bad shit happen to good people?" I sucked in a breath, then snorted. "He said I was good. I ain't good. I couldn't be good, or I wouldn't have thought of myself that night. I would have stayed, and you'd still be here giving me shit. Fuck." I swiped at my eyes roughly and cleared my throat. My damn bottom lip trembled. I pulled it in and bit down on it, ignoring the tears threatening again.

I wasn't good.

I was selfish and it cost me big.

Christ, if I could take back that night eighteen years ago, I would. If I could switch places, I would. In fact, I wanted to.

I wanted to be the one buried instead of my brother.

Never would I forgive myself for thinking of myself that night instead of him. I knew she'd been off her head, but that night I was too interested in chasing tail to think of anything else. That night the girl I'd been interested in would be at the party and I wanted to go and catch her attention.

Fucking dumb decision.

The wrong one.

It goddamn gutted me each and every bloody day.

"Christ," I hissed out and wiped at my face. Our fucked-up mother had a drug and alcohol problem. I'd been taking care of my brother, Shawn, who'd been three years younger than me, since he'd come into the world really. Mum was a bitch to live with, but I didn't want to get separated from Shawn if we got put in the system. Always my decisions that fucked up both of our lives. If I hadn't've been greedy and let him get a better life with another family, he would still be alive.

"Fuckin' hell," I whispered and fell back on my arse to the grass before Shawn's grave.

I'd never forget the night. Forget how I'd arrived home to find

Erin, our so-called whore of a mother, laying into Shawn with a knife on the kitchen floor.

At first, I'd gone through the front door with a smile on my face. A pathetic smile. Then it crashed, just like the pain in my chest, at what I'd seen. With a scream full of fury, I'd raced over and gripped the back of her hair in one hand. With the other, I'd taken her hand holding the knife and sliced it across her neck.

Sweat, tears, and blood coated my body, but all I could see was a lifeless Shawn staring up at me.

Fucking hell. *Fuck, fuck, fucking hell.*

The memory opened me raw, my chest, my throat, my gut.

I'd pushed her aside and kneeled over my brother, trying to stop the blood pouring from him, but there were too many wounds.

I didn't even find out why she'd done it; she died too quick by my hand. She deserved more, like I did.

I shouldn't have left him alone.

I'd never allow forgiveness to touch me over losing Shawn.

I wasn't good. I was pathetic, greedy, sad, and so damned angry.

I wasn't sure how long I'd stayed by Shawn's grave. Really, I didn't care how long it'd been since I missed our usual Sunday. Sunday had always been our day. A day when I hadn't worked or we both hadn't been studying. It was a day we'd treated ourselves to do fuck all and spend time with each other. Sunday had always been mine and Shawn's day, and I'd always, as long as I lived, go to my brother's grave every Sunday.

After leaving there, I headed back to my apartment to grab another bag of shit, and on the way back to Lan's, I called Dodge to see if there were any updates. There weren't. Frustrated, I asked if another brother could take a shift at Lan's for the next day so I could get out there to see if I could find anything. Not that the brothers weren't doing what they could, but I hated sitting around as if I were doing nothing. Thank fuck Dodge understood and agreed.

Stoke hadn't called, so I guessed he didn't care about how long I ended up taking. I didn't think I'd be gone all day, but I couldn't bring myself to leave Shawn's grave. Too much shit had been happening recently, and I hadn't been processing. I tried to while sitting in my silence. Still didn't make me any less pissed about the whole situation and Lan's lack of care about himself.

After parking, I grabbed my bag and got out of the car and walked to the front door. Before I had the chance to take the front steps, the door opened and Stoke stepped out.

"All good?" I asked, pausing.

"Fine, brother. Wanted to check on you."

I snorted. "I'm fine, I'd be better if that Miller fuckhead was caught and Lan was healed."

He came forward, enough to lean against the pole at the top of the steps. "Get the feelin' more is touchin' you than what's actually happened."

I tensed, and bit out, "I'm fine."

Stoke made a sound in the back of his throat. "Demons can fuck a brother up. Sure you know it as much as I do. Least I got the help of my brothers and a good woman to deal with my demons."

"Your point?" I asked.

"Just sayin' you ain't alone. You don't wear a cut, but you're still a brother. If you need to shoot the shit, any one of us will be there. Know someone else who would be as well. The man inside. He has your back. Has had it for a long time. Share stuff with him so he understands better, because he sure as shit didn't understand why in the hell you scolded him like he was a little boy."

"Reckless move and it pissed me off, that's all."

"It was reckless, but Miller'd know by now Lan's got our help. Sure, Miller wouldn't be stupid to come by again. He'd wait, bide his time for Lan to be out and alone."

"Can't say that for sure."

He nodded. "True."

Silence. If he was waiting for me to open up, he'd be waiting a while.

"Julian left with Nary earlier. My woman helped Lan to bed a while ago. You good if we head off?"

"Yep."

"All right." I started up the steps only to stop when Stoke straightened and grabbed my shoulder. "Lan's a brother, but he's also family. We got the same blood running through us. Do anything for that man in there, even when he pisses me off."

"I'd do the same."

"Know that. It's why I wanna thank you."

"No need for it."

Stoke chuckled. "Still felt I had to do it. Now it's done, and I gotta get my knocked-up woman home."

"Mally's expecting?"

His smile was a proud one. "Sure is."

"Congrats, brother."

"Thanks." We started for the door. "Just a note, Lan's back to being as high as a kite. You might want to ignore some of the shit that comes outta his mouth."

I snorted. "Pretty sure I know what you're talkin' about, and I knew."

Stoke grinned and shook his head. "Not sure you do, but I'm sure you'll see eventually. Just, he's a good man." He coughed. "Not bad lookin' even." Another cough and from the porch light, I saw him turn red. "I didn't know about his past, and I don't care now. He can like whoever he wants, but, I, ah, he's a good bloke... don't fuckin', I don't know, hate him for his attraction I guess."

I jerked my head back. Why in the hell would I care if he liked Easton? Jesus, I'd been standing at Easton's place when Lan confessed to dating him to Stoke and the others, and I didn't react then, so why was he saying shit now? "Told you I already knew. If I hated it, I wouldn't be here."

"Fuck," he bit out. "I... you... never mind." He opened the front door and called for his woman.

Mally came strutting out from the kitchen. I'd always found her attractive, like a lot of the Hawks women. She smiled warmly up at me.

"Stoke just told me."

She gasped, her eyes widening. "He did?"

"Ah, about the baby," Stoke said quickly.

"Oh, yes." She smiled and rubbed her belly. "Killer and Ivy are expecting too. We're hoping to deliver on the same day."

"Hell, must be in the water."

She laughed. "Must be. Um, Lan's a great guy, isn't he?"

"Love," Stoke said in warning, for some bloody reason.

They were acting damn strange. "Did somethin' happen when I was gone? Did Lan say or do anythin' I should know about?"

Mally laughed, but it was put on. "No." She shook her head, came forward, patted my arm and then tugged me down to kiss my cheek. "Thanks for being here for Lan."

"Yeah, no worries." I watched them as they looked at each other and then at me.

Just as I was about to question them again, Stoke clapped his hands and said, "We should go. Got a drive ahead of us. Take it easy, brother."

"You too, and congrats again to you both. Pass that on to Killer and Ivy."

"We will." Mally beamed.

"Talk soon," Stoke said, and with a tap on the back, they walked to the front door, out it, and gone.

What in the fuck was all that about?

I understood the knocked-up part, but the rest I didn't have a clue.

Shaking my head, I slid the bag from my shoulder and dropped it to the floor. I wasn't sure if Lan had eaten, but I was damned starving. I went into the kitchen ready to make something, but instead found a few dishes already made up. Some were of pasta, others meat and veg. Mally must have been busy cooking for Lan that day. Didn't mean I couldn't steal one. I grabbed some pasta and heated it. As I stood there and watched the plate turn around in the microwave, I couldn't help but wish I'd had a special someone in my life to want to take care of me in the way Mally did Stoke, or Low did Dodge.

Then again, having someone could lead to more hurt and heartache, because no doubt I'd do something to fuck it all up. Yeah, I'd rather stick to one-night stands.

CHAPTER FIFTEEN

PARKER

*A*fter eating and cleaning up my mess, I checked on Lan. I found him sitting up in bed, in his dimly-lit room from the lamp on the bedside table, blinking tiredly at nothing.

"Hey, you need something?" I asked, walking in and sitting on the edge of the bed. "You hungry? Need a drink? Shower?"

He smiled and then chuckled. "Sure," he slurred. Jesus, how much medication had he had? He must have caused more damage being outta bed and next door that morning than he thought and upped his meds. "You gonna join me?"

Snorting, I shook my head. "Wrong guy."

"Nope."

My brows dropped. Ignoring what he said, sure he thought I was Easton, I asked, "Thirsty?"

He sighed, ran a hand over his face once and then mumbled, "Dunno." He looked at me and blinked. A grin came over his lips. "Hey," he whispered.

I shook my head. "Hey. You okay?"

"Yeah." He nodded. He leaned forward. His hand gripped my shoulder and then slid to my neck. I froze. "Hey," he said again.

"Lan?"

"Sorry," he blurted.

"What for?"

"I did something, but it's not there."

I chuckled. "Man, you need some more sleep."

He laughed, gazing drunkenly at me. "Yeah." I felt a finger of his start to make circles on my skin. For a reason I couldn't explain right then my heart moved up a speed. When his eyes slid down to my damn lips, my body locked.

"I'm Parker," I stated roughly.

His smile widened. "Know." For a medicated guy, he was fucking fast. He pushed forward and touched his lips to mine. In my mind, I shouted, *What the fuck?* But I didn't do anything because shock had taken hold of my body and I still sat frozen.

That was until he slanted his mouth over mine more and touched his tongue to my lips. My brain shut down and for a half a second, I closed my eyes, opened my mouth and, fuck me, wound my tongue around his. Then I remember who *I* was and who *he* was and that I was kissing a guy!

I bolted off the bed with a rough, "What the fuck, Lan?"

He blinked slowly, cocked his head to the side and stared up at me.

"You... me... what were you thinkin'?" I didn't wait for an answer. Instead, I stalked from the room, grabbed my keys off the table near the front door and slammed my way outta the house. I made my way to Easton's by jumping the fence and then pounded on his door.

I heard frantic footsteps, and then the door swung open, "What's wrong?" he asked breathlessly.

I opened my mouth, snapped it closed and glared at him. He stood there in a towel, water still dripped down his body. Hell, he was fit for a paramedic and his tats.... Goddamn, motherfucking hell. Where was I going with that thought and why in the fuck was I looking at him? Fit?

Fit?

"Get your arse over to Lan's. You're it for the night. I got shit to do."

"But—"

"No. Fuck no." I ran a hand through my hair and shook my head, taking a deep breath. *"Please,"* I added.

"Okay," he replied quietly.

With a nod, I left and headed for my car.

My head was jumbled with thoughts. *Lips. Scruff. Hard lips. Soft tongue. What in the fuck?*

That wasn't me. I didn't kiss guys. Not that I kissed him. I didn't. It was the shock.

Fucking shock.

It'd caused me to freeze and not know what to do. Shock caused me to press back, to open my mouth. I didn't want to offend him. It was Lan.

Lan Davis.

A man I worked alongside.

I'd been stressed for a long-arse time. It was stress.

Stress fucking let that happen.

Somehow, I made it to the Hawks MC compound. Sitting in my car, I wondered what in the hell I was supposed to do. Would he remember? Could I flog it off and pretend he'd dreamt it? Then another thought occurred to me. It had me reaching over for my phone on the passenger seat. I snapped it up and pressed the few buttons I needed to.

"Yo," Stoke answered.

"You weren't worried about Easton before. What was that about, Stoke, and don't fuckin' lie to me?"

"Where are you?"

"Compound."

"You left?"

"He has someone with him."

"Easton?"

"Yes," I clipped, gripping the wheel. Fuck, maybe leaving Easton with Lan wasn't a good idea. Fuck that. I didn't care what happened.

"He ain't gonna protect him like—"

"Stop fuckin' messin' around. It was you not long ago said Miller'd be stupid to try again at the house. Now tell me what I wanna know."

"What'd Lan do?"

I tensed. "What do you mean?"

"He's done something to get you pissed. Not that it's hard." He paused and then, "He make a move on you?" He chuckled when I didn't answer. "Your silence is enough of an answer." He sighed. "Honestly, I didn't know if I should'a told you or not, but I guess now you need to know. I think he's, ah, shit, why is it me who has to have this conversation?" He cursed again. "He's got a thing for you."

I felt like barking out, "No he doesn't. Shut the fuck up," and then hanging up and hiding, but I didn't.

I forced a laugh, and said, "Yeah, sure. You probably got it wrong. He's hooked on Easton these days. We're friends and that's—"

"He said he thought you were good-looking and often looked at you, but he didn't want you to know because you would beat his arse," Stoke spat out quickly. "If you do beat his arse, that means I'll have to step in. I doubt he would have made a move on you unless he's high. Not sure if he'll remember it or not, but now it's out there, you'll just have to deal with it."

"Deal with it? What would you do if it was Killer and you?"

He thought for a moment and then chuckled. "Tell him I'm flattered, but I don't want to stick my tongue down his throat."

"This before or after you freaked out?"

"Yeah, all right. I know it's a damn shock, but you gotta ask yourself if that shit scares you, are you willing to back outta Lan's life forever?"

"How in the fuck did we come straight to losing Lan over this?

Of course it's a motherfuckin' shock. I only found out he was into guys a couple of days ago, and now you're saying he fancies me. Jesus Christ, Stoke, why in the fuck did you even tell me that?"

"That's what I thought you were calling to find out about."

Closing my eyes, I took a deep breath and tried to calm down. "I don't know why I even called."

"Relax, brother. Things'll be fine."

"Yeah." I nodded, only to shake my head after it. I was fucking lost to know if things would be fine. I had my goddamn lips on Lan's. What was I supposed to do with that? "Gotta go," I said, and then ended the call even as Stoke started to say something. It was a cunt move, but I needed a drink over anything else.

When I walked into the compound, I was greeted by every brother I passed. None of them stayed around to start a conversation, which could have been because of the scowl I knew I had going on.

I stopped at the bar, smacked the counter and ordered, "Shot."

"Anything?" Vicious asked. I nodded. He got me a shot of whisky. I sucked it back and then asked for a beer. "You all right, brother?"

"Fine," I bit out.

"I'm headin' to Pick and Billy's pub soon, wanna join?"

A squeal caught my attention. I turned to see Gamer with one of the club bunnies over his shoulder before he walked over to the couch to drag her to his lap and make out.

"Parker?" Vicious called.

"I'm good here," I said, my gaze travelling over the other brothers milling around playing pool or arcade games, and some bunnies trying to get their attention any way they could.

Maybe that was what I needed. A release to help ease some stress.

"You want another?" Vicious asked. I glanced over at him just as I drained the last of the beer in the bottle. Hell, I didn't realise I drank it that quick.

"Sure." I nodded, placing the empty on the counter.

"Last one I'll get. Help yourself next or Dallas'll be in later."

"All good." I tipped the beer back and took another long pull.

"You sure you're good?"

I tilted my head enough to glare at him and clip, "Fine."

His hands came up. "Got it. I'm headin' off. We run out here, come to the pub."

I gave him a chin lift in response. When he'd left, I leaned over the bar and grabbed the bottle of whisky. I'd repay it back next time I was in, but I wanted to de-damn-stress and whisky was calling my name.

"**H**andsome, your phone keeps ringing." The woman over me giggled and then ground down on my hard cock.

"I'll ring 'em back," I mumbled into her neck while I gripped the other side to hold her still enough to claim her mouth with mine. She was like a damn energiser bunny moving this and that way. Her lips were soft, wet, and sweet from her chapstick. They weren't hard and rough. She smiled against my mouth and moaned.

Fucking hell. I was hard, but I wasn't fully into it.

Why, Goddammit?

Usually it didn't take much for me to get going after having a good-looking bird grind over me, but as I kept thinking, I started deflating.

No, I need to get action tonight. I want this. Want her and her soft curves, her big tits. I ran my hands over the handful and my dick perked up once again.

It'd been a few hours since I'd arrived. I had a nice buzz going and a blonde dry-humping me on a chair in the corner of the common room at the compound. I wasn't the only one getting a taste that night. Another brother had one of the bunnies on her knees between his legs sucking him off, since none of the club women and taken brothers were around, and I was hoping my one would be up for doing the same soon.

My phone started again. I let out a frustrated groan. It was the third fucking time. Without looking at the screen, I picked it up from the arm of the chair and answered it, "What?"

"Where are you?" Lan asked.

My throat closed over as I froze. The woman on my lap pulled back to stare at me.

"Busy," I bit out.

"We need to talk."

Like fuck we did.

"Busy." I smiled up at the blonde. "Tell him, baby, how busy am I?"

She giggled, got close and said in a girly, high-pitched voice, "Very busy." Her lips trailed down to my neck where she bit.

Lan was very quiet on the other end.

"I didn't mean to...." He cursed low. "Have a good night," he said, and then hung up.

I gripped the phone tightly in my hand and lowered my arm.

Why in the fuck did I suddenly feel like an arsehole?

The blonde leaned in and sucked my lower lip into her mouth. I brought my eyes up to hers to find her smiling. She pulled back and licked across my lips. "We playing, handsome?"

Were we?

Why the fuck not.

"Yeah, baby. We're gonna play."

CHAPTER SIXTEEN

EASTON

I didn't like the look on Parker's face. At first, it had been angry, nothing new there, but then he switched it up, and I caught the confused, lost expression. I'd read it all in his eyes and pinched brows. Then when he added in the *please*, I knew I had to help him out. As soon as he'd left, I finished drying and quickly dressed, then locked the dog door so the dogs couldn't run amuck in the house while I wasn't there.

It was strange to find Lan's front door unlocked when I entered. I thought at least Parker would have locked it, so why hadn't he? What happened that caused him to rush off like his boxers were on fire? Especially since he'd not long been there. Not that I took notice of who was over at Lan's and for how long. I didn't. I just happened to see Parker arrive as I was passing the living room window.

After closing and locking the door, I went down the hall to check on Lan. He was lying back asleep. My brows dipped. Maybe Parker had a call from someone and something had happened to someone he knew.

No matter what, I didn't mind being there. At least Lan was asleep, and I didn't have to deal with... well, him.

Earlier, when they'd been at my house, and Lan delivered that last shock, Oliver had to drag me back inside because my body wouldn't move. It was stuck in a state of awe.

My mind still felt blown away by how he'd told everyone, and one being his cousin, we'd dated. Lan Davis admitted it in front of people he knew that we'd been a couple. People who were close to him.

He blurted those words out like they were nothing.

However, I could tell from the expression of surprise that crossed their features they knew nothing about Lan's past with men.

Never had I thought my heart could glue a piece back on itself, but hearing him say it felt like I'd gained some of my organ back from when he'd crushed it ten years ago. Although, my walls were still up. The darn devil man couldn't make me feel things for him again.

He couldn't.

He didn't.

Screw me up the nose, he had.

It was Lan Davis after all.

Making my way back out into the living room, I thought of Oliver's reaction. If he had anything to do with it, I'd be naked and already in Lan's bed. I was stronger than that, and with Chris's help, we'd made Oliver see reason as to why nothing had changed between Lan and me, no matter what he'd confessed in front of his friends.

Of course, it didn't stop them from making a bet on when I would end up sucking face—Oliver's words not mine—with Lan.

I sighed and flopped back on the couch. A sudden, strong scent of Parker wafted up and slapped me in the face. He must have been sleeping on the couch; only there were no blankets in sight. Had they not switched out the bloodstained mattress yet?

For an angry, annoying guy, he sure did smell delicious. It matched his chiselled, rough, sexy do-not-mess-with-me look.

Parker whatever-his-last-name-was confused me like no other person had. Maybe it was just me he didn't like, and he definitely showed it, yet I saw a different side to him with those Hawks bikers and even Lan. He didn't seem to care about the past Lan and I had. Yet, I still thought he didn't like me.

Leaning forward, I grabbed the remote off the coffee table and turned on the TV. Absently, I flicked through the channels, yet nothing really caught my attention.

I paused my flicking. Had Parker actually meant I was to stay here all night? At Lan's? Was he coming back at all? Dang it. I should have asked more questions and thought to grab extra things in case I was sleeping over. I guessed boxers would be good enough. I'd just have to find the sheets Parker had used…. Yeah, maybe not. A clean set of sheets would be better. Knowing the way my mind worked, if I smelled Parker all night, I would probably end up having a wet dream starring him, and that just wouldn't do. No matter how good-looking he was.

It was hours later when I heard loud cursing coming from down the hall. I quickly stood and made my way there. Stepping straight into the room, I found Lan sitting and pounding his fists on the bed.

"What did it ever do to you?" I asked.

He jolted and spun his gaze my way. "What are you doin' here?" His tone was curt, but I put it down to being surprised by my presence.

"You've got me here tonight. Parker had to step out," I said and then watched him pale.

That wasn't good.

"What happened?" I asked, shifting closer to the bed.

"Nothin'." He moved to flip back his sheet but winced.

I nodded to the medication. "Is it time for those? Parker didn't tell me when you had them last."

"No," he bit out, and then I saw him grind his teeth together.

I dipped my brows in confusion. "No what? It's not time, or you're not taking them?"

I stepped back when he slowly, using one arm, slid closer to the edge of the bed and then put his feet on the floor. "I don't need them," he stated.

"Lan, you don't need to be some macho—"

He stood and wobbled a little. "East, don't, please. I don't want or need them. I'll be fine."

"Said the guy who just winced like he tasted shit. Wait, you must have because I certainly smell bullshit."

He snorted. "Maybe you need to go back to being the shy Easton."

Thinning my lips, I reached up and flicked him in the ear. He cursed, and then I told him, "That Easton was too much of a pushover. This Easton isn't."

He studied me, a small soft smile playing on his lips. "I like both versions." My pulse raced when his hand circled my wrist, only to run his fingers up my arm. "I especially like the tattoos."

"Lan," I whispered.

"East," he said back just as quietly as his fingers slid to the back of my neck.

"What are you doing?"

His jaw clenched. He closed his eyes for a second and then he opened them. The warmth they'd held had disappeared. He dropped his hand and shook his head. "Nothin'."

Something was going on with him.

"What happened with you and Parker?"

"Do you know where my phone is?"

"Lan, you can talk to me."

He glanced away and then back. "I can't. If I do, I'll risk…. I'm a fuckin' idiot."

111

I rolled my eyes. "Tell me something I don't know."

He sat down on the edge of the bed and put his head in his hands. Only he didn't stay that way long. Straightening to sit, he looked up at me. He took my hand, my heart beating crazily as he pulled me closer, even between his legs.

"I messed things up between us so—"

"We don't need to talk about this—"

"I do. We do because I want to hope there could be something again between us." My eyes widened. He added, "Do I have the right to hope for that, East?"

"You don't know me now."

"I want to."

"How do I know...?" Where in the holy Jesus had my resistance gone? Some mushy words and I was already thinking about throwing myself at him. *Well, not fully. I don't think.*

"I can't promise I won't hurt you because what I have to say next could do that, but I'll still tell you. I'm messed up in the head, East."

I shook my head. "You're confusing me."

He snorted. "I'm confused myself."

"Are you sure you're not still high?"

He took my other hand in his and gazed at our hands. "I'm not," he whispered. "I shouldn't be asking you for anything. I don't have a right."

I licked my dry lips. "I can't promise anything either."

"I know." He nodded. "Can we just... see? Get to know each other?"

My throat was thick with emotion. I was nervous, scared, and yet so darn happy he was confessing to wanting something again with me. Still, fear outweighed it all and caused the hairs on my arms to rise. "What about, um, other people?"

He stood and leaned in to make sure he held my gaze with his. "I wouldn't give a fuck if the Queen knew you were mine. I wouldn't hide you, us. Never again."

My chest rose and fell rapidly with every breath I took as I stared up at him. "What..." I cleared my throat. "What about women?" I shook my head quickly and stepped back. His hands dropped from mine. "Don't answer that. We're not even there. I don't know what I can give when...." I looked to the floor and shook my head.

"When I hurt you in the first place," he supplied, and I caught his hands clench. "I'll earn your trust. I'll earn it, and I'll start now because this could—fuck, it could screw everything up already."

"What?" I asked.

He sighed, glanced at the ceiling and back to me. "I wasn't myself, but I was. I mean, I didn't know I'd do it and now I have I don't know what to fuckin' do."

I grabbed his wrist and slid my hand into his. "Lan, just tell me."

"Fuck." He screwed his eyes shut. "I woke up completely drugged up to Parker here and kissed him." When I didn't say anything, mainly because I couldn't since I was shocked to the core, he opened his eyes and looked at me, searching my face for an answer. I knew I wouldn't be showing anything on my face. I was blank. He tugged my hand in his. "East?"

Lan *kissed* Parker.

Parker. The most heterosexual guy I'd ever met.

Should I have been angry? Most would have been, especially after Lan talked a good talk about being with me and he'd already kissed Parker.

Parker I-wish-I-knew-his-last-name.

Really, I couldn't blame Lan. He *had* been high, and Parker, even though he was a butthead, was good-looking.

My lips twitched.

Lan kissed Parker. Who he worked with.

Lan's brows dipped. "East?"

My lips twitched again. I couldn't stop it. I cleared my throat and tried for, "What, ah, did he do?" Then I dropped my hands to my thighs and laughed heartily. "Oh, shit. You kissed Parker." I straightened and held a hand across my stomach; it ached. "Did he punch you?"

Then I sobered as the image of Lan in bed with Parker kissing popped into my mind.

I gulped.

That—I cleared my throat again—thought wasn't a bad one per se.

My stomach flipped.

Once more, for good measure, I cleared my throat. "Um, what did he do?"

Lan's eyes penetrated my mind, and I was sure he knew I'd been thinking about it. A smirk lifted his lips. He shook his head. "I've worked with him for a long time." I nodded. He went on, "He's nice-lookin'." I snorted, and he glared. "Okay, he's better than nice. Some type of feelin' was bound to happen." He ran his top teeth over his bottom lip. "But I didn't mean to kiss him."

I knew he wouldn't have. He knew, as well as I did, Parker didn't cross over his way or mine. Meaning he wasn't bi or gay. It would have been a big shock to them both.

"I'm surprised you still have a face."

He snorted. "So am I. Instead, he yelled and then left."

"No wonder he looked out of sorts when he came over," I mumbled to myself.

"Christ," he clipped, and started pacing with a slight limp. "What the hell am I supposed to do now? He's probably off throwing darts at my damn face somewhere. He's gonna hate me. Fuckin' hate me. Then..." He stopped to face me. "Then all I can think about is you, and I want to see if there could be something with us, but...."

"You're still attracted to Parker."

He dropped his head and nodded. "I'm a motherfuckin' arsehole."

"You're not." I sighed and ran a hand over the back of my neck. "Parker and you work closely together, and you do it in tough situations. I can understand your feelings." I nodded. "Oliver and I used to date and we work together." His eyes darkened. I waved a hand absently. "We're only friends now, and he's in love with Chris. What I'm saying is, I understand it. Besides, Parker's, um, you know, good-looking."

Lan's feet ate up the carpet to stop in front of me. "It doesn't matter if Parker is or not. Yes, I'm scared I just fucked up Parker and me as mates. But I worry more you'll walk out of this house and want nothing to do with me." His hands landed on my waist. Nerves twisted my stomach into knots. Still, I managed to lift my shaky hand to his forearms. Lan sighed. "I've never regretted something in my life more than letting you walk away from my place that night. Fuck, it eats at me still. Not a day goes by that I don't wish I could change it. I wished I'd stopped you and then come to your place sooner so you never left town." His eyes flicked down to my lips, but I wasn't ready for that. I wasn't ready to believe completely. Lan must have sensed it also because his gaze met with mine once more. I got a small, soft, yet sad smile, and he stepped back. "Maybe with time you'll learn you can trust me to never be so damn stupid again."

"I... ah...." I didn't know what to say. I wanted to trust, but that burn from years ago still lived inside of me. I nodded. His smile lifted a little from that nod. Needing to change the subject, I blurted, "You should call Parker."

His head jerked back a little. "What?"

What?

Why did I go for that? I could have said you should sit, eat, or anything else.

"Ah, I mean, you're worried, right? So you should call him. I mean, that's what you were going to do before, yeah?"

"Yeah." He nodded. I ignored his grin, aware he knew I was playing at changing the subject as I started for the door.

Over my shoulder, I said, "I'll grab your phone." I needed to distance myself because all I could think about was forgiving him, trusting him, and jumping him.

I was screwed.

Only it wasn't in a sexual way.

Though, it could lead down the track in a sexual way.

Dickwizzle idiot. I had to steer away from any type of sexual thoughts.

Especially thoughts about Lan kissing Parker because back there in the bedroom, that image I'd conjured had shot pleasure straight to my cock. Which was dangerous. Lan alone was enough to get me so darn hard, but I was sure that thought of the two of them could cause me to come in seconds.

I groaned, picked up Lan's phone I'd seen earlier, and made my way back down the hall thinking of everything but sexual thoughts.

I shouldn't even have been thinking of sex, coming, kissing, both men... I was a knobjockey, my dick already at half-mast. What I needed to get through my thick head, on my shoulders, not the other end, was that none of those thoughts were appropriate since Lan was in a deadly situation still, and healing.

Well, unless I was alone in my own bed at night. It was different then.

CHAPTER SEVENTEEN

LAN

I ignored my aching body, and my smile grew watching Easton walk from the room. Even though I was kicking myself repeatedly for how fucked up I was, I couldn't stop the grin because it was Easton. The man I could so easily fall in love with again. Yeah, we had to get to know one another once more, but I liked what I saw. I doubted there was anything that could turn me off from Easton Ravel.

He was something special.

I had to get shit sorted, get my life back on track, and prove to him I was worth trusting and spending time with.

Fuck the life I'd dreamed of... marriage with a woman. Easton was what I wanted, and in making sure I could have that dream with him, I had to forget my... attraction to Parker.

"Shit," I clipped to the quiet room. I'd kissed him. It was blurry in my mind, but I knew I'd done it as soon as I'd woken. What didn't make sense was how I imagined him pressing against my lips harder and opening his mouth, the touch of his tongue. I shook my head, then winced when it pulled at my shoulder and my face throbbed. I must have made that shit up.

Though I did remember him flying up off the bed, his eyes flashed with anger, and him yelling before leaving.

If I'd been more myself, I would have called him back and told him it was a mistake, pretended he was Easton maybe, and then barked at him to get over it. But I hadn't been; instead, I'd rested back with a smile and rubbed at my lips before falling back asleep.

What I did know was that I'd never take the damn pain pills again. They fucked with me too much. I'd ignored the sharp stab in my shoulder, the throb to my face, arm, and hip. The other smaller cuts weren't a problem. Nothing I couldn't handle, and shit, I'd handle the rest anyway. I'd have to.

What a fucked up few days.

Christ, it felt longer than a few days, but it wasn't, and yet so much had happened.

I'd need a bloody holiday after Miller got caught. He would. He had to. I wouldn't give up until he did. Maybe it was a good idea I let the pain meds go. That way I'd be able to do my own work. Seek information from my own sources.

A throat cleared. I glanced over at the door. Easton stepped in with the phone held out. I rocked on my feet, wanting to walk to him, pick him up, and crush my mouth to his. I didn't. I waited where I was and practiced patience. Something I would need until Miller was gone and Easton had accepted me back into his life, and bed. I'd also need patience to deal with Parker.

I sat on the bed, brought up Parker's contact and pressed it before I chickened out. When he didn't answer the first time, annoyance settled deep as the thought of him ignoring me drifted into my mind.

On the third try, he answered gruffly, "What?"

"Where are you?" I asked. I had to make sure he wasn't out beating someone senseless because of me. I could hear music playing in the background.

"Busy," he bit out.

Shit. Never had he been so cold to me. Yeah, he'd been curt, but

"Then you have to get back up and keep going." Easton reached out and squeezed my arm. "Things will start looking up."

The urge to drag him into my arms and claim his mouth was strong.

It was nothing else but the man in front of me and his words that calmed me and gave me a chance to see the possibility that things could be okay in the end.

Once everything had sorted itself out.

"Thank you." I nodded. I took a step closer to him and leaned in so my mouth was close to his ear. I wanted to bite it, lick it, or even suck it into my mouth, but I didn't, and, fuck it was hard not to. "No matter how you've changed, nothing you've done or will do could stop me from wanting to be with you. You calm me and drive me crazy. Never has another captured me as much as you, which is why I've never been with another guy since you." I pulled back, catching his gaze that flickered with emotions I couldn't read, but if I were to guess, it was desire. I then touched a finger to his bottom lip and trailed it across it before I gently tapped it. "I'll wait for as long as I live for you." I pinched his chin. "I'm going to go back to bed. Don't clean that up. I'll do it tomorrow. I know I said I have something for Parker, but what I feel for you has always been strong." Leaning in, I touched my lips to the corner of his mouth and then walked out of the room, leaving a stunned Easton there.

I didn't know if I was a dick for saying what I did so soon, but I couldn't stop myself. He needed to know. I needed to say it so he realised that no matter what, Easton was important to me, always had been.

Parker... well, I'd figure things out eventually. If he'd give me friendship again, I'd do all I could to never mess it up.

But Easton was it. Easton was mine already in my heart and soul.

One day, fuck, I hoped one day soon, Easton would realise it too.

Until then, I'd show him I wasn't the same man I used to be.

S unshine nearly goddamn blinded me when I woke. What came with it was more aching and soreness. I glanced to the bedside table for the time and instead found a note leaning against the digital clock someone moved from my room in there.

Lan

I had to leave early so I called a number I found in your phone. His name was Dodge, and any name like that told me he was a part of the Hawks bike club. He sent someone over. His name is Dive.

I'm sorry I had to leave after things were said last night. When I get back we'll talk more. I've programmed my number in your phone, call me whenever you want to talk.

I'll see you when I get back.

Easton

BTW, I had to head out of town because my father is apparently sick.

Also, since you refuse (which is silly) to take the heavier pain medication, here are some Panadol and Nurofen. Take them regularly with the antibiotics, please, and take care of yourself!!!

Disappointment dropped my gut, yet I still found myself grinning because he'd left his number. Sucked his dad was sick, but from what I remembered, the two of them didn't have much of a relationship in the first place. Whatever he was sick with must be bad to get Easton at his side. If I didn't look like Frankenstein, I'd find out where his dad lived and get there to be by his side, because I also remembered Easton saying something about how cunning his father was. I could only hope, if I called, he'd tell me if he needed help and no matter how I looked or felt, I'd get my arse there.

Fuck me. I'd give anything to be healed. Anything for Miller to be still in jail or at the very least known the motherfucker was out. I would have taken precautions if I'd known. Then I could have had a somewhat normal experience when I'd found out Easton was living next door. Things would have been different between us. I would've already asked him out on a date. Also, things wouldn't have crashed between Parker and me. I wouldn't have kissed him.

It sure as hell felt like Fate was shitting all over me. Hopefully, things would change once more for me, and soon.

CHAPTER EIGHTEEN

EASTON

*W*hen I woke to hear my phone ringing and it was still dark outside, I knew something was wrong. At first, I'd been a little disoriented wondering where I was, until I went to get out of bed and it wasn't my bed at all, but the couch at Lan's. I snatched up my phone from the floor and answered it in a whisper, "Hello?"

"Mr Ravel?"

My brows dipped at the uppity tone. "Yes."

"I am sorry to call you so early. My name is Andrew Harrell, I'm your father's executive assistant, and he's asked me to call you because he's gravely ill and would like to see you."

My father was gravely ill?

"Is his voice box ruined?"

Andrew paused long enough I was about to ask him if he was still there, but then he said, "Well, no."

"So he's gravely ill and wants to see me, but he can't call me himself?"

Andrew cleared his throat. "He's very busy right now."

I pulled my phone back and then placed it against my ear again. "At five in the morning?"

"Yes."

"I'm sorry. I won't be able to make it."

Just as I was about to end the call, Andrew shouted, "Wait, please."

Sighing, I rubbed a hand over my face, and asked, "What?"

"He has some things of your mother's and would like to give them to you."

"Post them."

"He'll not pass them along unless he sees you."

The manipulative bastard.

He knew I would come because whatever he had of Mum's I would want it out of his hands.

"I won't be able to arrive—"

"I've emailed a ticket to the last email your father had. If you don't receive it, please notify me. The flight leaves in a few hours. We'll see you soon, Mr Ravel."

Controlling prick. Somehow he would have known I'd put most of my money into purchasing a house. Fine. I'd take the arsehole's money. "Right. See you soon, and, Andrew, it's just Easton. My father's Mr Ravel."

"All right, Easton," he replied and then hung up.

Standing, I gripped my hair in both fists and screamed silently. Looked like I was heading to Queensland. He moved there a while ago and I'd been glad for it. Now I was running to him because he held something of Mum's for ransom. He wanted me to show my face, and I would, for her.

"Fucking prick," I muttered and went to check on Lan and found him sleeping. I couldn't leave him there alone. Someone had to take over, and Parker would be out of the picture. Then I caught sight of Lan's phone on the bedside table. I picked it up and went back out into the kitchen. I'd have to be quick to make it to the airport on time. I scrolled through the phone and paused when I came across a name that triggered a memory. Something being mentioned about Dodge being the president.

"Yo," he answered roughly.

"Um, this is Easton."

"Lan okay?" he asked, which I found sweet.

"Yes. Sorry to call so early, but I have to head out of town and didn't want to leave Lan alone. Parker's not here, and I don't think he'll want to come back right now, and I have to somehow pack, find someone to look after my dogs since I know Oliver won't, he hates them, which I don't understand how anyone could hate dogs—"

"Easton," Dodge clipped.

Goddangit, I'd just been rattling off to a club president. He probably ate children for supper and kicked people's arses for fun. Sweat formed on my forehead and back.

"Sorry," I squeaked.

He chuckled. Maybe he didn't want to kill me. "Relax, man. I'll get someone over there. His name will be Dive and to make sure it's him, ask him what he showed my woman's best friend the first time they met."

"Um, okay."

"The answer will be his junk."

"Say what now?" I asked in a whisper.

He snorted out a laugh. "His man jewels. He flopped it on out.... Anyway, I'll also get someone to care for your dogs. Leave a key at Lan's to your place. Don't stress. Just go do what you have to, yeah?"

"You will?"

"You helped Hawks out with Lan. We'll help you out."

"Ah, okay." I nodded, a nice warmth spreading through my chest. "Um, thank you?"

He chuckled again. "All good," he said and then hung up.

I closed my eyes and opened them slowly. Was I still asleep? I pinched myself. Nope awake, so that call had happened. Shaking my head, I couldn't help but think how I wanted to be a part of the Hawks club. They were pretty much amazing people.

People who didn't eat small children and beat others up for fun.

Andrew Harrell met me at the airport with a greeting of hello, and that was all. After I collected a bag, which I'd packed since I didn't know how long my father's game would play for, we made our way outside to a limousine. Andrew opened the back door, and after I climbed in, he shut it. He chose to sit up front with the driver instead of with me.

I got the message he sent. His loyalty lay with my father.

The drive took over an hour, and too soon we were turning into a drive that held tall electric gates and a long driveway which led up to an over extravagant triple-storey house. Shaking my head, I snorted. Why in God's name would he live in something like that when he was the only one in it?

Unless he liked to be lonely. Honestly, that wouldn't surprise me. All I really knew about Amit Ravel was how he loved to work and how he hated people who were different and didn't fall into the smart, rich, and stunning category. I'd lost count of the times he'd traded up for a new woman in his life because the recent one either got old or boring.

I hated him.

A lot would say hate was such a strong word when it came to a parent. In my case, it wasn't. All he ever cared about was himself. If we didn't fall under what he wanted or saw was right in the world, we didn't exist to him until we did something that made him proud. Even then his gratitude only lasted for an hour, tops.

The car stopped. I really didn't want to get out and go inside to see him, but for Mum, I would. No matter what he had of hers, I wanted it away from him.

The door opened, and I slid across the seat and climbed out. I started for the back of the limousine to grab my bag.

"Sir, Mr Geraldstine will collect your bag for you."

"Actually, how about we leave it in the car. I won't be staying here anyway."

Andrew's nostrils flared in agitation. I didn't give two hoots what he thought of my actions towards my father. He was probably new and didn't know him like I did.

"Very well." He nodded and swept his hand out towards the house. Sighing, I started my way up the path, stairs, and then through the front door, nearly knocking the man over who stood behind it, as if he were about to open it.

"Sorry," I offered, gripping his shoulders to steady him. I glanced back outside to find Andrew still near the car speaking on the phone.

"My apologies for not being outside to greet you."

"It's fine." I smiled. He didn't seem convinced. "Really, don't worry about it."

"Thank you, sir." He stepped back and waved me further in.

"Is Zachary still around?" I asked, glancing at all the fine art and overpriced furniture. Zachary had been the family's butler when I was younger. He'd been such a kind, caring man. One I looked up to more than Amit.

"I'm sorry, sir, but he left a long time ago."

It wouldn't surprise me if it was after I'd left. He'd been the only reason I stayed longer after Mum had walked out. I stayed until Zac advised me to get the hell out of dodge before Satan changed me. He'd also hated my father.

"I believe he's now living in the United States with his daughter's family."

Turning, I grinned. "Really? He always said he wanted to get back over to the States. Good to hear he did."

"Sorry, where are my manners. I'm Mr Luis Vanier. Head butler here at the Ravel Estate."

Ravel Estate.

Snorting, I rolled my eyes. Luis caught it. I asked, "Does Amit know he's not a part of *Downton Abbey*?"

Luis chuckled and then turned it into a cough. "A tickle, sorry." He cleared his throat. "I believe, sir, your father would know that."

"Easton. Just Easton please."

"Of course, and I am just Luis."

I grinned. "Thanks."

He nodded. "The master is in the library. Down the hall to the left of the stairs, the last door at the end. I shall bring refreshments in shortly."

"Got it," I said, and with a deep breath, I followed Luis's instructions. When I came to the door, I hesitated for a second thinking if I should knock, but that would be what he would want, and I didn't want to do anything he wanted.

I groaned inwardly because that thought was stupid since I was there because he wanted it. Right, from then on, I wouldn't do anything he wanted.

I hoped not anyway.

Opening the door, I strode in to see Amit Ravel sitting in a big leather chair like he was on a throne, not the dunny kind either. His eyes were already on the door, probably having heard my approach since the house was too quiet.

"Easton, son. Good to see you," he said without a smile.

"Amit." I nodded. His jaw clenched. He hated that I called him by his name. I didn't want to associate him with such a caring word like father or dad. After I approached, I sat opposite on the long couch. "You summoned, I came. Where's Mum's things?"

He frowned. "Really, son? It's been years and that's all you have to say?"

I leaned back and threw my arms out. "What do you want me to say?"

"Did Andrew inform you of my illness?"

"He said you were sick."

"I have cancer."

I waited. He said no more so I drummed my fingers onto the couch and waited some more.

"Easton, I have cancer. I could die."

I narrowed my eyes, leaned forward, and said harshly, "Mum had cancer and *did* die." I shook my head and sat back. "I don't know what you were expecting from me after that announcement. Did you want me to cry? To care? To live in despair that my loving and amazing father who took care of Mum and me could possibly pass from this life? What did you expect?"

"A softer emotion than what you're showing now at least."

I scoffed. "Are you serious? You told me I was no longer your son when I told you I was gay, and this was after Mum had passed away. Before that, Mum and I struggled each day with money and hospital visits. When we reached out to you, what did you do?" I waved my hand about. "Don't answer it. I will. You told us it was none of your concern." I stood. "Well, guess what, Amit? Your dying, your illness, is none of *my* concern. Where are my mum's things because as soon as I get them, I'm leaving."

A throat cleared. We looked at the door to find a pale Luis standing there. "I-I have refreshments, master."

Amit waved Luis in. He quickly set a tray of hot tea and small sandwiches on the coffee table between us and left.

Amit stared up at me. "Please sit."

I sighed. "What do *you* need from me? You could have just sent whatever it is through the mail. So tell what you need from me so I can leave," I asked, but didn't sit.

"You have a sister."

It was then I sat.

"What?" I whispered.

"She's five years old and her name is Jewel."

I swallowed and blinked slowly. I had a sister. "The mother?" I asked.

"My fiancée, Darlene, you'll meet her at dinner."

"What does this have anything to do with me staying and Mum's things?"

He stared. "I would like for you to stay a couple of weeks to get to know your sister."

What?

"What?" I breathed.

"Stay, get to know Darlene and Jewel while you're on your break from work."

My head jerked back a bit. "How do you know I'm on holidays?"

"Andrew told me since he called there looking for you."

"How did he know I even worked there?"

"I'm not an imbecile, Easton. I know where you work. You are my son still."

"You told me I was no—"

"Yes, well." He stood. "A couple of weeks, it's all I'm asking. For Darlene and Jewel's sake."

I shook my head at a loss of what to actually do. "I don't know."

"Go to the hotel, since Andrew informed me you won't be staying here, and freshen up. Come back for dinner and see how things go."

"If I refuse all of it?"

Another stare. "Then I refuse to give you your mother's things."

I snorted. "Figured. I knew you couldn't have changed that much." Shaking my head, I stalked towards the door.

"Andrew will contact you with what time dinner will be," he called. I had an urge to send him the middle finger back; instead, I gave a brief wave and kept on going.

Once in the hotel room, I paced the floor. I felt like a knobhead for even agreeing to come. Mum would have understood if I didn't.

I laughed to myself; she probably would have told me I was a fool to listen in the first place. Maybe even a small part of me thought since he got ill, he would have grown a heart. He hadn't. No, that was wrong. He had. It just wasn't for me.

This Darlene must have made a real impression on him, either that, or she was a pawn in one of his games to climb higher in the social ladder.

I never knew when it came to Amit.

My phone jolted me out of my thoughts and pacing. It couldn't be dinner time already? I went over to the bed where I'd thrown it and picked it up seeing a number I didn't recognise.

"Hello?" I answered.

"Hey." The voice was rough and deep.

"Lan," I muttered more to myself.

"Yeah. How you doin'?"

"I'm good."

"You don't sound it. Your dad okay?"

Sighing, I dropped my chin towards my chest. "Even if he wasn't, I wouldn't care. Is that bad?"

"No," he replied instantly. "Thinking it doesn't make you a bad person either. I remembered your dad wasn't good to you and your mum. Don't feel bad now because he got you there using guilt over him being sick."

I started pacing again. "He told me it was cancer and do you know what I said?"

"Tell me."

"I told him I didn't care because he didn't give a shit about me or Mum. Especially Mum when she had her cancer and couldn't beat it. He knew I wouldn't give two flying fucks about him, so he used another excuse to get me there. He's got some stuff of Mum's, didn't say what, but whatever it is I don't like it being left in his hands. That's why I came. It would never be because of him, and now I'm here, he blows a new hole in my life and tells me I have a sister who's five, and he wants me to meet her."

"Do you want to?" Lan asked.

"I don't know, Lan. I do but I know if I agree to stay the weeks he's asked for, for me to get to know my sister and her mother, his fiancée, then I feel like crap for doing something he wants when throughout his life, all he's ever done was treat Mum and me like we're worthless."

"Think of it this way. If you choose to stay, you're not doing it for him. You're doing it for you. It's because you want to meet your sister, you want to get to know her and hope there could be a future where you could support her in the end, if anything happens to him. Even if nothing does, you could be there for her when he throws her away if she disappoints him in some way, like he did with you."

"She would need me if that happened."

"She could."

"I want to get to know my sister."

"I could tell you did, East. Don't think of doing it for him. You're better than him because you left him, his money, his power behind to seek your own rich future with people you care about."

"I did." I nodded. He wasn't worth worrying over. I would do what I wanted. It didn't matter he'd asked. I wasn't staying because of that. It was my choice. "Thank you," I whispered. It felt amazing to be able to talk to him like I had in the past. He knew just what to say to get me out of any type of funk or situation I couldn't handle.

"Always here for you. You mind if I call each day to see how things are?"

Gosh darn it all. My heart just melted.

"No," I muttered. "I'd like that."

"Good." I could hear the smile in his voice.

"How are you feeling?" I asked.

"I'm all right, East. Took the pills you left and kept them up."

"I'm glad. Dive helping out?"

"Yeah, he's good. They've got Gamer stayin' at your place for the dogs. He's sleeping in the spare room."

"Do you know if the dogs were okay with him being there?"

Lan snorted. "Everything seems to love that guy. It's all good."

"The Hawks club, they have amazing people in it."

He grunted. "They do. Not as good as me though."

I laughed. "Not sure about that yet."

It sounded like he growled through the phone. "Then I'll prove that as well. For now, I gotta go. My maid just stopped in to give me food."

"Do you see a maid outfit, fucker?" I heard being yelled.

Lan chuckled. "Talk soon, East."

"Looking forward to it." Which I was. A phone call to Lan each night could possibly keep me from killing my father.

Maybe.

Hopefully.

CHAPTER NINETEEN

PARKER

*W*uss. I was a total fucking wuss. It's been a week since the last time I'd seen Lan. If I wasn't hunting down Miller, I was back out in the field doing surveillance on a new case the sarge at the station gave me. He'd also asked me how Lan was enjoying his time off. He'd been surprised when I said I didn't know anything about it. Like all of them at the station, they thought we spent all our time together. It wasn't like I lived with the guy.

Nope, instead, I was being a dickhead.

He'd kissed me. So what?

The longer I left time between the moment, the more I felt like a goddamn motherfucker.

"Huh, wonder if this was how Knife felt," I mumbled to myself after taking another pull of the bottle.

"You talkin' about me to yourself? About how amazin' I am? Sorry, brother, I'm one hundred percent taken," Knife, the grinning fool, said as he took a seat next to me at the bar.

Ignoring him, I asked, "Who's on tonight?"

He sighed. "Nurse is with Lan tonight. My guy, Dallas, and Handle are out hunting."

I'd taken the night off hunting because Dodge warned me if I didn't have a goddamn chill night and got the "I'm gonna kill you" look off my face, he'd take it off for me. Apparently, I'd been an even bigger arse since what happened.

"You gonna spill?"

"Don't know what you're talkin' about." With a tight grip on the neck of the bottle, I swung it up and downed the rest of the beer.

"So you muttering something about wondering if this was how Knife felt has nothing to do with your murderous looks and mood?"

Fucking cunt heard.

"Nope."

"You're a dickhead," he clipped.

I snorted. "Been told that many times before."

"Can I guess what happened?"

"Sure, why not?" I doubted he'd get it.

He leaned closer, and whispered, "Lan kissed you when he was high, and you freaked out over it."

I froze with the new beer Fang had slid my way halfway to my mouth. Out the corner of my eyes, I looked to see him grinning.

He chuckled. "Got it in one, didn't I?"

Slowly, I placed the bottle back down, clasped it between my two hands and stared at it.

His laughter stopped. "Why's it so bad? You hate him for it?" I glared at him. "What? You worried it's gonna fuck things up between you two now you know he thinks you're hot?" I narrowed my eyes even more. Knife rolled his. "Come on, I might be newly gay, but even I could tell by the way he looks at you sometimes. He's attracted to you, and now you know it. Is that the problem? You don't want to know it? Gonna make it awkward between you two?"

None of it was right. He didn't fuckin' know how screwed up in the head I was because all I could fucking think about was Lan and his lips against mine.

Fucking motherfucker.

That isn't me. I shouldn't be doing that. It isn't me, dammit.

I snarled out, "Just shut the fuck up. You don't know shit."

He laughed heartily then. Yeah, my words were stupid since he'd know more than anyone. Knife slapped the counter. "Fang, hit me up." Fang gave him a chin lift. Knife turned his attention back to me and shook his head. "Yeah, you know I know more about the situation than anyone. I just want to know why it's got you in knots."

"I don't want shit to change." I didn't. I wanted to go back to what we were before his lips touched mine. He could continue his thing with Easton, and I'd stick to one-night stands with women. Women were it for me, and that's all I'd ever want.

He nodded. "I can understand that. Look, I'm sure Lan is kicking himself for kissing you in the first place. Besides, I don't think it'd matter too much in the end. Not since he's got his Easton back in his life."

My jaw clenched.

"Hmm," Knife muttered.

"I goddamn hate it when people do that. Just fuckin' say what you're thinkin', arsehole."

"Nothin'." He smirked. "Nothin' at all." He took a sip of his beer. "But I will say, don't let things change if you don't want it to. Act normal, like it never happened."

"Is it that simple?"

"Sure."

"And how long did it take for you to realise that with Beast?"

He whistled. "Low blow, man. I thought we were friends. Yes, I freaked way the fuck out, but that was also because I liked what Beast showed me. It was a shock to my system when I couldn't stop thinkin' about it and wanted to try a taste of it again."

Was that why...? *Nope, fuck that thought right in the face.*

"So just act like it didn't happen."

"Yep." He nodded.

I could do that. Shit, I had to do it. I worked with the guy and wanted the awkward stage passed before he got back on the job.

"Right." I stood, grabbed my wallet, and slapped some bills to the counter.

"Where are you goin'?" Knife asked.

"Gonna go act like it never happened and see how Lan's doin'."

He punched me in the arm. "Good luck, brother."

"Yeah, thanks." *I think.*

My fucked-up gut turned and twisted as I got closer to Lan's front door. It was late. Maybe he'd be asleep and I wouldn't have to see him. I'd give Nurse a message I was there, and then at least Lan'd know I'd tried.

Goddamn, I felt pathetic.

All because he'd kissed me.

Sighing, I sucked in a deep breath and knocked on the front door. I heard heavy footsteps grow close and was sure my bloody heart beat just as loud, and then faster, only to then stop when the door swung open. Once spotting Nurse, it chimed back into its normal rhythm.

"Hey, man." Nurse grinned and stepped back.

I hesitated for a moment and then walked through. Glancing around, I couldn't see Lan anywhere. "Thought I'd pop in, see how things were," I said.

"All good and quiet here. Lan's in his room on the phone."

"Not a problem. I do gotta head off again, but I was in the area." In the damn area? Lan lived out in the fucking sticks. How was that in the area?

"Sure," Nurse drew out.

I cleared my throat. I acted like a wanker. "Might just pop my head in his door, wave, and then head off."

"Not a problem. Got my girl comin' soon. We're gonna watch *Hotels from Hell*. That Ramsey guy is a riot."

"Yeah." I nodded. "He is." Whoever he was. "Be back in a tick."

He shot me a chin lift and went back to the couch. I strode down the hall. Nearing the end, I heard Lan say, "Yeah."

His door was closed most of the way. Of damn course I thought it'd be all right to push it open a little, ready to just stick my head in, but I paused.

I didn't just pause. I locked solid. Shit, even my pulse stalled.

"Fuck, yes," Lan groaned low.

My eyes grew at the sight in front of me and my face heated. Laying back on his bed, boxers down low on his hip, Lan had his cock in hand while staring at something on his phone.

He jerked his cock up and down in a steady pace.

"Show me," a husky male voice said over the phone. Easton.

Lan tilted the phone down, so the screen would only show his hand tugging his cock.

Why wasn't I moving?

Why in the fuck wasn't I moving?

I'd never wanted to watch that type of thing before.

Why in Christ wasn't I backing away?

"Close," Lan groaned.

"Me too," I heard Easton say.

Holy fuck. They were jerking off for each other.

My gut tightened.

My goddamn dick twitched behind my jeans.

Why?

Someone needed to fucking explain to me why the fuck I felt a sudden pulse of desire.

"Now," Lan clipped and then, just as a moan sounded from the other end of the phone, I got a clear view of his cum shooting out and landing. "Parker." My name was cried out in shock.

My body jolted, I glanced up and clashed with Lan's gaze.

"What do you mean Parker?" Easton asked on the other end. "I knew we were starting things too early. I shouldn't—"

"East, don't. Please, just wait." Lan grabbed a tee from the bed and wiped at his stomach. He swung his legs over to the side, and that was when I started moving. I backed up again and again. "Don't," Lan growled out.

Turning, I bolted down the hall into the living room, I called, "See ya." On the way to the door, Nurse called something, but I didn't hear a damn thing. My ears rang in my head, my heart raced to tear its way out of my chest and my gut turned. I felt like I was going to throw up.

This was way worse than the damn fucking kiss.

I slammed the front door on my hasty retreat and jogged to my car.

"Parker," was yelled. I glanced up at the house to see Lan on the porch. "If you fuckin' leave right now, I'll goddamn…. Screw it, I'll do something really shitty."

I unclenched my jaw to snarl, "You think I goddamn care?"

He didn't say anything, but then we heard a car coming down the road. Nurse walked out the front door, headed my way just as the car pulled into Lan's driveway. Starr waved from the driver's side.

Nurse skipped past me, and called, "Later, brothers."

Stunned, I watched him open the passenger door and when I called out for him to wait—since he was supposed to be Lan's backup that bloody night—he slammed the car door shut and Starr started backing out of the driveway.

I glanced at Easton's house. Dodge had said something about one of the brothers minding his house while Easton was out of town on family business as payback for helping Lan out.

Before I could even make my way over there, Lan called out, "Gamer's not there. Gone out with one of his women. Won't be back until late."

No one occupied it, which meant I could hide out there and watch Lan's place from afar. It also meant I didn't have to deal with a fucking awkward conversation.

"Get in the damn house, Parker. Don't be a chicken shit."

I swung my narrowed gaze to his just as pissed one. We stood glaring at each other for a few moments more.

Christ. I had to man the hell up sooner or later.

Wished it'd be later, but I was stuck there now.

Cursing, I slammed my door closed and stomped towards the house.

CHAPTER TWENTY

LAN

*M*y head swirled. Jesus, I'd been on such a goddamn high, and then it crashed. Sailed right down into the pits of Hades. At least my body reacted as if I had. The reaction had been big when I'd seen Parker standing in the doorway. All of the oxygen had left my body, my gut had ripped open, turned and got shoved back inside of me. Fear over him seeing Easton and me jerking off together had me sweating in seconds. My hands had shaken as I'd cleaned up my gut and tried to get to Parker before the situation burned in hell.

I'd be sure he'd think it was worse than me kissing him.

Probably was. Hell, I didn't know what to think. He'd seen me wanking while Face Timing with Easton, and Easton had been doing the same. Parker would have heard both of our sounds, the pleasure we got from sharing that moment.

Why hadn't he bolted right away?

How long had he been standing there?

What in the fuck could I say to him?

What was I supposed to say? *"Hey, just forget I kissed you. While you're at it, forget you saw me jerking off to a guy on the other end of the phone."* Yeah, that wouldn't be damn awkward at all.

I took a seat on the couch. Parker sat in the chair, then stood, pulled something out of his jeans pocket, and tied his hair in a loose ponytail at the back of his neck. He plonked down, rubbed his hands down his thighs, and looked everywhere but at me. When his knee started bouncing up and down, I thought it time to get this shit out of the way and see if we could salvage some type of friendship.

"Do you hate me?" I blurted. It wasn't the first question I had in mind, but yeah, it was important still.

His gaze finally clashed with mine in a scowl that told me he was pissed. "Do you seriously fuckin' think a *slip-up*, when you were medicated, would have me hatin' you after the shit we've dealt with in work and from the club?"

I leaned back into the couch. It could have been a possibility, one I'd considered and had been on my mind near every hour of each day since I'd last seen him.

"Been a week, Parker. 'Course I'm gonna think it."

He cringed. "Yeah, ah, been busy."

"Look...." Fuck, I didn't know what to say.

Parker groaned as if he were in pain and scrubbed a hand over his face. "Can we just go back to before anythin' happened and never fuckin' mention it again?"

My lips twitched. "If you're willing, then yes."

"Good." He nodded. "Clean slate."

"Clean slate," I agreed.

"Great."

I nodded. "Good." Who were we kidding? It was going to still be awkward, for a while at least. However, I didn't want to lose him from my life. Besides, when I got back to work, it'd be hell if I had to find another partner. At least he was willing to try and get over this speed hump. I'd just have to picture him with a bag over his head or just replace it with Easton's image of losing control over the phone as he came.

Fuck me, that had been hot, and then I'd seen Parker at the door and blurted his name in shock. Thank fuck Easton had understood what was going down when I'd explained. He'd told me it was fine and that I'd better go sort shit out with him before he bolted again and ignored me for a few more weeks. Not that I'd reached out to him either because I didn't know what to say. I could have asked him about his lay with the Mickey Mouse-voiced woman, but that could have come across as me being jealous.

I still felt that twist my gut, the thought of him going off to get laid after my lips had touched his.

My gaze flicked down to said lips. I ripped them away to the TV. "Want a beer?" I asked.

"Sure."

Yeah, it would definitely be tense between us for a while.

At least things between Easton and me were building into something more. We'd been talking every day, morning and night, about anything we could think of. Especially about his dad and what he was dealing with being near his father. The motherfucker.

I pulled open the fridge door and peered in, with my mind on Easton I was smiling. When we'd reach the subject of wanking, my cock had gone from soft to hard in seconds.

As Easton laid back on the bed in the hotel room, he sighed. He'd not long come from the shower and only wore a pair of boxers. His inked skin had been on display, and I damn enjoyed looking at it.

"I think he's planning something for this dinner," he'd said.

"What could it be?" I asked.

"I don't know, but I don't like it. He gets this look in his eyes every time Darlene mentions it." Easton was coming back to Melbourne on the Sunday. Darlene wanted to throw a big party on the Saturday to celebrate him leaving. So far between them all, things had been civilised. He'd even enjoyed Darlene's company. She was young, but sweet and doted on her daughter, Easton's sister, Jewel. Easton had also loved getting to know the smart, but sometimes cheeky Jewel. He'd been thankful his father hadn't been around much. Busy with work, or as he'd told Easton, doctor's appointments. He'd even asked Easton not to mention his illness around

Darlene because she wasn't coping at all with it and would break down. He didn't want Jewel to notice because they hadn't told her. It sounded suspicious to me, but Easton didn't think it was because Darlene was such a sweet soul.

"Why don't you ask him?" I suggested.

His brows shot up. "I'd rather stick a fork in my eyeballs than have him think I care about anything he could be up to."

I chuckled. "Fair enough."

"Enough about him. Your bruises are looking better. I can actually see your other eye."

I smiled. "Smartarse."

"That's me. No seriously, you are looking better."

"Yeah?" I cocked a brow. "How much better?"

He rolled his eyes. "Are you looking for compliments, Lan?"

"Hell yeah I am. I've felt like a goddamn hideous monster for the last week."

He snorted. "You could never look hideous."

I smirked. "No?"

He laughed. "Stop fishing."

"Then I'll offer some instead. In the last ten years, I've missed seeing your handsome face, your goddamn stunning body, and listening to your voice. Do you know why I've rung every day?"

"No," he whispered.

Instead of sitting on my bed, I laid back, one arm behind my head while I still held the phone and the view of Easton on it. "Because I've gone too many fuckin' years without seeing and hearing you. I know this could scare you, but I still gotta say it, Easton. I don't want to go a day without you in it ever again."

"Lan," he uttered.

"Christ, I love hearin' my name come outta your mouth like that. Reminds me of all the times I was inside you and you'd say my name quietly on a sigh. Like you loved right where I was. You thought I belonged right where I was. In your bed, with you, and inside you."

"Y-you can't talk like that."

"Why?"

"It's too soon."

I shook my head. "Know you, East. Know all there is to know about you. Give me another reason."

"I don't know what I want."

"You do. It's okay to stall, to go slow, but you know what you want or else you wouldn't take my call every day, even a couple of times a day."

He grumbled under his breath. "Fine, Mr Know-it-all." He paused to bite his bottom lip, then licked it before he gained his courage to say, "Then you're making me hard and you're not here to take care of it."

Closing my eyes, I groaned. "Show me," I ordered, opening my eyes again to find his were like mine, hooded and heated.

"We shouldn't."

"Why?"

"It's too soon," he said again, but it wasn't as strong as before.

"East." I pulled my tee from my body and threw it beside me on the bed. "You wanna see?"

He thinned his lips and nodded.

Slowly, I tilted my phone down so his view would be of my chest, stomach, and then my boxers being tented by my hard cock. Easton made a noise in the back of his throat. I moved the screen back up slowly.

"Your turn," I said, and when he did, the sight was absolutely fucking hot.

"You can't find any?" Parker asked, coming into the kitchen.

Jesus Christ. I'd been staring off into the fridge thinking of the hot scene with Easton and had forgotten Parker was there.

How could I explain why I suddenly had a bulge in my boxers?

Fuck, fuck, fuck.

I grabbed two beers, shifted back to shut the door and then moved back some more, keeping my front hidden from his view. I felt like a goddamn horny teenager not wanting Mum to find out I got erections. I made sure the counter was between us before turning and placing his bottle on the counter and sliding it his way.

Parker picked it up, unscrewed the lid and flicked it into the sink. "Right, so I'll just add you hiding your boner to the list of things we forget and never talk about again."

Goddamn my life.

Sighing, I dropped my head, winced a little from the pain it pulled in my shoulder and closed my eyes. "Easton. I was thinking about him."

"Uh-huh," he muttered.

I snapped my head up and clipped, "I was."

Ah, fuck it. He could believe what he had. Hell, I'd been surprised he actually brought it up in the first place.

"Yeah, let's forget it. I'm gonna head back to bed."

He saluted me with the beer, staring down at the counter. "Night," he said, before walking from the room to plant himself on the couch.

I wanted to say more. Wanted to ask why he pointed it out when he could have just left it, but the little flare in his eyes made me think he'd been wondering the same question himself.

Instead, I took my bottle and made my way down the hall. At least he wasn't running out of the house again.

I closed my door all the way that time. I hadn't before because I wasn't expecting to jerk off with Easton. I sat on the edge of the bed, grabbed my phone and pushed in Easton's number.

"How did it go?"

"Well, he didn't shoot me or leave. I asked Nurse to give us a moment and then caught Parker in time before he bolted. He wants to forget anything happened and go on like normal."

"That's... good, right?"

I didn't know. I shrugged, then cursed under my breath. My damn shoulder, I'd used it too much earlier. Once more I wanted my hands around Miller's neck.

"I guess it'll sort itself out, and one day we'll get back to what we were."

"He saw you masturbating," Easton whispered, and then I caught his lips twitching. I narrowed my eyes. He gulped, then snorted. "Masturbating to me and this is after you kissed him." His lips twitched more. "I bet a straight guy hasn't seen as much action as this before." That was when he lost it and started rolling on the bed, laughing.

CHAPTER TWENTY-ONE

EASTON

"Good morning, Easton," Luis greeted as he opened the front door to my father's house. "I believe Miss Jewel is in the library with her mother before they start the picnic in the backyard."

Smiling, I nodded. "Thanks, Luis." I leaned in. "Is Amit around?"

Luis smirked and nodded. "He's in his study."

I rolled my eyes, patted his shoulder and made my way down to the library. Jewel loved to read and to have someone read to her. It didn't surprise me they were in the library, but what did was the male voice behind the closed door.

"He'll arrive when he does, Jewel. Now be quiet so I can work," Amit bit out, his tone frustrated.

Either Jewel ignored it or just didn't understand the difference. "Mummy said we were going to have a picnic. Do you want to come with us, Daddy?"

"No," he snarled. "Now shut up before I shut you up."

I swung the door open, strode in and picked up Jewel, whose bottom lip was trembling, and said, "I see nothing has changed with you."

He stood from the chair, his teeth grinding together. "Easton, you didn't hear—"

"I heard enough. She's five years old. *Five.*"

He threw out an arm. "I have a headache, and she wouldn't stop questioning me."

Jewel whimpered. I drew her into my chest more and rubbed her back. Glaring at what was supposed to be our father, I shook my head and walked out of the library.

"Son," he called. "Easton, do not tell Darlene about this."

He was such a dick.

Jewel was usually accompanied by Darlene, or if she were busy preparing a meal, because she loved to cook, Henrietta, Jewel's nanny or sometimes even Luis was with her. Darlene must have thought she could trust her own fiancée and the father to her daughter with Jewel. She couldn't. He would always be curt and find a child's company nothing but a nuisance.

Should I inform Darlene about it?

Would she listen?

When we spent time together, she hardly spoke of the man, but that could be because she could see how tense it was between us. After all, I hadn't been in his life for so many years.

"You okay, bubblegum?" I asked Jewel. Like usual, she let out a little giggle over the nickname I'd given her because she always smelled like bubblegum. Only that time it wasn't her normal happy one. "You know what I know about Amit?"

She shook her head, but before I could say anything she asked, "Why do you call him his name and not Daddy?"

I opened my mouth to answer and then snapped it closed trying to think of the best way to answer. "He *is* my father, but I don't know him too well, that's probably why. It might change when we get to know each other more." *Never.*

She looked up at me, and asked, "Will you call me Jewel when you know me more?"

I laughed. "Nope. Since I already know you and adore you, you'll always be *my* bubblegum."

She smiled. The darkness that had been there vanished. "I 'dore you too, East," she said as we entered the kitchen.

"Aw, that's the sweetest thing," Darlene cooed from behind the counter as she placed things in the basket in front of her. "You know she's going to miss you when you leave."

I placed Jewel back on her feet with a kiss to her forehead.

"Come, Miss Jewel. I have bubbles for us to blow," Henrietta called from the glass doors that led out onto the back patio.

Jewel glanced up at me. "Come with, East?"

"Soon, I'll just help your mum finish packing our lunch."

"'Kay." She grinned and took off.

"She talks about you all the time. Maybe if you and the gentleman Amit is setting you up with on Saturday night work out, things will be different."

Thankfully I was already near the counter. I gripped it as shock tore through me. "Sorry?" I whispered.

She smiled over at me, saw something in my expression and her smile vanished. "Amit told you, didn't he?"

I shook my head. "I don't know what you're talking about. Please tell me."

She pulled her lips between her teeth and searched my face. "I'm not sure. Amit may have wanted it as a surprise."

I needed to know what Amit was playing at. "Darlene, I need to be honest with you."

"Okay," she said hesitantly.

"Have you noticed Amit and I hardly speak to each other?" When she nodded, I went on, "He may have had a hand in making me, but he will never be my father. I have my reasons for it and don't want to say them because I don't want to sway your feelings for him in any way. However, what I will warn you is that you should never leave Jewel alone with him." Her eyes widened. I rushed on, "He's not violent. He would never hit a child, but he doesn't have the patience for them, and it can sometimes show in harsh words. Now, knowing enough, I need you to understand I would rather not have anything Amit considers as a surprise for me."

A stab of guilt flowed through me for warning her about the relationship between her own fiancé and their daughter.

She swallowed, and it looked like it hurt. "Okay." Her clear acceptance told me Darlene had already witnessed something between Amit and Jewel. She took a deep breath. "Your father has someone coming to the party Saturday night for you."

"What do you mean for me?"

"Well, you see, he's hoping you and this gentleman will hit it off, and maybe he could be a reason to have you come back here to live one day."

I stared and then laughed my arse off. I slapped the counter and snorted. Wiping my eyes, I shook my head, smiling at Darlene. "That's rich, especially when he disowned me for being gay in the first place. Now here he is setting me up with someone in the hopes I'll hit it off with them."

"H-he disowned you?" Darlene's voice shook. She may have been thirty-two years old, but she was sheltered and had no doubt been brought up in a loving household.

I waved my hand in front of me. "Don't worry about it. It's in the past. What I can't understand is how he thinks one look at a guy he picked would have me wanting to come back and stay in Queensland." He was up to something else. There had to be another reason for it because he didn't do anything without gaining something in return. "Anyway," I chirped. "Let's forget about it for now and enjoy the sun. I'm starving."

"Easton—"

I took her hand in mine. "I'm happy to be here. Happy I've had the chance to know you and Jewel. That's all that matters. He has one thing right. I will come back, but it won't be for anything he sets up. It'll be to see you and bubblegum."

She smiled softly. "Okay, and I know both Jewel and I would love to have you come back anytime you want."

"Good." I winked, picked up the basket, and started for the doors. I guessed Saturday night I'd learn what was behind Amit's sudden change of heart by accepting me being gay and trying to set me up with someone.

I walked out chuckling to myself.

"**H**e fuckin' wants to do what?" Lan roared through the phone. I flopped back to lie on the bed. I could even hear the heavy footsteps he took as he either started to pace or headed to another room.

"Where are you?"

"At the compound," he told me. He must be headed to another room for privacy.

"What are you doing there?" I asked.

"I went out with a couple of brothers on some leads we had with Miller. Didn't work out, so we're back here for a while."

"Should you even be out of the house? You're still healing."

"I'm good, East."

"Lan, you were shot and beat."

"I'm wearing the brace on my arm, so it restricts the movement on my shoulder. Promise, I'm good. Like you worrying though."

"Aw," I heard drawn out in the background.

I flew to sit on the edge of the bed.

He hadn't sought privacy.

He talked to me in front of people.

In front of bikers.

Warmth spread from my chest and out, all over my body.

"Fuck off," Lan clipped. There was laughter. Then he said into the phone, "Before these dickheads give me too much shit, tell me again why your fuckin' father is trying to set you up with someone."

"That's the thing. I don't know."

"He disowned you because you're gay," he stated, as if I didn't already know.

Rolling my eyes, I said, "I know."

"He's planning something. Some way to hold you to him still."

"I'm thinking that too, but I don't have a clue what. He should know none of it will matter. I've enjoyed my time with Darlene and Jewel, but come Sunday, he's giving me my mother's things and I'm leaving."

"I don't trust him," he said. Things quietened on the other end. Obviously people were listening now.

"I don't either, but nothing he can say or do will have me not coming back to Melbourne. Besides, I start back at work next Tuesday."

"Will you let me do some diggin' on your father?"

"How?"

"Gamer has a few skills with a computer. I'll see if he can find anything."

It would probably be for the best, might give me a chance to figure out Amit before Saturday night.

"Okay."

"I think I'll get a flight tom—"

"Lan." I laughed. "There's nothing to come here for. He's harmless in the end."

"You do not get set up with anyone."

I smiled. "Now who's the one worrying. Unless the guy is Hugh Jackman, I won't be fawning all over him. I'll tell him politely that I'm involved with someone, apologise for Amit being an idiot, and leave it at that."

"So you *are* involved with someone."

My pulse raced. "Yes," I whispered.

Silence for a few beats and then, "Wait, with me right?"

Laughing, I shook my head. "Yes, Lan. I don't masturbate over the phone with just a random person."

"Good, from this day and forever, I'll be the only one you do it with."

"You can't promise forever."

"I can." He sounded so certain. "I still think I should get a flight."

Grinning, I said, "No, Lan. I'm a big boy. I can take care of Amit Ravel."

CHAPTER TWENTY-TWO

PARKER

*W*hy in the fuck had I pointed out his goddamn boner? That shit just blurted out of my mouth before my brain could stop it. Thank fuck he'd left the room. Things were still tense between us, but with time, I hoped they would settle. Christ, they'd better.

I was over waking up dreaming of Lan's lips on mine. Worse was when it morphed into watching Lan *and* Easton on a bed kissing while I stood in the doorway.

Why? Fucking someone tell me why.

Why in Christ did I wake up harder than just a normal morning wood?

It confused me, but not enough to know I wanted his lips on mine again. I didn't. Hell no. Not at all. They were just stupid dreams.

Shaking my head, I walked into the compound on Thursday to pick up Lan. He'd been out hunting with the brothers, and when I'd called to say I was on my way to grab him before heading to his place, he told me there'd been more dead ends to the information we'd had on Miller's whereabouts.

It seemed the fuckhead had disappeared from Victoria. Dodge

had even talked to Talon, who put the word out to the other charters with Miller's full name and photo. Again, no one had seen or heard anything about him.

"Yo, Parker," Dive called with a chin lift as I entered the common room. I lifted my hand in greeting and spotted Lan sitting on the couch talking to Dallas, Knife, and Vicious. I made my way over and took a seat in the empty chair.

"How's it goin'?" Vicious asked.

"Same as always, brother."

He nodded.

"Want a beer?" Knife asked.

"Nah, I'll get back to Lan's first."

"Was just tellin' Lan, we're not sure his neighbour is gonna get Gamer outta his house. Never seen a brother in love with animals as much as that guy. He doesn't shut up about them," Dallas said.

"I should bring Neveah and Vin out there one day," Knife said.

"Sure," Lan agreed. "Make it when Easton's home. He's got more control over the mutts than Gamer." How'd Lan know that?

"After this shit is done with Miller, I'll have a barbeque. Invite everyone to get to know Easton."

"Rumours are true?" Dallas asked.

"What rumours?" Lan asked with a smile.

"That, you know, you and that guy."

Lan's lips twitched. "What'd you mean?" Lan asked, messing with Dallas.

Dallas glanced to all of us. We made sure to keep a straight face. He cleared his throat, red coating his cheeks. "You're with that guy," he blurted.

Lan chuckled. "Yeah. Knew what you were sayin'. Just messin' with you."

When had they decided to become a thing again? Knew it was in the cards, just didn't know it was official. Then again, seeing Lan.... Yeah, that was a good indication it was happening.

"Dickheads," Dallas grumbled, and took a swig of his beer while everyone else there laughed. Hell, I even smiled.

"I think it's awesome, and I know I can't wait to meet him," Low said, sliding up to Dallas's side. "Even though you got shit goin' down, I never saw you look content before, Lan. Loving it. The sisters are gonna go crazy. Shit, I better email them all. Get sorted with who's bringing what." She disappeared again.

"Now you're in deep shit," Dallas said with a chuckle. Once the Hawks women got something in their bonnet about any type of party, they were all over it. And usually, it ended up being something fucking big. Easton would freak no doubt. I snorted at the thought.

"Now all we need is Parker to hook up with someone to make him less broody," Knife teased. I shot him the middle finger.

"I could help with that," a woman said, and I recognised her voice right away. It'd be the bird I screwed the night of Lan's lips on mine. "Hey, handsome. You come back for seconds?"

Fuck.

My gaze locked onto Lan's. I was surprised to find him glaring with a clenched jaw.

Ignoring that thought for another time, I looked up at... fuck, I couldn't remember her name. She must have seen my dilemma and supplied it, "Bonny."

I offered her a rare grin; it wasn't her fault I was just about wasted that night. She slid onto the armrest and glided her hand over the back of my shoulders.

Shit, I shouldn't have smiled.

"Bonny, take a hike," Knife said.

We all glanced at him. Bonny giggled. "Don't be jealous, honey. Just because you've turned and are now taken, I'm sure our resident cop won't say no." She shifted her gaze to Lan. "Unless you want to have a go, sweetheart. I could take you both on."

"No," Lan clipped, his upper lip raised.

She winked. "S'all good, sugar, maybe another time."

"Barking up the wrong tree, Bonny," Dallas said. "And unless Parker shows interest, fuck off from here."

She rolled her eyes and glanced down to me. Her hand squeezed my shoulder. "What do you say, handsome? Feeling like some Bonny?"

"Not today, babe." I tapped her fingers on my shoulder, and she stood and walked off.

"That bitch is in heat," Knife commented.

Vicious grunted. "She'd just come from Elvis's room."

A look of disgust crossed Lan's features before he replaced it with a neutral expression. He tipped his beer up and drank the rest of it in one go.

My phone rang. I pulled it out and looked at the caller ID. Blackie. He was the president to the Venom MC. One I'd been undercover in a while ago. He'd known I was in the force towards the end and hadn't ratted me out. Instead, when Stoke and Vicious came calling to their compound for answers about Nary, he passed me back over to the Hawks. Stating that since he was in charge, they wouldn't need a snitch because he kept a clean club.

Fang, a brother of Hawks now, had also been a part of Venom but wanted away because he hated his father, and his pop used to have ties to the Venom MC. So did Fang's woman, which was why eventually Hawks and Venom had come to an agreement for allegiance between the two clubs.

"Yeah?" I answered.

"Heard you and the other cop are after someone."

I sat straighter and caught Lan's eyes. He shifted to the edge of his seat. "Know anything about it?" I asked.

Blackie chuckled. "Got a surprise out the front."

Hanging up, I stood. "Blackie's here. He's got a surprise for us," I told Lan. He straightened and followed me out. I knew he wouldn't be the only one coming either.

Out the front, Blackie leaned against a Hyundai iLoad. He grinned, moved away from the back door and slid it open. Someone crouched over something in the back. That something was rolled, and it tumbled out onto the gravel.

It was Miller.

"Surprise," Blackie said.

"How'd you find the fucker?" Lan asked, strolling over to crouch down beside an unconscious Miller.

"Stupid motherfucker came to the club. Asked for protection. Roda tasered him to the ground before he'd even finished speaking." A few chuckled. Roda was Blackie's crazy-arse woman; no one wanted to mess with her.

Lan's head came up, then glanced over his shoulder to me. "He probably thought Venom and Hawks were still on bad terms."

"Yep." Blackie clapped his hands. "Right, we done a favour bringing him to you. Means you detectives owe Venom now."

"Hold up," I called.

Blackie glared over at me. "What?"

"If I remember correctly, Blackie, and tell me if I get this wrong. But it was Lan and I at a house answering a call to help out in a Venom situation where you were shot, and we asked for nothing in return. We covered it all in fact. Do you remember that, Lan?"

He chuckled, stood, and nodded. "I'm recalling it now."

"We owe Venom nothing. If someone thinks we owe them, we don't like being told that. We don't do well with orders. Nice friendly requests are best for us, or we just get pissed. Got it?"

He glowered. "Fine."

"Good. Now you'll remember for next time if you ever do need our help with something how things happen. Just because we don't wear a patch of any kind doesn't mean we don't deserve respect."

"Not that long ago you were Venom, kid."

I shook my head. "I was never Venom, and you know it."

"Kinda wish I had'a made your time a little hellish when you were there now."

I grinned. "Too late."

"Fuck it," he grumbled and slid the door shut as the guy in the back swung over to the driver seat.

"We do appreciate your assistance, Blackie," Lan offered.

He eyed him and then looked back to me. "See, that's how you should do it."

I chuckled. "That ain't in me. It's why he's my partner."

Blackie snorted. "Yeah, I can see that. Later, arseholes."

"Later, Blackie," Knife called, as did a few others.

As soon as Blackie drove off, I said, "Let's get this fucker nice and comfortable in a room."

Lan grinned.

I threw the bucket of water over Miller and the chair he was tied to. He spluttered and coughed. Finally, he opened his eyes to see us standing around him. Immediately, he paled and started to beg. Nothing would help.

We'd already spoken about what we'd planned. What helped make that decision were the photos he had on him. We now understood how he got the teenage girl who had helped him at Lan's to cooperate. Through drugs. In one photo, they were shooting up together. In another, she lay on the couch with Miller over her. Her eyes told us she was out of it. We saw a few more photos we all wished we hadn't. The last was of the girl frothing at the mouth and yet he still.... Fuck, I couldn't even think what he'd been doing or I'd lose my lunch and temper.

I wasn't the only one who wanted a piece of his flesh by the time the photos were shown. Lan would go first, then myself. Knife, Vicious, Dallas, and Dodge would also be taking a chunk of Miller. We'd make him suffer until his last breath.

There'd been an option of sending him back to jail, but Lan made the final decision, and after he'd stared down at the photos for some time, he declared, "He'll die and be delivered to hell like the scum he is."

Since we were all in agreement, we set about making him pay.

His screams could be heard down the hall.

CHAPTER TWENTY-THREE

EASTON

*D*arlene supplied me with a suit for the final night I would spend with them because I hadn't brought one with me. My stomach swirled with nerves. I wanted to know what my father had planned by setting me up with someone. However, I also felt like something pinched at my chest as I hadn't heard from Lan. I'd tried calling him, a few times in fact, but he hadn't returned my calls. Worry weighed me down.

My phone chimed. I would never admit it if asked, but I dove for it on the bedside table in the hotel. Picking it up, I saw it was a text from Lan.

Shit, lost my phone down the fucking couch at the compound. Battery was flat. I only just got it back and charged it. Stupid me had thrown out your number and couldn't remember what hotel you stayed at. You still talking to me?

Smiling, I sent back: **Depends.**

His response was instant: **On?**

If you call me right now.

My phone started ringing, and I answered, "Hey."

"Miller's out of my life."

"What?" I breathed.

"A friend of a friend found him, brought him to us, and we dealt with it. Somehow, before all that happened, I lost my phone. Sorry, I saw your calls, knew you'd be worried, but everythin's fine here."

"Wait, go back. You've dealt with the guy who broke into your house, shot and beat you. How?"

"East..." He said my name as if it pained him. "I shouldn't even have said that. Just know he'll no longer be an issue."

Which meant he was dead.

Lan had killed a man.

I expected something like that would happen when Miller was found. He caused a lot of damage, but I had also thought that maybe with time, Lan would have realised death wasn't the only option.

"East?" Lan whispered.

I didn't know how it all sat with me.

My hands trembled at the thought of Lan up and killing a person.

Yes, the guy did hurt him... and would have killed him if I hadn't come along.

Lan would have been dead.

Miller would have killed him, no question about it.

"It's okay," I said into the phone.

"East," Lan whispered. "Are you sure you can live with that knowledge?"

I didn't pause. "Yes. He would have killed you if he'd had the chance otherwise." The room phone rang. "Shit, that's my ride to the party."

"Dinner. Tomorrow night. My place," he ordered roughly.

My stomach fluttered.

"I'd like that."

"Good. Call me if you need me."

"I will." I smiled into the phone.

The house buzzed with people, conversation, and music. While surrounded by so many people I didn't know, it seemed as if they all knew who I was; whoever I walked by either offered a greeting or a smile.

I had no idea how long I'd been at the party. It was at least a couple of hours, but it felt like a hell of a lot more. I hadn't yet found Darlene and Jewel, though Luis did know they were in attendance somewhere. Who would have thought a house would contain a huge-arse ballroom so big it was hard to spot the only people I went there for.

"Mr Ravel," Andrew called from the doorway I'd just passed. I walked over to him. "Your father would like to have a word in private please."

"Sure." I nodded and then followed him out. I took my phone out ready to text Lan as it was go time for a good laugh, when I noticed I already had ten missed calls from him, which had started a few hours ago. I checked the sound and found I'd somehow turned it down. Just as I upped the volume, it was taken from my hand. "Hey," I snapped, glancing up at Andrew holding my phone.

"I'm sure whoever it is can wait until after you speak to your father."

"Okay," I stretched out. Still, it was rude for Andrew to snatch my phone in the first place. I held out my hand. "I'll call him later, but I want it back."

Andrew spun on his feet and walked off. "I'll pass it back after."

"I want it now, Andrew."

"Yes, yes, but your father is waiting in his office."

Something was wrong.

"What's going on?"

Andrew didn't answer. He flew up the steps two at a time. I made haste to follow the long-legged dickhead. My phone started ringing.

"Why can't I speak to my friend?"

"You can, just later."

I could punch him in the kidney and take him to the ground for my phone, but I was curious as to why Amit needed a meeting at my farewell party. Unless it was for me to meet whoever he wanted to set me up with. But why would Andrew take my phone?

The whole situation was messed up.

What I wanted would be for Amit to give me my mother's things, see Darlene and Jewel, even say goodbye to Luis, and get the hell out of there. I started to feel like a flight that night would be good.

I wiped my sweaty palms on my dress pants and followed Andrew down the hall. A door opened, and Luis stepped out holding bottles of wine. He glanced from Andrew, who ignored him as he walked by, to me slowly. "Sir, did you find Miss Jewel?"

Smiling, I shook my head. Stopping in front of him, I said, "Not yet, but after this meeting with Amit, I'll be down to look for her."

His brows dipped. He glanced back at Andrew. "Very well."

I lowered my voice to say, "He took my phone, Luis. Should I be worried?"

Luis's whole body jerked. "I... I'm uncertain, Easton," he whispered.

"Mr Ravel, please hurry," Andrew called. We looked down to find him staring back with a scowl. "I'm sure the wait staff is very busy and has to get back to work or could be fired."

Jesus, I wanted to give him the middle finger salute.

Luis thinned his lips, but said clearly, "Yes, I must get back to work." With a nod, he started back down the hall the way we'd just come from.

With a frown, I caught up to Andrew. "Do you know you can be a dick sometimes?"

He huffed but said nothing, probably because we'd come to Amit's office. He knocked once.

"Enter," Amit called out.

Andrew opened the door, ushered me in with an arm to my back and stepped in behind me before he closed the door.

Then I heard the lock slip into place.

I glanced back to see Andrew stayed near the door, like some guard. He slipped my phone into his pocket and crossed his arms over his chest.

"Easton," Amit called, drawing my gaze from Andrew.

It was then I noticed two other people in the room. Amit stood behind his desk while another man stood beside him, and a woman, who could have been in her late teens, stood hunched beside the other man. Her eyes stayed glued to the floor.

"What's going on?" I asked, moving forward. It was my first time in Amit's office, and I should have known it would have been over the top. The space was the size of my living, dining, and kitchen combined. His thick, long wooden desk looked like it cost more than my house. Bookcases were positioned behind him, while to the left were floor-to-ceiling windows and to the right a massive fire-place where in front of it sat a couch and two chairs. The room could even be classed as a small apartment. All he needed was a bathroom, which looked like, if I guessed right, was behind the door in the corner of the room.

Amit gestured with his hand beside him. "I would like you to meet Mr Khatri and his daughter, Prisha."

"You never mentioned your son's name before Amit."

Amit sighed. "His Australian mother chose his name."

Mr Khatri's eyes widened. "How unfortunate."

"I agree." Amit nodded.

"I'm standing right here. Tell me how you really feel," I said, glaring at both. With a quick glance to Prisha, I saw her lips twitch, but she didn't raise her head or say anything yet.

Mr Khatri glanced at Amit. "He is willing?"

Amit shook his head. "I feel we will have to take drastic measures."

"Are you two insane, talking about me like I'm not here? What is all this about?"

Mr Khatri sighed. "Explain it to him, and we'll see how it will be handled from there."

Amit came around his desk to stand beside me. "Son, Mr Khatri has many companies in the Middle East. Companies he needs assistance with by my firm. I am in need of his business, so we have come to an arrangement."

My stomach dropped.

I knew what was coming. I just fucking knew it.

Turning to Mr Khatri, I said, "I'm gay. I won't marry your daughter."

"I have heard that from your father, but it matters not."

"Son, have you even tried to be with a woman?"

Shock caused me to laugh. It was ridiculous.

Shaking my head, I told them, "You're both out of your minds."

"We will make it worth your while," Mr Khatri said. He pushed some pieces of paper my way. "One million dollars."

"One million to marry your daughter even though I'm gay."

He nodded. "As your father asked, are you really sure you're gay?"

I snorted. "Yes, I'm sure. Sorry, Prisha, but women aren't for me." I shook my head again. "I can't believe I even said that in front of you lot. This is stupid." I turned to Amit. "I want my mother's things, and then I'm leaving."

His jaw clenched. "I need you to sign these documents."

"No," I clipped. "I'll not marry a woman to save your business and to get a million." I threw my hands up in the air. Then stilled. "Why do you need his business, Amit? Your firm is small and popular enough to gain clients. It's what you've always told me. So why?"

"That is none of your business."

"Is it because you're sick?"

"You're sick?" Mr Khatri demanded.

Amit paled. "No. I'm healthy."

Wait, what?

"What?" I bit out. "You don't have cancer?"

Amit rolled his eyes. "You rallied around your mother when she was ill. I thought it would get you here for me also. But no, I had to bribe you with your mother's things."

With a scowl, I told him darkly, "You know why that was."

He waved a hand around. "Yes, because I refused to help when she was ill. She left me, Easton. No woman leaves me."

I sucked in a sharp breath. "You're fucking kidding me, right? You held a grudge and didn't offer help to save her life because she left you? You treated her like shit. Then you disowned me because I'm inked and gay. You're messed up." I laughed humourlessly. "There isn't a chance in hell I would help you and sign that contract."

"What about your mother's things?"

Closing my eyes, I shook my head as sadness washed over me. She'd be cursing me more now. I walked right into his trap. She would have told me to forget whatever he had of hers, and I should have, but then I wouldn't have met Darlene or Jewel.

"It doesn't matter anymore." It didn't. I had my time with Jewel. I'd make sure Darlene knew I wanted to stay in their lives forever, but I would never want anything to do with Amit ever again. Turning, I said, "You can keep them."

Andrew straightened near the door.

"I'm afraid I can't let you leave until you sign the contract, Easton."

Laughing, I spun back. "You're kidding, right?"

"No."

I thumbed behind me. "Do you seriously think this dickhead could stop me?"

"Yes." Amit smiled.

I heard a gun being cocked and slowly faced Andrew.

"You won't kill me because then all this will be for nothing."

"True. But it doesn't mean he can't harm you. Come and take a seat. Let's all relax by the fire, have a drink and talk."

Did I believe Andrew would shoot to harm? I didn't have a clue because no way did I expect anything like this to happen. What was I supposed to do? Make a run for it? Tackle Andrew to the ground and bolt out of the room? But then I had a feeling Amit and Mr fucking Khatri still wouldn't let me leave. They seemed too smug, like Andrew wasn't their only plan.

I was stuck.

My chest tightened in fear because I suddenly saw no way out.

No. I'd think of something. I had to.

Nodding, I walked over to a chair near the fire and sat. I needed a plan.

CHAPTER TWENTY-FOUR

LAN

HOURS EARLIER

"He's not fuckin' answering," I yelled into the room. "That's it; I'm getting on the next flight." I started for the door, but then Parker stepped in front of me. He shoved me back gently.

"You're not thinkin' clearly."

"I'm not?" I clipped. "You saw what Gamer found on that motherfuckin' Amit Ravel. That damn email told me enough. I need to get the fuck over there to stop this bullshit and now."

"Do you really think Easton would marry some bird for one mil?"

"No. I know he won't. He wouldn't unless he absolutely had to."

"Guys," Gamer called from the computer.

"I can't see anything that douche had would get Easton to marry a bird. You're stressin' for nothin'."

"Then why in the fuck isn't he answering his phone, Parker?"

"Yo," Gamer called.

"Fuckin' shit," Dodge commented.

I ignored them and stayed glaring at Parker.

"Maybe because he's at some fancy dig and can't hear it, Lan. You're runnin' for no reason but an email where he gets one million for marryin' a woman."

"Motherfuckers," Knife boomed.

We both looked his way.

He pointed down at the computer. "There's been other emails before the contract one."

"What do they say?" I asked. Parker walked over with me as Gamer brought four of them up on the screen.

"They were in his deleted folder. The idiot didn't empty it out," Gamer explained. "It's not good, brothers."

"Explain," Parker ordered.

Gamer pointed to one. He glanced at me and asked, "Didn't you say he was sick? Cancer or something?"

"Yes."

"Doctor's results. He's in good health." He pointed to another. "This one tells us how his business will collapse because he owes the taxman money for his employees' pensions and shit."

"This one is a threat. From what I'm gathering, he slept with a prostitute. She knows he's from money and if he doesn't pay her in the next few days, she'll be sending evidence to his fiancée." He took a breath. "All of it tells me he'll be desperate to get this guy's business by making his son marry into the family."

"What does the guy he's gettin' money from gain from the deal?" Parker asked.

"A lawyer and his firm to do anything he wants them to do," Knife said.

"Fuck," Dodge clipped.

Gamer nodded. He pointed to the last email. "However, it's this one you need to worry about most."

"What is it?"

"If this fails with Easton and he doesn't sign, the father's hired a hitman for after he's married to the Darlene lady. Her family is fuckin' loaded. He'll go for her money."

"They have a kid together," I snarled.

"He won't care," Parker said, disgust in his voice. "Like Gamer said, he's desperate. Social and financial appearances mean everythin' to this guy. He's willin' to sell his son off to save his business. If that fails, he's gonna kill for it."

"Get me a flight, Gamer, and fuckin' now," I bit out.

A hand landed on my shoulder. "Do not fuckin' talk me out of it, Parker."

"I'm not. But it can't be you."

I faced him. "What the fuck, man?"

"You're not healed. Airports will ask questions."

Stepping up, I got in his face. "I don't goddamn care."

"Let me go. I don't look like I've been in some bar brawl. I have a badge, and Gamer will print out the evidence from the emails. He won't stand a chance."

"No one will give a fuck how I look. I'm not—"

"We're goin' after him. Don't you think he'll come after us? If he does, he won't find shit on me, but you looking the way you do, if things get put together, and people start asking where Miller, *your ex-partner*, is, don't you think shit could hit the fan? Then where would that leave Easton? He'd feel guilty as hell just because you couldn't take a breath and trust in me being right. We can't risk questions being raised with you looking the way you do."

"He's right," Dodge said. "Miller won't show to his parole officer so an investigation will start. You need to lay low until then. Heal. Not run off when you know Parker can handle it."

I pinched the bridge of my nose and breathed deeply, refraining from kicking some arse like I wanted to. I fucking hated they made sense.

Pulling my hand away, I clenched both fists. Nothing helped the fury boiling under my skin.

Parker stepped close, his hand landing on the side of my neck. "You fuckin' let loose in here, Gamer will lose the computers. The evidence. Calm the hell down. We got this. *I* got this. Gamer's gettin' me a flight already. I'll be over there and back with Easton. He'll be fine. Yeah?"

He shook me a little. I rolled my neck, goddamn wincing when it tugged at my shoulder and straightened before I nodded. "Yeah."

"Good." He faced the others. "I've got a bag in the car. I won't need anything else but those papers, Gamer."

"Printing now," Gamer said.

"What about work?" Knife asked.

Parker shook his head. "It'll be fine. Nothin's happening on the case. I'll tell Sarge I have to head out of town to help a friend out for a day, two tops."

"He good like that?" Dodge questioned.

"Yeah, he's pretty good," I told them.

"You're takin' backup," Dodge suddenly ordered.

Parker shook his head. "I'm a detective. If I show up with a brother from the club, it won't be seen well."

"You'll need someone with you. No brother, patch or not, goes it alone."

"Who?" Parker demanded.

Knife took out his phone. "What about a lawyer?"

"We're not taking a civilian into something like this. I don't even know what type of situation it'll be," I said.

Knife shook his head. "Liam's the fuckin' bomb at scaring people with words. He's a huge mofo too, and he's a black belt in karate."

"How do you know this Liam guy?" Parker asked.

"His partner helped me out in a situation."

"Parker, it's your call," Dodge said.

"He'll do. Make the call. Gamer, get him a ticket. Email it to him if he agrees and send mine to me. I'll meet him at the airport." Parker grabbed the papers Gamer had printed then strode out of the computer room.

"Be back," I said and followed him out. "Parker," I called.

He stopped and faced me. "Yeah?"

"Thank you," I said, stopping in front of him.

"You'd do it if I were in the same situation. Nothin' to thank me for."

"Just... after everything, ah, yeah." I nodded and felt like a fucking moron.

He snorted. "All good. See you when I bring him back."

I nodded. Unclenching my jaw, I added quickly, "Be careful."

His stare was hard to read because he wasn't scowling. He blanked his expression. Then he dipped his chin, turned, and walked off.

Parker

Knife'd been right. Liam was a huge mofo, and black. Jesus, the brother even towered over me, and I was tall. He stalked towards me with confidence in his pricey suit, holding a briefcase.

"Parker?" his deep voice asked, stopping just before me.

"Yep. Thanks for coming, Liam."

"I've been sent all the information. I'll read it on the way over. I've previously heard stories regarding Mr Ravel. He isn't a fair lawyer. He's an even worse human being. I believe in justice, Parker. I'll do what I can to help."

"Good. We'd better board."

He nodded.

Gamer had somehow got us a seat side by side. After take-off, I relaxed back for the two-hour flight. I felt Liam shift and opened my eyes to find him looking at me. His voice was low when he asked, "Knife didn't mention your involvement with Easton Ravel. Are you romantically involved?"

I scoffed, snorted, and then laughed. "No." I shook my head. Lan's lips popped into my mind. "No," I said again.

Liam narrowed his gaze. "Do you have a problem with—"

I leaned in. "Do not fuckin' ask me that question. If I had a problem, then I wouldn't be on this trip for my partner to help out *his* guy."

"Partner?"

"Probably like yours, meaning partner in work. The guy who helped Knife out."

Liam sat back, his lips twitching.

"What?"

"I have two partners, and it's not for work. Liberty and Damien."

Ding, ding, fucking ding.

Now I knew who Liam was. He was in a relationship like Pick and Billy were with Josie. Two guys and a girl.

"Ah, right." I nodded.

"There's nothing wrong with it. Will there be a problem?"

I sighed, ran a hand over my face, and said, "Why do people assume I'd have a fuckin' problem? Like and love who you want. I don't judge or give a shit."

Silence for a beat, and then he said, "It's the look you get on your face."

"What?" I clipped roughly, causing some people to look at us in our two seats at the side of the plane.

He shifted, giving his back to the other people on the plane. "Your eyes widened for a second in fear, then narrowed in anger. Your lips thinned in frustration, and then you rolled your eyes before you tilted your head in thought."

I froze.

"I'm a lawyer, Parker. I read people well. It's the fear and thought parts I'd want to know about. If you want to tell me, I'm a good listener, and if you ask me to keep it in confidence, I will."

Why did he tell me that? Who cared if he wouldn't say shit to anyone? I didn't. I had zilch to talk about. I just wanted to get to Queensland, punch Amit Ravel in the face before I arrested his arse and then get Easton back to Victoria for Lan.

176

Lan wanted Easton with him. They were together. Two men who annoyed the fuck out of me on more than one occasion. At least one of them I knew well, and I'd learned to take his teasing and the days he had attitude into account to know he was still a solid guy. The other I didn't know, wasn't sure I trusted him completely, but he had proven himself an okay guy.

Did I want to or need to talk?

Christ no. Besides, I couldn't think of anything I needed to talk about. Hell, I was fine. I had nothing on my mind. Nothing of which he'd understand. Besides, I didn't even know the guy.

"I'm fine," I said, and then leaned back, closing my eyes.

I felt Liam shift, heard a zip, and for some fucked-up reason, my heart jack-hammered in my chest until I heard the *tap, tap* of his fingers flying over a keyboard. I glanced out the corner of my eyes and saw him working on his laptop.

Jesus Christ. Had that thought actually popped into my head? The one where I thought Liam undid his zipper on his slacks. Messed up. So bloody messed up in my head.

Fucking hell, it was like I thought every guy was coming onto me after the thing that happened with Lan's lips.

Shit. I couldn't even say it. Think it.

I had to. I goddamn had to own it and get over it.

Lan kissed me.

Except that wasn't really it.

It was my reaction. For a split second, *I'd* kissed him back and liked the feeling of his lips—his man lips—on mine and what they were doing.

That damned split second was getting to me.

That second made me constantly think and dream about it.

Clenching my jaw, I tried blanking my mind. Thought about a brick wall, counted some fucking sheep, but nothing got me to switch off.

Rolling my head to the side, I sucked it up, and asked, "If you got a girl with you too, Damien the first you been with?"

His fingers stopped. He rested an elbow on the tray table and shifted my way again. "No. I'd been with others in my past. Again, both female and male. I'm bi. I like both. However, I was Damien's first."

It was too damn much looking at him; instead, I stared down at the seat in front of me. "First? As in he'd never been with a guy before?"

"Yes. Never. Hadn't even thought of it."

Surprised, I glanced at him, then back. Only to move enough to grab a band out of my pocket to tie my hair back. Then I sat forward, and then back. "Then how...?"

The refreshment cart got pushed by our seats. Then she stood beside us, leaned in, and asked, "Can I get you both anything?"

"Bourbon. Straight," I ordered.

"The alcohol costs, sir, it'll be—"

"Doesn't matter how much, sweetheart. Just grab me one," I said.

She smiled. Her gaze ran over me slowly, then Liam. If she could, she'd have a taste of both or either of us. She was stunning, so why wasn't I interested? Hell, being on a case never stopped me from getting some in a bathroom if I had a few spare minutes. Still, my cock didn't even twitch, even as I stared at her breasts as she bent over to give me an eyeful while passing the drink.

After she took my money, she asked Liam, "What about you, sir?"

"Water, please."

She nodded, passed a water, and offered, "If there's anything else I can get either of you during the flight or even after it, please don't hesitate to let me know."

Hello, dick, wake the fuck up. She'd offered herself up on a platter, and it seemed my cock was dead to the idea.

Fuck.

I heard Liam reply, but I got lost in my damn thoughts again. If I thought about Lan and those dreams of him and Easton together on a bed... my pathetic cock twitched and started to thicken. Why? I'd never thought about that shit ever before in my whole damn life. Why now? Why them? What in the fuck did it mean?

"You wanted to know how Damien knew he could be with a man?"

I jolted at Liam's voice, nodded, glared, and gulped back the bourbon like it was juice.

"He didn't until me."

I snorted. "You sayin' you changed his ways?"

Liam chuckled. "In a way, yes." He smiled warmly, like he was remembering it.

"He was straight. Completely?"

"Yes. One hundred percent." He nodded. "You see, he and I were interested in Liberty at the same time. We knew she liked both of us, and I didn't want to make her choose. I put it to Damien to give it a try, for her sake. Of course I found him very attractive too."

"And he did?"

Liam laughed. "Yes. It took a little time and a lot of thinking, but he worked out he liked it."

My brows dipped in confusion. How could a guy change just like that? Okay, Liam had said there was time and thinking, but Damien had been certain he was totally into women, and then he'd changed. How? Why? "So he's bi now, that right?"

Liam chuckled again. "If you ask Damien, he would say he's bi, but only for one man."

I shook my head and rubbed the back of my neck. "What?"

"Damien told me his friend Max tested him. He showed Damien pictures of other men, ones even half-naked to see if any of them interested him. They didn't. He said I was the only one who interested him in that way."

Liam was it for Damien.

In a fucked-up way, that kind of made sense. It wasn't until Lan kissed me that I'd thought of another guy's lips and they were his, only his. Okay, maybe fucking Easton's also. I wasn't wandering around looking at other guys and thinking about what it would be like if they kissed me. I wasn't dreaming of them. It was about a certain two men.

Thanks, motherfuckers, for confusing me.

Hell, it wasn't like I'd go and jump into bed with them.

But it might be all right to watch them together.

What. The. Actual. Fuck?

That thought flew out of nowhere.

Stop. Just stop thinking.

Jesus. My goddamn head hurt.

"Does any of that help?"

I jumped. "Huh?"

"Does any of what I said help?"

"With what? I don't know what you're talking about."

Liam sighed. "Parker, I'm gathering you like to bottle things up. It's not good for you. I can see something going on inside of your head, and it could be better to talk about it."

"Fuck. Fine," I bit out. Leaning in, I whispered, "Lan kissed me, and since then, it runs through my mind randomly. I also caught him doing something with Easton over the phone, and now I dream of it. Them."

I glanced to see Liam still held his neutral expression. "I'm going to take a guess. Did you like the kiss and seeing what you caught them doing?"

I clenched my jaw. "I don't know."

He nodded. "Even if you did, Parker, there's nothing wrong with it *or* you. Those incidences may have been ones you've never experienced before in your life so you're not to know if you would like them until they happened. Now they have and, if you did like them, it's opening your eyes. And for some people it's scary. Take time, work things out, or leave it, if that's what you think you'd prefer. Just don't beat yourself up over it."

Fuck me. He made sense. Though, I didn't know how to respond. I wasn't ready to admit aloud I enjoyed the kiss and watching Lan, even hearing Easton. Nope, I didn't enjoy it. I couldn't.

Christ, I had to work my head out first.

"How about we move on to the matter at hand?" Liam asked, and I nodded. "Right, I've done some digging and found that Mr Khatri owns many businesses in the Middle East. There have been charges against him for beating his wife and daughter. Charges against his sons, too, for doing the same to their own wives."

"Like father like sons."

"Exactly."

"I'll have someone contact the mother while Mr Khatri is away and see what else I can find out or help with. We should be able to get his daughter away from her father today since the files state she's actually only seventeen."

"Right. So we got not only one dickhead to deal with but two."

"Yes."

"You up for the challenge?" I asked.

"I believe I am. Are you armed?"

"My weapon has been checked. I'll have to pick it up."

"I have a feeling it could be needed."

"So do I." And I'd be ready to use it.

*a*n hour after walking in the room, I threw the papers to the floor and tried to reason with a new idea. "I didn't tell you, but I'm seeing someone. Do you think he'll believe I've just up and left him for a woman?"

"Enough of this stalling," Mr Khatri yelled. I caught Prisha cringe and whimper when he stood to stand over me as I still sat in the chair. "You've gone over the contract bit by bit, asked all the questions there are, and now you're telling us this lie about a new friend. Sign the papers, Easton."

I had been stalling. I just didn't know what for. I could sign the papers, but in them stated we had to stay married for five years, sire an heir, and live that time in Queensland. I also had a feeling they would keep us on a tight leash.

"I'm not lying. It's new, but I do have a boyfriend."

Amit sighed loudly. "Andrew, I thought you went over everything."

I shifted around to face Andrew. "What do you mean he went over everything?"

Andrew glared at me. "I did, sir. He's a paramedic, works rotating shifts. Had just moved into a ranch-style home with six dogs. Since his break-up with Oliver, he's been on a couple of blind dates, but nothing serious has come from them."

Spinning back to Amit, I snapped, "You had him investigate me?"

"Of course."

I scoffed. "Yes, of course you would. It isn't like you'd actually ask me anything or that you gave a shit about me. Ever." I sat back, crossing my arms over my chest.

"This is your last chance to sign, Easton, before things escalate," Mr Khatri warned. He moved to stand beside Amit near the fire.

"Why are you doing this to your daughter?" I asked.

"It doesn't matter why."

"It does to me. If she'll give me trouble, I need to know."

"She will be the best wife any man could have. She's pure and does as she's told."

He made me sick to the stomach talking about his own daughter like she was something and not a real person.

"He wants me to marry off because I love someone else. Someone in a lower social status," a soft, quiet voice said into the room.

"Prisha, keep your mouth shut." Mr Khari stormed over to her. His hand rose, and I knew he was about to hit her. I thrust myself out of the chair and over to grip his wrist before he could follow through.

"Do not touch her."

"Let go of me. Now," he snapped harshly.

"I will if you step away from her."

We stood glaring at each other when a knock sounded on the door.

"Honey, we have guests downstairs," Darlene called.

"We won't be much longer," Amit replied.

The door handle twisted and turned. "Honey, why is it locked?"

Yes, Darlene, get me out of here. Then I could call Lan to tell him everything, and he could somehow help.

183

"I'm in the middle of something," Amit said through clenched teeth.

Shit.

"Amit, people are waiting to see Easton. I know he's in there. I heard him. Please have him come out. It's been hours, and he has many people to see."

"Darlene, leave. We'll be downstairs shortly."

"At least let him say a quick goodnight and goodbye to Jewel before she goes to bed. She's here waiting for him."

Amit grumbled something. He waved at Andrew and said quietly, "Easton, go and say goodnight. If you try anything stupid, I'll have Andrew harm Prisha. You seem not to want to see any harm come to her."

Fuck. "Fine." I nodded. Dread twisted inside of me. Slowly, I made my way over to the door while Andrew walked over to where Prisha sat and stood behind her. My heart went crazy with each step I took. I wanted to scream, to run, to warn Darlene about the man she was going to marry, but I couldn't do any of it. My hands shook as I unlocked the door. I opened it. Only I didn't see Jewel or Darlene.

My eyes shot wide. I sucked in a ragged breath and almost cried at the sight of Parker.

"You all right?" he asked, his eyes running all over me.

I sniffed. Darn my stupid emotions. I nodded.

He smiled a very rare smile. "Then let's get you outta here and back to Lan."

"Easton, that's enough," Amit said. It was then I realised he didn't know who was at the door. I glanced back. I'd only opened it enough for me to see out, not for everyone else in the room.

"I can't leave," I whispered back at Parker, and whoever the intimidating, stunning man was beside him.

"I'm here to help with that."

"I'll help too," came a voice behind Parker. He shifted enough for me to see Darlene standing there. "I heard everything. Before Luis came to find me, he started a recording of it all." Her bottom lip trembled. "I'm so sorry, Easton. I didn't know—"

"Don't. He showed you another side."

"Easton," Amit barked.

"Step back please," the man beside Parker said. I did. He looked to Parker. "After you." Parker lifted his chin in return, and when I backed further into the room, Parker stepped in after me, then the other man, and finally Darlene.

"What is this? Who are you? Darlene, I asked for privacy," Amit declared. "Get out," he yelled and started striding towards us.

"Keep moving and you'll regret it," Parker warned, and it was in such a dark, rough voice Amit stalled midstep and slowly lowered his foot to the floor.

I shifted to Parker's side. Close to his side. I ignored him tensing because right then, I never wanted to move away from him in case he disappeared, and I was still stuck in the room without help. "Andrew has a gun," I told him. "The one behind Prisha."

Parker nodded, just a small one. "My name's Detective Parker Wilding. I'm here to collect Easton Ravel, and have incriminating evidence that goes against an Amit Ravel for forcing his son into a marriage contract, for conspiring with a Mr Khatri over this deal to gain money and business status, but more significantly, we have evidence of you agreeing to pay a hitman to murder your soon-to-be wife if this deal with Easton didn't go down."

"What?" I breathed. My body trembled with the amount of hate and dread coursing through me. "You were going to kill her?" I whispered harshly, and heard Darlene sob behind us somewhere.

Amit was going to kill her if I didn't sign.

Murder his fiancée.

Leave Jewel without her mother.

Hot rage burst forward.

It had my feet eating up the floor, rushing him. Amit's hands came up. He yelled something, but I didn't hear.

Someone else screamed something. There was more shouting, more cries.

I heard nothing.

I wrapped my hand around his throat and pushed him back until he hit the wall. I got close. My mouth right next to his ear as I squeezed his throat. "You were going to kill her. You're a mother-fucking bastard who doesn't deserve to live, but I'll let you live so you can rot in jail."

"Fuckin' drop it," Parker roared.

"He needs to move," Andrew screamed.

"Drop the fuckin' gun or I shoot."

Amit tried to choke through his words. I released him a little. "You'll never get your mother's things."

I chuckled. "I don't care. I have something better. Seeing everything you have go down the drain. That right there is victory for me."

I released his neck, stepped back, and smashed my fist into the side of his face.

Then I felt pain.

Pain sliced through my side.

Crying out, I dropped to my knees.

Sounds started to penetrate.

A gun was fired.

Parker yelled, "Stay down. Stay the fuck down. Liam, grab his gun. Everyone move to the corner there. Move. Now! Darlene, get Prisha over with you. Fuck. Easton? Easton?"

I chuckled. "I'm okay."

"Bullshit. Liam, stay on them," Parker ordered. He was as damn bossy as Lan.

I needed to see my own injury to patch it up. Andrew, the dick, must have shot me. Cringing, I slid off my jacket, untucked my shirt and pulled it up.

I jumped when Parker fell to his knees in front of me. He tucked his gun into the back of his jeans.

"Fuck, fuck, fuck," he chanted. His hands gripped my face. "You got shot. You got shot."

I giggled, adrenaline crashing in on me. I felt tired for some reason and giddy. "I know, but it's fine."

"It's not fuckin' fine," he growled.

"Parker—"

"Show me," he demanded.

"Parker it's—"

"Show me."

I shook my head, coming back to myself. The stinging throbbed at my side, just below my ribs.

"Parker—"

"East, show me the fuckin' wound," he clipped roughly.

East.

I'd always been Easton.

Not East, like Lan called me.

Lan. I wondered how he was doing. He'd be out of his mind with worry.

"Fuck it," Parker bit out. He lifted my arm, pulled up the shirt and then paused, staring at my scrape. The bullet hadn't even penetrated. It took off some skin for sure, but I would be fine.

Parker dropped my shirt, straightened and stared at me.

"Told you." I smiled.

He said nothing, but his hands were back on my cheeks and next, he tugged me in to plant his mouth on mine for a quick, hard kiss.

Whoa.

It only lasted maybe a second, but it was still long enough for my stomach to dip and my pulse to race.

He moved back, stared at me again, and then stood just as people burst through the office door yelling, "Police, nobody move."

CHAPTER TWENTY-SIX

PARKER

*a*ll the guests had left, and as far as I knew, none of them knew what had happened just above their heads. Easton sat in the corner of the room with Darlene and Prisha talking to the police. I'd already given them my statement, along with all the information we had. Darlene lied for us, saying she had found the emails since we hadn't had a warrant to even look through his computer.

Liam stepped up beside me. Thank fuck he'd been there. When I thought Andrew had shot Easton, Mr Khatri had tried to escape. Liam had taken him to the ground, and with the one punch Liam delivered, he'd been out like a light.

"Mrs Khatri has come through. She's over the moon happy to hear her daughter is safe and will stay that way with the information on her husband to put him away." He smiled.

I chuckled. "You got that information?"

He nodded. "In front of the police. I'm about to inform Mr Khatri he will be arrested for abuse, but also laundering money through a lot of his businesses. He'll be serving a lot of jail time."

"Good. Let me know if Prisha and her mum need a safe place to lay low."

"Thank you, I will." He turned, took a step and then spun back around. "Easton," he said.

"What about him?"

"Knife told me there was some hate and tension between you and Easton. At first, I was worried about it, until I saw that kiss."

I stiffened. "You were supposed to be watchin' the other people."

He chuckled. "I just happened to look back at the right moment."

I shrugged. "It was nothin'." It hadn't been really. My head was still stuck on repeat of, *What in the fuck did you do?* I couldn't understand what had come over me, maybe relief he was alive and only had a scrape. But shit, it had scared the fuck out of me. When I saw Easton drop to his knees, it took years off my damn life. Fucking years.

"I'm sure it was. He hasn't stopped looking at you."

I clenched my jaw. "I don't care."

Liam's lips twitched. "Of course you don't." He nodded, turned, and walked over to the cop who stood in front of Amit, Andrew, who had pissed himself when I'd fired my shot just above his head, and Mr Khatri. I started for the women and Easton.

Pulling up beside another cop, I said, "Think it'll be better if we get these people outta the room."

"Why?"

"No!" we heard snarled. "You have no right." Mr Khatri tried to stand, but the cop knocked him to the floor even while he kept ranting loudly over and over.

"Right. Is there another room where we can finish this?" the cop asked Darlene.

Even though the questioning had taken a damn long time, Darlene, Prisha, and Easton had wanted to get it over and done with. It saved them the trip down to the station the next day. With the evidence stacked against Easton's father, there was no doubt he'd see time behind bars, and none of it had anything to do with his son. So Easton would be allowed to leave Queensland and head back to Victoria. Only he would still have to come back for the trial. The cop also doubted they'd be granted bail. I fucking hoped so. If they did, I'd told him they'd better find someplace safe for Darlene, Jewel, Prisha, and her mum, who was travelling to Australia, to get away from her sons. I'd told them I had Easton covered in Victoria.

As they'd been finishing, I'd been sitting on a couch with my head back, pretending to sleep. My eyes felt grainy since it was damn near close to 5:00 a.m.

People left, the room grew quiet, but I could still sense someone close by, heard a rustling of clothes every now and then, but I wasn't ready to open my eyes until Liam came in and told me when our flight home would be. He'd gone off earlier to organise that and other things.

Someone entered the room again. "Is he your boyfriend?" I heard whispered. My ears pricked up at the question.

Easton coughed and then laughed. "No. No, he's not."

It'd been Easton in the room with me.

Huh.

"But that kiss—"

"I don't know what that was about, Darlene."

"Oh, um, okay." I could hear the smile in her voice. "It seemed like it was nice."

Holy fuck.

Would he answer?

Why did I want to hear his answer?

My chest ached with the waiting because my stupid organ beat wildly.

Why wasn't he answering?

Goddamn it.

"It was," he admitted quietly.

"Good. Anyway, I have poor Prisha in a room close to mine.

Would you like to stay here and sleep for a few hours? You can go back to the hotel before you fly out, but Mr Michaels said he couldn't get a flight out for the three of you until late this afternoon."

"I would love that, Darlene. It'll also give me some time with Jewel."

"Great. There's a couple of rooms just down the hall here that you and Detective Wilding can use. I've also already shown Mr Michaels to one." A pause and then she offered, "Try and get some sleep, Easton." I heard her start to walk off, until Easton called her name. "Yes?"

"I'm sorry about... him." It seemed he wouldn't say his name or call him his father. Not that I could blame him for it.

I heard her step closer Easton's way. "None of it is your fault, just like you told me it wasn't mine. I got played by a bad man. I'll learn and grow stronger from it." She sniffed. "It hurts. A lot, but I know I'll be okay because Jewel will be safe from him."

"She will be, and so will you."

"Yes. So will I. Even though we're still in the process of getting to know one another, Easton, I feel a great deal for you." Another sniff.

"I feel the same for you and Jewel. Neither of you are to be strangers in my life. We'll talk all the time on the phone, and I'll be back soon for the trials. You're stuck with me now."

She laughed, but her breath hitched too. "I'm glad we are." Her footsteps told me she left the room. I didn't know why I still faked sleep.

"Craptastic night," Easton muttered. "Except for...."

What?

Except for what?

He sighed. "Hey, Lan," I heard him say, must be into the phone. "Yeah, sorry I only got to text you earlier. We're all done now."

I'd called Lan a while ago and told him what went down. All of it. Okay, I only left out the kiss because it hadn't meant anything.

He'd told me to get Easton to call him and thanked me again for going over.

"Liam said he was going to call." He paused to listen. "That's right. I'll see you tonight, yes? Good. I can't wait to be home." Another pause. "He never said what he had of Mum's, but Darlene said she's going to search everywhere. Though, it wouldn't surprise me if it was nothing in the end. Yes. I'll get a couple of hours I hope. All right, see you then. Bye, Lan."

Easton sighed again, probably from exhaustion. Next, I jolted up, opening my eyes and sitting straighter when I felt a hand on my shoulder. I rubbed a hand over my face.

"Sorry to wake you," Easton said, hovering over me. "There's a bed down the hall that would be more comfortable to sleep in. Liam has flights ready for us late in the afternoon."

I nodded, stood, and stretched. Of course I looked to see if Easton was watching me. He was, down low, near my hips. I realised my tee had ridden up.

Fuck. Why was *I* looking to see if *he* was looking?

Wait, why did I care? Why did I *like* he looked? *Why* did my body react and my gut flip?

That shit was just weird.

Easton cleared his throat. "Liam dropped your bag there." He pointed to the floor next to the entrance of the room. "I'll, um, ah, show you to a room." He stalked out the door like I was chasing him. My lips lifted on their own. I found his nervousness cute.

Shit.

Following him, I picked up my bag on the way out and went down the hall until Easton stopped outside a door. He opened it. "Here. Uh, sleep well." He nodded, then thumbed over his shoulder. "I'll be in the next room. Um..." He raked his bottom lip with his top teeth. "Liam is over there." He pointed to another room, but I didn't look. Easton gulped. Then chuckled and scratched at his cheek. "So, yeah, ah, thanks for coming to help. Lan mentioned in his text why it was you and not him, and I'm glad you all talked Lan out of it.

That made sense. That he didn't come, and, ah, you did instead." He nodded again. "Um, goodnight. Well, good morning really, but... yeah." He nodded and then spun, walking to the room next to mine.

I could have gone easy on him and said something, but I found myself liking the way he'd acted all shy and nervous.

Shit.

Shaking my head, I went into the room and shut the door behind me. For a rich house, the walls were thin; I heard Easton shut his door as well.

I pulled off my tee, kicked off my boots, and dragged my jeans off. I needed sleep, and maybe with some shut-eye, I'd forget or even put it in the back of my mind how I felt about not one, but two men's lips on mine.

What in the hell was I doing?

Yanking back the comforter and sheets, I slipped into the soft bed and pulled the sheets back up to my waist. Lying flat, I put my hands behind my head and stared at the ceiling. There was a dim light already shining behind the curtains' edges. I wasn't sure I'd find sleep at all, even though I had to have it.

Groaning low, I rolled to my side and closed my eyes. That was when I heard it. Pacing. Easton was pacing in his room. Fucking hell, couldn't he just sleep? Or maybe his mind was running over the night. He could be worried about nightmares, but he'd proven himself to be a badarse when he'd gone after his father. Really, he shouldn't be awake worrying about it all.

Still, it wasn't every day a person heard their own father had committed crimes. One that would have led to the murder of a woman.

Yeah, that shit would have eaten at me if I wasn't used to extreme situations.

I would have got sleep eventually, after I blocked lips from my head, but it was useless to try when I heard each step he took.

Hell, maybe it was me overhearing shit.

Whatever it was it made me pissed.

Throwing back the sheets, I stormed to the room and to his door, where I threw it open.

Easton, in his boxers with tape across his side, let out a noise as he spun towards the door. He froze, both hands to his chest. I stalked in and stopped just before him, ordering, "Get in the fuckin' bed."

"W-what?"

Sighing, I ran a hand through my hair. The tie rolled out and dropped to the floor. I ignored it, and my hair fell around my shoulders. "I can hear your pacing, and it's driving me crazy. You need sleep. I need sleep. It's damn time to sleep."

He licked his lips, glanced to the floor, to the door, and then to me. "But... I can't."

Grumbling under my breath, I asked, "Why the hell not?"

He threw his hands up in the air. "I don't know. I keep thinking what happens if the cops decide to let him go. He'll come here and hurt Jewel *and* Darlene and then maybe even me before I can do anything. I can't do anything if I'm sleeping."

I gentled my tone. "He's not gettin' out."

"What happens if he does? Or Andrew?"

"East, you're safe. Darlene and Jewel are safe. You need to switch off and get some sleep."

He shook his head and crossed his arms. "I will when I get out of this town. When I get home."

I pinched the bridge of my nose. We both needed sleep, and I was damn sure going to get it. Turning, I went to the door, shut it, and spun back around to find Easton's eyes had widened. I walked back to him. I'd never taken in a man's body in the way I was then, in appreciation of his fucking fit body. That ink. That damn ink on his darker skin.

Christ. Stop.

Thinning my lips, I detoured to the bed instead of him and got in the other side from where the blankets had already been disturbed.

"P-Parker?"

"Sleep. With the two of us in here, one will hear something first and warn the other."

"Ah...."

"East, I swear to fuckin' God, if you don't go to sleep, I'll be the one harmin' you."

He said nothing, but I heard him approaching the bed. It dipped when he climbed in. I felt the separation between us as he lay down. Only since I had my back to him, I didn't know if he was on his back, stomach, or side... or if he faced me or the other way.

Bloody hell, I felt like I wanted to roll over to find out.

But I refused to. Instead, I closed my eyes and took a deep breath, relaxing my body. I couldn't remember the last time I'd slept in the same bed with someone. Fucking... yes, but I'd kick whoever it was out after.

This was different.

Fuck me, but it felt like more, even though we weren't touching or looking at each other.

"Thank you," Easton whispered.

"Sleep," I ordered gruffly and then heard him chuckle.

My mouth tugged up into a smile, and that was how I fell asleep.

CHAPTER TWENTY-SEVEN

PARKER

I'd been surprised when I'd slept like the dead. Only when I woke, I felt heavy and hotter than normal. Slowly, I opened my eyes, only for my drowsiness to evaporate immediately from my senses.

My body locked.

Locked tight.

That was because I had a body lying on half of me.

Holy fuck.

Jesus Christ.

Cue my damned heart noticing as it started to race.

Cue my damned breath to pick up, and my gut to tumble around like I was on a fucking roller coaster.

I didn't move anything but to peek out the corner of my eyes to see Easton's face near mine. His chin rested on the top of my shoulder, and he was asleep. Jesus, he smelled good. Had this always been his scent? I hadn't noticed... so why was my damn nose noticing now? Why was my body liking his heat glued to my side?

It didn't.

I didn't.

It was all in my messed-up head after what happened. I peeked at him again; he still slept.

Thank fuck.

Using my free hand—well it wasn't so free, but curled around Easton's wrist where his arm rested on my chest, while the other was under Easton's neck and flat on the bed—I unclenched my fingers from his wrist and slowly slid it down. I felt the bed and discovered I was on the very edge. Easton had moved in his sleep and moved far.

Right into my space.

What could I do?

Shit, I should have set the alarm or something.

Hell no, that wouldn't do. If we woke up at the same time, it'd be awkward. He'd probably choke on words as he tried to apologise.

I'd just started to relax a little when he stretched.

He bloody stretched. His arm glided across my chest to land on the other side, and then he hugged me closer to him.

There went my body's reaction again.

Fuck. Fuck. Fuck.

He slid his leg up from my thigh to my hip, and his knee grazed my already hard cock.

It was hard because it was morning wood.

Every guy got morning wood.

It was natural.

It wasn't hard and reacting to Easton.

Think, man, think.

His stretching could mean he was close to waking, so I had to do something. If I climbed out and ran, then it'd be worse because he'd know, and he'd feel like shit.

Goddamn it. Sucking in a breath, I relaxed my body.

I wouldn't be the first to wake.

Easton stretched again.

I made sure I regulated my breathing, closed my eyes, and turned my head away from him a bit.

Another stretch and then he froze.

Easton

T*its on a whale.* I was lying on Parker.
I was snuggled up to annoying, angry *Parker.*

What in the world was I doing half on Parker?

He wasn't awake. Thank the high heaven for small favours. But it meant I somehow had to get off him without him waking and thinking I'd been trying to jump him or make a move in some way.

When I shared a bed, I usually gravitated towards them. I should have warned Parker. No, I should have slept on the carpeted floor.

God, this would be so awkward if he woke.

I had to move. Slide away without… wait a second, was that his dick near my knee?

His *hard* dick near my knee?

Forget it, Easton. It doesn't mean anything. I have a boner.... Oh no, I have a boner resting against his side.

I squeezed my eyes shut and prayed he didn't wake and feel my boner.

Hang on. I had to stop freaking out.

No, no, no. Do not start to sweat. Was I panting on him? Oh fuck, was his hair moving because I was panting?

Get off, get off, get off, Easton.

My skin touched his. My body pressed against his.

Darn, he was good-looking.

Jesus, it isn't time to stare, Easton. Move. Besides, you have to get back to Lan, though Lan certainly doesn't mind staring at Parker, and it's not like I can blame him. He's worth looking at. If only he wasn't a jerk sometimes.

Hold it. I seriously had to stop thinking about it and get my arse into gear.

Slowly and oh so very gently, I shifted back inch by inch, until I had enough space between us where I could put my hand, the one that was on the other side of his chest. His wide hard chest. I begged to Karma and Fate and anyone else who'd listen that as I moved my arm from his chest, he didn't wake... and he didn't.

Yes, baby Jesus.

I sighed. Then I realised it blew his hair over his face more and that could cause an itch.

Shit, fuck, shit a darn dinosaur.

Instead of moving more out of the bed. I slid my hand up from under the sheets, hooked his hair with a finger and dragged it from his face. When he twitched, I froze. Even stopped breathing.

I would not get caught close to Parker. He'd probably either beat me senseless, throw me around the room, or yell in my face. Damn, the last one could happen no matter. He liked to yell and growl, and he looked good doing it.

Bloody stop.

I placed my hand between us again. Then I lifted my knee and leg away from his nice-sized hard dick before I pushed down so I could shift my body back more and more.

When I was finally on my side of the bed, I sucked in a big breath because I hadn't breathed until I'd been in the clear. I felt a little lightheaded from it too.

Unfortunately, I didn't realise how far I'd moved over until I went to roll to my back to sneak out and tumbled to the floor with flailing arms and all.

When I smashed down, knocking the wind out of me, I groaned.

I lay there trying to breathe when a face popped over the edge.

Whoa.

I'd never seen Parker half awake, hair everywhere with a smirk on his lips. He looked amazing.

His lips moved. I blinked slowly up at him. "Huh?"

He snorted. "I asked if you were okay."

He pushed back as I started to sit up. My back and side ached, but other than that, I was fine. "Yes, I'm okay. Uh, sorry to, um, wake you like that."

"It's fine." He rolled back over to his side with grace and then got out of bed to stretch.

Look away, Easton.

But I couldn't. His body, like Lan's, was a work of art.

"Easton?" Parker clipped.

I jumped. "Sorry?"

Before he looked away, I caught his lips twitching. "Gonna go get my shit."

Standing, I nodded, then asked, "Do you know what time it is?"

"Just after midday."

I chuckled, stretching myself with my eyes closed. When I opened them, Parker had been looking away. "How do you know the time? It that some detective thing?"

He glanced back with a deadpanned look and pointed at the bedside table behind me—where a digital alarm clock sat. Heck, I hadn't even noticed it.

"We'll shower, grab some food. You can spend some time with Jewel before we hit it."

We'll grab a shower. Did he mean together?

"Sure," I said in a near squeak. Then for added measure, I gave him a double thumbs-up. His brow rose, just the one, and then I saw a small grin before he shook his head and walked out.

I thumped my palm against my forehead and groaned.

Placing my hands on my hips, I glanced down at the bed. Parker and I had been in there together.

I had to tell Lan.

It was the right thing to do.

Reaching for my phone, I'd hit dial when Parker was back at my opened door, sticking his head in.

"Do you know where the bathroom is?"

I nodded. "Yes."

His lips thinned, but they wobbled a second like he was fighting not to smile. Why was he smiling more?

Maybe he was finding me humorous.

Maybe he was getting used to me.

Which meant great things for Lan and me.

At least then there'd be no tension at work between them.

It was too early to be thinking. I mean, of course he liked me a little to be able to help me out and then sleep in the same bed last night. He wouldn't do it if he hated me or if he didn't like I was gay.

"Easton?"

I jolted. "Sorry?"

He chuckled, then sobered. "Bathroom?"

"Right." I nodded, stood, and walked over to the door. He didn't move back much, but I used the space he gave me. Leaning out, I lifted my arm; it brushed against his stomach. I pointed down the hall, and whispered, "Second last door."

"Thanks," he said, and his breath washed over my hair.

I gulped and nodded.

My dick started to thicken.

No, no, no. Stand down, soldier.

This was wrong. *So wrong.* I shouldn't have been getting aroused by Parker. Not when I had Lan…. Crap, big mistake thinking of Lan. My dick thickened some more. I pressed myself against the doorframe.

"So, yeah, down there. Second door from the end." I pointed again. "That way. Enjoy. Get clean." I shook my head at my own idiocy and then banged it against the doorframe while willing my dick to deflate.

"You all right?" Parker asked.

"Dandy." I nodded, then reached out behind Parker and pushed him. He didn't move. The prick. "Off you go. Then I can have one after you. Leave some hot water for me."

Stop mentioning the shower, dickhead.

All I could think was both of us in there, and I felt guilty for it because Lan wasn't here.

Fuck, now I pictured Lan and Parker in the shower together.

"Ah, okay. Bye." I stepped back, shut the door hard and leaned against it.

Something in my hand knocked against my thigh. I glanced down as I brought my hand up.

It was my phone.

My phone where I had just pressed in Lan's number before Parker popped his head in.

Oh shit.

With a shaky hand, I brought my phone up to my ear. "H-hello?"

A deep chuckle sounded into my ear.

I blanched. "Lan," I whispered.

"Yeah, East."

"How much did you hear?"

"You stumbling over your words."

He wouldn't remember.

He wouldn't.

"What I wanna know is what got you flustered to begin with."

"What?" I yelled, then laughed. "I don't—"

"From what I remember, you're that way when you're attracted to someone, like you'd been with me, or as things progressed with us, you were that way when you had dirty thoughts."

Crap.

"Lan—"

"What were you thinkin', East?" His voice had dipped even lower, like each time he was turned on. No way.

"You like I had dirty thoughts?"

He chuckled. "So you did?"

"Um." Fuck it. Honesty was the best policy. "Yes. About him in the shower, and then I felt guilty about it and thought of you, which didn't go well because then I thought of you and him in the shower. I got hard. Had to hide it, and now I feel bad because I'd looked at

Parker the way I did. He even slept in my bed last night because I couldn't sleep, I'd been freaking out and was pacing. He heard, came over, and told me in his grumpy way to get in bed." I sucked in a deep breath. "He also kissed me when he thought I was shot. But I think that had to do with the moment. He was freaking out I was wounded badly. Maybe he thought you would have kicked his arse. So he grabbed me and kissed me. It wasn't a passionate kiss or anything. No tongue either. It was more a 'glad you're alive' kiss."

Silence.

With my fisted hand, I thumped it against my head over and over.

Stupid, stupid idiot.

"I'm sorry. I know none of it should have happened, because you and I—"

"East," Lan called loudly.

"Yes?"

"Calm down."

After another deep breath, I said, "Okay." At least I'd try; my organ in my chest wasn't doing too well.

"Don't stress about you and me. I know where we're at. I also know I kissed Parker and you're not grillin' my chops about it. You know I'm attracted to him. He's like that, gets under your skin without even really knowing he's there. I get it. Don't worry, okay?"

"I can't wait to be home," I said. Lan Davis just knew what to say to put me at ease. The man was amazing.

"Why's that?"

"I'd like to kiss you."

"Fuck," he groaned. "I'd like that as well."

"See you this afternoon."

"Looking forward to it."

CHAPTER TWENTY-EIGHT

LAN

I texted Easton earlier. He was going to come to my house first before we'd head to his to kick Gamer out and check on the dogs. I sat on my couch, bouncing my leg up and down in anticipation. He'd be here soon, and I damn well couldn't wait to actually see he was in one piece.

Parker would be dropping him off. Since Miller was no longer, I doubted Parker would stay, but I wouldn't mind if he did. I'd like to see him around Easton. I still couldn't get over the fact Parker slept in the same bed as Easton. Sure, he would have told Easton it'd be because he wanted to sleep, but deep down, and because I knew him, Parker would have done it for Easton's sake. He wouldn't have liked to see him worrying.

Just couldn't believe it led to them being in the same bed.

I'd have to ask Easton everything because I fondly remembered how when Easton and I previously slept in the same bed, I'd always wake with him sprawled over me. He was the biggest snuggler I knew. Had he done that with Parker too?

My cock throbbed at the thought of them together in bed. Throbbed painfully into hardness. Fuck, I'd have given my left nut to have seen them together.

I adjusted myself behind my jeans as an amused smile tugged my mouth up.

It would've been funny to imagine Easton's reaction or Parker's if he'd woken first. Those details I wanted to know.

Christ, I ran a hand over my face remembering how crazy I'd been not hearing from Parker or Liam when they'd got to Easton's fathers place. I'd been at the compound waiting with Dodge, Gamer, Knife, and Beast. It felt like it was more than the four hours it had been.

Tires rolling over the gravel road close to the house sounded through my ears. Standing, I ate up the distance to the living room window and saw Parker's car pull into my drive. I was out the front door in moments.

There wasn't a chance I could wipe the smile off my face.

Easton was here.

Home.

He knew we were something. He knew he was mine.

It meant I could walk down the steps and meet him at the car. Which was what I did. The car stopped, and I opened Easton's door before he could. I heard Parker open his own door and as I leaned in the car to Easton, I saw Parker climb out from the driver seat.

I smiled at a grinning Easton. "Hey," I said, reaching over him to undo his seat belt.

"Hi," he whispered.

"Fuck it. Can't wait," I told him. He laughed, but that stopped as soon as my lips hit his. I curled my hand at the side of his neck. The kiss started out soft, sweet, but as soon as Easton touched his hand to my side, just below my ribs, I switched it up and applied pressure. His mouth opened, and his tongue and mine twisted and wound around each other.

Jesus, he tasted good. He always had, and kissing him, finally after ten fucking years, brought up all the damn good feelings I had for him back then. It reminded me why Easton had caught my attention. Why I'd wanted him back then and again after seeing him for only moments. He'd been made for me. *Mine.*

Fuck, it was good to have him again.

He moaned into my mouth and ran his hand up to my chest, neck, and then cheek. He brushed his thumb against my skin.

I pulled back enough to capture his gaze. "Hey," I said again. We both grinned. "Let's get inside."

"O-okay," he stuttered. Maybe from the way he was feeling or it could be from whatever he saw in my eyes. Stepping back, I allowed Easton to ease out of the car. I couldn't take my eyes off him. He looked good. Shit, I wanted to run my hands all over him anyway to double-check he was okay, and other reasons.

I could touch him.

We were together, weren't we?

Fuck it, we were, and I refused to doubt it. Refused to doubt he'd second guess this. Me.

We'd been amazing together years ago, and we'd be better now.

Shaking my head, I smiled as excitement rushed through me over the thought of our future. I glanced over at Parker. He was at his boot grabbing out a suitcase. A huge sense of... shit, I didn't know, maybe happiness or gratitude settled in my chest. Whatever it was, staring at Parker had me feeling it because he'd taken care of Easton without letting anything stop him.

He set the case on the ground, and I got a nice view of his arse behind his dark blue jeans. I looked over to Easton and found him taking in the view too.

I chuckled. We could be pathetic together in our admiring Parker from afar.

Using the handle, Parker pulled the case over to us and stopped. Before he could say anything, I asked, "You comin' in for dinner?"

His eyes flashed; he hadn't expected an invite. Did he think I wouldn't want him around just because Easton was there now? That he could do a drop and run? Or that after putting himself in that situation for me and Easton, he could disappear without at least letting me show some gratitude with dinner and a beer?

"Nah, you two go ahead. I got some shit to do."

"Dinner and beer," I demanded. "Come on, man. You went all the way over there for me and East. Let me just do this."

Beside me, Easton reached out to run his hand down my arm and to squeeze my hand before dropping it. He also thought it was a good idea.

Parker shook his head. "I appreciate it, but I do have to get goin'. Another time."

I opened my mouth to bark at him about it only being one meal, when Easton gripped my wrist. He said, "Sure. Another time. That's good." He nodded. "Fine."

Parker lifted his chin in reply. As he started around the car, I called, "Thanks for everything."

"Not a problem, Lan."

"Hey, the women are putting something together in a couple of weeks. I know I'll see you before it, but wanted to make sure you knew about it. You're coming to it."

He snorted, then chuckled. "Sounds like I don't get a choice."

"Nope." I grinned.

Another chin lift followed before he climbed into the car. Easton grabbed his case and we made our way up to my house. Easton stopped at the bottom of the steps. "I'll leave this here for when I go over to my place."

"Okay," I said, only my attention was on Parker backing out of the drive. He didn't seem himself. Would it have to do with me kissing Easton in front of him or over him kissing Easton?

"He was quiet all the way home."

I looked down at Easton to see he'd been watching Parker as well, even as far as his car disappeared down at the road. "Parker?" I asked, to be sure.

"Yes." He glanced back at me. "Even Liam noticed and shot me looks. I tried to get him to talk, but I got his aggressive one-worded answers."

"He's more like that when somethin's on his mind," I mentioned.

"Should I have done something?" He turned to me with worry in his eyes.

Smiling, I shook my head. "Nope. Parker's just... Parker. Sometimes he just has to work shit out for himself." I just hoped that was the case here. Holding out my hand, I suggested, "Let's go inside, have dinner, make out, and then get you home to your brood."

He laughed, taking my hand. "Sounds like a perfect plan."

After dinner, where we talked about Easton's time away with Darlene and Jewel, we were on the couch together. Actually, Easton was straddling my legs, glaring down at me because he'd just explained what happened in bed that morning and I was laughing my arse off.

My hands landed on his hips as I tucked my face into his shoulder still chuckling.

"It's not funny. I nearly had a heart attack."

"Jesus, I would have loved it if Parker woke up while you were all over him."

Wait... maybe he had.

Maybe Parker had woken and then pretended to be asleep because he wouldn't want Easton to feel like shit for it. He'd do something like that. Even if he acted like a douche a lot, he still cared.

It could explain why he had to go in a rush and why he wasn't acting the same.

But then if he'd been awake, what did he think of Easton lying all over him?

"Where is your mind right now?" Easton asked, tapping my nose.

"First, you're looking a lot better, even after a couple of weeks. Now you can answer."

I smiled. "Thanks," I replied, then ran my hands up from his waist and around to his back so I could bring him closer to me. "And my mind was back in the bedroom with you and Parker in the bed."

His brows shot up. "Really?"

"Hell yes."

"You like that thought?"

"Is it weird if I do?"

He chuckled and shook his head. "No, because I liked the one of you and him in bed together."

Arousal shot right to my cock and hardened it. "Yeah?"

"Heck yes." He grinned.

"Only Parker. Never anyone else. I mean, I know we can't promise—" His fingers dropped against my lips, stilling them. Then he moved them so he could pinch my chin, all while staring at my mouth. "No one else ever. There's just something about Parker."

"I know." I rubbed my hands up and down his back. "Need you to wrap your arms around me, East. Want you close when I take your mouth."

He licked his lips. "Lan, your shoulder—"

"Is getting better each day. I know what I can handle, and your weight against me is fine."

"Your hip? Arm? Leg?"

My smile switched to a wide grin. "Fine, good and great."

"Lan—"

"East, keep your arms wherever you want them, so you don't worry about hurtin' me. But you need to hurry up and kiss me so we can go to your place."

His eyes softened. He melted more against me, and his hands went behind me to rest on the back of the couch. Repositioned, he whispered, "Okay."

As soon as he dipped his mouth close to mine, I placed a gentle peck against his lips while I met his eyes. Another followed as we both smiled. Then I flicked my tongue out to touch his lips. He stilled and then tilted his head to mold his mouth to mine. I slid my hands down to his arse and gripped, causing Easton to make a sound in the back of his throat.

Fuck. I loved kissing this man.

Easton Ravel was my world.

Fucked if I sounded like a damn woman. I didn't give a shit. My emotions for him consumed me more in that moment. When I pulled back to stare at him, he smiled lazily at me.

I had Easton back in my life. In my house and my arms.

How lucky could one man be?

"What are you thinking?" he asked.

"How lucky I am."

"Lan." His voice was a breathy sigh.

"If you hadn't forgiven me… I don't know what I would'a done. But fuck, East, thank you. Thank you so damn much for forgivin' me and being here. I promise I'll do everything in our world to never hurt you again."

"You can't—"

"I can promise it because I know if I did, it would gut me. I never want to see you hurt because of me again."

He nodded. "That means you have to keep yourself safe as well. If you hurt, then I will. Can you keep yourself safe?"

"I'd definitely want to so I can come back to you. But you have to do the same."

"My job isn't as risky as yours."

I raised my brows.

With a roll of his eyes, he responded, "At least nothing near as bad as yours. It's just the drugged out and scared ones we have to look out for. Plus, I'm not the skinny wimp I used to be."

I narrowed my eyes and squeezed his arse cheeks. "Never say that. You may have been slim, but you were never wimpy."

He grinned. "Note to self: don't put one's self down while around Lan Davis or he'll get cross."

"Damn right I will."

His grin widened. "How about we get back to my place. Kick Gamer out, and I make it up to you?"

"I'm down with that," I replied, smiling.

CHAPTER TWENTY-NINE

LAN

"You can't do this to me," Gamer cried and gave Easton sad eyes. "We've bonded. We're all one now. They're in my life, man. I'll need my fix."

Rolling my eyes, I left Easton standing over Gamer sitting on the floor with a pile of dogs around him. With a shake of my head, I walked into the kitchen for a beer, knowing it'd be stocked from Gamer being there, and I'd been right.

"I was gone two weeks." I heard Easton say, trying not to laugh. Once we'd come through the door, the dogs ran at Easton and greeted him like he was God, lavishing him with excited yips, licks, and whimpers. The whole time, Gamer had sat on the couch glaring at Easton. I'd started laughing, earning the finger from Gamer before he sat on the floor and called the dogs to him.

They looked at him, then up at Easton. However, they stayed by Easton, until he'd told them to go.

"I need visitation rights," Gamer announced.

I strolled back into the living room laughing and handed a beer to Easton. Then I took a seat on the chair down from Gamer.

"Of course you can come to see them. I can see how fond they are of you."

Gamer snorted. "Fond? They fuckin' love me."

Easton's lips twitched; then he thinned them. I just chuckled, getting another glare from Gamer.

"Just call me whenever you want to see them," Easton offered.

Gamer nodded. "I think it'll have to be three or four times a week to start with."

Easton's eyes flared. "Ah...."

"We'll have to get back to you on that, Gamer," I said.

"So you two are a thing now?" he asked.

Easton nodded, and I said, "Yep."

Gamer glowered at me. "Don't think you'll earn their love right away. It takes a special kind of someone—"

I whistled. Immediately, the dogs ran over Gamer to get to me and sit at my feet. I rose a brow.

"Low, man. So fuckin' low."

"How...?" Easton queried.

"I've been comin' over here to hang with Gamer a couple of nights. I guess your guys and girls found they liked me."

Easton's eyes softened, his smile turning tender.

Gamer groaned before standing. "I know when those I-wanna-get-me-some looks come out it's time for me to go. However, before I do, I need to state anytime you go away, I have the right to mind our dogs."

He walked past Easton, who looked at me and mouthed, "Our?"

I snorted with a shrug.

"Yes. Sounds good, Gamer, and thanks again for looking after them." Easton followed him to the door. Gamer clicked his fingers, and the dogs came running over to them. "You've been training Tin, Bell, and Buddy. Because usually, they'd been running in circles and not listening."

"Sure have."

"Thank you. How about you come for dinner tomorrow night?"

I snorted. Easton was so damned soft-hearted. He could see Gamer had actually bonded with the mutts.

Gamer grinned. "Shit yeah, I'd be down for that." He nodded and patted the dogs goodbye. Even went as far as leaning down and kissing them all on the head. "All right, be good for Easton." He straightened. "I'll see you guys tomorrow."

"Later, Gamer," I called, lifting my chin his way.

"Thanks again," Easton said.

"Anytime." Gamer lifted his chin and then walked out. Easton closed the door behind him and leaned against it.

"Why did it feel like I consented to a parenting arrangement with Gamer over the dogs?"

"Because that's what happened." I smirked.

He nodded. "Right. Okay." He started laughing. "I was pretty sure he was about to start crying over leaving them."

Chuckling, I nodded. "I reckon if you had of said he couldn't come back, he wouldn't have left."

"I had that feeling too." He made his way over to the chair I was in but stopped when I stood.

"You gonna drink that?" I asked, pointing to the beer he still held.

Easton glanced down to it, like he'd forgot he'd been holding it. "Uh, maybe?"

Taking his, I placed them on the coffee table then straightened. "I think I have a better idea instead of relaxing on the couch."

He smirked, crossed his arms over his chest, and asked, "Really, and what would the idea be?"

I didn't say anything at first. Instead, I dragged my tee from my body and threw it to the couch. Easton's eyes flashed with heat. He even grazed his bottom lip with his top teeth as he eyed my upper body.

"You want to work out?" the smartarse asked.

I chuckled. "Yeah, East. I want to work out. Naked. In your room. With you." I stepped forward. "We could work our bodies all over."

"Yes," he whispered, just as I stopped in front of him. I gripped the bottom on his tee and slowly pulled it up over his head and threw it to the couch with mine. "Working out is good," he said.

I ran my hands over his back, his shoulders, and over the front to his chest and stomach, which quivered under my touch. "It's very good. We'll get hot and sweaty."

He moaned, leaned in, and touched his lips to mine. He said against them, "I'm liking this."

"Yeah?"

"Yes. But it would be better if we were already in my room and if Nurse hadn't called me before I got back with an update, I'd be using the time to get you naked to inspect your injuries instead of… you know."

Smiling, I winked. "I do. So thank fuck for Nurse updating you." Sliding my hand to the back on his head, I pulled him close and kissed him hard and hot. His hands glided over my body and sent my pulse racing. I groaned against his mouth when he rubbed his hand up and down my length behind my jeans.

"Bedroom," he mumbled against me.

Shifting back, I ordered, "Dogs in or out?"

He glanced to the dogs sitting peacefully in their dog beds. "In for now. I'm sure I'll need a drink later, so I'll let them out then."

Smiling, I took his hand in mine and led him down the hall like I owned the place. Passing the spare room, I happened to glance at the door and then started laughing.

"What?" Easton asked. I pointed to the door. Easton snorted, then chuckled, shaking his head at the sign stuck to the door. It read *Gamer's Room*.

The guy was an idiot. But with a good heart.

Easton stepped close. He nipped at my shoulder, and all thoughts of Gamer vanished.

Once again, I was all but dragging him down the rest of the hall and into his bedroom. Nearing the bed, I turned, took his other hand, and smiled down at him.

"You don't understand how fuckin' amazin' this is for me. Being here with you in my life again means so damn much to me. An honest dream come true."

"Lan... I do know because it's the same as what I'm feeling."

Letting go of his hands, I watched as I ran my fingers up his arms, across his shoulders, to each side of his neck where I cupped his face in both palms.

We stared at each other as I gently tugged him forward. He tilted his head back, and I lowered mine to kiss the hell out of him.

CHAPTER THIRTY

EASTON

"What in the world?" I breathed, as I pulled into my driveway. Lan said it would be small. Lan told me only a few people would come.

This wasn't a few people.

There were at least twenty different vehicles. As I stopped my car, I glanced down at the extra ice bags Lan had asked me to go out and get before anyone showed while he got the barbeque cleaned and ready for our guests.

Nerves fluttered in my stomach. I wasn't ready to meet this many people in Lan's life. A couple of cars full, yes, bring it on. About twenty, hell to the no.

My hands already shook.

Maybe I could hide out in the car. No one would notice. Except maybe my boyfriend who was a detective. Oh, and my best friend who dropped down from the last step off my front porch and walked towards my car with a big smile on his face. He would know and be loving how I was all but shitting myself over the situation.

Lan and I had only officially been together for a few weeks. *I shouldn't have to meet this many people after a few weeks.* Yet, it was happening, and I couldn't think of a way out of it. I couldn't even fake work since it was mine and Oliver's weekend off.

I jumped and may have yipped when my door was thrown open. Oliver poked his head in, and said, "You can't hide. He knows you're out here because one of the women shouted your arrival."

Slowly, I turned to him, and asked, "Kill me?"

He laughed. Reaching in, still laughing, he undid my seat belt and had a hand in getting me out of the car. Oliver then shifted me out of the way and grabbed the three bags of ice before hipping the door closed and nudging me with his foot to my butt.

"How many?" I asked, making my approach slow.

"Ah… yeah, I won't lie. You see the vehicles, so you've already guessed there's a lot. By a lot, I mean over fifty."

"What?" I screeched and turned back around ready to make a run for it.

Oliver cackled. "Relax, a lot of them are kids, and I may be overexaggerating." He held up the ice bags. "These'll start melting soon. Suck in the fear and be brave. They'll love you. Some you've already met anyway."

"Is Parker here?" Since Lan had decided to take more time off work until he'd completely recovered, we hadn't seen much of Parker. After I'd started back at work, Lan went back to a semi-normal routine. That meant gym workouts at a gym the Hawks MC had recently bought out, not his usual one, one he'd gone with Parker to. When Lan had called Parker asking him to switch with him, Parker declined. Said he'd just paid for a new membership so he'd use that up and then rethink it. Of course, Lan mentioned he could probably get a refund. Parker's reply was how it'd be too much of a hassle, and besides, it was closer to his apartment.

When I asked Lan how he felt about Parker's actions, even how he'd declined dinner with us, Lan said it didn't bother him. Still, I could tell it did. There'd be times when we'd be sitting around or eating, and he'd drift off into his own thoughts with a frown on his face. It wasn't hard to work out it would be over Parker. They'd been close, and I couldn't help but think Parker didn't want anything to do with him over the things that had happened between us all.

I knew I was upset by it, but for Lan, it would be gutting.

"Yep, he's here." The way he said it sounded like he was upset.

"What's with that tone?"

"What tone?"

"The disapproving one." He went to open the front door and ignored my question, until I grabbed his hand on the doorknob to stop him. "Ollie."

He sighed. "He's a dick."

"I've told you he could be."

Leaning in, he whispered, "He brought a woman with him. He's been standing in a corner with her clutched to his side, glaring at everyone."

I snorted. "Sounds about normal for Parker."

"Seriously?"

"Yes." I laughed. Dropping my hand, I nodded to the door. "If I make a fool out of myself in any way, I expect you to make a bigger fool by saying or doing something so I don't look bad."

"Of course I will. Ready?"

"No. Yes. But—" Too late, he'd swung the door wide and stepped in. I had to follow him since he moved to the side, as if someone else waited to enter. But I really didn't want to. I still felt the urge to flee. Thinning my lips, I sucked in my fear, or at least I tried, and stepped through the door. I didn't do it for myself. I did it for Lan. He was introducing me to all of his friends because we were a couple. He made the effort to be open, caring, and darn wonderful, so I had to try and do the same without crapping my pants.

After I stepped through, the room full of people—adults and kids —grew quiet. I stiffened and was about ready to turn around when the sliding glass door off the dining area came open, and Lan stepped through. He spotted me and smiled. It seemed to me that no one else existed for him, except me. He made his way towards me through the crowd and leaned in and touched his mouth to mine. I heard a sigh from beside me and knew it was Oliver.

"You're back." Lan grinned.

"I am." I nodded.

"You look ready to bolt," he whispered.

"I'm still considering it. Lan, there's a lot of people here."

Lan chuckled. "I know. Blame the women. They always go overboard." I went to look around at them, but Lan cupped my cheek and brought my gaze back to his. "You gonna be good?"

I licked my lips. "Um...."

"I can get everyone to leave."

There was another sigh. Oliver.

I gripped his wrist. "No. I'll be okay."

"Yeah?"

"Yes. I want to meet all your friends."

His smile was outstanding. "Good." He leaned in again and brushed his mouth against mine.

"Come on," a female voice called; it sounded from behind Lan. "Enough monopolising his time. You can have him later."

Lan rolled his eyes and muttered, "If they're too much, tell me."

I chuckled. "I'll be fine."

"All right." He nodded before he turned to stand beside me. "Everyone, this is Easton. Easton, everyone... who I'm sure will introduce themselves. Don't scare him off. I want him to stay long-term."

"OMG, that is the cutest thing to say ever," Julian cooed. I remembered him from the day Lan confessed about us in the past.

Lan took the ice from Oliver and asked if I'd be okay on my own for a bit. Oliver said he'd stick by my side to help. Lan nodded, and with a final kiss, he went out the back again.

"Hey." A woman in her thirties maybe, with long dark wavy hair, came up with a friendly smile. "I know you won't remember all of our names, but I'd like to try and introduce you to those around here."

I nodded. "I'd like that."

"Great." She pointed to herself. "I'm Zara. Talon is outside with all the guys. He's the president to all Hawks chapters. I'll introduce you to him later. My tribe consists of Cody, who's outside with the men, Maya, Drake, and Ruby." She pointed to some of the kids. "Next to me is Deanna. Her two are Swan and Nicholas. That's Ivy, who's a couple of months pregnant. Same as Mally, who I've been told you already know." I nodded and waved at the already smiling and waving Mally, Lan's cousin's wife. Zara went on, "Clary, with her bundle of joy playing on the floor, Logan. My mum, Nancy."

The older woman stepped up, and I noticed Zara sigh and roll her eyes, before Nancy said, "You're damn handsome, young man. Are you sure you bat for the other team?"

I snorted out a laugh and managed a nod. "Yes."

"I don't," was called out. Everyone turned to look at Gamer, where he leaned against the hallway doorframe.

Nancy looked puzzled. "Don't what?"

"Bat for the other team." He winked. "Just thought you should know."

I caught Zara's eyes widen as she watched her mother blush. The room was utterly silent. Nancy then glared over at Gamer. "I'm old enough to be your mother. It's okay for me to mess about, but it's another story for young men to play people."

Gamer smirked, shook his head, and straightened. "Darlin', I ain't messin', and age is just a number." With that, he walked out of the room.

"Nancy, I think he was just coming onto you," Julian pointed out.

Nancy scoffed, glaring in Gamer's direction as he made his way outside, and then said, "Don't be stupid, Julian."

"He's not, Nance," Deanna said.

Nancy shook her head. "It doesn't matter if he was or wasn't. Richard was the love of my life, and no one could replace him."

"Doesn't mean you can't be happy," Zara said quietly.

Nancy studied her daughter with soft eyes. "I am happy, baby. Besides, I have the super-powered vibrator Julian got me."

"You got my mother a vibrator?" another man bellowed. He was holding a little girl in his arms. She looked up at him and giggled, slapping him on the cheek.

"Now, poppet," Julian cooed. "I love you, but our mumma bear has got to have some—"

"Julian! Mattie!" Nancy cried. She threw her hands in the air when men from outside looked in. "Great," she snapped. "Let's share that with everyone in the world, my sons."

Mattie held his free hand to his stomach. "This is why I stay outside." He handed the little girl off to Julian and stomped his way out the back.

"Mum, what's a vibrator?" Maya, Zara's older daughter, asked. Her lips twitched, so I had an idea she already knew, but she enjoyed playing with her mother and, from the way Nancy scowled at Julian, with her nana too.

"Yeah, Low. I want to know too," a little girl asked. When the black woman with a head of dark, wavy curls stepped back and looked to the door for an exit, I knew she must have been Low.

She straightened, and said, "Romania, come back to me when you're eighteen and ask again. *Then* I'll answer."

The little girl thought it over and then nodded with a smile. "Okay." She went back to building Lego with Swan, Drake, and Ruby.

Oliver leaned into me. "I think I'm in love with these people."

Grinning, I turned my head his way, and whispered, "So am I." I meant it. They were amazing. Right then, Zara and Julian, along with Deanna and Ivy, were huddled with Nancy, talking. Mally, her daughter, Nary, and Low took it upon themselves to introduce me to the others in the room. Oliver had already had time to meet the group while I'd been collecting the ice. Vi, Zara's sister-in-law, Mena, Dive's woman. Koda, their boy. Pregnant Della who was with Handle, and finally, Melissa, her man was named Dallas. The one I missed that day was Josie, but she was away with her men Pick and Billy, as in plural, lucky girl, who'd I'd already met.

What I did notice was that the woman, who was apparently with Parker, hadn't been in the room, which meant she was out with the men and not really a part of the group. I was happy she wasn't a part of this big, loving family and friends, but I kind of felt peeved she was out there, no doubt all over Parker.

Lan would see it, and I knew he wouldn't like it.

It was time to head out and meet the guys while seeing how Lan was reacting with Parker, and vice versa.

CHAPTER THIRTY-ONE

PARKER

*a*s I watched them all, I couldn't help but notice I was missing out. Nope, fuck that shit. I wasn't missing out. I didn't need anyone else. I didn't want a relationship. I liked to screw every now and then. That was it.

Easton grinned at the brothers as they came up to meet him from where he stood with Lan at the barbeque. He seemed at ease, but I was sure he would be panicked about meeting them. Hell, he probably was underneath it all. The brothers were good people though; they'd put him at ease. Lan knew it, which was no doubt why he'd organised such a huge gathering. Then again, it could have been the women taking over that did it all.

They would have thought it'd be easier to throw Easton in the deep end and see how he'd float with the pressure. From what I could tell, it looked like he was surviving.

"Handsome, I'm gonna go get another drink. You want one?"

"Sure," I slurred and nodded to Bonny. She unglued herself from me and swayed her hips over to the Esky. Why in the fuck did I decide to bring her? Oh, that was right. I thought she could be a good buffer between me, Lan, and Easton. I wanted to come, but I didn't want to have to talk to them much.

Why?

Because they were all I could goddamn think about. Even as I'd fucked Bonny hard before arriving, I'd been thinking it was Easton while Lan watched. As she'd sucked me off before we got into the fucking, I'd pictured it was Lan, and nearly blew my load from being overexcited about it.

What was wrong with me?

Why in the fuck did I have those images in my head?

Why did they excite me?

Christ, I was half tanked yet still managed to get a semi-hard cock over them.

How had they changed me?

Not that I was ready to admit the change. I still held out for something else. Something... normal. Thinking I wanted two guys wasn't normal. Thinking of guys instead of women in a way that was more than just a screw, wasn't normal. Not for me.

I wanted normal, yet I couldn't picture myself with a wife. Hell, and being with a woman long enough to want her as a wife was not on my radar.

But I could imagine something with them. My fucked-up head had imagined waking, sleeping, and walking around the same house together, as if we were all together in the same relationship.

Cursing, I scrubbed a hand over my face and glanced away from Lan and Easton to see Bonny flirting with a brother. Did it bother me? Not in the slightest. Instead, regret punctured my gut for even bringing her there. She was a club bunny. She'd never be anything else, and I'd pushed her on the women. The good women of the club. Fuck, only pricks did that.

I glanced over at Nary, which brought me to thinking of Josie. When she used to share my apartment with me, I hadn't been around much, having spent a lot of my time undercover on cases. The times I had been there, though, I'd thought of trying something with Josie. That was until I realised she deserved more. Even her, a good woman, one of the best and I couldn't consider having anything more beyond screwing. Damn glad to know and see she got her happily ever after with her guys.

My eyes drifted, but they always went back to the one spot.

Lan and Easton.

Lan had his hand on Easton's shoulder saying something with a smile. Whatever it was caused Easton to throw his head back and laugh.

Fuck. Even now I want to go over there and be a part of it. I want to stand with them, smile and laugh with them. Touch them like they do each other. With a gentle brush of fingers or a knock of the hip.

Why did I want that?

Suddenly, Liam was in front of me. "Quit glaring at them."

I snorted. "What the hell you talkin' about?"

"Only been here a short time, but in that time, all you've done is watch them and glare. What is your damn problem now? I thought things were sorted? I thought you'd come back and got yourself together. What's going on in your head, Parker?"

"Here you go, handsome." Bonny appeared at our side, holding out a beer to me.

Liam took the beer, glared down at her, and said. "Leave us for a moment."

"But—"

"Now," he demanded roughly.

"Fine," she snapped. "I'm going, Parker. You haven't spoken to me since we've been here anyway." She waited. Was I supposed to say something? She sucked in a sharp breath. Leaning in, she said, "You know, I totally faked my orgasm before."

"Bitch, like I give a fuck. I got off. That's all that mattered, and I'd heard you'd just come from Elvis's room anyway."

"You—"

Liam stepped in front of her. "Leave now."

She huffed, spun, and stomped off. Unfortunately, she'd gained the attention of people on her way, and they looked back over to me. I clenched my jaw when I saw Lan and Easton on their way over.

I wasn't ready for them.

With a wave, I announced, "Just remembered I have to be somewhere. Gotta go."

I was already near the side gate when I heard Liam say, "I'll make sure he gets home."

Once out front I realised I didn't have a ride. Since I'd been drinking at the compound earlier, Bonny had driven us over.

"You're stuck with me," Liam said, coming to stand at my side.

"You gonna lecture me all the way back?"

"Probably." He nodded.

"Hey," was called. We looked back, and a guy jogged towards us. "Need company?" he asked, eyeing me suspiciously.

Liam smiled fondly at him. "Parker, overprotective Damien. Damien, the detective Parker."

"Ah, that Parker." His hand came out and we shook. "Nice to meet you."

"Yeah, you too."

He faced Liam and winked. "Maybe next time you leave with a guy that looks like he wants to kill some people... no offense," he said to me, then back to Liam, "warn me it's all kosher and I won't freak the hell out."

Liam chuckled. "Got it." He grabbed the back of Damien's neck, tugged him close, and kissed him. It wasn't just a quick peck either, but for the life of me, I couldn't look away. Nor could I resist wondering what it would be like to do that to Lan or Easton.

Fucking hell.

Liam moved slightly back. "I like seeing you worry for me."

Damien grinned. "Don't be long."

"I won't." He stepped back and gestured with his hand to a sleek Mercedes. "I just have to knock some sense into Parker."

Rolling my eyes, I shot him the middle finger and went to the car since I didn't want to ask anyone else for a lift. No chance was I heading back inside.

Liam whispered something else to Damien and then came over to the car, hitting the unlock button. I got in and relaxed back in the seat, closing my eyes, and hoped he would just leave me and my pounding head alone.

"Seat belt," Liam ordered.

Groaning, I opened my eyes to grab the belt and click it in. Once again, I leaned my head back and closed my eyes.

Liam started the car and pulled out of the drive.

"Need to know where you live."

I told him and then shut up.

Liam sighed. "What's going on, Parker?"

"Why should I talk to you about it? Why should I talk about it at all?"

Liam laughed. "Like bottling it up is helping you. You've shared some with me before. I thought a recap with me on the matter again would be good for you."

Opening my eyes, I stared out the window and said nothing.

"Parker?"

I clenched my jaw and closed my eyes tightly. "It's not normal," I whispered into the car. "I'm fuckin' thirty-six years old, I should want to settle down with some woman, but I don't. I can't see myself married. I don't want to get married." I liked fucking them, but that was about it. I never went to a woman wanting a conversation about anything. I had Lan for that.

"What do you want?"

My baby brother would probably be ashamed of what I thought I wanted. The bitch who birthed me would definitely hate it.

"Something normal," I clipped.

"What's normal to you?"

"A man and a woman."

"So you're saying I'm not normal because I love two people at the same time? Two people who make me want to live, who cause me to laugh, smile, and enjoy each day?" I rolled my head his way to see him shake his head. "These days normal isn't set in stone. Women love women. Men love men. Who's the judge that says a person can't love two or more people at the same time? Who has the right to dictate how a person should love or decide what's right, what's wrong, and what's normal? No one but themselves. To me, it's normal to love Liberty *and* Damien. They think it's normal also. Damien's sister thinks it's normal to love her two men, as I'm sure Josie does as well."

He didn't understand. I didn't care people chose that life. "It doesn't bother me how you live or love. Not for any of you, never for any of you, but for me."

He looked over at me, then back to the road. "Because in your scenario it's two guys?"

Just say it, dickhead.

"Yes." Groaning, I leaned forward and dropped my head into my hands. "I don't understand how two guys can interest me when I fuckin' never wanted that in the first place. It's fucked up."

"For Damien, he told me once when we first kissed, it was like a switch flicked on inside of him. I'm sure it would be the same for you. What would you think if I kissed you right now?"

I straightened and turned his way. "I wouldn't be for it."

"Why?"

"Shit, I don't know. You're not it for me. You don't...."

"Don't what?"

"Don't get me excited."

"But Lan and Easton do?"

I thinned my lips.

"Parker?"

"Yes, they do. They goddamn do." I growled under my breath in frustration. "I can't stop thinkin' about them. It's fuckin' insane."

Liam laughed. "It's not insane. You're discovering something new, but doing it with two men. There's nothing wrong with it. Nothing wrong with you."

"What in the fuck am I supposed to do with this? How do I sort my head out?"

Liam shrugged. "You could find someone to move on with and forget them. However, I have a feeling your mind won't let that happen until...."

"Until what?" I demanded roughly.

"Until you test things with them."

"What?" I barked.

"I don't think I have to go into detail with what I mean." He grinned.

He didn't, but I wasn't sure if I could do that.

Although, if it meant I'd sort my head out and stop these thoughts... feelings, then it could be an idea. Maybe. Fucked if I knew.

CHAPTER THIRTY-TWO

LAN

*P*arker looked like shit. When he'd arrived, Parker had already seemed like he'd been up early drinking. He'd said a quick hi, hadn't bothered introducing the slut with him, and then picked a corner to brood in with his bimbo bitch. I couldn't goddamn believe the dick had brought her. The way she'd been all over him, him letting her hands roam without saying anything or even talking to her, pissed me off.

I'd finally started to relax with Easton at my side while we talked shit to the brothers around us. It'd felt bloody good to share that with Easton, and he'd settled after a while, only stumbling over a couple of words. Though, he did blush just about every time I touched him in a simple way. Then we'd heard the bitch huff about something and leave. I started to make my way over to see what the hell was up with Parker when he'd slurred a goodbye and quickly left.

Thank fuck Liam was there to help him out. If he hadn't offered, I would have gone out the front, asked what the fuck was wrong with him, and then if the dick answered, I'd have gotten him home safely.

Easton's hand slid up my back as I stared after Parker. "He didn't look good, Lan. What do you think's going on with him?"

"I don't know. Me maybe. Us? I don't fuckin' know. But I want to know. I need to know. If the idiot would just talk to us...." Facing Easton, I told him, "Before everyone arrived and you came home, I got a call from Sarge. Parker's given his four weeks' notice."

"What? Why?"

"Sarge doesn't know. He was shocked I didn't know anything about it. But he's guessin' Parker's just had enough. Of course, I can't help thinkin' it's because of me. He wants to get far enough away from me as he can."

"He said he doesn't judge people."

I shook my head. "He doesn't. It could be because I—"

"Wait, hang on. Sorry to interrupt," Violet, Talon's sister and a private investigator, said, stepping up to our sides. We shifted her way. "But I thought you knew what was going on."

My head jerked back. "What do you mean? What's going on?"

"Parker's quitting because of the offer I made... but it was for you and him. He told me he talked to you about it and would get the ball rolling.

"What offer?" I asked.

"I'm looking to branch out my PI business and was hoping to take you and Parker on board for my new branch here in Melbourne."

Why wouldn't Parker tell me? Glancing to the ground, I clenched my fists. That was right, because he wasn't talking to me.

"Violet, right?" Easton asked.

"Yes."

"You're a PI?"

I didn't hear the rest of their conversation.

Confusion rolled around and around inside of me. Mixing with it all was hurt. I wasn't sure what was going on with Parker, but I had to find out. I'd put hearing him quitting behind me because I'd wanted to enjoy the barbeque, but I was determined to know why. I wasn't messing the day for Easton and me, though. He was sweet enough to distract Violet while I got lost in my head, and Easton was what was important.

I curled my arm around Easton's shoulder and tugged him close. He smiled up at me. "Vi, thanks for the offer. I'll just need some time to think about it."

She smiled. "Of course. I'm going to get another drink. You guys want anything?"

Easton shook his head, and I said, "We're good, thanks."

When she walked off, I brought Easton to the front of me and wrapped a hand around his wrist. "We're going to enjoy this barbeque and the company we have. Later, we'll talk about Parker and Vi's offer. That sound okay?"

"Sounds good, and thank you."

"For what?" I asked, smiling.

He shrugged. "For today. For being you. For sharing your friends and family with me."

I shook my head. "You don't need to thank me for any of that. But I appreciate the thought and you gotta know, I'm thankful for all that from you too."

Mally leaned into me on the patio setting while others talked around us. "Can I be honest with you?"

"Yeah, honey."

"I've seen you around a couple of women, on dates and such, but I've never seen you so happy. You're talking, but your eyes don't stray far from him."

I grinned. "That's because I fear what Julian could be telling him."

She giggled. "He'll be safe."

"He'd better." I nudged her shoulder with mine. "When East and I were together long ago, I knew he was something special, and when I messed shit up between us, I've regretted it each and every goddamn day. When I saw him for the first time after all of these years, it hit me hard. I believed it was a second chance to redeem myself and a second chance to have my own chance of happiness." I looked at Easton when I spoke those words to Mally. Catching me staring, he smiled warmly over at me, but his brows dipped when he glanced at Mally. I looked at her and found her crying. "Honey?" I wrapped my arm around her shoulders and brought her in close.

She sniffed. "That's just so amazing. It's like you two were destined to be together."

"Yeah." I grinned. "I like to think that."

"How did you first meet him?" she asked.

"Shush everyone, Lan's about to tell the story of how they met," Ivy yelled.

"Cupcake," we heard sighed.

"Lan, after they're finished pecking over you, we'll be inside watchin' the game," Talon said. I lifted my beer in return and the brothers shot off inside. All except one.

"You goin' in?" I asked Stoke.

"Hell no. I want to hear how my cousin lost his nuts to the one... what did you say, love? Destined to be together?"

Mally blushed. "Yes." She wasn't the only one blushing, so was Easton. I grinned over at him and winked.

"Let's hear it then," Stoke said.

Didn't bother me he wanted to hear it. However, Easton thought it did. He blurted, "It really wasn't so special. We met, we ah, um, got to know one another and then, ah, dated. The end."

I laughed. "East, it was a bit more than that."

He gave me wide eyes, as if to tell me he was giving me an out, but I didn't want one.

Shaking my head, I then said, "It was. First, there was the time I saw Easton but didn't speak with him. When I was living in Ballarat, my boss had a friend at Melbourne University. He wanted an officer to visit his class to talk about being in the force. I was lucky to attend and Easton was in the class. While other career people talked, I looked around at the students but paused on Easton. He captured my attention. I remember thinking how I'd never seen anyone that damn good-looking before. Too bad he was so young." Everyone laughed. Julian shoved Easton in the shoulder, and Easton smiled shyly, still blushing. He glanced back over to me. I went on, "I tried to make sure I didn't linger on him, and then when it was over, I looked for him in the halls but couldn't find him. I had to head back to town anyway. About a month later, I happened to be in town and met up with a woman I used to hook up with."

"I knew it." Easton smiled.

"Yep. I'd told him she'd just been a friend. I met her at a pub and Easton was there sitting at the bar studying. Well, pretending to. I kept catching him looking in the mirror behind the bar watching me." Some of the women oohed over it. "As soon as I saw him, I remembered him from the university."

"You never said you remembered me."

"I'm loving this," Julian cried, his hands clutched in front of him under his chin.

"I didn't want to scare you. You were so fuckin' cute *umming* and *ahhing*, scared you'd upset me in some way. Do you remember what I first said to you?"

His smile widened. "Yes. I was about to leave because I'd been bummed you were with a woman. But then she left, and as I was packing up, you walked up to the bar and said, 'So, you're just going to leave and not say anything after watching me most of the night?'"

"I did and acted as if I didn't know you. Then you mentioned about uni and rambled on because you were so nervous."

"I was. I couldn't believe you were talking to me."

"I couldn't believe I saw you there that night. There wasn't a chance I'd pass up the opportunity by not saying anything. As luck would have it, you were taken by me."

"I was."

Everyone was silent. Hell, even Stoke. It kind of felt awkward, but again, I didn't give a shit. I loved the man across from me, and I'd have everyone know it if I could.

"Well shit. That's pretty awesome and sweet, and all that crap. I think I need a beer and to watch the game to get my man card back." Stoke came at me. He clasped my shoulder. "Happy for you, cousin."

"Thanks, man."

"Drake, no," Zara yelled. "Put the dog down."

"But, Mum, he wants a bath." It was then I saw Ruby had a bucket ready for her brother.

"No," Zara said. Drake took a step closer with Buddy in his arms. "Drake, I mean it," Zara warned.

"It's okay, Zara. I can just dry him later. My dogs are mellow; Buddy won't hurt him."

She shook her head. "I'm more worried about him hurting one of them. He's a hooligan like his father. Drake, stop." He made a run for it. Zara bolted up and after him. Deanna followed to help.

I rested my attention back on Easton because he'd risen and started my way.

Mally saw and said, "I'll go see if the men are wrecking Easton's house." She leaned in, kissed my cheek, and stood. As Easton stopped beside the table, she kissed his cheek too. "Good to have you in the family," she said, and before he could reply, she moved off.

Easton stared down at me, warmth in his eyes. "I kind of want to kiss and hug you right now."

I turned on the bench seat to straddle the middle. "Come at me, East. You say it, so do it."

"But...." He glanced around at the rest of the women, and Julian with Mattie, talking amongst themselves.

"Babe, I don't care what they think or see. You want a piece of me, you take it, no matter who's around. Get down here." I grinned when he moved and sat facing me, shifting his legs over mine on the bench so we were close.

He dipped his head, his forehead touching my good shoulder.

Once settled, he whispered, "You make my heart beat crazy, Lan Davis." I caught Mally rounding others up to head into the house, leaving us alone.

"You do the same to mine." I slid my hands slowly up his arms to his shoulders, only wincing a little from pain in my shoulder.

He pulled back to have my eyes and glide his hands up and down my thighs. He glanced around to find everyone gone. "Did Mally make everyone disappear?" he asked.

"Yeah."

"You have good people in your life."

"I do now. I didn't back then. The friends I thought were friends were nothing but dickheads."

He nodded. "I need to say something, but can you wait until I'm done before responding?"

"Okay," I agreed, a little worried from the serious tone.

"You hurt me a lot when you treated me like a stranger in front of your friends." I opened my mouth, and he laughed as his fingers pressed against my top lip. "Let me finish." I nodded, taking his hand in mine and holding it between us. "I'd never felt hurt like that from other guys I'd been with." I glared at the mention of other guys. He smiled and then rushed on, "All of that tells me you mean more to me than anyone else. You've also mended the hurt and changed it into hope, into love. I know it sounds all mushy, but what you said before, how you described seeing me and then at the bar, it overwhelmed me hearing your side of it all. I never thought you were taken with me like I'd been with you. It meant a lot hearing it. So much so I need to tell you...." He bit his bottom lip when it wobbled. "Darn it all to hell. I'm not usually a mess when talking about feelings, but you bring it out in me, and I can't help but feel so much for you."

"East," I interrupted.

"Yes?"

"Tell me," I ordered.

"Really it's not the best time. The house is full of people. People we're supposed to be entertaining."

"No offense to any of them, but fuck them. They can entertain themselves. The man I love was about to tell me that he loves me. I want to hear that more."

He stilled, his eyes filling with tears. "You love me?"

I grinned. "Yeah, babe. I love you."

He sniffed. "I love you, too."

It was then I caught Oliver and Julian at the kitchen window watching us and hugging, both with tears in their eyes.

Fucking hell.

Still, I ignored them and bent enough to claim Easton's lips with mine.

CHAPTER THIRTY-THREE

EASTON

A few nights had passed since the barbeque, and I was out with Oliver, Chris, and a few of his friends, while Lan had gone to the compound. Clubs weren't usually my scene, but of course, it was hard to say no to Oliver, especially since it was his birthday.

"How's hot-stuff Lan going?" Oliver shouted in my ear.

Grinning, I said, "Good."

Oliver studied me for a moment, then leaned in. "You know, I don't think you were ever this happy with me."

"Ollie—"

He shook his head. "Relax. I like it. Seeing you this happy. He's the one, like Chris is mine."

I nodded. "I like to think so."

"Speaking of Chris, I'm going to go help him at the bar. If Patrick and Niall ever get off the dance floor, tell them we're getting this round."

I gave him two thumbs-up instead of shouting. While I might still be young enough to go to nightclubs, I knew I'd regret it tomorrow with a pounding headache. Also, if Oliver had anything to do with it, I'd be stumbling out of there by the end of the night with the amount he wanted to drink. I was already halfway tipsy. He was such a bad influence at times.

Patrick slipped into the booth puffing and panting. He waved his hand in front of his face and said something.

"Sorry?" I yelled.

He moved around the booth and got close. "It's so hot out there. Niall's gone to the loo and getting some drinks."

I was about to tell him to find Niall to tell him to forget the drinks when someone gripped the top of my arm and dragged me up to stand beside the booth. I spun to face a fuming Parker.

He got in my face. "Lan know you're here whisperin' sweet nothin's to some dude?"

"We weren't—"

"Say goodbye. I'm takin' you home."

"Parker, I'm not leaving. I'm here to celebrate Oliver's birthday."

"Bullshit. You're steppin' out on Lan."

Now I was pissed. So I pushed his chest. He didn't budge. "I would never do that," I yelled, and just in case I could take him off guard, I tried to shove him again. His hands wound around my wrists and held them against his chest. My stomach twirled like a fancy ballerina dancing for the first time.

No. I couldn't, *wouldn't,* let him and his good looks and firm chest distract me. Neither would the way his hands loosened on my wrist and... was that his thumbs brushing over my skin. I shook my head to clear it.

"Ah, Easton, is everything okay here?" Patrick asked, loud enough to be heard over the music, kneeling beside us on the booth seat.

Parker ignored him, and asked, "If you're here for Oliver and not to pick up, then where in the fuck is he?"

"He's getting drinks, not that it's any of your business." Sheesh, that sounded familiar, like I'd said it to him before. I rolled my eyes, fully aware I had.

"It is my business," he clipped loudly.

"How?"

His jaw clenched, his glare narrowing even more.

Oliver stepped up to our other side. "Hey there, scowly. What's going on?"

I raised my brows at Parker. He said nothing.

"Um, what's happening here?" Oliver asked.

"Nothin'," Parker snarled and dropped my wrists, stepping back.

"Wait," I called, grabbing his arm before he could take off and getting in his space so I didn't have to yell too much. "You need to talk to Lan."

His gaze travelled over my face before meeting my eyes. "Why?"

"He's worried about you. We both are. Have we done—"

"Don't," he bit out.

"What? Don't what? Ask about you? Ask what we could have done to have you steer clear of us? Is it because of me? Do I annoy you that much you have to stay away from your friend? Or is it because Lan kissed you? While I'm at it, why did you kiss—" He covered my mouth with his palm, and I glared up at him.

My eyes widened when his expression softened. His gaze moved lower, on his hand over my mouth. He moved his hand and slid it across so his finger grazed against my mouth. He stopped with his finger at the edge of my mouth and then ran it down to my chin. He tapped it a couple of times before resting it there.

"Yes," he said.

"Yes what?" I asked, more confused than before.

He shook his head and dragged his eyes up to capture mine, and I sucked in a shocked breath when I saw desire pooling in his eyes. He smirked, turned, and left through the crowd. While I stood there, frozen to the spot.

What. Was. That?

What *was* that?

"Are you okay?" Oliver asked, threading his arm around my waist.

"Ah…."

"That was the hottest thing I've ever seen," Chris said from the other side of me. Oliver nodded, agreeing with Chris.

"What are you talking about?" I asked Chris.

"I was coming back with drinks. I saw the whole hand on mouth and trailing his finger, tapping your chin and resting it there." He gulped his drink.

"I saw the look in his eyes. Easton, honey, he wants to eat you alive," Oliver said.

"I got that same feeling from just seeing a touch," Chris said.

Shaking my head, I told them, "You two are crazy."

Oliver spun to me. "You can't tell me you didn't get the vibe off him wanting you. Don't lie to me, Easton."

I shrugged.

Chris patted my shoulder. "Does Lan know?"

"I, no, there's nothing… I—" I threw my hands up in the air. "I don't know what he needs to know. Yes, it was a hot look and touch, but I don't know," I cried.

"There, there," Oliver cooed, rubbing his hand up and down my back. "Come on, let's go have a drink, and we'll call Lan to come pick you up."

I shook my head. "A drink yes, but I'll text Lan and tell him I'm Ubering it home. This place is too far out of his way."

"Do you think that's wise? He'd hate it."

"It'll be fine. I'm a big boy. I can take care of myself, and Ubers are safe."

"Plus," Chris said. "It'll give you time to think about what to tell Lan."

"No, that's not why. He won't care. Not that there's anything to care about, but he was fine when Parker kissed me the first time."

"Parker kissed you and you didn't tell me!"

Now I knew I'd need not one but two drinks. One for my rattled mind and body, and another for the Parker conversation with

Oliver. I still couldn't believe that look. His eyes had smouldered. It sounded so lame, and something from the eighties, but darn it, that's exactly what they did. Smoulder.

As I took my drink from Chris, I couldn't help but wonder why Parker was there in the first place. Had he been looking to hook up with some random woman or could he have known I was there and wanted to see me?

I laughed at that thought and shook my head. That thought was just stupid.

Or was it?

With the outside light shining, I could easily see Lan waiting on the front porch as the Uber pulled into my driveway. Smiling, he leaned against the house with his arms crossed over his chest. As soon as I was out of the car, he straightened and started towards me.

"How drunk are you?" he asked, coming down the front steps.

Grinning, I tilted my hand side to side. "So, so." Once close, he pulled me into his arms. "What about you?"

"I'm fine, drove home. Already been in. Dogs are out in their kennels. I've got water in our room ready for you."

I laughed. "Am I going to need it?"

"Oh yeah, you'll be very parched when I'm done."

My heart stumbled, only to stop. "I saw Parker tonight." Lan's head jerked back in shock.

"And?"

"I... he... strange."

"What was?" he demanded.

"He got angry with me because he thought I was stepping out on you."

Lan snorted. "Seriously?"

LILA ROSE

"Yep." I nodded. "When he realised I wasn't, he went to leave, but I got in his face, blurted stuff out, asking if he hated us or just me for being with you. He didn't really say anything, but he did put his hand over my mouth. Lan, Ollie and Chris saw it, but I don't know if it's for real. I thought it was just me seeing things and maybe feeling things, but they think it's true."

He shook me a little. "What?"

"There was a moment."

"A moment?"

I nodded.

"What kind of moment?"

"An intense one."

Lan studied my face. "We need to talk to him. See what's going on." He shifted, curled his arm around my shoulders and started us up the steps.

"We do."

We both turned at the same time when we heard a car coming down the road. My breath caught when I saw it was Parker's.

I took a step down, and Lan's arm slipped from my shoulders. He moved behind me more.

"Why would he be here?" Lan pondered.

"I don't know. He left the club, but didn't mention he was coming out here."

Parker parked, got out, and strode towards us with stiff movements. His eyes scanned over both of us, and he kept clenching and unclenching his jaw. It looked like he could even be grinding his teeth. Still, even with the dark look upon his handsome face, he was unbelievably attractive in the light of the porch.

Okay, maybe I did have too much to drink.

"Parker," Lan greeted.

"Lan." Parker lifted his chin and moved his eyes down to me. "Easton."

"Ah, hey." I waved lamely.

244

It could have been my eyesight, but I was sure I saw his lips twitch. Of course it didn't last.

"What's goin' on?" Lan asked.

He glanced over to the side, then down at his feet. I heard his intake of breath before he peeked up at us. "I want to watch."

Say what now?

"Watch what?" Lan asked cautiously. He was probably wondering what I was: Did he mean me and Lan together?

Holy fuck, did he?

Would he?

Would I want it?

My dick was screaming *yes, yes, yes*, while my mind was… all right, I was also thinking hell to the yes. I loved Lan. Being with him was something special each time, and to share that with Parker would be amazing, especially since it was Parker. A man we were both attracted to.

"You two," Parker clipped, probably annoyed Lan was questioning him, but we had to know.

"Why?" Lan asked.

He opened his mouth, closed it, and mumbled under his breath before sighing and staring down as he shuffled his foot into the gravel.

Oh my God.

Parker Wilding was curious.

He thought he could be interested in men. Maybe in us. He didn't know; he was confused.

Was all this the reason why he stayed away from us?

Was it why he was being such an arse to Lan?

It must have been.

"Parker?" Lan bit out.

I knew one thing, if Parker had to talk about it first, it would freak him out even more. He was an action man. If I didn't take control of the situation, Parker would leave, and I wasn't sure something like this would happen again if it came to Parker.

Turning to face Lan, I reached up and cupped his face. His eyes crashed down to mine. I mouthed, "Trust me." Lan nodded slightly. I smiled and slowly dragged his face down so I could touch my lips to his.

CHAPTER THIRTY-FOUR

PARKER

*T*hey were kissing. Kissing right there in front of me. Goddamn, it was hot to watch. My chest fucking ached with how crazy my heart beat. My gut swirled with nerves, but I kept watching them. Lan made a sound and wrapped his arms tightly around Easton, pulling him up to the step he stood on.

My hands shook at my sides, so I fisted them. I hadn't thought I'd have the strength to actually show. Knowing Easton would head home to Lan and, since he'd been drinking, he'd want a piece of his man.... I wanted to see it to finally figure out if it was something I'd be into. I'd looked at some gay porn the last couple of nights. It didn't do shit for me until I thought of Lan and Easton as the actors.

Easton let out a moan that my cock responded to. It jerked behind my jeans.

Lan slid a hand down to grab Easton's arse cheek. He tugged him forward and ground his, *fuck*, cock into Easton's.

They'd be hard. From one kiss and already they'd be up and ready to go.

Shit, I'd never really had that. It'd take me some groping and shit to get me going with women. Yet, watching them, I was nearly so damn hard I wanted to palm my dick and tug one out.

Jesus, they'd only just started.

Lan pulled back. He shot his darkened eyes over Easton to me, before he straightened, unwinding himself from Easton and taking his hand to lead him to the door and then inside.

He left the door open for me.

This was it.

I was going to see them fuck.

Christ.

Fear had me gulping for air and rubbing at my chest. My gut spun, despite the shots of desire shooting into my balls.

All I had to do was walk up there to get what I wanted.

Lan

"You're okay with letting him watch us together?" Easton asked. With already our shoes and socks off, we stood near the couch while waiting to see if Parker would walk in the house or if he'd be getting back in his car. I still couldn't believe he was there and wanting to watch us, but Easton had just told me this could be why Parker had been steering clear of us... because he was scared. He thought he wanted us.

Fuck me, my chest expanded in excitement over the possibility of it.

I cupped Easton's cheek and nodded down at him. "As long as you are."

"Yes." He grinned.

"Nervous?"

"Very much, so if I say or do anything embarrassing, please stop me."

I chuckled. "No way. I love you doing those things."

He came up to his toes to kiss me. Anytime I had his mouth, I wanted more of it, more of him. I moved my hands under his tee and lifted it up so I could see, feel, and taste more of him. When I threw it to the floor, I happened to glance over at the door and found Parker stepping in.

Easton also looked over, and we both watched him close the door to lean against it. Parker wanted a show. I would give him one, and then he'd know for sure if he wanted this.

I fucking hoped he did in the end.

Resting my hands at Easton's waist caused him to jump. His eyes came back to me. He smirked, and I grinned down at him, then shifted my hands around to his front where his jeans were. Easton sucked in a sharp breath when I undid his button. He shuddered before he kissed my chest and I unzipped him. I stepped back a little, gripped the top of his jeans and pushed them down with his boxers. I bent, helped him step out of them, and ran my gaze up his naked body. His long, thick cock stuck straight out. Unable to resist, I kissed the tip before standing.

Parker

*F*ucking *hell*. I was going to come in my jeans. I breathed in and out rapidly, my cock throbbing in my jeans. My balls were already tight, begging for a release. But I wouldn't give it.

I enjoyed the show of Lan removing Easton's jeans and then seeing Easton naked. His body was a damn nice sight. I'd never get bored of staring at his tattooed artwork.

Fuck me, how could my attraction to him be more than anyone's? I'd seen many, so bloody many tatted up men, but none of them got my cock leaking.

It was both of them. *Just them.*

Lan, I'd seen naked. But I'd never thought about it, about him and his body until that moment and I found myself wanting to see him, all of him again. He was taller than Easton, wider, and a little more muscled. Both of them, their bodies, captured my whole attention.

Lan stepped forward, closer to Easton. I saw his hand move between them, and I goddamn knew he would have his hand full of Easton's dick.

Shit, fuck. I wanted to see Lan jerking Easton off.

"Sit down," Lan ordered. If it was to me, I couldn't move. But then Easton shifted. He turned and I got my first sight of his front. He was hard, long, and thick, but so very bloody hard. He sat back on the couch.

I glanced to Lan to find him watching me as he palmed his thickness behind his jeans. His eyes were low on my body. I knew he'd see the erection I sported behind my jeans. He grunted, turned, and got to his knees, between Easton's spread legs.

Crap, fuck me. Lan was going to suck Easton off.

I bit down on my bottom lip to stop myself from moaning at the sight of Lan bending in, taking hold of Easton's cock for a taste. Almost as if in slow motion, he reached under Easton's thighs and pulled him down the couch a little. His hand went back to Easton's cock, all while Easton watched him through hooded eyes.

I wrapped my arms around myself and fisted my tee to hold onto something. My body thrummed with desire. I'd never wanted to come so badly in my bloody life.

Easton threw his head back into the couch when Lan glided his mouth over Easton's cock. *Christ. Jesus Christ. Yes. Suck him.*

I leaned more into the door. My legs weakened when Lan licked, sucked, and skimmed his mouth and tongue up and over Easton's dick. Seeing it slide in and out of Lan's mouth was fucking amazing. I wanted to be where Easton was. I wanted my dick sucked by Lan, and yet, I wondered what it would be like to suck both of them. What their reactions would be if it was me giving them head.

Easton's legs widened, and I caught my breath when Lan licked and spat on two of his fingers. When I saw him reach between them, my dick ached so fucking hard because I knew he'd be playing with

Easton's arse. From the way Easton panted and moaned, he was lost in the feel of Lan. Lost in the thrill and loving every damn second of it.

Something came over Easton. He clutched Lan's hair in his hand and drew Lan up, still while grinding up, down, and around. When Easton kissed him firmly, I nearly lost my shit and went over there. But then they moved. Lan knifed up, his back muscles bunched and moved, and the sight of them pleased me like they never had before.

He helped Easton stand and then took something out of his pocket, his wallet. He opened it, produced a condom and handed it to Easton while he grabbed something else. My eyes drifted down Easton's body to see he'd already ripped open the packet and slowly, Lan ran the condom down over Easton's erection.

Lan leaned into him, and I pulled my gaze back up to see Lan kiss Easton's neck and say something low against it. Easton stepped over to the chair opposite the couch and kneeled on it. I had a nice view of Easton jutting his arse back, offering it to Lan.

I looked at Lan. His eyes were on me already. He undid his belt, his button, and then slid his zip down before he pushed his jeans and boxers down his legs. He didn't even bother to remove them fully.

He palmed his dick and stared at me. My fucking heart kicked it up a notch. They made this, *me* feel so damn much. Everything felt fiercely thrilling.

"You want to see me fuck Easton?"

I glanced at Easton. He had his elbows to the back of the chair. His head was down until he heard Lan's question, and then he glanced over to me. His eyes slowly ran over my body, a small smile playing on his lips.

"Parker?" Lan barked.

I unclenched my jaw to clip, "Yes."

Lan smiled, and it was shameless. He stepped up behind Easton, leaned over him, and asked, "You ready for me, babe?"

"So ready," Easton whispered.

Lan kissed Easton's shoulder before straightening. Running a hand down over Easton's back, he stopped at his hip before removing it and picking up a packet of something again. From where I stood, I could see Lan ripping open the packet, gripping his uncovered dick and squirting some lube onto it and then rubbing it around before touching his fingers to Easton's hole. Easton pushed back on his fingers, showing he was eager. As was I.

Lan leaned in to give another kiss to Easton's shoulder, and Easton glanced over to smile at him. Lan winked. He gripped his dick again and aimed it at Easton's hole. Easton sucked in a breath, and fuck, I wanted to watch him, but I couldn't fucking look away from Lan gripping Easton's hips and slowly sliding his dick inside of Easton.

Fucking Christ.

Fucking hell.

Jesus.

Easton groaned. With his head thrown back, a look of pure bliss lit his face. Suddenly, he opened his eyes and turned his head my way. His body shifted forward and back as Lan moved in and out of him.

"So good," Easton cried.

My cock ached, my balls as well. I needed to come. Watching Easton being fucked was more than I ever expected. I liked it. No, I goddamn loved seeing it.

Lan clenched his jaw, his hands running over Easton's body as he moved in and out of him.

"Yes," Easton cried. "Harder," he snapped. Lan did. Fucked him so hard Easton's hold tightened on the chair. He moaned and whimpered. There was no concealing it. He loved Lan pumping his cock into him.

"God, Lan—"

"Not yet," Lan ordered.

"I can't hold back," Easton said with his eyes on me. Did that mean me being there turned him on more?

"I know," Lan grunted. He pulled at Easton's hips, tugging him back to slam his arse onto his cock more and more. "Fuck, East," he yelled.

"Now," Easton cried. I shifted my gaze down to see, even without touching himself, Easton shot his load into the condom. He moaned through it, took hold of his dick and jerked it more, still coming. Lan growled from deep within and bent over Easton, wrapped his arms around him and thrust again.

"Coming," he clipped. "Fuck, yes." He pumped Easton again and again, then stilled.

Both were breathing hard, just like I was. I'd been so close to coming in my jeans. Jesus, excitement still rushed through me, although fear was there as well. I didn't know if I should leave or what I wanted.

Lan stood, slipped from Easton, and helped him to his wobbly feet. Easton giggled, high on his own release.

Holy motherfucking hell.

Lan put his hands around Easton's hips, down to Easton's cock and removed the condom for him. He tied it and threw it to the floor and then glided his hands back over Easton's body. Easton's dick jerked.

"You're hard, Parker," Lan stated, his voice low and rough.

I swallowed but said nothing.

Over Easton's shoulder, Lan stared at me while he kissed Easton's neck. Easton arched for him, but he was also looking at me. Lust still swirled in his eyes.

Lan rested his chin on Easton's shoulder. "Want East to take care of it?" Lan asked. Easton gasped, bringing his hands up to hold Lan's over his stomach. He was already growing hard again.

Fuck, I did. I wanted that.

"East would love to suck you, Parker." He grinned when Easton shivered. "You want that?" I nodded once. Lan shook his head. "You have to say you want it."

Bastard. When I narrowed my gaze, he chuckled.

Through clenched teeth, I bit out, "I want it."

When Lan dropped his hands, Easton walked over to me. Each step he took, my head swam, my lungs seizing. I uncrossed my arms and dropped them to my sides, straightening. Easton stopped before me, that small soft smile still playing on his lips. He reached out to my jeans, undid the button and lowered the zipper. He didn't push them over my hips. Instead, I sucked in a sharp breath when he slid his hand inside my jeans and boxers and gently pulled my hard cock free.

Easton stared up at me as he licked his lips and then dropped to his knees before me.

Christ. Fuck me, just my luck I'd faint. My body ached so badly.

Easton licked the tip. I jolted and widened my eyes when I realised I definitely wanted this. When he slowly sucked me into his mouth, I ground my teeth together when a moan wanted out. His mouth and tongue teased and tasted my dick as he withdrew it from his lips.

"More?" Lan asked. Again, I jumped, not having noticed he'd approached until he was right next to us.

Easton stared up at us, his mouth inches from my dick, but he didn't move, and I knew he wouldn't until I answered Lan's question. I glared down at him. "Yes," I admitted.

Lan nodded. Easton grinned and then opened his mouth, placing my dick on his tongue and then ran his tongue around my knob.

"Fuck," slipped out of me.

"He's good," Lan growled out. I noticed his jeans were up, covering his dick, but still undone. Then my attention went back down to Easton as he sucked harder up and down my length.

"Jesus," I ground out. I knew he'd be tasting my precum and knowing it shot my balls up inside of me. I was too damn close already.

"Parker," Lan called. I hadn't realised I'd closed my eyes, so I opened them and turned my head his way. Christ, his eyes were filled with hunger. He enjoyed watching Easton suck me. His hand came to the side of my neck.

Fuck me.

He leaned in slowly, enough time for me to stop him, but I didn't. On the first touch of his mouth on mine, I pulled up my arm and wrapped it around his shoulder, dragging him close and groaning into his mouth. He grunted out a moan in return, his hand landing on my stomach. I used my other hand to thread into the back of Easton's hair as he bobbed faster and faster on my dick.

I was going to come, but I didn't want any of it to stop. To feel was okay. The sensation of being close to release was so fucking perfect knowing it was Lan and Easton, but then I knew reality would crush me once it ended.

I could only hope it didn't.

Sliding my tongue over Lan's bottom lip, I panted into his mouth.

"You close?" he asked, his voice harsh with arousal.

I nodded, tucked my forehead into his shoulder while I still held Easton. I gripped my other hand to Lan's neck and tightened it again on the first shot of my cum into Easton's mouth. I grunted, groaned, and goddamn growled as I kept coming. Lan gently rubbed my stomach as I sighed when the last drops shot into Easton.

Fuck.

Shit.

What did I do now?

I couldn't get enough oxygen in. Pain stabbed at my chest.

Easton moved off me with one last lick. I sensed him standing. Clenching my jaw, I straightened, cleared my throat and tucked myself back in. Shit, I even did up my jeans. I had to get out of there. I couldn't even look at them.

I liked it.

No, I fucking loved it, but I was still goddam motherfucking scared.

Turning, I faced the door, my hand touching the handle.

Lan stopped me. "Wait. Fuck, Parker. Don't run. Did you not like that? Did—"

"Lan," Easton said. Then there was silence for a few beats before Easton rambled, "You can stay in the spare room. It's late, so maybe, if you wanted to, we could talk in the morning or something."

Did I want to stay? Talk?

Everything in me screamed to run and hide.

But fuck that. Screw feeling that way because I had to sort this shit out. Sort myself out.

Drawing in a shuddering breath, I faced them. Easton covered himself with a tee. They stood away from me, worried I'd freak out again.

"I'll stay," I said.

"Good." Easton smiled. He took Lan's hand and pulled him towards the hall. "The spare room has clean sheets. It's all ready."

"Thanks," I said.

Easton did a dorky wave thing, blushed, and was the first down the hall.

"Lan," I called. Lan stopped, nodded at Easton in the hall, and then turned back to me.

"You okay?"

Was I?

Right then, even though I had freaked, I still felt good. My release had been hard and oh so fucking good.

I nodded and walked towards him. He started down the hall and I followed. At the spare room door, right next to Easton's like the layout of Lan's house, he opened it for me.

"All right. We'll talk in the morning." He nodded, more to himself.

He began to move off, but I stopped him with a couple of my fingers hooking into his jeans. When he froze, I braved it enough to run the back of one of my fingers up and down his skin at his hip.

"I did enjoy it," I said, and then dropped my hand. Stepping back into the room, I closed the door. After staggering over to the bed, I sat on the edge.

"Fuck," I whispered. "Holy shit," I added. I'd just come in Easton's mouth, kissed Lan's, and the whole scene had been out-of-this-damn-world hot.

Until I freaked.

Shaking my head, I pushed my anxiety to the back of my mind and thought of what happened. Easton's hot, wet mouth. Lan's hard, demanding kiss.

A laugh escaped me. I clamped my lips shut, but I did it smiling.

Christ, I wanted that to happen again. Thinking about it caused my dick to stir. Thinking about them in their room, in bed, naked together, had my dick hardening.

Yeah, I wanted more of Lan and Easton, and I wouldn't be sure when I'd ever get enough of them.

CHAPTER THIRTY-FIVE

LAN

*D*azed, I walked into the bedroom. The shower ran in the en suite a few moments longer before it switched off. Needing one myself, probably even a cold one, I made my way into the bathroom. Easton stood outside the shower drying himself. He saw me and smiled.

"How do you think it went? Do you think he'll disappear into the night or will he be here in the morning?"

Chuckling, since Easton was just as worried about Parker running off in the night as I had been, I kissed him quickly and reached around him to open the shower door. "I think he might just surprise us and stay."

"What makes you say that?"

"He just told me he enjoyed it."

Easton spun to face me. "Really?" He smiled wider.

I grinned. "Yeah. I'm guessin' you liked it as much as I did?"

"You're hot on your own, but having him watch and then watching you kiss him…" He shook his head. "It was *fucking* hot." He moved the towel away from himself. "Look." He nodded down at his dick sticking out, ready and hard.

I shoved my jeans down, my erect dick springing free.

Easton moved into me. "I could jump in the shower with you."

I smiled, nipped at his neck, and said, "In bed."

He turned and made a beeline for the bedroom. "Hurry up then," he called. My chest felt like it'd grown bigger, wider with the amount of fucking happiness coursing through me in that moment. Parker had watched Easton and me. He hadn't looked disgusted or scared at the time. Never disgusted, but somewhat scared at the end. More than that, though, he'd also stared at us, mesmerised with raw desire. His cock had already been hard when he'd walked into the house. I'd been surprised I'd lasted as long as I had, having been so close to coming when Easton and I kissed with Parker watching.

Parker.

He'd kissed me like he wanted to devour me in the best way possible. Christ, the noise he'd made, the ones I'd eaten with my mouth on his. My dick throbbed from thinking of them.

This was Parker.

Hell, he was in the room next to us, and I was about to ask Easton something with him not far from us. Fuck me, I even wanted him to hear us.

I started to get myself ready for Easton and nearly blew my load when images of what happened in the living room wouldn't stop playing over in my mind. So I shut off the shower, quickly dried myself and walked from the room naked. With the light from the en suite, I easily saw Easton lying on his back with his eyes on me. I went over to the bed and slipped between the sheets. Resting my elbow on the bed, I placed my head on my hand and grinned down at him. Honestly, I couldn't stop smiling, and it seemed Easton was having the same problem.

"That really happened?" I asked.

"It did." He nodded.

I slid my hand to his stomach. It trembled under my touch. I glided it down and found him still hard. "Need something from you," I told him.

"Hmm, what's that?" He smirked.

I kissed him, and said, "Want you to fuck me."

He stilled. His eyes darkened, his nostrils flared. "Roll over," he ordered, and Christ, his harsh tone went right to my balls. I didn't offer it often because I loved being inside Easton and he enjoyed it even more. Still, there were times I needed it, and right then was that moment.

After a quick kiss, I rolled over, resting my head on my curled-up arm. My shoulder ached and tugged a bit, but I ignored it. Instead, I listened to Easton open our drawer; he'd be grabbing out the lube. No condom, never a condom between us since we both knew we were healthy and hadn't taken another without protection before. I also knew for a fact Parker always wore a rubber as well with anyone else. It was like his religion. No chance did he want little Parkers showing up. It was how I'd let Easton suck him off without talk of it beforehand.

Easton's hand touched my hip having moved closer behind. "Lay on your back. Let me get you ready," he whispered.

I shook my head. "Already ready."

Easton moaned and bit my shoulder. "In the shower?"

"Yeah, babe."

"But it's been...."

"Ten years, I know, but I want this."

He kissed my neck. "Love you, Lan Davis."

"Fuckin' love you, East."

When the blanket moved off him, I looked over my shoulder to see him lathering lube onto his stiffness. He angled towards me and applied more to me. Facing forward, I then heard the tube of lube hit the end of the bed, and Easton shifted closer, pulling the blankets over our waists. Once on his elbow looming over my back, I pushed my arse back onto him and heard his intake of a quick breath when his tip hit and slid into me.

"Fuck," I moaned and pushed back more.

"Lan," Easton bit out. He gripped my hip, holding me still while he pushed inside me, past the resistance. I groaned low when his dick hit my prostate.

"Fuck yes," I clipped. That was what I needed. Him inside of me, feeling him.

Easton moaned and curled his arm under mine to my chest while I placed mine back so I could grab his hip and force him in and out of me faster, harder.

"Lan, slow," Easton said. "Or I'm going to come."

"Christ, East. Can't, need it hard. Want it hard."

He thrust in hard. We both froze when we heard the door open with a squeak. Easton glanced down, and I looked over my shoulder to see Parker standing there only in his boxers. In the light of the en suite, I saw his chest rise and fall rapidly.

"Ah... God," Easton moaned.

I'd begun sweating even before Easton shifted back slightly and then pushed back in. I tightened my grip on his hip.

"Parker," I groaned when Easton pulled out and then pumped in. Parker walked around the bed to my side.

"He fuckin' you?" he asked roughly.

Shit. Crap. He sounded like he wanted the answer to be a yes, especially with the way his boxers tented, so it was lucky Easton was fucking me. "Yes," I hissed.

He licked his lips, his eyes on the blanket at our waists. I didn't say anything, wanting to see what he would do or say. Easton also stayed quiet; instead, he kissed and bit at my shoulder and neck while slowing his thrusts down to glide in and out of me.

"Hell," I groaned.

Parker reached out and flipped the blankets off us to see Easton pushing his cock in and out of me. Easton didn't stop either. He kept pumping his thickness in my tight hole while using his mouth on my skin.

"Fuck," Parker clipped. He reached into his boxers and palmed his own dick.

"I'm going to come," Easton whispered against my neck. I

nodded. I was so fucking close as well from seeing Parker pleasure himself while he watched us.

I gripped the end of Parker's boxers and pulled them down. They fell to the floor, and we got to see Parker jerking his dick up and down fast. He sucked in a sharp breath.

"Y-yes," Easton cried, his cum warming my arse as it fired out of him.

"Babe," I said. I needed to come and I was still so close.

"Lan," Easton sighed, his thrusts slowing to a stop. He pulled out of me and, in a flurry of movements, he was rolling me to my back with a hand to my shoulder. He flipped the rest of the blankets off the bed, grabbed Parker's arm and tugged until Parker fell onto the bed on his knees. Easton shifted, gripped Parker's hip on one side and pulled him so he had no choice but to climb over my leg so he didn't fall on me.

"W-what the fuck...?" Parkers eyes were wide, his breathing erratic. Still he was somehow hovering over me, a hand to each side of my shoulders. He stared down at me, my spread legs around him, his gaze travelling up to my face with shock.

He hissed, lips pulled back on his teeth as he looked between us. Easton had a hold of his dick and using his other hand, Easton pushed at Parker's back.

Fucking what?

Oh hell.

Oh shit.

Holy fuck.

Parker's tip hit my hole. We both froze.

Easton leaned into Parker. Against his ear, he whispered, "Lan needs you to finish him. Fuck him, Parker."

Parker gulped, closed his eyes, and dropped his head. Easton smiled down at me. He then sucked Parker's earlobe into his mouth. I saw a flashing of his teeth biting into it. Parker groaned and pushed forward.

"Christ," I growled. Pain and pleasure shot through me. Pain from him forcing himself in, pleasure when he hit the right spot straight away.

I opened my eyes to see him staring down at me with wide eyes.

"Good," Easton whispered, before running his tongue down Parker's neck and back up to his ear. "He liked that. See his eyes, how hot they are for you? He wants you to move, Parker. Move inside of him. Fuck him hard, Parker. Lan wants you to fuck his arse."

I grabbed Parker's arms and glided my hands up. One to cup his neck, the other to slide my thumb into his mouth, touch his tongue and then drag it out to wet his lips.

"Jesus," Parker hissed. He pulled out and thrust in fast, pulled out again and thrust back in. "So fuckin' tight. Hot, wet."

"Yes," Easton said. "He feels great, doesn't he?"

Parker nodded and moaned while fucking me harder.

"Christ, Parker," I grunted, digging my feet into the bed, taking him deeper. "Feels so good."

"What does?" Easton asked.

"Parker."

"Hear that, Parker? Lan likes the feel of you inside of him. You like knowing that?"

"Yes," he hissed, and still thrusting, he rested all his weight on one arm and the other, he grabbed Easton and kissed him hard. Easton whimpered into his mouth. I wanted to close my eyes, get lost in the pleasure building so fucking big, but I didn't. I watched them kiss, followed the sweat on Parker as it trailed down his body and I looked between us. I saw Parker's hips moving in and out, again and again, drilling his cock into me.

It was too much.

An overload of arousal.

"I'm coming," I clipped. They broke apart, both looking down to see the first shot of my cum out of the tip, landing on my stomach, spreading, dripping as I tugged the rest out of me.

"Fuck," Parker growled roughly. His arm dropped from Easton

and he fucked my arse harder, staring down at me, clenching his jaw.

"Come, Parker," Easton whispered against his ear again. "Come inside his arse. He wants to feel it. Fill him."

Parker unlocked his jaw and snarled out a curse as his cum did as Easton said: filled me.

CHAPTER THIRTY-SIX

EASTON

*H*alf asleep still, I stretched, not really wanting to wake up. My body felt sore, but in the best way. Smiling, I stretched again and then realised my cheek rested on a chest, but I also felt warmth at my back.

I opened my eyes in a flash and stared at a throat. Slowly, I moved my head up and saw Parker's sleeping face. It wasn't his chest I lay on either; it was his arm. His other was thrown over me. I didn't feel his hand at my back, which meant he had it on the other man snuggled into my back. I was sandwiched between two men. My morning wood throbbed.

I liked the feel of it.

Both of them.

Last night had been... honestly, there weren't enough words to describe how fantastic it had been. I still felt giddy, my stomach agreeing by dipping and swirling. What was more significant was the memory of when, after it all, Parker didn't leave the room. He'd crashed to the bed between us and said, "Talk in the morning." After that, he pretty much fell asleep. Somehow though, I'd ended up in the middle of them both. I wasn't sure how it happened, but I liked being there.

Lan pushed his erection into my butt, which told me he was awake. Shifting inch by inch, I glanced over my shoulder. He kissed my temple and then whispered against my ear, "Think it'll be best if he woke alone." I nodded. Lan added, "Gonna grab some clothes for you and me, you shower, get brekkie on. I'm gonna take the dogs for a run."

He pulled back to see if I'd agree. I glared and shook my head. His lips twitched as his brows dipped in confusion.

I rolled my eyes. "Get the clothes, talk out there."

Lan winked and gently unfolded himself from around my back and climbed out of bed. Of course I watched him. Who wouldn't watch the stunning naked man walk around the bedroom as he grabbed clothes that he kept here?

When he walked out of the room, I started my MacGyver manoeuvres to get out of bed undetected. I lifted my head first, then moved my butt back by pressing my weight onto my hand between Parker and myself. It felt similar to when I woke half on him in Queensland, only this time, he was facing me. He could open his eyes any second and find me sneaking out. Then I would feel bad if he thought I wanted to leave because of him. I mean, in a way I was, but it was so he didn't feel overwhelmed with us in there when the night before crashed into his mind.

Lifting the sheet behind me, I made sure all of my body parts were clear of his and rolled like lightning, landing on the floor in a crouch. I glanced at Parker. He still slept.

I did it.

Then I heard chuckling from the doorway. Lan stood there, holding a hand over his mouth and one on his stomach. I glared, shooed him away, and then slowly stood. The floor creaked. I froze. Lan choked on his laugh and moved away from the door down the hall. How in darnation had Lan missed that creak, but I didn't?

Thankfully, Parker hadn't opened his eyes. I tiptoed out of the room, shutting the bedroom door quietly after me. Lan waited in the hall, and I immediately smacked his stomach.

"You could have helped me," I whisper-hissed.

"That was too funny to help." He followed me into the spare bathroom. I found some track pants and a tee waiting for me on the side of the basin.

I started the shower, and while it warmed, I turned back to Lan. "How did I end up in the middle last night?"

He grinned. "I'd got up to have a shower, you must have rolled over Parker, and somehow, he ended up on the other side of the bed. One day he'll figure out you're a clingy shit in bed."

I huffed, shot him the middle finger, and turned my back on him. His arms came around me. "You know I like it." He kissed my neck. "From the looks of it, Parker didn't mind either or he wouldn't have slept like the dead."

I chuckled. "He did crash hard."

Lan snorted out a laugh. "Guess we wore him out."

"Do you think...?"

"Not sure what to think, can only hope. But that's as long as you're down with three in the relationship or even trying for one."

"I'm in love with you, Lan, but I do feel something for Parker."

He squeezed me gently. "I'm the same, babe. We just gotta wait to see how this morning goes."

Turning in his arms, I said, "Which reminds me. You are not going for a run and leaving me with him alone. How am I going to handle it? He could wake hating everything, freak out, and leave. We'll never see him again. I'm not going to know what to say or how to act. Shit, I'm already worried about it."

Lan chuckled. "Relax, you'll know what to do and say." He kissed my lips quickly. "You'll be fine." He smacked my arse and then started for the door.

"Lan Davis, do not leave me."

"You want the dogs to miss their run?"

"Yes!" I winced when it came out too loud.

Lan winked. "See you soon, won't be long." Then he was out the door. Maybe I could just hide in the bathroom until he got back.

I had braved it and stood in the kitchen waiting for the kettle to boil. I'd never had a coffee machine since I liked instant coffee, something Lan hated, but he'd put up with it, or if he really wanted a cappuccino, or whatever his machine did, he went to his place for it.

The dogs were gone with Lan, so I didn't have them to distract me. Instead, I leaned against the counter nibbling at my thumbnail while staring at the floor and willing the kettle to boil already. Then I wondered what Parker liked for breakfast. If he even ate breakfast or if he was like Lan and preferred one of those shaker shitty drinks instead.

Just in case, I went to the pantry to have a look. I had cereal, oatmeal, toast, and bagels. Surely he'd like one of those. I was pretty sure I had bacon as well. I'd check the fridge.

"Hey," was called.

I yipped, spun, and saw Parker standing in the kitchen with jeans and wet hair. He must have taken a shower or else he wouldn't have wet hair, right?

"Um, morning. Coffee? The kettle's freshly boiled. I'm about to have one." Without looking away from him, I backed into the counter, turned, and grabbed two mugs from the cupboard above. I knew I'd suck at this. I didn't know what to say. Certainly, *"Hey, last night was amazing, can we do it again?"* wouldn't work... or would it? *Nope, throw that idea out of your head, Easton.*

"Ah, Lan's gone for a run. With the dogs. He'll be back soon." I glanced over my shoulder to find him closer. I smiled. "How do you take your coffee?"

"Black."

"Sugar?" I asked.

"No."

"Milk?"

Silence. "Black," he repeated.

I closed my eyes and sighed. "Sorry, I'm an idiot. So anyway, do you want breakfast? I have toast. I mean, I can get some bread in the toaster in a couple of seconds if you're hungry." I turned with his coffee and held it out to him. He stared down at it. I stared down at it. "Don't like green mugs?"

His eyes came up to me. "I thought I was supposed to be the nervous one."

Sighing, I placed our mugs on the counter and started pacing. "I can't help it. I told Lan I wouldn't be any good with you alone, how I'd say or do something stupid... and you probably want to leave now." I threw my hands up in the air. "I mean I can understand why. Last night was wow, but a lot to take in for a first-timer." When I spun to pace back, Parker stood in my way.

His brow raised. "Last night was wow?"

Heat hit my cheeks. "Well... yes."

"I probably would have left if it had've been the two of you out here waiting to question me. But it wasn't. It's just you. Lan knows what he's doing. I like your reaction, how nervous you get. It calms me down."

"Lan knew what he was doing?"

"Yeah." He nodded. "He knows me too damn well sometimes."

"Okay then."

"You'll chill now?"

"I will." I smiled. His eyes dropped to my lips while mine went to his chest, his stomach, and those fine hairs just under his belly button that dipped down into his jeans. Flashes of last night played through my mind. My dick thickened, and wearing tracksuit pants wouldn't hide anything. I cleared my throat and grabbed his mug again. I practically forced it into his hands and turned away from him, heading for the pantry. "So, um, toast? I also have a few cereals, even oatmeal, and, ah, Lan keeps those shakes he likes in the morning if you prefer one of those."

He didn't answer.

"Are you even hungry? Some people don't even eat breakfast, but it's important—"

Hands landed on my waist. I jumped like my cock did. Parker's breath washed over the side of my face when he asked, "Why are you nervous again?"

My breath caught in my throat, and I laughed shakily. "Uh, I'm not. I was just thinking—"

"Easton," he clipped.

I groaned, frustrated. "Because you're half-naked in my kitchen."

He chuckled. "You serious? My body is makin' you nervous?"

Clearing my throat, I nodded. "I-it's distracting and, ah, yeah."

"And, ah, what?"

Closing my eyes, I dropped my head and shook it. "Parker." I said his name in a way that sounded like a plea for him to leave it, but having him close, and how his hands ran up and down my waist slowly, gently, sensually had made my reaction worse. I now sported full wood.

"East," he said with his rough tone.

He wanted to know the problem and wouldn't leave it alone. Then I'd show him. Reaching up, I took his hand and pulled it down, pressing it against my stiff cock. "You half-naked is a problem because last night is very fresh in my mind." I hissed when his hand tightened around it.

"I see," he said, and it sounded like his voice held humour. I glanced over my shoulder to see his lips were fighting not to smile. "You always have this problem with half-naked men?"

I glared. "No, you prick, just Lan, and it seems you apparently."

His hand snuck under my pants. I stopped glaring and gasped. His hand wound around my dick, and he pulled up and down. "This help?" he asked, his voice light.

"Y-yes." I nodded. It did, but I was about to blow my load because it was Parker.

Parker touched me like he didn't care I was a guy. He wanted to touch me. *He* had been the one to slide his hand under my pants for my dick.

He wanted this.

He liked it.

Liked me.

"You like touching me?" I asked.

His gaze met mine, even as he kept tugging me. "I fuckin' do." His lips slammed down on mine. I shifted around and wrapped my arms around him, one at his shoulders, the other at his waist.

The kiss was wet, heavy, and delicious. I moaned into his mouth, pulled back to suck in some air. "Shit, you're going to make me come."

He smirked, and my stomach twirled from seeing it. His lips touched mine once more before he said, "That's the point of it."

I put my hand over his to stop him. I sighed. "I want to. I so really, *really* want to. But we need to talk first."

What I expected from Parker was anger or annoyance; instead, he chuckled. "Worried I'd be using you for a quick tug?"

"No, that's not—"

"Chill, I know. Seems I couldn't resist messin' with you, and I hadn't expected it to lead here when I started." He bit the edge of my ear. "Besides, I heard waiting makes it so much better."

I gulped and nodded. "However, it could also cause me to lose myself very quickly."

Parker laughed again. "You might have to sit back and watch for awhile then."

"Watch who?" came from behind us.

I jumped in surprise. Parker didn't. He gave my cock one last tug, then lifted his hand out of my pants. He turned, and I stepped up beside Parker, grinning over at Lan. Then my heart stalled because he was topless and sweaty. Out the corner of my eyes, I saw a tinge of red coating Parker's cheeks. My eyes widened for a second before I acted as if I hadn't noticed the colour or the way Parker looked over Lan's body.

"You gonna have a shower before we talk?" Parker asked, ignoring Lan's question.

He studied Parker, then glanced at me and raised his brow in question. I just kept on grinning.

"Yeah, sure. Be back."

CHAPTER THIRTY-SEVEN

PARKER

I couldn't believe I'd crashed and slept so goddamn hard. It might have been because I'd come twice the night before and did it so fiercely it took all my energy with it. There was even the possibility it had something to do with the men I'd fallen asleep with.

Whatever it was, I'd needed it.

Shit, I'd also woke with a smile. I'd never done that. Not since before I'd lost my brother.

Although I felt great, I'd still been shit-scared to head down into the kitchen after my shower, but Lan knew me too well. Knew I'd freak in some way, would think of running straight for the front door. I had, until I noticed Easton alone in the kitchen. Then he started rambling, wouldn't look me in the eye, only my body, and I couldn't help but like the fact I had some type of power over him. Power that caused him to blunder around all shy and nervous.

It was fucking cute *and* hot.

Calmed me right down.

So yeah, Lan knew what he was doing. If it had've been the both of them straight up and they'd bombarded me with questions, I would have got my back up.

Even when I bloody loved what happened the night before. Although, before I'd gone into their room, my gut had been churning and I'd been sweating up a storm in fear to take that leap when I heard some moaning happening. At first, I wasn't going to go in there, instead just listen to them, maybe jerk off to what I could hear, but it got the best of me. I'd wanted to see.

Then, fuck me, there was no way I expected what happened to happen.

If it hadn't been for Easton manoeuvring my body, I would have missed the chance to be inside Lan.

Christ. I'd been *inside* Lan.

My friend.

My co-worker.

Lan Davis.

I'd come inside of him. In his tight, hot, slippery hole. Come inside him after Easton had too. Jesus, just thinking it made me hard and my gut twist in the best fucking way. I wanted it again. Wanted both of them again.

I'd surprised myself when I'd put my hand down Easton's pants before, but he'd been looking at me like he wanted a taste, and I wanted him too, but I knew he wouldn't make a move because he'd been worried I'd freak. It was still in me to do it, to turn and run out of the room... but I couldn't. No, I wouldn't let myself, which was why I was damn grateful Lan had planned that morning.

"I'm going to make another coffee," Easton said after Lan walked out of the kitchen. I nodded and made my way over to the kitchen table to sit.

Easton fluttered around the kitchen and I noticed he still had a semi-hard cock, one I wouldn't mind seeing. Out in the open, nothing on him. Naked. I wanted to see East naked sitting on the table where I sat, right in front of me, so I could study his body, his cock, and maybe even see if I'd like to suck it.

My dick throbbed at the thought.

Everything was still so goddamn new to me, but I definitely

found myself interested in wanting to try all different things with the both of them. Fuck, I could even imagine as I sucked Easton off, Lan storming over to take control of the situation. I wasn't sure I'd give myself over to the complete loss of control, but I'd like to see if I did in the heat of the moment.

A mug was set in front of me. I blinked out of my daze to see a grinning-like-a-maniac Easton sitting in the chair next to mine, facing me. "What are you thinking?"

I dipped my brows. "Why?"

He shrugged, but his eyes danced. "For a moment you had a dreamy look on your face. Made me wonder what was on your mind."

"You," I said.

His eyes widened. He hadn't expected me to answer truthfully.

"Also Lan."

"Really?" he asked, taking a sip of his coffee.

I dragged mine close, held it between my two hands and nodded.

"What about Lan and me exactly?"

Smirking, I shrugged.

He frowned and then glared. "Not fair."

I chuckled.

Fucking hell, I hadn't felt so light in my head and chest in a damned long time.

Was it them?

Had they done this to me?

It was a good guess to say it was, and I wanted to keep this feeling for a very fucking long time. But what would people think?

Shit, I shouldn't even care because it wasn't anyone's business. Besides, it wouldn't be like we'd flaunt it down the street. It could be just our business, and if our friends didn't like it, they could go and fuck themselves.

Hang the fuck on... I was already thinking of being with them? After one night, I'd concluded I wanted to be with them? Forever?

It was a bloody long time. I could maybe want rug rats in the end. Fuck, I was overthinking yet again. I had to stop, go back to feeling like I had only moments before.

I wanted to stay that way and give my middle finger to all the other worries.

First, I had to see how this talk went. Hell, it could even be they didn't want me for anything but the previous night.

East and I turned towards the entrance of the hallway and Lan stepped through in bare feet, jeans, and a tee.

"Your shake's on the counter," Easton called.

"Thanks, babe," Lan replied.

Like normal. This was their normal for a morning. Did it mean I was intruding on them?

"Did you make Parker one?" Lan asked as he walked to the table and stopped on the other side, glancing down at Easton. My heart tumbled.

I caught Easton screwing up his face. Then he faced me. "You *do* drink those as well?"

My lips twitched, and once again, I felt at ease. "Yeah."

Easton groaned. He shouldn't have; it reminded me of last night, and my cock throbbed like it hadn't come in ages. Easton pointed at me. "Can I sway you into a normal breakfast? Lan said he wouldn't budge."

I snorted. "Lan's particular with his routine. I like to switch it up a bit. So yeah, East, one morning I'll have breakfast with you."

Had I said too much?

I made it sound like I wanted there to be more mornings with the three of us.

Fucking hell, had I screwed up?

Then I looked to both of them.

They stared at me with warmth. Easton whispered, "Okay." He smiled sweetly before he sipped his coffee again. I let out a slow, relieved breath, pretending I was blowing on my coffee and then took a gulp of it, watching them both over the rim. They glanced at each other. Lan winked at Easton, who smiled in return.

Christ, I can easily watch them all day.

That was weird to think and made me straighten at the realisation of the passing thought.

Lan cleared his throat. I looked from the table to him. He said, "Let's get something outta the way first." I nodded. "You've quit."

"Yeah," I replied.

He rolled his shake between his two hands on the table. "Why? Better yet, why in the fuck didn't you tell me about the offer Vi's giving?"

"Lan," Easton said gently.

I shook my head at him. I'd been expecting this, just didn't realise it'd be up first. Then again, it probably would have been the same with me if he'd quit and didn't tell me. I'd have been pissed like he was.

Leaning back in the seat, I crossed an arm over my gut and held my coffee with the other. "Vi talked to you?"

"Yeah. I know you've been... I don't even know, but you still could have talked to me. We were close, Parker. Been through a lot and after—"

"Lan," Easton snapped. "Calm down, and maybe Parker can explain."

Lan glared at Easton who in return gave Lan an apologetic smile.

"It's all good," I told East. "I know I fucked up, but my head's been a mess."

"Why?" Lan clipped.

I rose my brows. "You want to know that before the other stuff now?"

He rolled his eyes. "Don't be a smartarse." His eyes lightened. "I want to know it all because you've goddamn worried us. I just had to voice that shit now."

Sighing, I straightened and put the mug on the table. I crossed both arms over my chest. My leg bounced up and down. I hated this talking shit, but I knew I had to give them answers if we were to get anywhere, because it'd been me confusing and pissing them off with how I'd acted. I was just bloody nervous to say the shit I had to.

Easton's hand slid towards me; it was what brought my head up from the table. He smiled. "You don't have to—"

I shook my head again. Fuck, it was sweet of him to want to protect me, console me, but I had to tell them. "It's good. I'm good." Easton nodded and sat back in his seat, cupping his mug with both hands in front of himself. "Hell, I don't get nervous, but over this shit, I am." I swiped a hand over my face and then tucked my hair behind my ears. I scooted my chair back from the table and leaned forward, elbows to my knees, hands clasped together down in front of me. I stared at them because I couldn't look at Lan or Easton. "That kiss Lan landed on me started everythin'. Fuck, man. I never thought you went that way, and even if I had've known, I wouldn't have cared. But that kiss, it's like it did somethin' to me, and then I couldn't stop thinkin' about it. It was strange, messed up." I glanced up with wide eyes. "Not that you two—"

Lan waved his hand. He smirked. "We get it. Go on."

I nodded and glanced down again. "Never thought of a guy before. Then there was Easton. He got me lookin' at him, thinkin' what made him special for you to be with." I snorted. "Let's just say I had so much runnin' around in my head I didn't know what to think or if it was right. But when I thought Easton was shot, it gutted me." Lifting my head, I looked to Easton. He stared back. "You were right. I kissed you out of relief, but I didn't stay in your bed that night just because I wanted to sleep and stop you from pacing. I was worried about you. After realising that, I thought how in the fuck could my head and body change what I'd always known to something else. I like fuckin' women. I still do. Actually did it just a few nights ago because I'd been scared, worried my head was just messin' with me, and I actually wouldn't like anythin' with a guy. But even as I screwed her, I couldn't get you two off my mind. I had to see…. It's why I came here last night."

"What did you find out?" Lan asked with a frown on his lips, maybe at the confession of being with a woman a few days ago. I didn't know, but I kind of liked to think it was over that. Over him being jealous.

"I liked it," I said roughly.

He tried to keep a straight face, but a grin twisted his lips up. "Yeah?"

"Yeah." I nodded. "Not sure what this means, where I go from here, but I had to be honest with you both and with myself." I went to grab my mug again but forgot it was empty. Easton noticed and got up to boil the kettle again. "You need a coffee machine," I suggested.

Easton froze when Lan started chuckling. Lan grinned over at me. "That's what I've been telling him. Saves boiling it all the damn time."

Easton grumbled under his breath, hit the button, and stood at the counter waiting for it. "I prefer the taste of instant coffee." He paused, and we heard the click of the kettle. "Look, didn't take too long to boil now, did it?"

I liked this. The ease of it all. The light banter. Them.

I liked them both.

Fuck me. I goddamn liked two men at the same time.

If anyone had said I would months ago, I could have shot them in the head for being too fucking stupid, but there it was. There *I* was sitting at the table with two men I'd tasted and without a doubt, I wanted to taste again and again.

Go figure.

CHAPTER THIRTY-EIGHT

LAN

I watched Parker looking at Easton as he complained about something to do with the coffee machines. He smirked, but it was his eyes that held most of my attention. Besides his naked chest, which was damn distracting. Still, his eyes fascinated me the most as I hadn't seen them so bright before. Maybe it also had to do with how he hadn't clenched his jaw or fisted his hands in annoyance or anger since we started talking. Even when I got pissed at him over quitting and not talking to me about shit.

He seemed calmer.

It was so fucking good to see him like that.

Yeah, he had his good days when we worked together. He wasn't always broody with me, but this was more than even those good days.

It looked as if a weight had been lifted off him.

Had we done that?

If we had, I didn't know how. Hell, maybe it was the norm for him after shooting two huge loads of cum the night before. Whatever it was, I damned enjoyed seeing him this way.

I wondered if he even noticed the change in himself. Did Easton notice it?

Couldn't believe he'd stayed, though, but I still reckoned it had something to do with me not being in the house when he woke. He would have been edgy as fuck, but I'd known Easton would have eased him in the best way by acting his usual shy, nervous, and goddamn cute self.

Easton came back to the table with two mugs, Parker's and his. I swallowed the rest of my protein shake.

"Black," Easton said, handing it over. Parker nodded, leaning to grab it and I noticed Easton's eyes on Parker's chest and stomach. His brows dipped. "I'll be back." He put his coffee down and headed out of the room.

Parker glanced to me, his brows arched. I snorted. "I think you're about to be clothed."

Parker's eyes widened before he laughed. Shaking his head, he told me, "He said I was distracting."

"You are," I said.

His laughter subsided. He stared at me. "Another thing I never thought I'd like."

"What's that?"

"You likin' the way I look." He sat forward, elbows to the table. "I do like it, but what happens if Easton doesn't like you lookin' or the other way around? I won't get in the middle of what you two got going on already. I should have thought of it last night but...." He shook his head, pink tinting his cheeks. He'd been too eager to see what would happen without thinking of the consequences. Luckily, Easton and I were already cool about it.

"You don't need to stress. East and I have talked."

"Talked?" he questioned, a smirk resting on his lips.

"Yeah." I smirked back.

"We're both attracted to you," Easton said as he came into the room carrying Parker's tee from the night before. He thrust it out to Parker. "Please."

Parker chuckled, grabbed it, and slipped it over his head. He sat back with his coffee. "How can this feel...?"

"Normal? Easy?" I offered.

Parker nodded.

"From the start you and I got along. We were already good around each other. East"—I smiled at him—"creates a serene zone around him."

"Especially when he's nervous," Parker added.

I chuckled and tipped my cup his way. "Exactly. Makes a person feel calm."

Easton glared at us both. "Are you two done? I have attitude as well."

"Oh, I know. I remember the first time you got in my face," Parker said. "I like that too. Both of your attitudes." His brows came down as he shifted in his seat. Seemed he was uncomfortable telling us that, but hell, I liked it. A lot.

A phone rang. Easton's work tone. He groaned. Still, he got up and went to the counter to grab it. "Hello? Can't another team do it? Have you called Oliver? He said yes?" He closed his eyes, jaw clenched. He didn't want to leave. "Okay. Yes." Still, he'd do it. Only I knew he wouldn't be doing it for himself, but to cover whoever couldn't make the shift before his and for the people who'd be in need of a paramedic. Unfortunately, it also meant he'd be doing a double shift. He wouldn't get home until tomorrow morning.

Fuck it.

He hung up and faced us. "I've got to go in early."

"You gonna be right?"

"Yes. I've done a double shift many times." He smiled warmly. "I'll need to grab a few things before I go. Sorry to have to leave, but I know you two can get everything sorted. Besides, you both have to talk about work." He tipped the rest of his coffee in the sink. "I'll get my stuff, be back."

Easton already knew I was going to take Vi up on her offer even if Parker hadn't liked it.

"Why did you quit, Parker? You took Vi up on her offer without talkin' to me? Didn't you want to work alongside me anymore?" I asked. Before the previous night's action, I'd presumed it was to get away from me. Hoping I wouldn't hear about the offer or take the job. But after last night, I wasn't sure anymore.

Parker looked into his mug, then drank the rest before putting it on the table. He sure did know how to make a man wait for an answer, or was it because he didn't know what to say or he didn't want to hurt me from what he had to say?

Fucking Jesus. I just gave myself a headache.

He leaned into the table, picked up the salt shaker Easton always left there and started playing with it. He didn't look at me when he answered, "I quit because you've been talkin' about slowin' down, wantin' a change for a long time. I knew you'd snap up Violet's offer. I wanted to be sure, before you found out about it, I'd be in the position to follow you. Knew you'd try and talk me out of quittin' because you'd think I'd want to stay being a detective, but I wouldn't if you weren't there. I want to still be able to work with you." He shrugged. "Slowing down sounds good to me. Means we get the chance to help out the brothers more if they need it. Also, Vi's like us, follows her own rules."

Holy fuck. I was still stuck on I want to be still able to work with you.

"You chose to do it even before last night," I stated.

He nodded, then shrugged. "I'm used to havin' you in my life."

A cruel thought messed with my mind and put doubt in there. "That's not why...." Why he stopped by last night? Why he thought he could change? For me, for Easton... all because he didn't want to work with anyone else?

His scowl made an appearance. He stood, fists on the table and glowered down at me. "Do you seriously fuckin' think I would do that? Change my life, take a risk, all so I wouldn't have to work with anyone else because you know I don't work well with others in the fuckin' first place? You think because of that I would come here and mess with you two, get between you two, just for goddamn kicks to make sure you'd still work with me?"

"It crossed my mind briefly," I admitted.

"Fuck you, Lan. You should know me better." His fist pounded on the table. He straightened, crossed his arms over his chest and breathed hard through his nose. His temper was back in full force, and it'd been my damn fault it made an appearance.

"Everything okay out here?" Easton asked, walking over to stop beside my chair in his full uniform. He glanced from Parker, who glared at the kitchen, down to me and raised his brows.

Parker unclenched his jaw and snarled, "Lan thinks me being here was a play to keep workin' with him. That I fuckin' used you both."

"I didn't—"

Easton's hand landed on my shoulder and squeezed. He then moved over to Parker, stood at his side and forced him, with his hand on Parker's crossed arms, to turn his way. Parker glared down at him.

Easton scowled back up at him. "Lan can be a fool sometimes." I snorted. "But he knows when to apologise when he's wrong, and he's wrong in this instance. Aren't you?" Easton looked over at me.

"Yeah. Shit, yes," I said, standing also.

"It would have been a passing thought because we never expected for last night to happen. Now don't be a dick and get all huffy over it. I have to go to work, and I want things to stay good between you two or I'll kick both your arses for cracking it over shit that can be sorted by talking through it."

I waited. Parker remained staring down at Easton while Easton stared back. Then Parker lifted his head to look at me. "Does his scoldin' make you want to laugh as well?"

Easton growled in the back of his throat. My lips twitched. "Most of the time."

"Well, screw the two of you," Easton clipped, and stomped off into the kitchen to grab some snacks.

"Well, it's either laugh or...," Parker said with a smirk.

Easton stopped and faced him, arms crossed. "Or?" he bit out.

Parker smiled. "Guess you'll find out one day."

If I had to guess, Parker was thinking either about kissing or fucking Easton. I'd felt that a lot around Easton, even when he was getting in my face about something.

"Okay," Easton whispered. He picked up his bag and made his way over to me. I ducked my head to gain access to his lips. I kissed him hard and wet. It was long enough to get my dick pumping of blood. Fuck, he could kiss, so could Parker for that matter.

Easton gave a last peck, pulled back, and stared up at me. "I have to go."

I smiled. "So go."

His grumble made me chuckle. I grabbed his arse cheek, squeezed, and told him, "More of that when you come home tomorrow morning."

"The dogs—"

"I've got them. You know that."

He nodded and nipped at my lips again. "All right," he said. He stepped back and slowly glanced to Parker. He'd be wondering what the situation was for goodbyes with him. Would it be like with me or something else?

I fought my lips twitching as Easton waved his hand at Parker. "Guess, I'll see you, ah, I don't know." He shrugged and then stuck his hand out Parker's way. I snorted when Parker looked angrily down at it then up at Easton, who was blushing. "Thanks—" He gasped. "I don't mean thanks for last night, just that... shit, I don't know why I said thanks. I don't know what to do or say. I didn't even think I'd be the one leaving early so—" He let out a sound when Parker took Easton's hand he still held out and used it to drag him forward. Their chests collided, and Parker leaned in and claimed Easton's lips. I heard Easton sigh and Parker then growled into his mouth.

Fuck me, it was an amazing sight.

Parker pulled back from a dazed Easton. "Like your attitude, but like you nervous more. That's how, in this home, we'll all say goodbye to one another." Then Parker blanched, dropped his arms and looked over at me. "Unless—"

My hand came up. My chest expanded. He wanted this. Us. That was what counted. "Don't even. Before East goes, we'll get it out. I want both of you. See how it goes at least. Are you both willing to try? That's all I'm asking for... is to try."

Easton nodded, smiling. "I want to try. As long as you both don't piss me off."

I laughed. "No fun in that." I lifted my gaze to Parker. "You?"

"I'm for trying."

Easton's smile grew. "Okay. Good, ah, yay." He rolled his eyes. "I didn't mean that yay. Shit, ignore I did that, I have to get to work." With a quick peck to Parker's lips and then to mine, he walked out of the house with a new spring in his step.

He was happy.

Hell, I felt happy, and from the way Parker's eyes were back to shining, he did too.

We'd just have to see how well the three of us would go.

"So," I started after Easton had left. We both still stood at the table. "Wanna sort out this new change if we're both willing to take Vi up on her offer?"

He grinned, nodded, and then walked towards the cupboards, calling, "As long as I can have one of your protein shakes."

"Help yourself."

He stopped, turned, and asked, "How in the fuck is it not weird between us after last night?"

Surprised by the question, I laughed. "I don't know, but I'm glad it's not."

"Yeah." He nodded, his eyes drifting away in thought. Then he straightened and went to the pantry, adding, "I'm thankful for it too. Means things won't be weird after it happens again."

Knock me the fuck over with a feather.

CHAPTER THIRTY-NINE

LAN

*P*arker and I talked out the PI job and then rang Vi to confirm more shit about it. Once we told her I was also on board, she got excited and told us she'd just found the perfect place to set up the second business. She was going to get Warden to send us the details so we could take a look, along with the information we needed to get our own PI licenses. Though Parker had already looked into it. It would take at least between four to six months to gain our certificates; we would have to do forty hours of class time with the rest online.

A change seemed scary, but it wouldn't be too big of a change already. Really, it'd be for the better and make our lives a little safer. I was just damn happy I'd be making such a big leap with a person I trusted without question to have my back.

After the call, we would check out the place, get a feel for it, and then head to the compound to tell Dodge about the change. I also had to call Sarge to tell him I'd be giving my four weeks' notice. Which meant I might have to go back to work for a couple of weeks before my long service leave ended. He'd be pissed, but I knew that once we told him our next move, he'd support us. The guy was solid.

The best part about the morning was that Parker and I were normal around each other. We were back to our old selves, despite him having his dick in my arse.

Fuck. Cue my damn boner.

"The place looks good," Parker said from the driver seat of his car. He went on to say something about perimeters. I nodded, my other head doing the thinking for me.

Right, that was what we were doing, examining our new office not thinking about how good it was to have Parker fucking me after Easton had finished, or how I goddamn loved watching Parker wank over watching Easton fuck me.

Christ, I'd never get over the look of lust in his eyes as his cock slid in and out of me, nor how he'd watched me come over my gut, keeping his eyes between us as he entered and exited me.

"Lan?"

I nodded. "Sounds good." What would be better was to know how soon Easton, Parker, and I could get naked again. Maybe the next time could lead to Parker sucking either one of us off. Hell, I'd love to see that. His lips wrapped around either of our dicks. I wasn't fussy over who, because one way or another, I knew I'd get off.

"Lan!" Parker barked.

My whole body jumped and I glanced around at him. "What?" I snapped, pissed he'd dragged me away from a good thought and, of course, my eyes zoomed in on his lips.

"Now I know where your head's at." He smirked.

I pulled my eyes up to meet his amused ones. "Huh?"

"What were your thoughts?" he asked, his chin tipping up towards the building.

"Yeah, good. We'll need cameras outside though."

Parker snorted. "Sure," he deadpanned.

"What?"

"I said that already. Jesus, man, get your head outta the gutter and into the now."

I glared and started to lie, "I wasn't—"

"Don't even fuckin' try it." He chuckled.

"Shit, okay." I moved my gaze back to the building and pushed my filthy, thrilling thoughts aside and got back to business. "We'll get Dodge, if Warden can't make it here, to put in the security system. It's good the place next to it is just storage units and takes up a lot of space. Means we could tap into their camera feed for extra protection. We'd just have to keep an eye on the shops on the other side since they're all selling," I said while wondering why the three shops on the other side of the building Vi was looking at were for sale when the area was a good one. Should even be a popular one. I'd have to look into it.

"Something we could look into before we give Vi the go-ahead on the place. Though, the properties could be something Hawks'll want to invest in later."

I nodded. "Could be. We'll bring it up with Dodge and then check out the real estate agent."

At the compound, hanging in the common room with Dodge, Knife, Beast, and Vicious, the place was pretty quiet.

"I'll get Gamer onto the properties. Texas is currently settin' his goals towards tattooing. He'll need a place to set up eventually, and I like the area already."

"Plus, Nary and Josie are gonna set up a place soon for abused women to get some help at. If it's near a PI place and has brothers close by, it'd be better," Vicious suggested. "How many shops you say were up for sale?"

"Three," Parker told him.

"If it works out, we could look at connectin' two of the buildings. It'd help if Nary and Josie get women with families needin' someplace to stay until they find them other places."

"Until we fuck over the dicks who messed with them in the first place," Dodge muttered.

Vicious smirked, and it wasn't a nice one. "Or that."

Knife announced, "Just sent Gamer an email to get onto it."

Beast snorted. He grinned as his hands moved around and signed, *That's if he'll be alive long enough.*

"What's that about?" Parker asked. He leaned into the bar beside me.

"Wildcat told Talon that Gamer tried to get in with Nancy. It didn't go down well with Talon. Even though Rich has been gone three years, he thought highly of the guy and doesn't like to think of Nance as dateable," Dodge said. "Gamer's layin' low."

"Even though Talon's in Ballarat?" I asked.

Beast chuckled and nodded, signing, *However, I caught the guy texting Nancy.*

I snorted. "Did she respond?" My hand shot up. "Wait, don't tell me. I don't want to know what Nancy gets up to. She's been like a mother figure to a lot of us."

Parker grinned. "So you don't want to know if she's bonin' someone my age?"

I glowered at him, then put my hand on his shoulder ready to warn him I didn't want to hear another word when he froze under my hand. Panic drowned out the amusement, and he shrugged off my hold.

He faked a laugh. "Guess Gamer is up for some trouble if he's still reaching out to Nancy."

"I think it's great for Nancy," Knife said. They went on to talk about other shit, but I couldn't help notice Parker had gone silent. A scowl marred his features. The way he'd acted and now how he was lost in his thoughts told me he wasn't ready for people to know about the change between us. I got it. I really did. I understood it more than anyone, but it didn't mean it didn't hurt.

Hell, it wasn't like I was holding his hand, groping him or any other type of public display of affection. Fuck me, we weren't even at the level in private where I'd think I could show him I cared by kissing him or reaching out to touch him, or fucking hug him. So of course I knew he wouldn't be down for it in public.

How-fucking-ever, I only placed my hand on his shoulder.

One simple touch and he reacted like I had rabies.

Shit, now he was probably thinking about getting out of the whole situation between the three of us. I'd gone and fucked it all up without even knowing a hand to the shoulder could do it.

Jesus bloody Christ.

My gut spun before it dropped to my feet.

How was I supposed to know one touch could cause him to freak?

"Parker," Knife called, only it grabbed my attention too.

"Yeah?" he asked.

"You good, brother?"

"Fine." He straightened. "Just gotta get someplace." He turned to me without even looking at me. "You good to get home?"

Hurt slashed across my chest.

"I'll be good. Sure Beast'll give me a lift."

Beast nodded.

"Good, later guys." He gave a chin lift before walking out of the common room.

It was after he'd gone, Dodge said, "Thought he'd been in a better mood today, guess I was wrong."

I'd been wrong too, apparently.

Maybe this with Parker, me, and Easton wouldn't work out after all.

After Beast dropped me off, I'd headed into Easton's to feed the dogs and sat on the back porch drinking a beer while I threw multiple toys around for the crazier dogs. The three calm, lazier ones sat on the porch with me watching the others with a bored expression.

I glanced down to Nero, sure he was glaring at the others, thinking they were nuts for being excited over toys. Nero was a favourite of mine, had been ever since he came barrelling into my room that first day and scared the fuckers away. I was sure he kind of knew it too. He lifted his head to stare up at me. As if he sensed my mood wasn't the best, he got to his feet and came over, resting his head on my thigh.

A smile tugged up my mouth, even though I didn't feel like it, and I patted his head. Parker hadn't come back to the compound. I'd waited like a pathetic idiot with tension radiating out of me, and a lot of the brothers gave me a wide berth or strange looks as I helped them in the garage so it didn't look like I was waiting.

I was at a loss.

I didn't know what to fucking think or do about Parker Wilding. I felt like shit for putting him in that situation, then angry because it wasn't really a situation in the goddamn first place.

Fuck it, I'd stick with anger.

A hand on the damned shoulder was nothing. Fucking hell, no one would have got the information he'd been screwing me the previous night from one single hand on his shoulder.

Grumbling, I gulped back the rest of the beer. I wanted another and then another. Maybe a drunk brain could figure out what went wrong with Parker or I could just forget about it altogether.

However, the kitchen was too far away and Nero was enjoying the attention I gave him. Until he lifted and turned his head with a snarl pulling back his upper lip.

Parker stepped around the side of the house. Nero stopped growling and settled to the floor beside me with a grunt.

Christ, now I wished I had a full beer, or ten, to drink.

I shifted my gaze away from his approach and out onto the land. Did I honestly have a right to be shitty? This was all new to him. I'd freaked out with Easton, and that led me to lose him for ten fucking years.

"It's fine," I offered before standing and walking towards the glass door. "I get it. You freaked, wondering if they knew we screwed, but I can tell you they can't read it over an innocent touch." Goddamn it. "Fuck, that sounded judgy. I didn't mean it." I stood at the glass door, my hand on the handle to pull it open. I could see his reflection, where he stood at the bottom of the steps looking up at me with his jaw clenching. "It's all good." I nodded. "Maybe we can catch up tomorrow?" I didn't wait for an answer. I slid the door across and then pulled it shut after I'd stepped in. I made a beeline for the fridge to grab those ten beers.

I felt the need to apologise to Easton again for what I did those years ago.

Fuck, I'd been a cunt. I wanted to punch myself for it once more. What I didn't want was to talk to Parker about any of it because I just wasn't in the mood, and I didn't want to hear he'd made a mistake.

But then I heard the door sliding open and shut. I grabbed a beer and unscrewed it before flicking the top in the sink. I turned, leaned against the counter, and stared at Parker while taking a pull from the bottle. He stood on the other side of the counter, his hands landing on the top of it, and then he lifted one to brush back his hair.

"Man, I said I understand, and I do. I reacted worse with East those years ago, and he didn't even do anything but show at my place unannounced when I had friends over. I knew I was bi, but I hadn't told anyone. No one knew until East came back into my life." I sighed, glanced out the kitchen window and then back to him. "What I'm gettin' at is that I know why you reacted that way. It's all good, but it's gettin' late, and I'm about to hit the bed. You'd better head off."

There was his out. He could take it or not. I didn't know what he'd pick, and I'd like to say I didn't care, but I fucking did.

CHAPTER FORTY

PARKER

*M*y heart beat so fast it felt as if it wanted to crawl up my throat and out of my body. I'd fucked up and knew I had, yet I'd walked out of the compound like a fucking coward. I was a dick. An idiot.

It was great to hear Lan understood. I *had* freaked over him touching me, wondering if they'd notice how it felt, like it was more than just a normal touch because I'd been with him the night before.

It was goddamn foolish to think it in the first place, but my head liked to mess with me.

As soon as I'd got outside, I wanted to turn myself around and go back in. I didn't because it would have made me look like an even bigger idiot. I wasn't ready for any type of display of affection from Lan or Easton in front of people. Fuck, I was still figuring myself out. Us out. If we'd all work. There'd be a big chance they'd get sick of me and then get rid of me.

I'd never had a relationship. I didn't have a fucking clue what it involved to be in one. But I still wanted to try.

The thought of walking away from them both clogged my throat and chest.

I had to see where it would go.

I deserved something good in life, right?

At least I thought I did.

I wanted to try for something good. Lan and Easton made me want to try. I just had to get past the other issues that'd come and go with being with two guys.

When I'd left the compound, I'd driven to my brother's grave, searching for answers. I didn't get any, but I did figure out walking away from them didn't sit well inside me.

I tried picturing just being around them as I'd been with Lan before anything happened, and I didn't like what I saw. I wanted to reach out to them, run a hand over them, even kiss them if I wanted to. But for now, it had to be in private. We had to give this, us, a chance before anyone else knew. We had to see if it'd work first.

Then maybe others could know it wasn't only Easton and Lan in the relationship, but me as well.

Only the thought of that sent my heart fucking spinning in my chest.

Why did it freak me?

I knew the people around me would accept it. Hell, they were fine with Josie, Pick, and Billy. So what if it was different for me because it was two guys instead.

Shit. This leap scared the fuck out of me still, but I wouldn't stand down. I wouldn't walk away. I had to keep reminding myself I *was* meant, and fucking allowed, to have a good life. A happy one.

Happiness for me was Lan and Easton.

I couldn't look past them and search for anything else. My head and body had been consumed with them for a long time. No one else had captured and kept my attention like this before.

"What I'm gettin' at is that I know why you reacted that way. It's all good, but it's gettin' late, and I'm about to hit the bed. You'd better head off," Lan finished with.

He was giving me an out. Did he want me to walk out and forget everything? Didn't he know I couldn't? I just needed time to deal, time to learn, time to adjust, but I didn't want to do any of that away from them.

Shaking my head, I glanced down at the counter in front of me.

He'd expect me to walk out, run away from this. But I wouldn't.

Sucking in a deep breath, I lifted my head. "It freaked me out because when you touched me, all I could think about was being inside you. I had to walk, get away, worried they'd see me get hard." I shook my head and started around the counter, stopping to lean against the counter beside him. "I just need time to get used to it all. You gonna give me that time without gettin' pissed at me if I react in a way that could hurt you?"

His eyes flashed wide before he blanked his surprise over me not going anywhere. Instead, he said, "I wasn't hurt."

"Bullshit," I clipped. "I saw your face, the flash of hurt. I didn't mean for that to happen. It was an unexpected reaction for me as well."

He sighed. "I know."

"So?" I asked harshly.

"So what?"

I growled under my breath, faced his way and bit out, "Time, you willin' to give it?"

He dropped his head, his eyes to his feet. That action had me worried. Maybe he didn't want my hassle already. He couldn't be bothered putting up with me adjusting to something I didn't have a clue about because he already had Easton. He was already happy with one man.

He tilted his head my way and asked, "You sure you want to try with us?"

Fuck. He thought *I* wasn't sure.

He was wrong. I *was* sure about them.

Moving quickly, I stepped in front of him, and his head came up. I placed a hand to the side of his neck and one to his waist. "Yes," I clipped. "I want to try. Don't question that. I just need patience in it all. I've never done any of this stuff before."

His pulse raced under my finger at his neck. "I could do patience," he said quietly.

Jesus.

My cock throbbed, my heart lurched, and I goddamn had to have his mouth to show him I loved his answer. My hands shook with nerves, but I could do it. Smiling, I leaned in, and tested it, touched my lips to his once, twice, all while we kept each other's eyes.

Resting against him, from chest to groin, a groin I felt thicken against my already hard dick—shocking me how his body reacted to me and turned me on—I said, "If I ever fuck up, pull me up on it."

He smirked. "I will."

"You gonna kiss me now?" I asked.

"No."

"No?" I parroted and frowned. "Fine then," I said and then tightened my grip on his neck and waist before I took his mouth with mine. It wasn't gentle, and when he opened his mouth under mine, it was wet and fucking perfect as our tongues played with tasting and taunting.

When my nerves flew out the window, I ran my hand from his waist lower to his arse and forced him against me so our groins rubbed. He groaned into my mouth, and I ate it down before responding with a growl.

Christ, he made me hard, made me needy with desire.

All from a kiss.

Fuck, that wasn't true. It was from a look, a thought, and I was ready to go for him, and for Easton.

Lan pulled back and we both breathed heavily. He cursed, "Fuck."

"What?" I asked.

He laughed. "You're Parker."

I smiled. "Last time I checked, yeah."

He shook his head. "No. You're Parker." His hands tightened on my hips. "You're the man I've been checking out secretly for years.

Now you're in my arms." His smile widened. "I just had my tongue in your mouth."

I snorted, leaned in, and whispered in his ear, "I also had my dick in your arse last night, and I liked it. I liked kissin' you while Easton sucked me off. I liked watching you fuck Easton and then him fuckin' you."

He shuddered and groaned low. "You're driving me fuckin' crazy."

I straightened, grinning, and enjoying the fact I drove him crazy with lust in the first place. It gave me confidence. "Does that mean we can fool around in bed before we crash?"

Lan's eyes rounded, his mouth dropped open, and I started laughing.

Only it stopped when Lan pushed me back. I moved and watched him walk to the back door and lock it. He went into the living room and checked the front door, which I already knew was locked because I'd tried it when I'd first arrived. Then he stalked back to me, took my hand, and dragged me out of the room. Chuckling, I said, "I'm takin' that as a yes." Then my gut burst to life in nerves and excitement.

Lan's reply was a grunt, making me smile.

"Do you think Easton will mind?" I queried when we entered the bedroom.

Lan pulled his phone out and pressed something. He put it on speakerphone, and the ring filled the space. I yanked my hand out of his, and yelled, "What the fuck? You can't ring him at work." I dove at him, trying to grab it. He dodged, but I managed to knock him to the bed. He landed on his back, and I slid up his body, still trying to wrestle it from his hands.

"Fuck, your shoulder," I barked and started to gentle my movements.

He mumbled. "It's good, nothing but a twinge every now and then."

"Good," I stated, and reworked my struggle to grab the phone, all while having a smile on my mouth and a lightness in my chest.

"Hey, hello? Sorry, I left my phone in the ride... Lan?"

I shoved Lan's head into the bed so he didn't say shit. He still managed a muffled laugh. When his elbow connected to my ribs, I cursed, dropped sideways and lost my grip on the back of his head.

"Hey, babe," Lan called, his voice holding humour.

"What's going on?" Easton asked suspiciously.

I smacked Lan in the back of the head. He cried, "Ow, fucker, that hurt."

"It was supposed to," I clipped.

"Parker?" Easton called.

"East, where's Ollie?" Lan asked.

"Still inside the diner. He went to the bathroom, why?"

"Nothin'," I called and went for the phone again. Lan must have been expecting it because somehow, he was up, diving at me and then straddling my waist. He held the phone up high and used his other to stop me from trying for it.

"We have a question," Lan said.

"No, we don't," I yelled.

We heard Easton chuckle. "What's the question?"

"Nothin'," I shouted and went for a different distraction tactic, slipping my hands under his tee. His heated eyes dropped down to me.

He smirked. "That ain't gonna work, but keep trying." I glared, and he chuckled. "East, the question is, do you mind if Parker and I fool around?"

Shock stilled my hands on his sides. He just blurted that shit out like it was a natural thing to say, to ask. Easton was Lan's first man, and he was asking him if he minded Lan and I fooling around without him.

"Fool around how?" Easton queried, his voice took on a huskier tone.

Holy crap, was he getting turned on?

Lan rocked against me, and I realised my growing dick was positioned right under his arse. He grinned when I grew harder and rocked against me once more.

"You know, a kiss, a suck and then see where it leads."

"This is not fair," Easton complained.

"See," I mouthed at Lan.

He shook his head. "What's not fair, babe?"

"Being stuck working while I can't watch you two."

Wait... what? Easton would be okay with this?

Lan raised his brows at me. "How about Park and I get each other off with our hands and mouths and save the fuckin' until you get home."

My body fucking hummed at hands, at mouths, and then at Easton home and fucking. Christ, I pressed my dick up. Lan's molten eyes burned into mine.

Easton groaned. "Yes, hell yes— shit, Oliver, warn a guy next time."

We heard Oliver laugh. "You would have seen me if you weren't staring off into space. Who you talking to, Easton?" Oliver laughed again, then some more.

"What?" Easton demanded roughly.

"It has to be Lan on the phone or else you wouldn't be springing a boner at work."

"Shut the fuck up!" Easton yelled, and then he added, "I have to go, see you bo... ah, bright and early in the morning." He caught himself from saying see us both.

"Or maybe we should talk about this boner you've got going on?" Lan teased. I snorted.

"Bye," Easton shouted.

Lan hung up the phone, dropped it to the bed, and then we both laughed. "Oliver will give him a heap of shit for that," Lan said and went to roll off me, but I tightened my hold on his waist and shook my head.

"He doesn't mind?" I asked to be sure.

Lan put a hand at each side of my head and looked down at me. "No. I knew he'd be cool with it because if it were the other way around, I'd be fine with it too. Would you?"

Hell, would I?

If I wasn't around and they made each other come without me seeing… I wasn't sure. I'd want to be there for each one, but then that'd be selfish of me because I'd want time one on one with each of them also.

Like now.

I was enjoying it was just Lan. Seeing him in his flirty, fun way with just me was good.

"I think I'd be all right," I told him.

He smirked. "We can all learn to share together. Something new for all of us." He dipped down, his face not far from mine. "I'm fucking lovin' seeing you on the bed under me, your hair everywhere… just like I'd imagined." He touched his mouth to mine. Lan's words had my cock pounding, wanting a release. Lan pulled back, and asked, "You cool? With me? *Just* me?"

He was worried him on his own wouldn't get the same reaction as both of them. Fucking idiot.

I removed my hands from under his tee, to the end of it, and started to pull it up. He smiled before he lifted his hands, and the tee came all the way off. I threw it to the floor. My eyes roamed over his body, loving the sight of him. I rested my hands against his shoulders, then ran them down his arms and back up. Lan watched me as my hands slid to his chest, my fingers tracing his nipples. He rocked down on me, sucking in a sharp breath. Grinning, I glided my fingers lower to his belt.

Glancing up at him, I undid his belt, his button, and the zipper. I said, "Yeah, I'm totally fine with *just* you."

"Fuck," Lan clipped when I pulled his cock free and ran my hand up and down it. He shook his head, watching my hand. "Never thought I'd see this. You touching me, wanting to touch me like this."

I chuckled. "Guess you and East worked your magic on me." For a second, I paused as I took that in. It *was* like they'd worked their magic on me because there I was, with Lan, touching him and knowing I wanted more with him, his lips, his body, his moans. I wanted it all, and I wasn't scared from it.

He grinned. "Sorry it fucked with you, but I'll forever be grateful for kissing you. No, for gettin' messed up by Miller in the first place or else none of this would have happened."

He gasped when I tightened my grip around him. I glared and frowned up at him. "Don't be thankful for that motherfucker."

Lan chuckled. "I'll see what I can do."

I nodded. My glare drifted away when I looked down and watched as I jerked Lan off. Couldn't believe I was getting off by touching another man's cock.

I had another man's dick in my hand, and it was like it was normal. I goddamn loved the feel of his smooth skin, the veins, the look... all of it in my hand.

What would I be like if I sucked it?

What would Lan be like?

I wanted to know. "Can I suck you?" I asked without looking at him, then added, "Try at least?" I lost my grip on Lan as he climbed off me.

My brows dipped in confusion, but then he grabbed my arm, hauled me up and ordered roughly, "Get undressed. Now." He then went about taking off his jeans and boxers. When he saw I hadn't moved, he growled impatiently and tugged my tee up and off. He worked my jeans until they were undone and down my legs, my dick springing free. "Kick them off," he clipped.

I did, with an amused smile on my face. He liked the idea of me giving him my first try at head with a guy.

He gently backed me to the bed again. "On your back," he demanded.

I did, wondering how he wanted this to happen.

He stood at the edge, his dick in hand, stroking himself while eyeing me all over. "Fuckin' gorgeous."

"Yeah?" I asked. He'd told me he liked to look at me, but it still surprised me how I turned him on. Guessed he'd feel the same since he did that to me too.

"Christ, yes." He nodded.

I lay flat, gripped my dick and dragged it up and down. "So are you. Gorgeous."

"Goddamn," he bit out. He walked around the bed and climbed on.

"What…?" I shut up when I realised what he was doing. He lay facing me, only his face was at level with my dick when I rolled his way, and I had an eyeful of his junk.

Christ, I was about to suck my first dick. I licked my lips, wanting to please him. My body jolted when he took hold of my cock and licked along the tip.

"You taste good," he said, and then took me all the way in, deep, until the tip of my dick touched the back of his throat. I groaned.

I wanted to pleasure him like he was me. He sucked me hard and fast, and I pushed my leg back a little for more room. Reaching out, I grabbed his dick and pulled it down to my mouth. Slowly, I stuck my tongue out and ran it across the tip of Lan's leaking cock. I brought my tongue back in and rolled his taste around before swallowing.

I liked it.

Lan gripped my hip and jerked me back and forth, fucking his own mouth with my cock.

"Fuck yes," I growled out. I pulled his dick down to my mouth again and licked around the knob before gliding my lips and swirling my tongue over it as I slid my mouth up and down on his hard length. He groaned encouragingly, and it got me going more. I grabbed his hip tightly and sucked Lan in and out of my wet mouth.

Fucking hell, I was giving a blow job.

Giving *Lan* a blow job.

The way his hand ran over, up and down my body told me he was enjoying everything I did. I teased his tip, flicked my tongue over the end before drawing him in again. Up and down, I pressed my head and mouth onto his huge fucking dick.

He groaned. My dick lost his mouth as he groaned again, but his hand jerked me over and over while I saw him look down his body to me, lathering his cock with attention.

"Christ. Yes, Jesus, Park, that feels goddamn good."

My balls shrank, my gut twisting in the best fucking way. I was going to lose it because I liked the desire, the lust on Lan's face as he watched me suck him off.

"Fuck," I cried. "Coming," I yelled, coming up for air. Lan managed to get his mouth back around my tip just as the first load shot free. I couldn't help it, I pumped my dick into his mouth and kept coming, losing it all inside Lan's mouth.

Opening my eyes, I realised I was still pulling Lan's cock in my hand. I went to take him back in my mouth when Lan moved. He got to his knees; his eyes burned brightly as he leaned over my head, offering his dick to my mouth.

"Suck me, Park," he clipped harshly.

I spread my lips and then clamped around him. He slowly slipped his cock in and out of my mouth. His breath came out rapidly as he slid his dick back in and then out. "Fuck." He watched me, his eyes never straying from my mouth. "Latch tighter." I did. "Yes," he bit out when he pushed his cock back inside my mouth. "Like that." He nodded. I swirled my tongue, sucked him hard, and when it came back to the tip just near my lips, I ran my tongue in the slit. "Christ," he cursed. He thrust harder into my mouth and pulled back out just as fast. "Coming. Chest or mouth?" I didn't give him an answer; instead, I ran my hands from his thighs up to his arse and gripped him to me. He lost it and fucked my mouth, groaning as he climaxed.

For my first taste of a mouthful, it wasn't too bad. It was a taste I could definitely get used to.

Lan pulled his dick out and sat back on his hunches. His breath seemed hard to grasp. "You sure you've never done that before?"

I snorted, rolled my eyes, and sat up. "No."

He moved in, kissed my lips, a hand tangled into my hair where he pulled. Against my lips, he said, "Fuckin' loved it."

I grunted. "Good."

"Now we got a problem," he said.

"What?"

"I had a big day and came fuckin' hard. I need a rest."

A chuckle escaped. "Okay." I touched my lips to his with a peck.

He let go of my hair and shifted to pull the blankets down. "Also means we're spoonin'."

I didn't mention I wasn't usually one to ever spoon, but it seemed with Lan and Easton, I was willing to do anything.

Jesus, how could I feel so full by feeling so damn much inside?

I didn't know, but I fucking loved it.

CHAPTER FORTY-ONE

EASTON

*M*y feet dragged as I made my way up to my front porch. I was dog-tired but also thrilled knowing I would walk into my house to two men.

Two men.

One I already loved.

One I liked a darn lot.

After opening the front door, my eyes landed on Lan standing in the kitchen with one of his shakes in his hand as he leaned against the counter. He only wore running shorts and looked all sweaty and delicious with a smirk on his lips.

My heart skipped a beat.

I made my way over to him. Ignoring the sweat, I dropped my bag to the ground and wrapped both arms around his neck. One of his went to my waist while the other still held the shake.

"Hey," I whispered.

"Hey, babe. You look wrecked."

"I felt it up until I walked in and saw you."

He chuckled. "I like being here, in your house when you get home."

"I like having you here in my house when I get home."

He reached behind himself and put his shake on the counter. Placing that hand on my waist, he tugged me closer and bent, taking my mouth with his.

He nipped at my neck. "You need some sleep, East."

I nodded and blinked slowly up at him. "How'd last night go? Is Parker still here? I didn't even notice if his car was out front."

Lan grinned. "He's still in bed. I tried to wake him for a run. He grumbled and went to hit me." I laughed. "Last night was good."

"And?" I drew out.

"Let's just say Parker has given his first blow job."

Hearing it went right to my dick; it twitched behind my pants.

"Really?" I breathed.

"Oh yeah, he liked it too."

"Did you by any chance film it for me?"

Lan threw his head back and laughed. "Sorry, babe, but I didn't think of it at the time."

I huffed but then smiled, knowing I would get to see it one day.

"You need anything before you crash?"

"You and Parker." I grinned.

Another laugh fell from his mouth. "Get some rest, and we'll see what we can do." He kissed me. "I'm gonna grab a quick shower, head out for some food. I'll leave a note for Park in case he wakes."

"Park?" I teased, liking the new shortened name he used. Like he did with mine.

Lan smirked. "Yep."

"I like it," I told him and then yawned. Pushing away from him, I said, "Just a quick nap and wake me in a few hours."

"Sure."

"Lan, I mean it," I stated, undoing my shirt and slipping it off. "I don't want to sleep all day. Maybe we could all go see a movie or something later... ah, if Parker wants to." Lan had messaged me and told me about Parker freaking out. It was good to have a heads-up like that in case I'd reached out to him in some way without knowing he didn't want any public intimacy.

"Okay, I promise, and that actually sounds fuckin' good. Haven't been in years."

"Awesome."

As Lan detoured to the spare bathroom, I went down into my bedroom to find Parker still asleep in the middle of the bed. He lay on his back with an arm above his head and the other thrown out wide. The sheet sat low on his hips, and I couldn't tell if he had boxers on under that sheet or not.

Stripping out of my clothes, I left my boxers on and went to the bed. I could have gone to the spare room so I didn't disturb him, but I wanted to climb into bed and sleep beside him.

I pulled the sheet up and slipped in. I bit my bottom lip to keep from groaning aloud when I spotted Parker completely naked. His morning wood called for my touch, but I refrained because, no matter how excited my body was—and it was excited, I was already hard—my head felt foggy and tired. I needed my nap so I could be coherent for later.

Still, I wiggled down a little and over. Getting as close as I could to Parker, I rested my head near his and gently placed an arm over his waist. Sleep took me under within seconds.

Voices dragged me awake. I stretched and wrapped my arm tighter around a waist.

"He always like an octopus? I woke earlier to him practically lying on me with both arms around me."

A chuckle sounded. "Yep, always been that way. How come you didn't get up?"

The chest under my head shook with laughter. "I did get up, but in a different way." Parker paused, and then added, "I didn't want to move him."

That was hot and sweet. It seemed Parker was going to surprise me each day about something.

"He wouldn't have woken. He sleeps like the dead."

"Except for now," I mumbled. I opened my eyes and lifted my head. Lan stood leaning against the doorframe talking to Parker, who was still lying in bed with me. "How long did I sleep?"

"It's just after lunch," Lan said.

I stretched again, flopping to my back; it cracked. I hummed under my breath, still not fully awake. That was the problem with a double shift; it took me a while to wake when I usually had to stretch and open my eyes, but I felt like I wanted to close them and drift again.

"Wake him," I heard in the background.

"You. He must need it."

"He didn't want to sleep all day. He can catch more tonight. He wanted to see a movie or something with us."

"A movie?"

"Yeah, that okay?"

Parker paused. "Haven't done it for a fuckin' long time."

"Me either."

I rolled his way again. "You'll go?" I asked, opening my eyes. They both laughed.

He lifted his chin. "Sure."

"Great. Brilliant. What movie? Can we grab some food first? You haven't had lunch or breakfast so you'd have to be starving. I better shower." I flung the sheet back and got out of bed. "I'll be quick. Then we can get going."

"You think he's excited?" Parker asked, amused by me. I didn't care because I wasn't sure if they realised, but to me, this would be our first date. Even if there was no touching involved, I got to take them out in public, enjoy their time, watch a movie, eat, talk... all of it with them and I couldn't wait.

"Marvel or DC?" I asked, walking out of the theatre. We decided to have a quick something to eat at the house since the movie we'd agreed on started shortly. We'd luckily just made it on time.

"Either," Lan said.

Parker shrugged. "Doesn't bother me."

I stopped and stared at them both. I unclenched my jaw, and stated, "We're Marvel people. Remember it and there won't be a problem."

Parker snorted. "Got it," he said with a salute.

"Sure thing, babe." Lan chuckled, only it wasn't funny. He came to my side, spun me to face forward, and put his arm across my shoulders. "Before you get your boxers in a twist, I'm now starving. Popcorn didn't fill my gut. I need food."

Parker stepped up on my other side. I huffed at Lan. "I don't get my boxers in a twist like some chick and her panties."

"Uh-huh," he muttered, his lips twitching.

Parker hid his smile behind his hand. Only then he dropped it completely when something caught his attention. "Fuck," he clipped.

I glanced over to where he was looking. *Tits on a whale.* It was Bonny. She was smiling sugary sweet and swaying her hips Parker's way. He'd had her, been with her, fucked her, and it looked like she wanted it again, even after how she'd stormed off from the barbeque we'd had.

"Hey, handsome," she cooed, stopping at Parker's side.

My phone picked that moment to ring. I slipped out from under Lan's arm, and said, "I better get this." I stepped away and answered, "Hello?" Any type of distraction was better than having to see her grope Parker.

"Easton, honey," Darlene's voice came through the line.

"Darlene, how are you? How's Jewel and Luis?"

"We're all good, honey. But I have some news. They were going to call you after they did me, but I said I'd tell you."

"What is it?"

"Amit's court date is set for next month on the twenty-ninth. He didn't get an option for bail, honey."

"Good," I clipped. He didn't deserve it.

"Only, Andrew did. He's out."

"What?" I yelled, spinning to face Lan and Parker. Parker said something to Bonny; it looked nasty from the way his face screwed up. Her mouth dropped open, but I didn't see anything else because Lan and Parker filled my line of sight as they made their way over. "How?" I whispered into the phone, clutching it tightly to me.

"Amit testified he was to blame for Andrew's actions. Threatened Andrew with killing his family if he didn't do as Amit said."

"I don't believe it."

"I don't know what to believe," Darlene said. "However, I've taken more security on. I think you should do the same. I don't know what Andrew is capable of, or what Amit would have him do since it's obvious I never knew my fiancé. We need to be careful."

I nodded, because I never really knew my father either. I wouldn't put it past him to try something, though I was lucky to be in Victoria. Darlene and Jewel weren't though. "I'll talk to Lan and Parker, see what they say. Maybe we need someone to follow him, make sure he gets on with his life and forgets us. I thought this shit would be over."

"It might be," she said.

"Do you honestly believe that? Do you think he'll walk away from Amit and his orders?"

She said nothing for a few beats. "No."

"I'll ring you back."

"Okay."

"Stay safe, Darlene. You, Jewel, and Luis."

"We will, same to you, honey."

I ended the call, dropped my arm, and said, "Amit testified that Andrew was innocent against all charges. Said he'd threatened Andrew, so he's been released."

"Fuck," Lan clipped.

"When?" Parker asked.

"Today. Amit's going to trial on the twenty-ninth. He didn't get bail."

"At least there's that," Lan said roughly, though he still didn't look too pleased.

"From what we heard, you think he'll be trouble?" Parker asked.

"I don't know, but I need to be sure for Darlene and Jewel's sake."

"And yours," Parker bit out.

"I'm here. He's over there. I doubt—"

"Never doubt with people like this," Lan ordered.

I nodded. "What can we do?"

"I like your suggestion. We'll find a PI over there, a trustworthy one. I'll call Vi, see if she knows of any. We'll get someone to follow him. Find out his moves and if any lead to harming you, Darlene, or Jewel, he gets taken down." After Parker delivered that, he pulled out his phone and turned away from us. His harsh tone clipped into the phone when Vi answered.

"What did he say to Bonny?"

Lan moved his gaze from Parker down to me. I saw his eyes drain with worry and shine with amusement. "He told her he'd rather suck our cocks than ever see her again."

Even after all the drama, I smiled.

CHAPTER FORTY-TWO

LAN

*P*arker organised with Vi that a PI she knew would tag Andrew. She'd told him it was a priority and to start right away. After Park had finished the phone call, I suggested takeaway instead of a dinner out someplace. Though Easton wouldn't have it. I could tell Parker, like me, didn't like the idea, but we went for Easton.

"Guys, he only got out today. I don't think he'll be jumping out from behind any bushes anytime soon. Not that there are bushes around," Easton said as we walked to the front of the pub Easton picked to eat at.

I glanced at Parker to find he was doing what I had been, scanning the area for any type of trouble.

Easton sighed. He took my hand then went to grab Parker's but stopped. "Relax, both of you. He can't do anything to me here in Victoria."

"You're gonna have to give us a pass for being paranoid," Parker said.

"He's right. We're gonna be on edge until we know for sure Andrew won't do shit. We've seen a lot, East. Some people are fucked up."

"I know," he said. "Okay, I'll stop hounding you two about it. Besides, it's kind of sweet you both want to protect. Let's just eat, then we can get home."

"To do what?" I queried with a smirk.

Easton blushed. Parker caught it and grinned. Looking to his feet, he shook his head. Then Easton went ahead and started muttering, "You know, I mean, we don't have to do anything, and I'm not even sure Parker will..." He looked around and leaned in to whisper, "...stay the night. We can't expect it every night and really, are we all rushing into this? Since we got back from Queensland, Lan and I haven't slept apart. Have we jumped straight into—"

I grabbed his arm and spun him my way, laying a hard kiss on him. Pulling back, I asked, "You good?"

His chest rose and fell rapidly. He nodded. "Yes. I think things just got on top of me and... I don't want to mess this up." He glanced at Parker. "With either of you."

"You won't," Parker replied. Easton opened his mouth to say something until Parker shook his head. He rocked back and forth on his feet with his hands in his jean pockets. "How about we talk while we eat?"

Easton nodded. I leaned in and kissed his neck. Taking his hand, I tugged him in through the pub door after Parker.

We got led to a table in the bistro area. I sat on one side with Easton, and Parker sat opposite. We all ordered a beer and asked the waitress, who was eating Parker up with her eyes, if it was too early for dinner. She told us it was fine before she skipped off to get our drinks.

Easton flicked the menu open and studied it, but I knew he wasn't really seeing anything; he'd be thinking of what he said outside. Worrying if he went too far with putting it out there. As far as I was concerned, we weren't moving too fast. And as for Parker, I'd been interested in him for a long time, and in my opinion, Easton and I had ten years to catch up on. Hell, I wasn't getting any younger. I just didn't know how Parker felt.

The waitress came back and placed our drinks on the table, brushing up against Parker. She must have been a fan of long hair because she even flicked it off his shoulder with a giggle when he gruffly said thanks for his beer.

"He's not interested. Can we just order?" Easton snapped. Parker and I both looked at him. "What? I'm hungry." He gave his order to a glaring waitress. I said mine, and then Parker ordered. The woman stomped off with a pout after Parker ignored her fluttering eyes.

Easton took a gulp of his beer, set it down on the table and then pulled his fork closer to spin it. I watched him with a smirk. Parker looked on with his lips twitching.

"All right," I said. "I'll start. No, I don't think we're rushing. I don't want to go for even a night with sleepin' in a bed alone. I like having one or both of you close to me because I see this could be something good. Even with the times we'll argue."

Easton bit his bottom lip and nodded. "I feel the same. However..." He glanced at Parker. "You're new to this, and this, meaning the three of us, is a lot to take in, so maybe we need to back off a little. I mean, it's only been two nights together, and Lan's already talking about living in a house together, the three of us. I know it's too soon, so I want you to know if you feel it's too much, please tell us, and we can take a step back."

Parker listened to us both as he stared down at his beer, gliding his fingers up and down his glass. "Couples do sleepovers. It's what we're doin' until we know for sure this'll work." He glanced up to Easton and then me, his eyes warm. "It's good to fuckin' know you both think about me in your futures. But for now, let's just take each day as it comes. Hell, I could freak out about somethin' tomorrow, and you guys could get over havin' to placate the newbie. We just need to see how shit works. There'll be nights I won't get a chance to spend the night, but it won't be tonight."

He wanted us that night and we'd give it to him. Whatever he wanted.

He leaned forward. "What I do know works for me is your reaction when women get too close, but you both don't need to worry about that because all I can think about, and see, right now is you two."

Fuck me. That was hot to hear.

"Do we have to eat?" Easton whispered.

Parker smirked and sat back. "Yeah." His smirk morphed into a big smile. "Tell us how much shit did Oliver give you for gettin' hard?"

Easton groaned. "It was sweet to call, but next time don't. I don't think I'll ever live it down because I kept thinking about it all night long, so my problem didn't go down until we got a call to Mr Hinkson's house."

"What happened there?" I asked, resting my arm along the back of his seat.

Easton shuddered. His lips thinned and he shook his head. "I can't talk about it really, but let's just say no man should stick what he did up *there*."

"I'm good without hearing all the details," I said.

"Fuck. Wasn't he eighty?" Parker asked.

"Yep." Easton nodded.

Even after the shit we'd heard about Andrew getting released, the meal ended up being good because it was shared with two people I cared for. We talked about random things, work for Easton, the new careers for Parker and myself. We argued about football teams. We laughed together, we smiled, and we just enjoyed each other over the course of the meal. I fucking loved every second of it.

It was how I pictured many meals to come in our future. If it was together, I could really see how happy I'd be.

With them.

Sounded soppy, but I didn't give a shit. I was happy. Never thought I'd be so damn happy, but there I was, smiling and thinking about the two men with me as we made our way into Easton's house.

Parker stepped aside after he entered and I walked through the door, shutting it behind me and locking it. Easton already headed for the kitchen. Parker rubbed his stomach and groaned. "I seriously need to hit the gym tomorrow. You in?" he asked me.

"Sure." I nodded. Easton came back out with three beers. I took mine with a smile and sat on the couch, flicking on the TV. A game had not long started. "What about you, East, want to work out with us tomorrow?" I asked.

He shook his head, taking a seat next to me, and Parker sat in the chair. "That could be hazardous. I'd be too busy watching you both and end up hurting myself. I'll stick to the one at work for now."

Parker snorted and glanced at me, grinning. Now he knew. "You were checking me out those times you were supposed to be spotting me with the bar."

I took a sip before answering, "Yep." His eyes changed, darkened. It seemed he liked knowing how he distracted me.

Then they changed and got serious. He stared down at his beer and announced, "Sundays I go to my brother's grave."

I stilled, shocked he'd shared that when he didn't talk about his family at all. Fuck me, he was opening up. Easton went to say something, but I clamped my hand on his knee. He looked up at me, and I shook my head before refocusing on Parker.

He still studied his beer bottle. "We had a shit life." He shook his head. "Fuck that, our lives weren't shit, our ma was. We made what we had better. We had each other, and to us, that's all that mattered." He glanced over at the dogs out the back. "I was eighteen, and I wanted one night for myself. One night where I could get off with the chick I'd been into. I shouldn't have left. I didn't fuckin' think, too busy worryin' about my dick than the amount Erin... my ma had drank that day." His jaw clenched over and over. "I got home to find Erin over Shawn, stabbin' him." Easton gasped; his hand flew to cover his mouth. "I'd never felt that type of fury before. It took over.

All I could see was my brother lying dead on the floor in a pool of blood, but she was still layin' into him." He sucked in a shuddering breath. He faced us, his eyes hard. "I went over there, grabbed her hair, then her hand with the knife and sliced her throat open." He stopped, staring at us as if trying to tell us something or perhaps waiting for us to run from the room yelling murderer.

It wouldn't happen, and he shouldn't have expected that. Especially from me. We'd seen and done shit by helping the Hawks MC that wasn't legal, but we still thought was justified in our own eyes.

"W-why are you telling us?" Easton asked.

His eyes sliced to Easton. "Because I need you both to know everything about me. If this goes to where... if it stays like this between the three of us, you need to know who you've got in your bed."

"Who do you think that is?" I asked.

"A murderer. You know I don't follow the rule book, Lan."

"Yeah, and you know I don't either."

He shook his head. "I killed a drunk. She had an addiction, a disease that could have been helped, but I ignored it and kept livin' my own life with my brother."

"She was the adult. She should have helped herself for her children's sake," Easton said harshly.

"I sliced her throat open and I still don't care about it. If I could go back, I'd hurt her in a different way, in a way she could suffer for the rest of her life." He stopped, glared and stated, "I'm not a good person."

"I don't care," Easton whispered. "You did what any eighteen-year-old would have if they'd seen the same. No matter if she was your mother or not."

"East's right. We don't care." My brain began to put together all of the missing pieces, everything that I knew about Parker, the small gaps where I'd struggled to make sense of his behaviour and actions. "This why you hold yourself back from so much? You don't want to get close in case someone fucks you over in some way and hurts

you? Or that you'll be worried you'd have to hurt them for something they do?"

He shrugged.

He lived a life so damn guarded. Christ, my heart ached for him.
For him feeling he had to hold back from people because of his cunt
of a mother.

"How didn't you go to jail for it?" I asked.

"Told them I got home to find them like that. They investigated
and concluded she killed her son in a fit of drunken rage and then
killed herself after it."

"Christ, Parker. I'm sorry you went through that."

He sat forward, shaking his head. He put his beer on the coffee
table and stood. His hands threaded through his hair. "I shouldn't
have left him there. It's my fuckin' fault he died. I'll never forgive
myself. I—" He growled in the back of his throat. Tears threatened
to fall from his eyes. "I need to leave." He started for the door.

"Parker," I called, pulling my keys from my pocket. "Don't drive,
here." I threw them at him, and he caught them. "Stay at my place,
but don't go far."

He looked down at the keys long enough for Easton to stand and
walk over to him. Easton reached up and slid his hands to Parker's
neck. "The memory of that is not something that will ever go. But it
doesn't mean you can't forgive yourself for trying to be a teenager.
It sounds like you loved your brother very much, so I know he
would have loved you back just as much. It's how I know he
wouldn't want you to carry that guilt forever. He also wouldn't want
you to think you're not a good person because you killed someone
who was supposed to love you unconditionally; instead they
harmed, they... murdered someone very important to you."

Parker stared down at Easton, with a look of awe on his features
over Easton's truthful words. Guilt was a fucking bitch and stayed
with a person until they could work it out or learn to forgive.
Parker was holding onto it as he blamed himself for his brother's
death. I could understand why, and I wasn't sure if he would ever let

go. But the least Easton and I could do was help him, show him he deserved to be happy, no matter what he did back then.

Fuck, it explained so much. His standoffish, cold attitude. In the last couple of days, I'd seen a new side to Parker, and the selfish bastard I was loved it too much to let him take it away from us, especially because of a misplaced sense of guilt where he'd convinced himself he didn't deserve to feel happy.

"Parker," I said gently. Easton stood back, his hands dropping. But rather than backing away, he took one of Parker's hands in his. Parker glanced over, turmoil shining in his eyes. He didn't know what to think or say. "Appreciate you sharing with us. Just know we take you for who you are, not what you've done. You've told us, and we're still gonna want you. Nothing changes. You still want time, you take it, but we'll be there for you in the end."

His chest rose and fell quickly. He closed his eyes and sucked in a sharp breath, letting it out slowly. He shook his head before he opened his eyes. "I'm gonna stay. You both make me want to stay. Make me want to believe, and trust, and fuckin' feel."

CHAPTER FORTY-THREE

PARKER

I felt raw. Like I'd sliced myself open and let everything show on the inside, yet they still wanted to know me. It shouldn't be unbelievable since Lan travelled the same path as mine with the law. But what I'd done to Erin was different. She'd birthed us. She'd been sick. She could have gotten help, but after what she'd done, her crime, I'd become the judge, jury, and the executioner. I'd never forgive myself for leaving Shawn. I'd carry that guilt probably forever. Yet there they were, within moments, consoling me. Telling me they'd stick by my side after what I aired... what I hated most about myself.

I grabbed the back of Easton's neck and slammed my lips down on his. When I forced his mouth open with my tongue to tangle with his, he moaned and played with mine back while gripping me to him.

Using my other hand to slap down on his arse and tug him forward, I ground my cock against his. Both ours stirred, and I felt him grow with mine. Christ, it didn't take much and lust overrode any other sense.

Hands at my waist caused me to jump. I came up for air from kissing Easton to find Lan behind me. He shifted my hair to the side, bent his head and kissed my neck. He grabbed the bottom of my tee next and lifted, pulling it from my body and throwing it to the floor, along with his, and then Easton also removed his own, dropping it with ours.

I shifted, wanting to see both. We stood bare-chested admiring each other. I lifted my hands and trailed one over Easton's stomach and chest, the other over Lan's. Both quivered under my touch.

"Never thought I could like this."

"What?" Lan asked. He already knew, but he wanted to hear it.

"Touchin' you both, how it turns me the fuck on from just the feel of your skin." I glanced down to their pants, wanting them off. "Remove your pants, both of you," I ordered roughly. Lan dragged his top teeth over his bottom lip before kicking off his shoes, undoing and pushing down his jeans. He flicked them off with his boxers and socks. He stood proudly in front of us with his erection in hand. Lan's eyes moved from my chest to Easton. I shifted my gaze to see Easton running a hand over his chest, stomach, and dipping down into his jeans. There was an outline where he grabbed his cock.

With my pulse racing, I looked back at Lan to see him watching Easton while fisting his cock up and down. I heard a zip being slid down. My eyes moved back to Easton as he dropped his jeans. His hard dick sprang up. Reaching out, I took it in my hand and then held my other out for Lan. He stepped closer, and I wrapped my hand around his erection as well. He sucked in a breath while Easton moaned as I jerked both of them off at the same time.

Christ, my dick leaked as I watched my hands glide up and down their lengths. Lan leaned in and kissed my neck while Easton's cool hands touched my stomach and back. He moved them over my body, driving me insane with his touch.

Lan cupped my cheek and turned my face his way. Our mouths met, touched, tasted and played with one another. Kissing him, kissing them both was fucking amazing. I groaned against his lips when Easton snuck his hand down the front of my pants and squeezed my dick.

Lan knocked my hand away from his cock and stepped back. He took my hand and led, with Easton following. Our hands still wrapped around each other, we manoeuvred just a few steps over to where the back of the living room couch was.

"Hold on to the back," he said. I did, looking on with a hooded gaze as he reached in and undid my jeans, pushing them down. Easton's hand roamed down to my balls and rolled them gently around while Lan got to his knees. He pushed my legs back a bit and slid between the couch and me.

My pulse raced, and I wouldn't be surprised if they could see how fast it beat under my skin.

Easton used his other hand to stop mine on him. He smiled and moved behind me as he still played with my balls at the same time Lan took the tip of my dick into his mouth. "Fuck," I clipped, pushing my hands into the back of the couch more as a thrill raced up my spine. Easton kissed my back while Lan sucked me deeper into his wet, hot mouth. I shuddered, rolling my head around, lost in the pleasure from both of them.

Letting go of the couch with one hand, I placed it at the back of Lan's head as he blew me faster and faster.

"Spread your legs," Easton ordered gruffly. I did, unsure why, but it was Easton asking so I would do it. His hands rubbed over my back, my shoulder, and down again to my arse cheeks. I dropped my head back, moaning from their combined touch.

Lan licked the underside of my cock, right down to my balls where he sucked one into his mouth and played with the other.

"Christ," I hissed.

When one of Easton's hands slipped between my arse cheeks, I froze. He kissed my back and ran the hand up my spine. "Relax, promise you'll like it. Trust me?"

Licking my lips as I still watched Lan, I nodded. Easton hummed under his breath. "Thank you."

Lan winked up at me before he glided his tongue back up my dick and then sucked it in as Easton's now slick fingers ran inside my arse cheeks. I tensed up for a moment, until Lan sucked deep and Easton ran his tongue over my ear, then drew my earlobe into his mouth.

He traced his fingers over my hole, and while Lan's mouth drove me crazy, I pushed back on Easton's fingers, losing control. I wanted more of them, wanted it all.

Lan cupped my balls, rolling them softly as he bobbed up and down. He hummed and it vibrated over me. Unable to look away, I cursed as I kept watching him. And when he palmed his dick, rubbing it up and down in rhythm with his mouth on me, I was sure I'd explode.

Easton's lips ran to my neck, momentarily distracting me. I tilted it to give him more access while his hand on my hip pushed me back a little while his finger pushed in. I tensed.

Easton nipped at my shoulder. "Relax," he whispered. "Give me your mouth." I did, and he kissed me, lulling me to relax. His finger slipped in further. Only Lan picked that moment to hum around me again. I groaned when East pushed in more, hitting something inside that had me gasping into his mouth and moaning low in the back of my throat.

"Fuck," I clipped, dragging my mouth away.

"Yeah." Easton smiled. He withdrew his finger and pushed in again, rubbing against what I was sure was my prostate. Fuck, I'd heard stories, but never in a fucking million years had I figured this was what it would feel like. I backed onto his finger, searching for the thrill. "Hell, yes," I groaned when pleasure shot to my shaft as he ran his finger over the same spot.

I removed my hand from Lan's head and slammed it down onto the couch to support myself. With my head buzzing and my body vibrating, I rocked into Lan's mouth and back onto Easton's finger. I throbbed all over.

"Need to come," I snarled, closing my eyes for the first time.

Easton grabbed my hip and upped the sliding of his finger. I groaned loudly. Lan sucked me deep and swallowed around my tip... and I was lost. Cum squirted out of me. My knees wobbled as I groaned again and again. "Yes, fuck." I lost Easton's finger before I finished coming in Lan's mouth. He sucked me hard until the last drop slipped out.

Never thought it possible to come harder than I had the night before, but I swore to God, I just goddamn did.

Lan shifted out from between the couch and me and stood. His heated eyes shone as he leaned in and kissed me. I straightened to wrap my arms around him and tasted myself on his tongue. It was fucking hot.

Lan broke away to order, "East, bed now."

Easton stopped stroking himself and walked off without saying a word.

Lan gripped my chin. "I'm gonna go in there and fuck him. You gonna come watch?"

"Fuck yes."

He took my hand and led the way down the hall into the bedroom. Already on his back, Easton looked fucking magnificent and needy. He threw something at Lan who caught it. Lube.

I went over to the bed and climbed on while Lan opened the bottle. Grabbing Easton's calves, I forced his legs apart so I could move between them. With my eyes on his, I leaned in and kissed his leaking knob. He sucked in a shaky breath, and when I skimmed my mouth over his thickness, he moaned low and gripped my hair, holding me to him. Only I wasn't staying there, too eager to watch Lan be inside of him.

I licked my way around him all the way up to the glans again, drawing out the precum and swallowing it before I kissed his pelvis and his stomach, which quivered under my touch. I kissed his ribs, his chest, his shoulder, and neck. Finally, I pressed my mouth against his and wrapped my arms around him, lowering my body against his hot skin. My cock was once again hard, even after coming not long ago. It was what the two men did to me.

They got my blood pumping, my pulse racing, my heart hammering in a way everything they did excited me.

Christ, I hadn't been this horny since I was in my teens.

Easton tightened his legs around me when I ground my erection against his.

"Park," he sighed.

"Love hearin' that from you and Lan." Speaking of Lan, I glanced over my shoulder. He stood at the end of the bed watching us with a clenched jaw and lust-filled eyes. He didn't touch himself though, which made me wonder how close he was. I kissed Easton again, then said, "Someone's waitin' to be in you."

"Hmm," Easton moaned. I rolled off him gently and looked at Lan as he climbed between Easton's legs. He grabbed the back of Easton's knees, lifted them, tugged him down the bed and lowered his hips. His hand went between them. Then, as he bent to kiss Easton, I heard Easton groan and knew Lan was entering him.

Lan's hips surged forward, and Easton cried out, his head pushing back into the mattress.

"Fuck, Christ. Jesus, yes," Lan muttered. "So fuckin' tight." Easton grabbed him, hauled him down, and claimed Lan's mouth. They groaned against each other. I got to my knees, sat back on my haunches and left my gaze on Lan's hips pounding into Easton. I wrapped my hand around my cock and stroked, listening to the slapping of their skin against each other.

"Fuck, fuck," Lan bit out, straightening his arms to loom over Easton. He glanced at me, saw me jerking off and groaned again. "Sucking Park off got me goin'. I'm close."

Easton nodded. "Faster, babe. Please," he begged.

"Shit, ah, fuck. I'm—" He closed his eyes, dropped his head and groaned so loud and long I knew he was coming. He slid out of Easton, picked him up with a grunt and turned him, facing Easton's arse my way. I shot up to my knees, grabbed my dick in one hand

and Easton's hip in the other and fed his arse my dick. Inch by inch I watched it slide inside of him. He panted, whimpered, and then moaned once I was fully in.

I ran my hand over his back, his fucking sexy-as-sin back with all the fantastic ink. "Fuck yourself on me," I ordered.

He looked over his shoulder, his eyes hooded as he reared forward to force himself back on me. "Yes," I hissed. He did it again and again.

I goddamn loved it. Watching his body move, feeling him surrounding my dick, so damn tight and wet. He fucked himself on my cock and seeing it had me groaning, had my balls shrinking.

Lan lay on the bed, scooted himself under Easton's body, and I heard the sucking. Easton cursed, moaned, and glanced under him, at Lan taking his dick in his mouth.

"Fucking hell," Easton yelled. He slammed back onto me, and rolled his hips around, panting. One of his hands left the bed, went under him, holding Lan's head against him. He rocked his arse on my cock over and over.

"I'm close," I warned.

"Hmm, yes." Easton sighed. "I'm... God, coming... now!" he cried. His pace picked up. Up and down his arse went on me, causing me to lose my second load for the night, only that one was in his arse, along with Lan's.

"Christ," I hissed, gripping tightly to his hips as I emptied myself fully.

Out of breath, I brought Easton back to rest against me, kissed his shoulder and then slowly, while supporting him, slipped out. "Best fuckin' sex in my life," I commented, before dropping to the bed totally spent.

"Shower soon," Easton mumbled, and then both of my guys laughed tiredly, and the way they rested around me, one on each side, was a perfect end to the night.

CHAPTER FORTY-FOUR

LAN

A couple of nights later, I opened the front door to a grinning Gamer. "Where are they?" he asked.

I snorted. "Hey, Lan, how are you, Lan? Good, Gamer, how about yourself?"

He rolled his eyes. "Yeah, yeah, all that. Now, where are they?"

Laughing, I stepped back and let him in, then closed the door behind him. I followed when he made a beeline for the back sliding door. He quickly pulled it open. "I'm here, guys and girls. Your second daddy is here." The dogs came barking and racing excitedly towards him. He greeted each one of them with a pat and cooed words, while I watched Easton walk our way from the back shed.

"Hi, Gamer."

"Hey, how they been?"

Easton smiled softly. "Good."

Gamer nodded. "So, what's for dinner?" He straightened and crossed his arms over his chest, then glanced down at the dogs and squatted again, giving them more attention, which they lapped up.

"Steak, salad, and baked potatoes with chives and sour cream."

His nose scrunched up when Easton mentioned salad, and I chuckled. "East made it. You'll eat it, man."

"Even the salad?" he questioned, like it wasn't what I'd been talking about in the first place.

"Yep."

"Fine. Need help with anythin'?" He may come across as a dick sometimes, but Gamer was a good brother. From what I'd heard around the Hawks MC compound, he'd had a shit life until he became a brother. Another thing I heard, and still couldn't really believe because of how he was these days, but apparently, he'd been a brooding arsehole to start off with. Just went to show that people could change around the right group, and especially family.

"I'm about to grill the steaks, you can spend time with the mutts while I do it," I suggested.

"Sounds good to me."

Easton sidled up to my side and placed his hand on my back. "I'm going to check the potatoes and set the table." He tilted his head back, and I leaned down and touched my mouth to his, smiling.

After Easton closed the door behind him, Gamer said quietly, "Used to have dogs when I was a kid. Instead of beating on me one night, my fuckin' father lined up my dogs and shot them in the head for punishment because I didn't take out the garbage. I had to bury them myself in the backyard."

Holy fuck.

"Brother—"

He stood, shook his head, and said, "Appreciate Easton lettin' me mind his house, bondin' with his dogs, and you both givin' me time in your lives. But if I'm intrudin'—"

"You're not," I stated. "You're always welcome here, Gamer. Never doubt it."

That type of shit would fuck anyone up. Hell, no wonder he didn't have any pets of his own. To him, it'd be safer to make a connection with someone else's pets. He probably thought if something happened to them, he wouldn't be as affected, but he'd be wrong. Still, I wouldn't tell him that.

His whole demeanour changed from serious to playful in a

blink. "Cool. Say, do you think Talon will kill me if Nancy and I ever go on a date?"

Shaking my head, I chuckled and gave him the out he wanted, to change the subject. "Yeah, it's possible."

He nodded. "That's what I was thinkin'." He shrugged. "She'd be worth dying for though."

"Brother, why her?"

He looked at me like I'd lost my head. "Have you not seen her? She's fuckin' stunnin', and smart, and funny. My dick—"

"Do not finish that."

He laughed. "Sure. You gonna grill those steaks or what?"

Shaking my head, I spotted Easton through the kitchen window just as Parker stepped up behind him. Shit, he'd told us he'd be staying at his place because the case he was working on was taking him into the night. Yet, there he was, startling Easton with a kiss to his neck.

Gamer went to turn, and I yelled, "Steaks. How do you like yours?"

Gamer's brows shot up. "Wow, you're suddenly excited about steaks. I'll have mine medium."

I nodded. "Right." As I walked over to the barbeque, I noticed Easton and Parker were no longer in the window.

Easton

I watched Lan and Gamer through the kitchen window as I did some dishes. For a second, it had looked like the conversation turned serious, but they were back to smiles. Lan glanced my way, his eyes widened just as I felt heat at my back and lips on my neck.

Gasping, I spun and dragged Parker down to crouch on the floor.

Parker thinned his lips. "What's wrong?"

"First, you can't just sneak up on me like that. I could have hurt you." He laughed, but then I covered his mouth with my hand. "Second, Gamer's here for dinner. Didn't you remember or see his bike out front?"

His tired eyes snapped closed. "Fuck," he clipped and opened his eyes. "I've been doin' long hours. I thought it was Lan's ride over here and fuckin' forgot about Gamer. Been buggered, just wanted to come here, spend time with you both and crash."

My heart swelled and warmth flowed through my chest.

He was busy, but he wanted to see us. Wanted to spend time with us.

Hearing it was like—as pathetic as it sounded—like cupids singing a sweet harmony.

"Why are you blushin'?" Parker asked and smirked.

"It wasn't a dirty thought," I blurted.

His smirk morphed into a wide grin. "Doesn't matter what it was. I just know it'd be about me in some way or Lan, and I like that." He glanced away, as if his admission surprised him, but then looked back to me and took my hand in his before standing. He ran his thumb over my wrist before dropping my hand and stepping back. "Think there'll be enough food for me?"

"Yes." I nodded.

"Good, I'm starved, but then I'll have to crash..." He looked outside to see Gamer standing with the dogs surrounding him while he talked to Lan. "Shit. Guess I'll have to head to my apartment after all."

"No," I yelled. The men outside looked towards the window. Gamer lifted his chin to Parker in greeting, which Parker returned. I lowered my voice and said, "I mean, he might leave early, and then you can just sleep here. You shouldn't really be driving while you're so tired. It's not safe."

He faced me again. His bloodshot, exhausted eyes roamed slowly over me, stopping on my lips. "Want to kiss you," he admitted.

I glanced out the window to find Lan and Gamer busy talking

again. I grabbed Parker's wrist and pulled him out of the kitchen and just inside the hall where Gamer couldn't see. I turned, and told him, "You can't say things like that, all cute like, and not actually end up doing it."

He smiled lazily. His hand threaded around the back of my neck and he pulled me close. His other hand went to my waist, just above my hip, while I rested my hands on his chest. His heart beat fast under my touch.

Parker leaned in close to me so our lips brushed. There he said, "Like that you want my kiss as much as I want to give it, East."

"Do you?" I whispered, meeting his gaze.

"Oh yeah," he growled low, and then crushed his mouth to mine. I melted against him, and yielded to his lips, his tongue, and then groaned as he kissed me like he hadn't done it in years. As I slid my hands up and curled my arms around his neck, his hand on my waist drifted down to cup my arse. He dragged me close to rub his erection against mine.

Unfortunately, that was when we heard the back door open.

We pulled apart, and I panted, trying to catch my breath.

"Where's the guys?" Gamer asked.

Parker and I stared at each other, breathing hard. I placed my hand against my chest and sucked in a deep breath. Then I made sure my tee covered my hard-on and whispered, "Follow my lead."

"East—" Parker clipped low.

A little too late to stop me though because my mouth was already open and I said, "So that's the type of mattress you should buy." I rounded the hall and waved awkwardly at Lan and Gamer.

Lan dropped his head back, eyes to the ceiling, and I caught his lips twitching while Gamer stared at me strangely. There was a long sigh behind me, and I sensed Parker step up to my side, only I didn't look. He huffed, then replied, "Yeah, looks good. Dinner ready?"

Lan tilted his head back and nodded. "Sure is."

"What type of mattress is it?" Gamer asked as Parker and I

approached the table I'd already set out. I stumbled and gripped the back of a chair.

"Ah...."

Lan coughed over his laugh. "It's a Luxury DreamCloud one."

"Yes," I said and pointed to Lan. "Brain fart for a second there since it was only moments ago I told Parker the brand."

"Babe," Lan called. "The potatoes."

"Right. Forgot them, I'll go get them." I raced over and grabbed the bowl, busying myself so I didn't stuff anything else up.

Turning with the bowl clutched to the front of me, I caught Parker walk around the table to sit next to Lan because Gamer was already sitting on my side. I also saw the way Parker's hand trailed over Lan's back discreetly before he sat down. I spun my gaze to Gamer. Had he seen?

Nope, he was looking at me with a smirk to his lips. Did he know Parker and I had just been kissing?

Slap a dick, had I screwed things up for us already?

Slowly, I made my way over to the table and sat down, hoping I could refrain from acting like an idiot for a while longer.

Parker

Later, as I lay in bed, I rolled towards Easton, who still sat up in the middle of the bed with a book and a book light shining down on his pages.

He glanced down. "Sorry, am I disturbing you?"

"No," I bit out. "But I want you to tell me what you're thinkin'."

"How do you—"

On the other side of Easton, Lan sighed long and loud. "That's how." He lifted his head and got to his elbow.

Easton winced. "Sorry."

"What's wrong, East?" Lan asked.

"I like this," he whispered.

"What?" I queried.

"This. Us. All three of us. The connection we have started, how it's not only about the hot sex, the *very* hot sex, but the times we share together. The small touches, the kisses, the talking, hugging. All of it, and I don't want to be the one to stuff it up."

I knew what he'd been thinking, of his actions around Gamer, wondering if he gave away our relationship. The thought of Gamer knowing kind of twisted my gut. I wasn't ready for people to know. However, Gamer was one person. It wasn't like he'd just talk shit about us anyway so in that moment, I relaxed from the thought. Instead, I knew I wanted, no I had to, reassure Easton because even if he had slipped and blurted out about us, I wouldn't blame him. It'd just mean he hadn't thought in that moment because he was happy with what we had. I couldn't blame him for being himself.

Reaching back, I felt for the cord and switched on the bedside lamp. Then I took his book, turned off his book light, and put it on the bedside table. "Come here," I ordered, while tugging on his arm. He slid down to lie between us.

I also got to my elbow to loom over him. I shared a soft smile with Lan. I had to agree with Easton. This was what I wanted. Both of them. I couldn't imagine not being able to share moments like this with them.

With the sheet down to our waists, I watched as I slid my hand to Easton's stomach. It clenched under my touch. I grinned, glancing up to him. "Nothing you do or say could ruin what's buildin' between us. You don't need to worry. Okay?"

"But—"

"No," I stated. "No buts. Not allowin' them."

Lan chuckled. His hand came down over mine and I gripped it. We stared at each other and I told him, "I like this a hell'va lot. I won't let little shit get in the way." Meaning, if it came down to it, I wouldn't care too much if people found out, but I still wanted to take things slowly. Get us sorted, even though I already guessed this would last between us because I wouldn't want it any other way. Then I'd tell the damn world about us without a care so long as I knew they'd be with me.

"I know." Lan nodded.

I looked down to Easton. "Yeah?" I asked.

"Yes." He smiled. He wrapped his hands around Lan's and mine. I dropped my gaze and looked at our joined hands. My gut rolled in a good way from what I saw. Hell, I liked being with them, liked sharing the same bed, and having them close.

Yeah, I already wanted this to last a fucking long time.

"Can we get some sleep now?" I asked teasingly.

Easton rolled his eyes. "Fine."

Smiling, I leaned in and kissed his chest, then his chin, and finally his mouth. After I knew he was breathless, I pulled back and turned to Lan. He moved in over Easton a little and met my lips with his. When I felt Easton tuck my hair behind my ear, I shifted back with a final peck to Lan's lips.

"I thought you wanted to sleep," Easton said with a smirk.

"It's overrated anyway," I replied, my gaze on his mouth.

"Nah-uh. You're too tired for my liking."

"East's right, you need more sleep and I know if we start we won't stop." Lan flopped down, curling closer to Easton. But we both knew it'd change through the night and somehow Easton would be over both of us in one way or another. Not that it bothered me.

Sighing, yet still smiling, I switched off the lamp and lay back down. I took hold of Lan's hand and again, Easton's wrapped around both ours. I pulled them up over Easton's heart and that was how eventually we all fell asleep.

To a lot of guys it would be a cheesy, sappy action, but in that moment, to me, it was everything right.

EPILOGUE

EASTON

A knock sounded on the front door so I started for it. Lan was out back readying the yard for visitors. We were hosting another barbeque since Low announced it was our turn again. Parker was off working some things for a case they'd started, but he said he'd be back for it, only he could be late. Not that anyone knew he was ours, nor did it matter. I just loved having him around, even when I couldn't reach out to him in front of people.

Even though it had been three months after Andrew got released —and from what the PI told us from Queensland, Andrew made the call to go about his days as if having never worked for my father— my guys still didn't like leaving me alone at home. When I worked, it was fine since there were other people around me. And after Parker and Lan told Oliver about Andrew, Oliver wouldn't leave my side. He'd go as far as following me to the toilet. At least we knew Amit and Mr Khatri were out of the picture. They'd both been sentenced to a long time in prison. Both their businesses were closed, and people learned just what type of men they were. Prisha and her mum were safely hidden still here in Australia, in case Mr Khatri's sons were going to seek any kind of revenge for sending their father away. Though, from what I heard, they were too busy sorting out their own problems with their own wives, who had decided to press charges against them after everything about their father became public in the Middle East.

It seemed things were settling nicely in our lives. Lan had also received a call from his old boss in Ballarat informing him of Miller's release, a little too late, and the fact Miller had disappeared but to keep a look out just in case. None of us could believe they'd never questioned Lan about Miller's disappearing act in the first place. However, it worked in our favour.

At the front door, I looked out the side panels and saw Mrs Bridge standing there smiling. She waved when she spotted me. I opened it, and before I could greet her, she said, "Hello, Easton dear, I hope I'm not being a bother, but I remembered you saying you were a paramedic. My John has had a tumble, and I'm not sure if he should move. I told him not to get up the ladder anymore because of his bad leg, but he won't listen to me."

"Of course, Mrs Bridge. I'll just let Lan know where I'm going."

She looked next door and then back, "Yes, yes, please be quick. My John is a bit of a sook."

I chuckled. "I will." I quickly went to the back door, slid it open, and called out to Lan, who was fixing the ride-on mower near the back shed. "Lan," I called.

"Yeah, babe?" he yelled.

"I'm just heading next door. Mr Bridge had a fall. Mrs Bridge is at the front door waiting for me."

"Take Nero with you."

"Lan—"

He looked up. "East. Take Nero." He glanced down at Nero and ordered, "Go." Then lifted his chin in my direction and somehow, our smart boy knew what Lan was saying and trotted my way. Though, since Lan had moved in, all of the guys got spoilt. They were now allowed to sleep in the house through the night, and since Parker spent most nights with us, they loved the attention we all lavished on them while we lazed around watching TV, reading—

mainly myself and Parker, to my surprise, liked suspense and horror books—or just talking. The only time Parker didn't stay was if he was too beat after being out of town on a case. Instead, he'd crash at his place. It never stopped him from calling us though.

When Nero was at my side, we walked back to the front door, and I opened it. Mrs Bridge had been frowning, but it quickly changed to a smile.

"Are you okay, Mrs Bridge?" She gave a wary glance down to Nero. "Don't worry, he's harmless."

She nodded. "I'm fine, dear. Just worried about my John." She took my offered arm and we walked around our shared fence because I wasn't sure I could pick her up and help her over without hurting her. While walking, she chatted about her plum trees out the back, how I had to grab some before I left because there were too many for her and John.

"Mrs Bridge, I've been meaning to have you and Mr Bridge over for dinner. I haven't been very sociable, I'm sorry." I would have to have them visit when it wouldn't be too crowded. I wasn't sure they were ready to be around a rowdy bunch of bikers. I'd warm them up first.

She patted my hand and I was sure I saw her eyes well. "It's fine, dear. I've seen cars coming and going all the time. Though, there's been a certain couple of men who seem to stay a lot."

"Ah, yeah, they're my friends."

"I'm old, dear, not dumb. You know John and I used to attend swinger parties."

That wasn't something I could unhear.

"Um, okay, that's cool. Is John inside or out?"

"Inside." She glanced back to my house. "Dear, I wasn't hearing things. You did say one of your men is home now?"

"Lan, and yes, he's working out the back."

She hummed under her breath. We made it up to the front door where she paused and glanced down at Nero. I offered, "He can stay outside if you prefer?"

"No," she whispered. "He'll be fine." She opened the door and stepped in. "John's just in the kitchen."

As soon as I was through, the door slammed shut with Nero on the outside. He went crazy, barking and scratching. I started to turn to the door, but something smashed into my head. I gasped and stumbled to the side, gripping my skull.

Mrs Bridge cried out, and I blinked her way to see a body standing over her. "You stupid woman, you let him bring a dog?"

Blinking again, things cleared and I couldn't believe who I saw.

Andrew stood looming over Mrs Bridge. Shaking my head to clear it, I saw him point a gun down at her. "No," I yelled and went to grab him, but he swung the gun my way. I stopped moving. "What are you doing here?" I stepped back. Mrs Bridge slowly shuffled on her bottom to lean against the wall.

"As ordered," Andrew laughed.

"But...."

"The people you had watching me? I'm no fool, Easton. I know how to manipulate people into thinking they saw me when it's really someone else."

"What's my father got over you to make you—"

"Make?" he yelled and laughed again. "No, he isn't making me. I wanted to do this because you've ruined our lives. I looked up to Amit. He was like the father I never had, and you, his own flesh and blood, got him put away." He growled under his breath like the madman he was. Gone was the tailored, poised, and stuffy Andrew. In his place was a dishevelled, crazy man. He waved his arm around with the gun. "Shut your fucking dog up or I'll shoot it."

"Nero, heel," I yelled. Nero settled, then whimpered. "Where's John?"

When Mrs Bridge sniffed, I glanced at her. "H-he knocked him out in the kitchen. I had to come and get you, dear. I-I had no choice. He would have killed my John."

I nodded. "It's okay, Mrs Bridge. This is my fault."

Andrew laughed. "That's right. Your fault, everything is your fault, and now you can watch me kill them before I take your life."

The window crashed just behind me, glass raining down and slicing me in places. Wide-eyed, I stared at Nero as he landed on the glass-littered floor. The instant he was on all four paws, Andrew fired the gun. I screamed, Nero snarled, and another shot fired just before Lan jumped through the window and barrelled into Andrew, taking him to the ground in a grunting mess. With fear clawing at my throat, I watched on, relief flittering through me when Andrew hit his head hard, his eyes closing.

Lan straddled Andrew, gripped his tee and tugged his body up. "Motherfucker," he clipped harshly, disappointed Andrew was out for the count. He dropped him. Andrew hit his head again.

Lan glanced my way. His eyes stormed in fear and anger. "East?"

"I'm good," I told him. I glanced at Mrs Bridge, and that was when I saw him.

Nero lay on his side surrounded by blood.

"Nero," I yelled. I stumbled over and dropped to my knees. "No, no, no." I ran my hands over him, pressing my hands to a bleeding chest wound. He panted and stared up at me. "Nero." A sob caught in my throat. "Nero," I cried. I shook my head. "Puppy, my baby."

Lan crouched next to me. "Ma'am, please call the police." His hand rested on my back, and he rubbed up and down. "East."

"No!" I yelled. I patted Nero's head, rested mine against his and told Lan, "Kill Andrew. Kill him, Lan."

"East—"

"No."

"I'm sorry," Mrs Bridge cried. "I'm so sorry. But, Easton dear, John can help him."

I snapped my head up and my eyes landed on her where she sat on the floor still. "What?" I whispered.

"He can help Nero. He was a vet."

I glanced to Lan, who nodded and said, "I'll go check on John. Stay with him."

340

"I'll call the police," Mrs Bridge said in a small, but hurried tone, but all my attention went back down to our brave boy.

Parker

Three months we'd been *dating*.

Three months of dating two guys and, fuck me, I was happy.

It was the longest relationship I'd ever had. It was one I wanted to make sure stuck for as long as I lived. That was why I was gonna tell them, not ask—I wouldn't give them a choice—that I was moving in. Besides, I hated the nights I stayed in my apartment thinking it'd be good to give them the night to themselves. Not that they ever asked for one; I just thought it was good for them. However, now we'd have to sort out a different routine because I'd travel all the way around the world if I had to, to get home to them. To sleep beside them each night.

They calmed me. Made me realise there was light at the end of a dark guilt-filled tunnel. I was healing because of them. Learning to forgive myself because of them. I still had a way to go, but I finally knew it was possible.

I couldn't see my life without them in it.

I never wanted to.

My phone rang through the Bluetooth system in the car. The caller ID read Dodge. "Yeah, brother?" I answered.

"That Andrew motherfucker showed."

"Where?" I snarled.

"We're at Easton's—"

"I'm on my way," I clipped, and ended the call. With my heart in my throat, I sped the rest of the way home. I didn't want to hear over the phone how bad it was. I couldn't. If either Lan or Easton were harmed, I'd fucking lose it.

Vehicles surrounded the place, but all I focused on was the ambulance. I parked at Lan's place, shot out of my car, and ran. Jumping the fence, I bounded up the steps then forced the front door open. It hit the wall and all eyes landed on me.

"Parker," someone said, but it wasn't the voice I was after.

I spotted Lan standing behind the couch. My eyes ate him up, and he looked fine. I settled a little, but it wasn't enough. I then focused on the ambo leaning over someone on the couch in front of where Lan stood. My chest ached, my hands shook, and my gut twisted in an ugly way. I stalked over, ignoring everything else, and pushed the guy aside. He cried out.

Things got blocked out as I looked down at Easton. He had a bandage over his temple, a few cuts and scrapes, but other than that he looked fine.

"Parker," he said gently, his eyes flicked around us, and I knew he was worried for me as we were surrounded by people we knew and I didn't want people to know about us.

But fuck it.

I dropped to my knees, cupped his face and leaned in, claiming his lips.

Gasps and curses started around us. Then Lan bit out to someone, "Leave him."

The place quieted. I pulled back and ran my thumb over Easton's bottom lip. "You're good?"

"Yes," he whispered, his eyes warm.

I nodded, stood, and shifted beside Easton to grab Lan by his tee and pull him forward. "You're good?"

"Yeah, Park." He smiled.

"Good," I clipped, and then kissed him just as hard. My relief was immediate, my soul settled, righted itself. My men were okay.

"Holy shit," was drawn out from someone.

I didn't give a fuck. I needed this, them. While my mind and body eased after getting the crap scared out of me, Christ, I still trembled.

Lan's hand threaded into my hair and he tugged my head back. His eyes met mine. "We're fine, yeah?" He knew the way my brain worked, knew the reality of them being okay was sinking in. I nodded. He rested his forehead against mine. "You gonna be okay?" I knew he meant with people knowing.

"Fine," I said.

Easton came to our sides, and we straightened, facing the people in the living room together.

"The three of you?" Stoke asked the obvious.

"Yep," I said.

Silence.

"Well…." Dodge started.

"Who gives a fuck," Knife said. "Two guys, three, four. As long as they're happy."

Dodge rolled his eyes. "I was gonna say that, dickhead."

Knife chuckled. "Thought I'd get in first."

"Look, we'll get over the shock eventually," Stoke said. He eyed his cousin. "You couldn't just have one. You had to pick two."

Lan laughed. "They couldn't resist me."

I scoffed.

"I think it's brilliant," Julian announced. He turned to Mattie.

Mattie's hand came up. "No."

"But—"

"Hell no."

Julian huffed, "Fine."

"Glad you all agree this shit's good, but even if you hadn't, I wouldn't give two fucks," I told them.

"You'd just get those two fucks," Dive yelled. Mena, his woman, elbowed him in the gut. People laughed.

"Whatever," I said with a smile, then offered Dive the middle finger. "Can you give us a second?"

"Everyone out with Nance and the kids," Griz, second in command from the Ballarat Charter, yelled.

"Wait, where in the fuck is Gamer?" Talon snarled.

343

"Honey," Zara said, starting after him since he was already on his way out.

As soon as everyone was gone, I faced Easton and Lan, and placed one hand on Lan's hip and the other on Easton's. "What happened?" They explained everything, even down to the point I arrived.

"Where's Nero now?" I asked.

Easton smiled. "Gamer's actually in the spare room with a resting Nero. He doesn't want to leave his side. But John thinks he'll be fine," Easton said.

"Good." I took a deep breath. "That fucker better not get bailed out."

Lan shook his head and rubbed his palm up and down my arm. "He won't. The Bridges will testify, and they heard the whole story. He won't get off this time."

I nodded, closed my eyes and sighed. I ran my fingers through my hair. "I've never been so fuckin' scared."

Easton's body slammed into mine. "Sorry you got that scare. I promise we're fine."

I grabbed the back of his neck with one hand and reached out for Lan's. "I know. I can see it, and I'll calm eventually."

Lan tugged on my hand. "We'll help you later."

I smirked. "Lookin' forward to it."

"People know now," Easton stated.

I glanced down at him. "Yeah, they do, and I'm good with it. It also means we don't need to hold back anymore. I'm happy and fuckin' proud of who's in my life, because I damn love you both."

Easton sucked in a shocked breath before he leaned up and kissed me deep and long. Against my lips, he whispered, "I love you, too." He glanced over to Lan, running his hand down Lan's stomach. "Both of you."

Lan stepped up behind me to press his lips to my neck. There he murmured, "Love you, Park." He reached out, took Easton's hand, dragged it up to his lips, and kissed the back of it. "You know I love you." He smiled and then shook his head. "Don't understand how I got damn lucky in life to have the love of both of you, but I do. It's mine, and no one nor anything will fuck it up. You two are my for-fuckin'-evers."

He was right. It was exactly how I saw them. As my forevers.

Fuck normal.

I was happy being different, especially when it meant I'd have Lan and Easton by my side.

SNEAK PEEK

FUMBLED LOVE

CHAPTER ONE

REAGAN

The day was going to be a terrible one. I knew it the moment I woke up late, having slept through my alarm again. I really had to get one that sounded like a freight train going through my house because when I slept, I did so deeply.

To make matters worse, I raced from my room, skipped around the Pomeranian named Fozzie, and then slipped in still warm poop.

Gagging and cursing him black and blue, I quickly used some paper towel to wipe it off my foot and I let him out the dog door, which was already built in the door when I bought the house. Thankfully, Fozzie was my parents' dog, and it was my last night minding the little fella.

The cleanup took longer than I thought, which added extra time on my lateness. But I refused to leave my house stinking like dog doo-doo. It wasn't like I could go to work smelling like poop. I could already imagine the less-than-creative names my students would come up with.

Finally managing to get out the door without another incident, it was then I realized I'd put on the panties I should have thrown away a dress size ago. Yes, those deadly small panties. It meant the whole walk to work, they kept making friends with my butt crack. Midstep, I glanced down and groaned; I'd also managed to pick out the worst outfit ever. A long red skirt, which had a tear in the middle, and a *rainbow*-colored tee. Not only did I look homeless, but it was like a Skittle had thrown up on me.

Of course, as I ran through the halls of Radley High School, where I taught English, the principal stepped out of nowhere, and I nearly collided with him.

With just one look at me, Tom Gallegan's eyes widened. "What happened, Reagan?"

"A rough morning." I hadn't even had the chance to inhale my much needed three morning coffees.

He cleared his throat, apparently not wanting to touch on the fact a unicorn farted rainbows all over me. His lips twitched. "Right, ah… I need your help. It's school assembly in a few minutes and Khloe is out sick. You'll need to fill in on stage."

And the morning just got worse.

Khloe was Tom's assistant; she regularly stood on the stage in assembly and, well, assisted with whatever she had to do. I didn't take much notice of what she actually did. I liked hiding in my corner with Brooke, my friend from college, who happened to get a job at the same school as me. We stood in the back and… to be honest, we bitched. Mainly about Elena, the witch I'd gone to high school with, and who'd made my experience hell. She also, unfortunately, worked at the same school as us as the family and consumer science teacher. I'd spent probably far too many hours considering other meanings for FACS, which seemed fitting for Elena. Though, my favorite was: Facts About Cockup Slags

"Erm, I can't."

Tom crossed his arms over his chest and rested them against his beer belly while he stared me down. We all liked Tom; he was a great guy to work for, like a father figure in a way, but there wasn't a chance I was getting up on that stage and pretending I wanted to be there. Tom tended to drone on and on and on. Once, Brooke had even elbowed me hard in the ribs because I'd dozed off standing up.

I could take him on in the stare down.

I really could.

With my hands on my hips, I leaned in a bit and stared right back.

Neither of us blinked, and my left eye started twitching seconds in.

The man was a master at the stare down. Damn him.

Sighing, I blinked a few times, and said, "Fine." I started stalking off, ignoring his grin of triumph.

"You're going the wrong way," he called.

"I need to see if Brooke has a spare top or I'll never live it down with the kids," I called over my shoulder.

I loved my students, and they loved me, but they could also be little shits. One time, I'd somehow managed to go to class with my slippers on, and a Twix chocolate bar stuck in my hair. I blamed the *Supernatural* marathon I'd had the previous night. However, I'd heard their murmurs of how they'd thought I'd been dumped and was wallowing in depression. Then there was also the day I'd got caught, after a quick visit to the restroom, with my skirt in my panties. They'd thought I'd ducked out for a romp with the phys ed teacher. After I'd swallowed the bile in my mouth—because no one would want to romp with stinky Steve, who I was sure didn't own deodorant, regardless of how many times Brooke and I chatted about how good deodorant was in front of him—I assured them it was an accident. I'd been rushing back so they wouldn't get into too much trouble. Or more specifically me, as I really should not be leaving the classroom unattended. But when I needed to pee, nothing was getting in my way.

I managed to catch Brooke as she was leaving her office. She was the school counselor.

My dear friend took one look at me and started laughing. "Oh God, Ree. Did you not look in the mirror this morning?"

"I was running late. Do you have a shirt I could borrow? I have to take Khloe's place on stage."

"Yeah, sure. It's in the locker." She stepped away from the door and started down the hall. "I'll see you on stage. Apparently, I have to help with something too," she yelled back.

Thank the high heavens I wouldn't be alone up there.

Quickly, I slipped into her office and took out a black shirt, then cursed. Damn Brooke was only a size smaller than my size fourteen, but I was larger in the chest area. My boobs looked like they wanted to burst free from the buttons. At least it was a bit better than my rainbow tee. I squished the girls down, so I didn't look like a tramp, and made my way into the gymnasium.

Bustling along with the other teachers and students, I managed to make it on stage just as the final bell rang. Tom ushered us to the left, near the opened curtain, and placed a huge-ass trophy in my hands. It also covered my chest nicely, thank God. Then he placed a small banner into Brooke's hands before he shuffled off. Brooke and I looked at each other. She then read what was on the banner before I could.

"Oh," she whispered.

"Oh? Oh, what?"

"We forgot."

"Forgot what?" I asked snappishly, because her concerned tone was freaking me out.

"That Carter Anthony was coming today." She winced at my face paling, and I knew it was because I suddenly felt sick.

Carter Anthony.

How could I have forgotten he was showing?

Maybe because I'd put it at the back of my mind, in the *very* back of my mind.

"It'll be okay. You don't even have to talk to him."

Nodding, I replied, "There is that. And anyway, it's not like he'll remember me. I was a nobody back then. We didn't even talk." He'd just been my high school crush, the popular football player, and I'd let my infatuation last for years. My love died once I heard him join in with his jock friends laughing at plus-size girls. It also happened to be just before he left town, accepting the big football scholarship with some college out of town. Apparently, he was still a star player and two years ago, he got transferred to one of our city's NFL teams, whatever they were called. Only he still opted to live away from his home stadium, picking to travel the few hours drive instead. Although, it could be possible he already had a place set up back where he was and didn't want to leave it. I'd also heard some talk he was thinking of moving back to settle down. While I knew next to nothing about the sport or even teams, I wasn't surprised by his success. He'd been a brilliant player even in high school. The most recent news I'd overheard was that Carter was finishing up his final year playing, and that he wanted to coach at a local college.

Not that I stalked him. I didn't. It really was the gossip around town.... Okay, so it was one night—two months ago when we found out he was going to do a talk at our school—Brooke and I were drunk and she'd googled him.

Shifting from one foot to another, since my tight panties had ridden up, again, I took the steps needed to move to the spot Tom gestured us to with an annoyed look on his face; we were off to the side, near the curtain.

"Stupid tight panties," I grumbled under my breath. I hadn't had a chance to pull them out discreetly. I scanned the audience and spotted Elena standing on the floor by the stage at the opposite end to us. She appeared eager, and I knew why. Carter had been her high school sweetheart for two years before he'd moved away.

Snorting, I took notice of her outfit, and I'd been worried about my top. Her breasts were close to popping out to say hello.

"What are we snorting about?" Brooke asked discreetly.

"*Her.*"

Brooke looked at Elena. "Oh, *her,*" she snarled. Elena was the worst. One of the coldest people I'd ever met. It was as if she was stuck back in high school and still thought she shit roses.

As Tom finally took to the microphone, I leaned into Brooke, and said, "Her boobs are so perky they're like a Disney Princess's on crack." Brooke coughed through her laugh. "Actually, I bet she'd want to be Dora the Explorer right about now."

She glanced at me, then back out to the audience of pubescent teens. "Why?"

"She'd want to be the first to explore Carter's whole body with her tongue."

She snorted. "Would she be the only one?"

"Yes." I nodded. I rolled my eyes as Tom went on and on about the great Carter Anthony. I was sure Tom had a guy-crush on him, like a lot of males all around the country. Even some of the male staff were salivating for a peek at Carter. Except for Larry, one of the math teachers, who I wasn't sure had moved out of his mom's yet, despite being thirty-seven.

"Why are you moving like that?" Brooke hissed at me. "Do you need to pee?"

"No, I have a wedgie," I whispered.

"What?"

"My panties are riding up my butt. You need to pull it out."

She swung her gaze my way and looked at me as if I'd lost my mind. "Come on," I pleaded. "I can't continue like this the whole time. It's so uncomfortable. My panties up there making out with my butthole. This thing is too heavy to hold with just one hand while I fix the problem."

"I am not—"

"Remember the time you had me check your boob for a lump? I fondled it for a good while and only found a pimple under it."

"But—"

"Or the time you broke your arm and had trouble dressing, showering, and going to the toilet?" Looking over to Tom, I pretended to pay attention, and snapped in a low tone, "It's only a piece of fabric, but it's annoying the heck out of me. Can you please...?" I felt fingers on my bottom, and then sweet relief. My panties were adjusted. Only what was strange was when my friend patted my ass after it. Still, I said, "Thank you." Then I glanced back to Brooke who had wide eyes. I added, "See, it wasn't that hard."

"Reagan—" Brooke bit out. However, Tom then boomed through the room, "And here he is. Please welcome, Carter Anthony."

Cheers and claps erupted. I shifted my gaze to the far side and behind the curtain, only Carter didn't step out.

My body tensed as I felt a presence step up beside me. "Anytime you need help, I'll be there," Carter's deep voice said out the corner of his mouth while he waved to the audience. Then, as he walked toward Tom, he glanced back and winked.

I felt the need to vomit, pee, poop, scream, and cry all at the same time.

He couldn't have been the one who'd pulled my panties out of my ass.

Nope.

It wasn't him.

"Reagan—"

"No!" I hissed through my heavy breathing as I tried to calm myself. "It was you," I stated in my do-not-screw-with-me tone.

"Oh, got it. You're playing dumb. Right, yep it was totally me who had my hand on your ass adjusting your panties and then patted your rump." She scoffed. "I also whispered that my helping hand was willing to do it again and then winked at you."

She quickly looked away.

Huh, guess my death glare does work sometimes.

God, how long had he been standing behind the curtain?

Shit, shit, shit. I didn't, *couldn't* think about it, or about what he heard.... Did he hear me talk about Elena? Had I said her name? She was currently sending him sultry "come screw me" eyes while he was on stage talking about how awesome his life was.

Actually, I couldn't hear what he was saying because my ears were ringing while my blood pumped frantically through my body because I was having a breakdown.

"Reagan," Brooke barked lowly.

My body jolted. "What?"

"They're calling you."

I froze. They were? Glancing at the microphone, I saw Tom glaring at me while he waved me over. Carter stood beside him smirking. At least Gerry Understock, a top sports student was smiling.

Leaning in a little toward Tom, I whispered-yelled, "What?" I rose my brows at Tom. He sighed and thumped his forehead.

"The trophy in your arms is for Gerry," Brooke supplied.

"Oh, right."

She laughed. "Get it over there before Tom strangles you."

"Reagan." Tom hurled my name at me as if he were praying it would catch me on fire.

I snorted to Brooke. "He's thought it many times, but he would never do it. He loves me too much." I started toward the microphone. In fact, I was sure Tom thought of me as his adopted kid.

Stopping in front of my adopted dad—who I just claimed, something I would tell him later when he tried to kill me—I smiled. He covered the microphone and clipped, "I'm going to staple information about assemblies to your forehead. Then maybe you'll remember what's going on."

Okay, I was his *annoying* adopted child.

"*I'm* usually down there." I gestured with my head. "Bad move on *your* part to have me up here. I get bored easily." The only way I didn't get bored was when I read or watched movies and TV shows. I'd even taken up walking on those random days nothing else satisfied me. Brooke had checked my temperature when I told her that. However, after the first few times, I realized I enjoyed it.

Gerry snorted out a laugh, until Tom scowled at him, then he quickly shut up. And Carter—the sexy mountain-of-a-man Carter— stood off to the side smirking once more. I narrowed my gaze his way; his smirk changed into a shit-eating wide grin. Did I have something on my face? God, his eyes were mesmerizing. I suddenly felt an urge to paint or draw them. Although, I still hadn't passed the stick-figure pictures, so I knew I'd totally suck at it. While I could explain the difference between a simile and metaphor, my artistic credentials sucked.

"Reagan, pass the trophy over to Carter," Tom snapped.

Shaking my head to clear my mind from stick-figures, I then nodded, "Right. Of course." I nodded again like an idiot, and stepped up to Carter, practically throwing the heavy trophy at him. I did it all without meeting his hypnotizing gaze.

"Reagan," Carter called, in his sensual voice.

Goddammit all to hell. The man was sex on legs. He knew it; heck, *everyone* knew it, and I didn't want to fall into his trap. The one where he'd undoubtedly captivate me, then *BAM*, he'd friend-zone me so fast I wouldn't know what hit me.

It was not happening. So, ignoring his call, I tapped Gerry on the arm, and said, "Congrats on your, um, award, trophy, thingy, Gerry. Top notch, young boy. Brilliant job." Shit. I needed to get out of there. I patted Gerry's arm once again and then made my getaway back to Brooke.

Facing the audience, while they listened to Tom and then Carter talk again, I whispered out the corner of my mouth, "Did I look like a total idiot that whole time?"

"Sure did."

"Thanks. I thought I had. Can you please bury me this afternoon?"

"Can do. I'll even bring wine and say something nice after you're in the ground."

"You're sweet."

"It's what best friends are for."

ACKNOWLEDGMENTS

For all the readers who were excited for Lan, Parker, and Easton. I hope you've enjoyed their story and thank you for all your support. I wouldn't be where I am without YOU!

To Becky Johnson at Hot Tree Editing. Thank you for always being a part of the process of writing. I couldn't do it without you. Also, Peggy, Donna, and Randi, thanks heaps, ladies.

Amanda Berry and Lindsey Lawson, thank you so much for all your help with Out of the Blue. Amanda, I'm so glad you were willing to join my Beta team!

Craig and our monsters, love you all so darn much.

Leah Sharelle and Colleen Snibson, your friendship means the world to me. So glad you both live in Ballarat. Love you, ladies.

MariaLisa deMora, I freaking adore you. There aren't enough words to describe how much you mean to me, woman.

My sister, Rachel Morgan. You've always been such an amazing, supportive, positive role in my life. Love you always.

To all the ladies at Give Me Books Promotions, thank you for everything you do.

Wander, you are a genius at what you do. Thank you for such a beautiful cover photo.

Ryan, the cover model who I based Parker off, thank you for your support, I really appreciate it. You rock! (Readers, be sure to follow Ryan on Instagram @ryanwhat03)

ALSO BY LILA ROSE

Hawks MC: Ballarat Charter

Holding Out (Free)

Climbing Out

Finding Out (novella)

Black Out

No Way Out

Coming Out (m/m novella)

Hawks MC: Caroline Springs Charter

The Secret's Out

Hiding Out

Down and Out

Living Without

Walkout (novella)

Hear Me Out (m/m)

Break Out (novella)

Fallout

Romantic Comedies

Making Changes

Making Sense

CPSIA information can be obtained
at www.ICGtesting.com
Printed in the USA
BVHW052352060223
658028BV00011B/401